Double the Heat

Double
the Heat

Lori Foster

Deirdre Martin

Elizabeth Bevarly

Christie Ridgway

BERKLEY SENSATION, NEW YORK

THE BERKLEY PUBLISHING GROUP
Published by the Penguin Group
Penguin Group (USA) Inc.
375 Hudson Street, New York, New York 10014, USA
Penguin Group (Canada), 90 Eglinton Avenue East, Suite 700, Toronto, Ontario M4P 2Y3, Canada
(a division of Pearson Penguin Canada Inc.)
Penguin Books Ltd., 80 Strand, London WC2R 0RL, England
Penguin Group Ireland, 25 St. Stephen's Green, Dublin 2, Ireland (a division of Penguin Books Ltd.)
Penguin Group (Australia), 250 Camberwell Road, Camberwell, Victoria 3124, Australia
(a division of Pearson Australia Group Pty. Ltd.)
Penguin Books India Pvt. Ltd., 11 Community Centre, Panchsheel Park, New Delhi—110 017, India
Penguin Group (NZ), 67 Apollo Drive, Rosedale, North Shore 0632, New Zealand
(a division of Pearson New Zealand Ltd.)
Penguin Books (South Africa) (Pty.) Ltd., 24 Sturdee Avenue, Rosebank, Johannesburg 2196,
South Africa

Penguin Books Ltd., Registered Offices: 80 Strand, London WC2R 0RL, England

This book is an original publication of The Berkley Publishing Group.

Contents

Hart and Soul
Lori Foster

1

Breaking the Ice
Deirdre Martin

87

Double Booked
Elizabeth Bevarly

199

Original Zin
Christie Ridgway

271

Hart and Soul

Lori Foster

One

Hart Winston tried to prepare himself, but with every breath his anxiety level ramped up until he felt sweat on the back of his neck.

What did she want? In his gut, he knew it had to be something important for her to be so persistent in seeking him out. Lisa Vogle wasn't a woman who chased any man. For sure she wouldn't chase him.

He had his suspicions about the message she had to give, and mixed emotions kept him tightly coiled with the possible consequences.

He wasn't a coward, damn it! He would face up to his responsibilities as all the Winston men did.

Yet, he continued to sit in his car in the blistering parking lot in front of Lisa's apartment building, trying in vain to sort through his feelings, not only about Lisa but also about the life ahead. To his twin, Dex, he had denied caring about Lisa. He'd even denied being attracted to her. He'd called her "plain" when that adjective could never be applied to a woman with her vitality, her intelligence, and her grace. No, she didn't look like most of the women he dated. She didn't act like them either.

And that, in part, was what unsettled him.

Enough. Turning off the car, Hart braced himself for what lay ahead and stepped onto the burning blacktop. Waves of suffocating heat wafted up to amplify his already churning emotions.

He'd make it work, he told himself. So Lisa wasn't like most women he knew. In many ways, she was better.

It didn't matter that he'd considered her a one-night stand, a moment of weakness.

He couldn't lie to himself; he'd thought of her often even before she began tracking him down. He enjoyed her company. He'd really enjoyed sex with her.

It'd be fine.

Might as well get on with it. Dexter expected a full report, as did his cousin Joe. Hell, if his suspicions were correct, the whole damn family would know his private business in no time at all.

Staring through mirrored sunglasses, hands on his hips, Hart surveyed Lisa's building. From the parking lot he could see the side of the balcony where she liked to sit in the evening, drinking hot tea. Not a beer, never that. Not even a cola. She held those dainty teacups with all the grace of a queen.

He smiled at the image, caught himself, and scowled again.

Other than a light that shone from behind closed curtains, her place looked empty. Hell, it was only eight o'clock, but Lisa was the "early to bed, early to rise" sort. She was also a dentist, of all things. Conservative, uptight, and buttoned down, very proper—in a hundred different ways, their personalities and lifestyles would clash.

But he'd slept with her in a moment of lust-inspired insanity, a moment that had plagued his thoughts ever since. And now she'd tracked him down for a reason, so he had to address the repercussions.

Damn.

Before he could change his mind, Hart strode up the front walk and into the building. Air-conditioning chilled his skin as he bounded up the stairs and to her door, where an artificial summery wreath hung. It was homey, domestic—like Lisa.

Hart cursed under his breath and knocked.

He knew she had to be home, but she didn't answer the door. Scowling, determined to get the uncomfortable confrontation over with, he knocked again, harder this time.

The door jerked open, but only as far as a chain allowed. Without showing herself, Lisa said, "Go away, Hart Winston, and stay away."

Out of sheer instinct, Hart thought to poke his foot in the space before she could close the door.

She smashed his foot hard, and kept on smashing, hoping, no doubt, to encourage him to remove the obstacle.

He put his shoulder into the door. "You're breaking my foot, woman."

"Remove it if you don't want to lose it."

He grinned at the surprise sarcasm. She always did that to him, amusing him at the oddest moments, drawing him in . . . turning him on. Again, he shook off the unfamiliar feelings. "We need to talk."

"I have nothing whatsoever to say to you."

Baloney. He added some pressure against the door to relieve his poor foot. "Then why the hell did you track me down?" His voice rose in annoyance. "You called my brother several times. You called my cousin—"

"Brother? I didn't even know you had a brother. Now get lost."

Hart drew a breath and tried to sort his way through her odd behavior. She was usually so proper; she wouldn't have told an intruder to get lost. And he was not an intruder. "Come on, Lisa, listen to me. I'm sorry it took me so long to get back to you—"

"No big deal. It doesn't matter, not anymore. Leave with a clear conscience."

Hart's blood ran cold. What had she done? Had he taken so long to contact her that she'd given up on him? Damn. "What does that mean, Lisa?"

She stopped pressing on the door, but still didn't show herself. More composed and with less anger, she said, "It means just what I said: it doesn't matter. I was going to tell you something, but . . . I've changed my mind. So just . . . go away. Forget I ever called."

His stomach knotted. "Sorry, but I can't do that."

"Try."

So she thought to cut him out? Hart sought his own measure of control. "I was out of town. I can explain where and why if you let me in. But the point is that I couldn't get in touch. The messages you left for me went to my twin, Dexter. He was sort of filling in for me so that no one would know where I was, and—"

Her face appeared between the door frame and the door. "You seriously have a twin?"

Hart stared. "What the hell happened to you?" He studied her, but even beyond the massive curlers in her brown hair, and the fact that she had her glasses off, she looked . . . funny. Sort of unbalanced, somehow.

"Since when do you have a twin?"

"Since . . . birth?" He frowned. "What did you do to yourself? Is something wrong?"

Her brown eyes rolled. "Move your foot and I'll let you in, but only for five minutes."

"You promise?" If he pulled his foot out and she locked the door, he'd lean on the bell until she caved.

Lisa narrowed her eyes, which only made her look funnier. "Move. Your. Foot."

Hart moved it. The door clicked shut, he heard the rattle of the chain, and she opened the door again.

"Come in before my neighbors start to complain." She stood to the side, holding the door for him.

She wore a long robe, and under it Hart saw a peek of pink lace on her bra.

Lisa wore pink lace?

She noticed the direction of his attention and clutched the lapels of the robe together. "Now," she said. "I *had* wanted to talk to you, but you were such an ass, and so much time has passed, that I've changed my mind."

Hart gestured at her face. "Something's not right."

She rolled her eyes again. "I have makeup on one eye, so I'm lopsided." Her frown pinched with accusation. "You interrupted me."

Yeah, that was it. On her right eye she had shadow and liner and mascara. The other eye looked small and mean in comparison. His brain scrambled from that to the idea of her wearing makeup.

From what he recalled, Lisa went without cosmetics, and it suited her. With her dark eyes and lashes, her glossy light brown hair, she didn't really need much makeup.

So why had he considered her so average? Shaking that off, Hart went over to the couch and dropped down to sit. "Interrupted you from what?"

Both eyes widened. "Don't you dare get comfortable, Hart Winston. This conversation is over, and you have to go." She fluttered over him. "Get up."

She forgot to hold those lapels together. Her generous breasts overflowed the sexy lace cups of her bra. Hart sprawled back, his arms spread out, his jeans-covered legs relaxed. "That's some sexy-looking underwear for you, isn't it?"

She didn't blush. But she did look ready to flay him alive. She tightened the sash on her robe, inadvertently emphasizing the narrowness of her waist and the lushness of those full breasts. "Get out, Hart."

"Not yet. You have something to tell me."

"Wrong. I *had* something to tell you—but not anymore."

"I want you to tell me, anyway."

"Tough. You should have shown up when I first called."

Unable to keep his brain on task, Hart found himself studying her body. He needed to know what she had to tell him, even if he had to insist, but he just couldn't stay focused. "I never figured you for sexy lingerie."

Well, hell. Hart watched her face and grinned to himself. Not exactly to the point, but all the same, he waited for her reply.

Her back went straight and her mouth pinched. "I have always worn feminine underwear."

Cocking a brow, Hart said, "Really? Because I don't remember you—"

"You turned out the lights, goofus. How could you have seen anything?"

Goofus? Well, that was rude. He sat forward with a frown. "I turned out the lights for *you*." She was shy, right? Timid and modest. He'd been trying for consideration, hoping to put her at ease.

"For *me*?" Lisa laughed—a sound devoid of real humor—and crossed her arms under her breasts in a belligerent stance. "I wanted the lights on, bud. I wanted to see you. I wanted to see *everything*."

Hart felt his dick twitch at that telling admission.

Lisa shrugged. "But hey, when you turned them out, I didn't

say anything because I figured you had insecurity issues about your body or something. I didn't want to embarrass you."

He was off the couch before he realized his own intent. "You're kidding, right? I do *not* suffer from insecurity of any kind."

She looked at a fingernail. "Can't prove it by me."

Losing all semblance of civility, Hart pointed at her and said, "You came twice, lady."

She shrugged. *Shrugged.* Hart couldn't believe her insouciance.

"Yeah, so? What's your point?"

Seeing red, he moved closer to loom over her. At five-nine, she was tall, but he stood a good five inches over her. "You screamed, Lisa. Hell, you damn near deafened me. *And* you bit my shoulder."

"It was dark," she said. "How could I know what I was biting?"

His eyes rounded. "You enjoyed yourself."

Another shrug. "I plan to enjoy myself tonight too." Those lopsided eyes glared at him. "If you'll just go away, so I can finish getting ready . . ."

Oh, hell. He felt flattened. Laid low. Taken off guard.

She had a *date*? And she planned to get laid?

At his expression of utter chagrin, she shook her head. "Come on, Skippy. Pack it up and get on out of here, will you? I have things to do."

Skippy? Hart held his ground. "What the hell has gotten into you?"

That must've been the proverbial last straw, because she exploded. "Well, excuse me if I figured sex entitled me to the courtesy of a return phone call when I let you know—repeatedly—that it was important. But oh, no, not the lady-killer Hart Winston. He can't be bothered with something as mundane as a phone call from a one-night stand he hoped to never set eyes on again!"

Ah. He'd hurt her feelings, and because of that, he felt like a cad. He reached for her, saying gently, "I'm here now."

With a loud "Ha!" she shoved him away. "You insufferable ass, is that supposed to matter to me? I want nothing more to do with you."

Well, that didn't sound promising. Solemn now, Hart sighed. "That might be tough, don't you think?"

"What?"

"Having nothing to do with me." If his suspicions were correct, they were tied together for life.

She shook her head, rattling those big rollers loose. "It will be incredibly easy if you'll just *go away*."

Not likely. "Tell me why you called me." Once she did, they could sort through things. After an abject apology, she'd forgive him. He hoped.

"Fine." Lisa drew a shuddering breath, let it out slowly. "Misplaced concern. Nothing more. That's why I called." Her smile pinched. "Now leave."

Instead, Hart went back to the couch and sat down again. He could wait her out. If she wanted to be rid of him, she'd have to 'fess up first. This was too important for him to let either of them avoid it.

"Hart," she warned.

"So you have a date?"

She stared at him, all but vibrating with irritation, before she turned on her heel and stomped away. Hart waited, but she didn't return, so he went looking for her.

As he went from the living room through the kitchen and dining room to the hallway, he took inventory. Her pristine apartment looked the same: warm, welcoming, very organized, like the lady herself. It was cozy, with little touches like knickknacks, matching curtains and pillows, potpourri, and healthy plants.

He liked it. It wasn't at all like his chrome, glass, and leather furnishings, and it felt more comfortable.

Peering into her bedroom, he saw the made bed, the uncluttered dresser and chest, the closed curtains.

He remembered that bed only too well. She'd been something else, something unfamiliar. Special. Unsettling.

He also remembered slipping out of the room early the next morning.

Yeah, he was an ass. But he was a determined ass who needed answers to questions. He found Lisa in the bathroom, the door ajar as she finished her makeup, using a magnifying mirror in place of her glasses.

Leaning on the door frame, Hart watched her slick lip gloss on her soft mouth, then smooth it with her baby finger. With that done, she started removing the curlers.

It was uniquely intimate, watching Lisa's feminine routine. Course, he hadn't known Lisa had a feminine routine. He'd seen her only in professional clothes or a white lab coat, her hair twisted up, her face clean of makeup.

On Lisa, the austere look had been sexy enough. But this was pure seduction.

Interesting.

The more Hart watched her, the more he thought about the future, maybe with Lisa, and how it wouldn't really be bad at all. In fact . . .

He cleared his throat. "I'm not going anywhere until we talk."

"Suit yourself. I trust you not to steal anything after I leave." Then her eyes—now matching—narrowed in his direction. "At least, you better not."

Would she keep stabbing him with insults the entire night? Probably. And why not? He had it coming.

Hart's curiosity gnawed on him. "So who's the lucky guy tonight?"

"You wouldn't know him." She dabbed on perfume, touching it to her throat, her wrists, and her cleavage.

Hart tried to picture it: Lisa with another man; her burning up the sheets . . . with the damn lights on; her biting someone else.

He didn't like it.

Annoyed as much at himself as at her, Hart crossed his arms. "You're saying he doesn't run in my circle, huh?"

"Hardly." Her expression turned smug. "He's an oral surgeon."

Lifting a brow, Hart said, "Sounds . . . romantic." *Not.* Why the hell did she want to get sweaty with some stuffed-shirt medical type? Lisa was prim, no two ways about that. But she was also open and caring. "You two have a thing?"

"This is our first date."

Both brows lifted. "And you plan to jump his bones? Lisa, Lisa. I thought you were more discreet than that."

"You also thought I wanted the lights off."

Hart winced. She was in rare form tonight, sharper tongued than he recalled.

Maybe if he explained things, she'd soften a little toward him instead of beating him down with her mockery. "I'm sorry, Lisa. I really am. I couldn't get in touch sooner because I was fighting."

She paused in the middle of brushing out her hair. Her big brown eyes met his in the mirror. "Fighting? With whom? What did you do now, Hart Winston?"

"No, it's a sport. The SBC. Supreme Battle Challenge. Have you heard of it?"

She continued to frown at him for a few seconds, and then seemed to accept his explanation. "Ah, I guess that makes sense." She went back to her hair. "It's like that fake wrestling stuff the youths enjoy?"

Annoyance crept up his neck. "No, not like that at all." Her brown, usually straight hair now fluffed out in sexy waves. His fingers twitched with the urge to touch it, to stroke it.

He remembered tangling his fingers in her hair while he drove into her, and then, later, feeling it drifting over his shoulders, his chest.

He cleared his throat and shoved his hands into his pockets. "There's nothing fake about it, believe me. It's a serious sport, and it's growing fast in popularity."

"If you say so."

Why it was so important for her to understand, Hart didn't know, but he forged on. "I'd been training for a while in mixed martial arts, and I decided to go professional. You called while I was away at a camp."

"Oh, just like Boy Scouts."

She was out for blood tonight, and even knowing that, Hart took it on the chin. "No, smart-ass." He jerked his T-shirt up to his chin. "Do these look like the abs of a Boy Scout?"

Lisa stared. She reached for her glasses on the side of the sink, slipped them on, and stared some more. Her look was so intense, Hart could practically feel her gaze on his stomach, up to his pecs, then back down again . . . way low, lower than he had exposed, damn it.

Her lips parted a little. She took two quick breaths.

Stoked by that intimate gaze, he suggested, "Your turn."

She laughed. Then she cleared her throat and slanted her gaze at his face. "You missed your turn on that one, Skippy."

"What the hell is with this *Skippy* business?" Such a stupid nickname. But damn it . . . didn't most nicknames start in some basis of fact?

"You know," Lisa said, interrupting his musing, "I find it very odd that you'd flaunt your body now, but felt so shy and insecure when we had sex that you had to hide from me."

Heat flooded his face. "I did *not* hide."

"You turned out the light."

"Damn it, woman!" She slandered his masculinity to suggest such a thing. "Accuse me of insecurity again, and I'll strip right here, right now."

Blinking, she turned to face him—and appeared to consider taking him up on that challenge. Then she picked up her watch and put it on. "Tempting, but sorry, no time. I'm going to be late as it is."

She'd been tempted? Hart followed her into the bedroom.

She stopped and turned to face him.

He held his ground.

Lisa pointed toward the door. *"Leave."*

"Not until you tell me why you called."

Fury brought a becoming blush to her cheeks. She looked at her watch again, crossed her arms, and said, "It doesn't matter anymore."

Damn, that possibility really bothered him. Time to get it out in the open. Maybe if he said it first, she'd discuss it with him.

Trying for gentle understanding, Hart cupped her shoulders in his hands. "Lisa . . . are you pregnant?"

Her jaw loosened. *"What?"*

Undeterred, Hart squeezed her shoulders. "Are we having a baby? Because if we are—"

"Are you *insane*?" Lisa jerked free, went to the other side of the bed—far away from him—and laughed. Hard. "Do I look like an idiot to you?"

That had to be a trick question. "No." Confusion swamped him. "Look, I know we used condoms, but they aren't foolproof, so—"

"No, they aren't, which is why I'm on the pill." Aghast, her back ramrod straight, she glared at him. "For your information,

I would never, ever, take a chance on unplanned pregnancy, but most especially not with you."

He was relieved, he really was, but still . . . Hart propped his hands on his hips. "Why not with me?"

"Oh, my God, Hart!" Her made-up eyes looked enormous behind her glasses. "Are you serious?"

Was he? Yes, damn it. Hart gave a firm nod, but said, "I think so."

"You're not father material."

Now that hurt. "Who says?"

"Every woman you've ditched after a quick lay?"

Ha! He had her on that one. "It wasn't quick, now was it, Lisa? We spent hours in that bed." He pointed to the bed between them, and stressed again, *"Hours."*

More color flooded her face, and her teeth gnashed. "In terms of minutes, no, it wasn't all that fast. In terms of life, it was no more than an afterthought for you."

Hart struggled to assimilate all that she said with the way that she said it. He believed her that he wasn't going to be a dad. Yay. What a relief!

Right?

To hell with that. He didn't like thinking about it, so he went back to more familiar ground. "You enjoyed yourself, so stop acting like you didn't."

"I won't deny it." Her shoulders lifted, her robe slipped, and he again saw that tempting pink lace. "You were fantastic. Spectacular, even."

That was more like it. Hart nodded with satisfaction—and glanced again at that comfy bed right there between them.

"But I am not," Lisa said, regaining his attention, "and have never been, pregnant."

Shit. Back to square one. "Fine. Not preggers. Got it. So if there's not a little Winston bun in the oven, what was so hellfire important that you had to hunt me down, call a dozen times, and pester my relatives?"

Fury narrowed her eyes. "You don't have to worry that it'll ever happen again. You have my word."

Holding up his hands, Hart apologized. "I'm sorry. That came out wrong. I just meant that you made it, whatever *it* is, sound so important that I sort of resigned myself to big news from you, and now—"

Her snort of irony stopped his apology.

He sighed. "Look, Lisa, you have something to tell me that's important enough for you to attempt to track me down, despite my lack of availability at the time. I'm here now, so if you would please just tell me, I'd appreciate it."

Judging his sincerity, she chewed it over, and finally said, "If I tell you, then you'll go away?"

"Yes."

"And you won't argue about it?"

Probably not. He worked his jaw, and nodded.

"And I'll never have to see you again?"

Damn it, why did she have to keep pushing him? "Maybe." But he doubted it. By the minute he found her more fascinating than ever, and all the reasons why he'd wanted her in the first place were suddenly pounding through him again.

Accepting his lackluster response, Lisa moved to the foot of the bed and sat down. She drew a deep breath, looked at Hart, and said, "Someone wants to hurt you. Bad."

"What?"

"I overheard two men talking in a bar. There can't be too many Hart Winstons walking around, so it had to be you, right? I didn't completely understand at first, but now that you say you're fighting, it makes more sense. It was something about ensuring you wouldn't win. They have a conspiracy against you, and somehow a woman is involved, I think as a distraction or to get you to the right place where these other men can jump you, and effectively take you out of the running."

Hart stared at her. Okay, he hadn't seen that one coming. "Are you serious?"

She nodded. "There. I've done my duty and warned you, so you can leave." She stood again and edged around him to leave the room. Without looking at him, she added, "And Hart? Don't let the doorknob catch you in the butt on the way out."

Two

Of course she didn't get far before Hart caught her arm and whirled her right back around. He took her off guard, and she fell into him.

He didn't set her away.

And blast the man, he felt delicious. Rock-hard and solid and so hot . . . Regaining her wits, Lisa shoved away from him.

"Keep your mitts to yourself, buster."

"Don't you mean Skippy?"

Oh, she wanted to sock his smug, all-too-handsome face. But she didn't want him to see that much emotion from her. If she couldn't convince herself not to care, she could at least convince *him* that she didn't. "Leave. Now."

"You *have* to be kidding."

He took the seat she'd vacated at the foot of her bed—and damn him, he looked good there. "I'm serious as a heart attack."

Lounging back on his elbows, he studied her. "At least give me details."

Impossible to do with her heart in her throat and her pulse racing. Even breathing seemed difficult, when she really wanted to pant. And fan herself.

Why did he have to be so scrumptious? Not just his body, but his carefree, fun attitude, his openness, his sense of humor, and confidence? He was smart and talented, funny and sexy. All wrapped together, Hart Winston made one incredibly appealing package.

But she couldn't forget that he saw her as only a one-night stand.

Jerk. She had to get him off her bed and out of her apartment. ASAP. "I'll make you a deal. Leave now, and I'll tell you all about it—later."

"What if this evil plot goes down before you tell me? Hell, woman, I could be killed."

"I don't think they wanted to kill you. They said something about a ball bat and doing stuff just dire enough to take you out of commission."

When she finished, Hart looked half sick.

He dropped flat to the bed and put an arm over his eyes. "Christ, I can handle myself, Lisa; I hope you know that. In a straight-up fight, no problem. But if some prick is planning to jump me from behind or something . . ." He moved the arm from his face and caught her staring at his lap. He grinned. "Come on, Lisa. Do you really want that on your conscience?"

She sniffed, a believable sound of indifference. "You're nothing to me, Hart. A quickie fling, no more. I did my duty and warned you, and now it's up to you."

"But you do have more details, right? Information that'll make it easier for me to defend myself?"

"You're insufferable."

Gently, he said, "I know."

"And obnoxious."

He nodded as he slowly got off the bed and came toward her.

Knowing her voice went too high, she said, "You certainly don't deserve any special consideration from me."

"Of course not." He stopped in front of her, let his knuckles brush her cheek, the side of her neck, as he smoothed her hair over her shoulder. "But you're a really kind, caring woman with an enormous heart."

It was a curse. "I really am," she agreed without modesty.

He took her hands in his, then bent his knees so he could look into her eyes with masculine appeal. His rough thumbs coasted over the backs of her fingers again and again in a seducing caress. "I don't deserve anything from you, Lisa; I know that. But this is important, and I'm asking as nice as I can—"

Reality kicked in and, again, Lisa jerked free. "Ohhhh . . ." She moved away from him to stand behind her rocking chair. "Just stow the sex appeal, Skippy. I'm not buying into it, not ever again."

He studied her, came to some conclusion, and propped his hands on his hips. "All right. But as pissed off as you might be with me—"

"I'm not," she denied with disdain. "I don't care at all either way, period."

"—we both know that you don't want to see me pulverized through some sneak attack." He leveled a look on her. "Right?"

Her heart thumped. How could he understand her so well when he'd spent little enough time trying to know her? She glanced at her watch, and gave in. "Fine. We can talk. *Later.* But for now, use extra care. Don't take any chances, and if you can keep it zipped for once in your life, try to avoid any women you don't know particularly well."

His blue-eyed gaze heated as he looked her over with suggestive intent. "I think I can manage that, all things considered."

What did that mean? No, she didn't want to know. She fashioned a stern expression and said, "Good-bye, Hart."

He smiled. "All right, I'll go. But Lisa? Don't do anything that I would do, okay?"

It took her a second to realize what he'd said, and then she heard the front door open and close. To be certain, Lisa went to the door and locked it, then dropped back against it with a heartfelt sigh.

Hart Winston. Man, oh man, but he packed a wallop to her emotions and her libido.

Calling him "Skippy" was her way of keeping his penchant for running off at the forefront of her mind. Hart was a man who took his pleasure, then took off before emotions could get involved. If she poked fun at him, then he couldn't know how foolish she'd felt after sleeping with him. Foolish because . . . well, it had felt like something very special to her. Different. More powerful than casual sex.

She was a twenty-seven-year-old independent woman with experience, a career, and plenty of intelligence. She should have known better than to build expectations around a casual night of spectacular, mind-blowing sex, or to think, even for a second, that the infamous Hart Winston had felt the same magnitude of sensation that she had.

But still, she'd been surprised that he skipped out the next morning without a word.

Fool, fool, fool!

Turning to look in the foyer mirror, Lisa made a face at herself. After that tumultuous, surprise visit, the last thing she felt like doing was suffering the company of another man, a man she was seeing only to try to get out of her funk.

A long, hot bath and a good book seemed more appealing, but she'd promised herself, so she stuck to her guns, put on her nice dress and heels, and went out to her car.

Starting the night was no fun at all, not when she already knew exactly how it would end—thanks to Hart Winston.

Having moved his car to the other side of the lot, Hart watched from his inconspicuous vantage point as Lisa hustled out in sky-high heels and a body-hugging dress.

He felt like a stalker. Like a pathetic kid with a bad crush.

But Lord have mercy, Lisa looked good. Better than good.

He'd felt that body, every inch of her, and as sweet as that had been, touch didn't quite do justice to the visual. The woman had done a fine job of hiding a killer body. Course, she'd done a good job of hiding that smart mouth, too, and all that stinging sarcasm.

He couldn't help but grin. Truth be told, he'd enjoyed sparring with her. He'd even enjoyed her insults.

He'd known Lisa Vogle for damn near a year, had talked with her numerous times, and had always enjoyed her company. Not once had she ever unleashed her displeasure on him. In fact, she'd always been beyond proper.

When he thought of Lisa, it was intelligence, kindness, and manners that came to mind. Well, and amazing sex too. He would never forget the sex.

But even before they'd slept together, there'd been something about her, something that taunted and teased him to the point that, before he'd realized his own intent, he'd asked her out on a spontaneous date.

Even more surprising, she'd accepted. In too many ways to count, he didn't seem like her type, and vice versa. But he'd felt the sexual chemistry between them as they rode in his car to a restaurant. Hell, they'd even run into his cousin Joe and his wife, Luna. Lisa had not been dressed then as she was now.

No, that night Lisa had worn a black suit and a simple white blouse with comfortable pumps. Her hair was still in that twisted, stately bun on the back of her head, and not a single speck of makeup had shown on her face.

And somehow, when he'd gotten to her door, all that prim and proper staging had blown his mind. Her naked mouth drew him; he'd meant only to kiss her good night, but she'd kissed him back, and his hands had somehow tumbled her hair, and the next thing he knew, they were in her apartment going at it hot and heavy and . . .

He felt edgy again, just thinking about it.

It was pretty freaking incredible.

Too incredible. Hart hated to admit it, because it made him sound like a wuss, but Lisa Vogle had intimidated him.

Never before had he been on a date with a smart woman who conversed easily, laughed honestly, greeted his cousin with impeccable manners, and then scorched him in bed.

That kind of perfection was enough to spook any die-hard bachelor. Right?

And now, adding her sharp wit and ease at banter, well . . . could the woman be more flawless?

He watched as Lisa drove out of the parking lot without ever once noticing him. So Romeo wasn't picking her up? What a chump.

Knowing what she had planned, Hart stewed. His thoughts were in turmoil. Was Lisa really that sexual by nature, or had she exaggerated to irk him—not that she could have guessed he'd be irked, considering how he'd cut out on her.

Damn it. He felt mired in guilt. She'd been trying to warn him, and he'd put off contacting her to finish his training camp. The camp was important, but he could have eked out some time to call her.

He'd make it up to her, Hart decided. At the same time he denied that his motives were anything but altruistic, never mind the jealousy gnawing on him.

He'd never been jealous, so he gave himself some leeway in dealing with the unfamiliar sting.

Let her have her fun tonight, sick as it made him feel. Tomorrow he'd give her the sincere apology she deserved, and they could start over from scratch.

This time, he'd do things right, and Lisa Vogle wouldn't know what hit her.

At barely eleven P.M., Lisa dragged in her front door with relief. What a bust, as far as dates went. And it was all her fault.

She kicked off the arch-murdering heels and carried them into her bedroom. Pausing at the entrance to the room, she remembered Hart sitting on her bed, at his leisure, teasing and flirting.

Her shoes hit the closet wall with a thump.

Of all the men out there, why did he have to be the one who got her motor running?

She could curse him and call him unkind names, but it wouldn't be truthful. Hart was a great guy, friendly to everyone, courteous, talented.

As an artist, he showed great sensitivity.

As a lover, his instincts were remarkable.

He enjoyed being a bachelor, and she couldn't very well fault him for that. After all, he'd been honest and up-front about everything. She knew before she slept with him that it would go nowhere.

And she'd thought that would be enough.

She almost ripped her dress in her haste to remove it. The long, hot shower did little to ease her tension. And when she tried to sleep, visions of Hart Winston's sexy abs played in her mind.

Lordy, when he'd lifted his shirt to flaunt that too-perfect body, she'd wanted only to touch him. But therein lay additional disaster to her heart, so she'd laughed it off instead.

She wasn't laughing early the next morning when she woke before sunrise.

Needing the exertion, she stuck her hair in a ponytail, dressed in a sports bra, T-shirt, running shorts, and her favorite sneakers. Hitting the pavement always served as a good way to relax her. And this early, she wouldn't run into many people.

More than an hour later, damp with sweat and breathing hard, Lisa returned to her apartment—to find Hart sitting on the front steps with a box of donuts and two carryout cups of coffee.

No. Blast the man, she'd just shaken off the coiling need, and then, with only one look at him, everything inside her tightened again.

Though mirrored sunglasses hid his eyes, she felt certain that he saw her. The corners of his mouth tipped up in that too-sexy way of his, and a new alertness showed in the set of his shoulders, the tilt of his head.

Slowly sitting up from his sprawled position on the steps, he waited for her to reach him.

Lisa considered turning around and jogging away again, but that'd be too obvious. She ran from no one, definitely not from Hart Winston.

Instead, she strode up to him and, as she went right on past, asked, "What are you doing here?"

He picked up the food and followed after her. "I came to see you, naturally. To talk."

Lisa could feel him right there behind her. Probably looking at her behind in the snug shorts.

Oh, God.

"You should have called first, Hart. I'm busy." He stayed far too close.

In a voice too deep, he said, "So I see."

A quick glance over her shoulder confirmed his interest. He'd removed the sunglasses and was indeed looking at her backside. Breath escaped from her lungs. "Now is not a good time. I need to shower and get dressed—"

"Want some help with that?"

Yes. *"No."* After unlocking the door, Lisa turned to face him. Without benefit of heels, she felt extra small compared to him. Not only was he tall, but he was also broad shouldered with a solid chest and impressive biceps.

She stared up at him, got sidetracked by his mouth, then by the glossy darkness of his hair. Her chest hurt. "You'll have to come back later."

Juggling everything into one hand, he stretched out a long, muscled arm and flattened his hand on the wall beside her head.

She felt caged—and, shamefully, liked it.

"Come on, Lisa," he cajoled. "Cut me some slack. I even brought donuts as a peace offering."

As if the man needed a bribe. "I'm a mess, Hart."

His gaze moved over her face, down to the sweat-damp front of her T-shirt, then down to her legs. "That's not quite how I'd describe you." He looked into her eyes, smiled, and said low, "You grub up real good, woman."

How could he make that sound like such a sensual compliment? Lisa forced a benign smile. "Don't be ridiculous. I have sweat on my sweat."

"You smell earthy and warm. I like it."

He could *smell* her? That broke the spell. Horrified, Lisa pivoted on her heel to make a hasty entrance into her apartment. "I need to get a shower."

Before she could get the door shut, he stepped in behind her. "Fine. Don't mind me. I'll wait for you in the kitchen." She was about to protest that when he added, "Hard as it'll be, I promise to behave myself. I'll even save you a donut or two, so take all the time you want."

Yeah, right. No way would she feel comfortable lingering naked in the shower while Hart Winston moseyed around her place unattended. "Stay in the kitchen," she ordered.

He crossed his heart and grinned like the rascal she knew him to be.

Rather than waste more time debating it with him, Lisa went into her bedroom, gathered a change of clothes, and ducked into the bathroom. When the lock on the door gave a loud click, she heard Hart laugh.

Her reflection in the mirror was the stuff of nightmares. Sweaty, lank hair that had escaped her ponytail stuck to her neck and temples. Exertion turned her complexion ruddy. Heat had left her soft T-shirt limp and shapeless. She looked like a hag.

So why had Hart acted so turned on?

Lisa answered her own question—because the man was always ready, no matter what.

The sooner she answered his questions, the sooner she could get him out of her life again. Much as that thought dismayed her, she knew it was the wisest choice.

In record time, Lisa showered, washed her hair, and brushed her teeth. Dressing in her favorite pair of stay-at-home faded jeans and a beige tank top, she girded herself with a pep talk. After combing out her wet hair and leaving it loose, she put her glasses back on and was ready to rejoin Hart. Not more than fifteen minutes had passed.

The second she came into the hall, he left his seat. For an extended moment in time, he just stared at her, from her bare feet to her snug, comfy jeans, to her beige tank.

Lisa lifted her chin, almost daring him to comment.

Instead, he cleared his throat and held out a chair for her at the kitchen table.

She shook her head. No way was she getting that close to him. Not yet. Not with that particular gleam in his eyes.

Sounding a little hoarse, Hart asked, "How do you like your coffee?"

"In someone else's mug." She'd never quite gotten the taste for coffee. She preferred tea.

"That's what I thought, so I put the teakettle on to boil." He no sooner announced that than the kettle began to whistle. "Where do you keep your tea?"

That he offered to wait on her took her by surprise. "Sit down, Hart. I'll take care of it."

"But this is my treat—my way of apologizing."

"Not necessary." But it was still nice that he went to so much trouble.

Did he really feel that bad about sneaking out the proverbial morning after, or was this more about him wanting her cooperation in sharing the details of what she'd overheard?

He didn't go to the table, choosing instead to prop his big body against the counter. Lisa inched around him to reach for a cup from the cabinet and then found a tea bag in the canister beside the stove. As she poured boiling water in the cup, she glanced at Hart.

The man had the most tactile gaze imaginable. She felt his attention, and it unnerved her.

"You have a good time last night?"

"Hmmm?" She stirred her tea to buy herself some time.

"Last night. Your big date?" He studied her. "Things go as planned?"

"I didn't have a plan." Not after Hart had dropped in on her.

"You were going to jump his bones, remember?" His brows came down in consternation, and he sidled closer. Softly, as if in commiseration, he asked, "Didn't quite work out, huh?"

Of all the . . . "None of your business."

Scrutinizing her, he drew his own conclusion and let out a relieved breath. "Right you are." He gestured toward the table. "Let's take a seat and chat."

Since that served her purpose, Lisa didn't argue. "Fine, let's."

He held out her chair first, then seated himself, lounging back in easy comfort and gazing at her with expectation.

Lisa cleared her throat. "I thought about everything last night."

"While you were with the other dude?"

Why did he keep pressing her on that? If she didn't know better, she'd think he was jealous. "No, after I got home," she lied.

"Mmmm." His fingers tapped the tabletop. "When was that, exactly?"

Exasperated, Lisa gave him a long look that showed her impatience with his attempts at prying.

Hart held up both hands. "Sorry." He tipped his head to watch her. "So after prolonged consideration, what did you decide?"

"I accept your explanation about being busy and out of touch. I overreacted, I think, in getting annoyed that you hadn't called back." She fiddled with the teacup. "Truth is, I realize things are different for you."

One eyebrow lifted. "Different?"

Lisa gestured. "Most people return phone calls as a matter of

common courtesy. But I assume you get a lot of calls from a lot
of women—Hart Winston, you can wipe that smug grin right off
your face."

He laughed. "I'm sorry, but you're cute."

"Now you're just being condescending." Her appearance had
improved with the shower and clean clothes, but she'd deliberately
left herself as plain as possible. Nothing cute in that.

He leaned forward. "No, I mean it. You're so damn nice all the
time that you're even willing to make up excuses for me."

"You're saying you don't have women calling all the time?"

Almost as if on cue, his phone rang.

They locked eyes. Hart winced; Lisa sighed.

"Answer it."

Chagrined, he glanced at the number and shook his head. "Ah,
no. It's not important."

Unbelievable. "That was a woman, wasn't it?"

He hesitated. "Yes?"

"You don't know?"

"It feels like a trick question."

Of all the idiotic . . . "My point is," Lisa said, determined to
get this over with, "you probably thought I was trying to hit on
you after we'd *both* agreed that our time together was a one-shot
deal."

"Not really, no."

Her head started to spin. "What does that mean?"

"It means that you're wrong, that I didn't blow off your calls,
assuming you wanted another go-around. It's just that I really was
busy with a training camp and—"

His phone rang again. Apologetic, Hart glanced at the number,
then put the phone back down without answering.

Lisa's teeth clicked together. "Is there a reason you don't just
turn it off, seeing as you don't answer anyway?"

"There's a reason." He sipped his coffee before answering, then met her annoyed gaze. "Family has this number, as do some of the fight promoters and my training coach."

"I see." Apparently everyone was more important than the women he dated.

Lisa wanted to throw her tea at him, but she refrained.

He wedged a hand into his jeans pocket, pulled out his wallet, and withdrew a card. He slid it across the table to her. "I don't think I ever gave you my cell number."

No, he hadn't. She'd had only his apartment number and the number she'd found for his cousin Joe. "Thank you, but I no longer have any reason to call you." And then, because she couldn't help herself, she added, "Not that you'd answer anyway, right?"

He looked far too serious when he said, "If you call me, Lisa, I'll answer. I swear."

That rattled her. She didn't understand him or why he said the things he did.

His card lay on the table between them.

"So . . . to get back to the point here. I realize now that I over-reacted. Getting angry with you serves no purpose at all."

He slouched a little more. "And?"

"I'm happy to share with you what I overheard."

"No kidding?"

She nodded. "You're right. I don't want any injury to you to be on my conscience."

His brows pinched. "And that's it? Your conscience is the only reason you're willing to warn me?"

"What else did you expect?" Unsure of his swift moods, she sipped her tea and waited.

"I don't know, exactly." He stewed in silence for a few moments, then snatched up the box of donuts and offered them to her.

Lisa shook her head. "No, thank you. I try to avoid that much sugar."

He didn't remove the box. "Live a little." Eyes darkening, he said, "Again."

That flustered her enough that she picked out a cream-filled donut before she knew what she was doing. Hart set the box down, put his elbows on the table, and leaned toward her, waiting for her to take a bite.

As soon as she did, he smiled. "Good?"

It was. "Sinful, almost."

"Yeah." He watched her so closely, she felt self-conscious. "A little sinfulness is good for you."

"Depends on the sin, I'd say."

"And who you're sinning with."

Okay, enough of that. She couldn't banter with him. Not this early. "Let's get started."

He went very still. "Yeah, let's."

"You're incorrigible." She couldn't help but laugh at him. "Now, have any—"

The ringing of his cell cut her off.

Again he glanced at the phone, then at her, and he shrugged. "Sorry. Go ahead."

Curiosity burned her. "If it's the same woman calling, then perhaps—"

"No."

Maybe she'd throw her tea at him after all. The cup was small and dainty, so it wouldn't hurt him overly, and the tea had cooled, so . . .

"Lisa?"

She gave up on that particular fantasy. "Have any new women come on to you?"

"Define 'new.'"

Her eyes narrowed. "A woman you aren't already familiar with. A woman you haven't dated before."

"Or slept with?"

Meaning he slept with women he hadn't formally dated? Of course he had. "Yes."

Hart hesitated. "Maybe, but like I said, I've been busy training, and *not* dating."

He had to be kidding her—but he didn't look like it was a joke. "Not dating?"

He shrugged. "Aka, not seeing anyone."

Lisa snorted. "Aka, not—"

"Sleeping with anyone. Exactly."

Astounded, she dropped back in her seat. "You're telling me that you've been celibate? Since when?"

"For far too long, honey." He left his seat and moved toward her. "Since I slept with you, actually."

Three

Hart saw Lisa's chest expand with a sharply indrawn breath. He knew what she expected him to do, but he was done being predictable. She thought she had him all figured out, and he wanted to surprise her.

He paused beside her, smiled, and moved on past to get a napkin off the counter.

When he returned to his seat, she still looked shell-shocked.

And his stupid phone rang again.

Cursing under his breath, Hart glanced at the number with disinterest. "Lisa, I don't want you to think—"

"No," she said, and she scurried from her seat to get a notepad and pen. "This is good."

She sounded rattled—which he counted as a good thing. If he confused her enough, maybe she'd give up her rock-solid and not-too-complimentary impressions of him, and really get to know him.

She tossed the pad and pen toward him. "Start keeping track of the women trying to reach you. And you'll have to answer, to see who wants to hook up."

Damn, but she looked good today. He'd never imagined her in jeans, but the casual clothes suited her. And her sexy little toes . . . she must keep up on her pedicures, because her feet defined femininity: narrow and soft with a high arch . . .

"Hart, are you listening to me?"

"I was fantasizing about your feet, actually. Sorry."

She stared at him. "My feet?"

"Yeah." He shook his head. "You were saying . . . ?"

After snatching up another donut, she pointed to the paper. "You need to track any woman who is interested in you."

Smiling, Hart picked up the pen and wrote down a name.

She peered across the table, trying to see, so Hart turned the pad for her to read.

She saw her own name written there, and laughed. "Uh, no. Scratch that."

He shook the pen at her. "I know women too well, Lisa. You're interested, all right. But you're denying us both because you think I'd just play you."

After a long look, she let out a breath and folded her hands in her lap, as if in preparation for a serious discourse. "Hart, really, the thing is, you're fun to play with."

"Fun?"

"Definitely. I did enjoy our night together. But I'm a serious woman with serious responsibilities, and we've had our one-night fling."

Meaning one night was enough for her? Too bad. He'd already decided that he wanted more. A lot more.

After that short lecture of hers, and his lack of response, she settled back, content to eat her donut.

Hart didn't mind the silence. With Lisa, it was pleasant. Comfortable. His phone stayed silent, sunshine slanted through her kitchen window, the coffee was good, the donuts were better.

"This is a real nice way to spend a Saturday morning."

She turned thoughtful. "It is." With her donut finished, she wiped off her hands and considered him. "But we need to get down to business, so think—who would want to hurt you?"

"No one. People like me." He was the type of man other men found easy to befriend, and women had always shown a preference for his company. Even after things ended, women—other than Lisa—didn't hold it against him.

She stewed in her own thoughts. "As much as you get around, is it possible one of your . . . *lady friends* has a disgruntled husband—"

"No."

"—or boyfriend or—"

"I don't poach," he told her, dead serious.

Skepticism lifted her brows. "Ever?"

Insulted that she had to ask, Hart scowled at her. "I do not poach. Period. If she's involved in any way, that's a big red flag. And besides, I told you I haven't been with anyone since you."

Tapping her fingernails on the tabletop, Lisa studied him, and finally said, "Knowing you, that's just a little hard to believe."

"You should try living it." He made a face. Celibacy was not a sport he enjoyed. "But it's still true."

"If you say so."

Umbrage rose. "You don't believe me?"

She tried a laugh that sounded flat to him. "It's been weeks since we were together."

As if he didn't know that. "All right, let's get something straight, okay?"

She checked the clock, shrugged. "Shoot."

Her disinterest in his irritation irked him all the more. "I do not lie." He stood from his seat and went to hers. "I admit I have more than enough faults for one man, but lying isn't one of them."

"Fine. Don't get your feathers ruffled."

His teeth ground together. "No, it's not fine." Knowing she was only placating him, Hart braced his hands on her chair seat, at either side of her hips. The position put him nose to nose with her. "I told you up-front that I wasn't looking for a long-term relationship, right? I didn't lie then, and I'm not lying now. If I wasn't doing without, I sure as hell would admit it."

Emotions flashed over her face, starting with intimidation, then awareness, and ending with anger. "Back off."

In direct contrast to her expression, her voice was small, breathless. When he straightened away from her, she drew in a shaky breath.

"Lisa?"

Slowly, she licked her lips, closed her eyes a moment, then opened them again. "I believe you."

Hell, seeing her all flushed and breathless had wiped his brain clean of everything but desire. He forgot what they were talking about. "You do?"

"You were celibate. Goody for you."

"Let's don't go overboard, okay?"

She gave him a look—and this time it was her phone that rang. "Excuse me."

Hart listened in as she picked up a receiver in the kitchen and spoke quietly for a few minutes. Apparently someone had a dental emergency, which meant his time with her was about to be cut short.

Sure enough, as soon as she hung up, she began hustling him out of the kitchen. "I need to go to the office."

"Everything okay?"

Impatient to be on her way, she rushed through an explanation. "One of my patients, a young man, fell and broke a front tooth."

"Ouch." He opened the front door, but didn't step out. "We need to finish discussing this."

"The rest of my Saturday is taken."

She'd said that a little too fast. "Are you free tomorrow morning, then?"

Her sleek brown hair bounced as she shook her head. "Tomorrow is fine, but I like to jog on the weekends, so I prefer later in the day."

"Let's plan on lunch, then. I can pick you up at noon." When she hesitated, he lowered his voice and said, "Or would you prefer we stay here, at your apartment?"

"No, a restaurant is fine. But I'll meet you there."

"Because?"

Her brows leveled out. "I prefer to have my own car handy."

In case she decided to run out on him, probably. But he could live with that. "Not a problem." He named a restaurant convenient for both of them, and then, before she could guess his intent, he leaned in and kissed her.

He'd meant for it to be no more than a quick good-bye peck. But she froze, so he didn't pull away, and the touch of their mouths lingered, grew heated. Hart inched closer to her; she didn't object.

He turned his head just a little; her lips parted.

Breath hitching, he slowly took hold of her shoulders and drew her to his body. He felt no resistance at all, only giving and excitement and astounding heat.

Silly woman. Their one night would now just be the first of many.

Rather than press his luck, Hart gently pulled back. Her eyes were still shut, and a pulse raced in her throat. He had to kiss that, too, and in the process of tasting her soft skin, he inhaled the sweet scent of her.

"Tomorrow, Lisa." When he touched her cheek, her thick lashes fluttered up, showing her dazed eyes. "I'm looking forward to it." Right before he turned away, Hart saw her gaze sharpen with fresh understanding of what had just happened.

The door slammed behind him, but it didn't diminish his grin. Now he knew he would definitely get her under him again, and he could hardly wait. But when it happened, he'd damn straight leave on the lights—and he'd see everything.

Dressed in her stuffiest clothes, her ugliest "sensible" shoes, and with her hair in a severe twist at the back of her head, Lisa stared at the entrance to the restaurant. On a hot Sunday afternoon there was no real reason for her to wear the very plain beige suit jacket and skirt with a buttoned-up white blouse, complete with a collar that tied shut, except that she wanted all the armor she could get between herself and Hart Winston's irresistible appeal.

The man had already proven how quickly her weak defenses crumbled when he turned on the charm. If she wanted to survive this newest encounter, she had to come prepared.

Clutch purse held under her elbow, Lisa straightened her jacket and headed into the restaurant, hoping to be seated before he arrived. But to her dismay, she'd gotten no more than a few steps inside before she spotted not only Hart, but another large, impressive male at the table with him.

Heavens. Her jaw loosened, her eyes widened, and she stood there as the air-conditioned air that should have cooled her didn't.

The guy with Hart looked . . . *dangerous*—in a very sexy way. He was older than Hart, probably by two decades, but that didn't lessen his impact at all. Even sitting, she could tell that he stood well over six feet tall and was rock-solid. Inky blue-black hair showed only faint traces of silver at his temples. When he pulled at his ear, Lisa noticed a small gold hoop.

Suddenly, maybe because of her stare, he turned to look at her, and she got ensnared in flinty, dark blue eyes heavily fringed with black lashes.

Lord have mercy.

The man nudged Hart, and they both pushed back their chairs as if in preparation for her joining them.

Only her feet wouldn't move. She did, however, get her mouth shut. How embarrassing.

Rallying herself, Lisa straightened her glasses, chided Hart with a frown, and made her way to the table. Taking the initiative, she said to Hart, "You could have told me you were bringing a guest."

He cleared his throat. "I, ah . . ."

Lisa looked at him again, and her eyes flared. "You're not Hart."

One brow lifted. "You sure?"

"Well, of course I'm sure." She snorted, embarrassing herself again, then held out a hand. "You must be the twin he mentioned."

Her hand got engulfed as the brother treated her to a broad smile that was gorgeous, but not quite as cocky as Hart's. "Dexter. And you must be Lisa."

"Nice to meet you, Dexter. My, but you're almost the spitting image of your brother, aren't you?"

"Or vice versa." He gestured to the big fellow next to him. "This is our cousin Joe Winston."

Flustered all over again, Lisa girded herself and faced the big man. Along with that edge of menace, he oozed raw sex appeal.

Was this what Hart would look like in his prime? If so, then

God save her, because he'd be even more devastating in his midforties than he was in his late twenties.

Fashioning a smile out of her stiff lips, Lisa said, "Hello, Mr. Winston."

"Damn, now I do feel old." He used her proffered hand as a leash and hauled her in close to brush a warm kiss to the cheek. "Just call me Joe."

A swoon threatened.

And then Dexter laughed. "No reason to blush. Joe has that effect on everyone, even his wife, who you'd think would be used to him by now." Dex held out her chair.

Before her legs gave out, Lisa sat.

As the men took their seats, Dex asked, "How did you know?"

She raised a brow in query.

"That I'm not Hart, I mean."

"Oh." Lisa shrugged. "You're not Hart, that's all. There are differences."

Joe smirked. "You don't know the half of it."

"What differences?" Dex wanted to know.

She had to give it some thought, and admitted, "It's subtle. But Hart has some singular expressions, a certain air about him, and he holds himself differently, with more negligence." She looked around. "Where is Hart, anyway?"

With a toss of his head, Joe indicated the back of the restaurant. Lisa saw Hart making his way to their table.

"Sorry," he said. "I had to take a call, and I couldn't hear up here."

A call from a woman? Lisa did her best to hide her reaction to that, but she did say, "This better not have been a test, Hart Winston."

"Or what?" He raked his gaze over her, frowning at the neat

bow tied at her throat, and dropped into his seat. "What's with the matronly duds again? Is that your idea of a chastity belt?"

Everyone froze. Lisa gave serious consideration to throwing a glass of water in his face.

Joe chuckled. "Thus, one of the differences. You see, Dex has some class. Hart—nada."

"I have class," Hart argued.

Dex rolled his eyes. "A weight class, but that's about it." He slugged his brother in the shoulder. "You just insulted the lady, you idiot, in front of your family."

Hart looked at her, his blue eyes smoldering, his mouth curving into a grin. "Ah, sweetheart, did I? Insult you, I mean?"

For answer, she fried him with a look.

A waiter came for their drink orders, breaking the icy tension. Dex asked for a cola, Hart kept his water, and Joe requested coffee. Lisa declined anything, determined to keep this visit as short as possible. Whatever bug had gotten to Hart's butt, she wouldn't put up with him by extending this visit any more than necessary.

Laying her napkin on the table, Lisa turned to Joe. "You're here as added counsel about the attack planned against Hart?"

"My specialty," Joe concurred.

A curious statement, but Lisa didn't question him. She wanted only to finish this and be on her way. "A week or more before I contacted you, I was at a bar in town—"

"With who?" Hart asked.

Lisa paused, considered several cutting replies, and chose instead to ignore him. "I was sitting somewhat in the corner, and next to me, at another table, were two men. They were conversing very quietly, but when I heard Hart's name, I started to listen. Not that I normally engage in eavesdropping, of course."

Dex said, "Of course not."

Hart slid down in his seat and crossed his arms over his chest in a sign of disgruntlement.

Joe gave him a sideways glance, hid a smile, and said, "Go on. I'm listening."

"The men said that Hart was an obnoxious ass—or words to that effect—and though I agreed, they spoke with a certain vitriol that alarmed me."

Hart nudged Dex, saying, "She speaks like you write."

They *all* continued to ignore him.

"The men agreed that Hart needed to be taken down a peg or two, and they decided the best way to accomplish that would be to ensure he wouldn't win, rather than leave it to the judges." Lisa frowned as she recalled the conversation. "At the time I didn't understand what they meant by that, but they didn't appear inebriated, so I took the threat seriously."

"He has a fight coming up," Joe said. "A big one, sort of his major debut as an SBC contender. Maybe his popularity was a little quick for some to like it."

"Did the men look like fighters?" Dex asked.

"I don't know what a fighter looks like," Lisa told them. "I certainly never suspected that Hart, who I knew only as a painter, would engage in such a thing. But I'd recognize the men if I saw them again."

"I have an idea on that," Joe confided. "But first, let me hear the rest."

Lisa nodded. "One of the men, the more muscular of the two, said that he could arrange for a 'skirt' to get Hart alone."

"A woman," Dex said.

"I took the derogatory comment to mean that, yes." Lisa frowned at Hart, and he gave her a look that asked, *What did I do?*

She shook her head. "And then he—the other man—said he

would hit Hart in the leg, or perhaps the arm, with the intent of disabling him. I believe a baseball bat was mentioned as the weapon of choice."

Hart winced. "Damn. My leg?"

Dex frowned in worry.

"He said that with a busted elbow or knee, Hart wouldn't be able to fight for a while, but that it'd look like a mugging, not anything more." She glanced at Hart. "The other fellow suggested that perhaps it'd be prudent to take out both the knee and the elbow, just for good measure."

Joe sat back. "It almost has to be someone in your weight class hoping to scale down the competition."

"Thinking back, I agree." Lisa mused over the comments. "There was a ring of jealousy, and I believe that with Hart out of the running, the man thought he'd have a better chance of 'walking through' his weight class."

"I thought they all liked me," Hart murmured, clearly disturbed by the deviousness.

Lisa almost felt sorry for him. But not enough to offer genuine sympathy, not after that crude comment he'd made on her attire—true as it might have been.

The comment had been especially stinging since she'd struggled with wanting to dress sexier for him, to see his appreciation again. But she was not a stupid woman, and saw no reason to prod his interest.

She turned to Joe Winston for a distraction. "So how do you play in this? Are you a police officer or something?"

Joe grinned. "Nah. I run a casual resort on a lake with my wife and kids."

Dex laughed. "Don't let Joe fool you. He's been everything from a bounty hunter to a private eye and a bodyguard. He has unique skills that come in handy in situations like this."

"Meaning he thinks as ruthlessly as the criminals do," Hart pointed out. "Until he met Luna and settled down into marital bliss, he was a real hell-raiser."

"Still is," Dex said, "when the situation calls for raising some hell."

But Lisa barely heard Dex. Staring at Hart, she said, "You believe in marital bliss?"

Lounging back in his chair, fingers laced over his stomach, Hart treated her to a slow, knowing smile. "I'll have to introduce you to my other cousins. They've all settled down and started families, and they're the happiest bunch of ex-bachelors you'd ever want to meet."

Joe bobbed his eyebrows suggestively. "Very happy." He nodded across the table. "Old Dex here will be tying the knot soon enough too."

Amazing. Lisa forced her gaze away from Hart to his brother. "You're engaged?"

"Funny story," Dex said, "but I met the right woman while pretending to be Hart. Talk about awkward . . ."

The men all laughed over some inside joke.

Fascinated, Lisa wondered how in the world Dex ever managed such subterfuge. The differences between the two men, in her mind, were quite noticeable. "How did you fool her?"

Hart perked up at that, but before he could say anything, the waiter returned with their drinks. When he asked for their orders, Joe told him to give them a little more time.

As soon as he was gone, Dex leaned forward to share the story with Lisa. "Hart wanted some private time to train without the family knowing, so I moved into his place, and just claimed to be him. No one suspected a thing—except Christy. She picked up on differences right off."

"I'm sure she did."

Hart looked between them with heightened awareness.

Dex slanted a look at his brother. "She barely knew Hart, and what she did know, she didn't like all that much."

Lisa grinned.

"When I behaved differently from Hart, it confused her."

"Especially his pursuit of her," Hart pointed out, "given that I'd made a point not to get too friendly with any of the women in my apartment complex."

"I think when she found out the truth, she was more relieved than anything." Dex smiled. "She forgave me, and finally started calling me by my name, instead of Hart's."

Lisa could only imagine how uncomfortable that had to have been for both of them. "But you were truly able to fool her?"

Dex shrugged. "You had the advantage of already knowing that Hart had a twin brother."

Brows drawn in confusion, Hart leaned forward, saying to his brother, "Did she—"

"She did," Joe told him.

Hart stared at her. "You knew he wasn't me?"

She rolled her eyes. "As soon as I approached the table, yes."

"How?"

Lisa gave him a long look, considered explaining, but then narrowed her eyes instead. "I'm really not talking to you right now."

Affront straightened his back. "What the hell did I do?"

Dex elbowed him before saying, "Christy is planning the wedding, but in the meantime, she lives with me instead of next door to my brother."

"Dex doesn't trust me," Hart said.

And Lisa agreed. "I don't either." She pushed back her chair.

Joe forestalled her with a hand to her forearm. "We haven't even ordered yet."

And she wasn't going to. Sitting across from Hart, knowing the indifference he felt, was nearly painful. Her demure clothing might dissuade him from lascivious thoughts, but it did nothing to make her yearning ebb. "I didn't really come to eat, just to share what I know, and that's done."

Joe stood, too, as did the brothers. Dex looked uneasy; Hart, frustrated.

"What are your evenings like?" Joe asked.

Boring, but she wouldn't admit it. "Why?"

"I'd like to get everyone together at this place where the fighters hang out. Maybe the guys will show up there and you'll recognize them."

"Oh, um . . ." She did not want to spend an evening with Hart. "Why not just report them to the authorities? Surely they could investigate."

"We can't prove anything. They could say you misunderstood their conversation—but I don't think you did. I want to catch them in the act."

"Yeah," Hart grumbled, "and I have to trust everyone that I won't get maimed."

"Sissy," Dex accused, surprising Lisa with the insult until Hart laughed.

She said, "Don't worry, Skippy. I'm sure you'll do fine." But *she* was worried.

"Skippy?" Dex repeated in confusion. "Hart 'Skippy' Winston. I like it."

"Don't start," Hart said with a dark scowl.

Lisa stewed. Would Hart be injured? Could he possibly even be . . . killed? Hoping for reassurance, she said to Joe, "Do you have a foolproof plan?"

"Actually, it's Hart's plan, but I don't see a problem with using him as bait. At the very least, it'll be expedient." Joe squeezed her shoulder. "We need to expose the guys, or Hart will forever be looking over his shoulder. And I can tell you from experience, anyone determined to get to him will manage it eventually. So can I impose on you to join us?"

She didn't want to, but what choice did she have? Without looking at Hart, she nodded. "Yes, of course."

"Great. Let's get started tonight, say nine o'clock. Does that work for you?"

No way would she admit that most nights, nine o'clock found her in her pajamas on the couch watching DVDs. "That would be fine."

Joe gave her brief directions on how to get to the bar. "We'll hang out till midnight, unless you spot the guys before then. And if you don't . . . we'll go back the next night."

"I'll pick you up," Hart told her.

"Actually, you won't." Without another word to Hart, she bade Joe and Dex good-bye and made what she hoped appeared to be a steady exit when in truth, conflicting emotions left her churning. She'd be with Hart tonight, and every night until they found the guys.

Given her weakness around him, maybe she *should* buy herself a chastity belt.

Four

Lisa no sooner walked away than Hart slouched back down in his seat.

Dex gave him a pitying look. "You should have walked her out."

"So she could snub me some more?"

Joe laughed. "She's not what I expected."

Immediately on the defensive, Hart turned to him. "She's gorgeous when she lets herself be."

"That's plain." Joe smirked. "I'm not blind or anything."

Dex laughed. "Remember, brother, Joe sees through feminine disguises."

"Wasn't much of a disguise, if you ask me," Joe said. "In fact, I always took more sedate clothes as a dare, if you get my drift."

"I get it," Hart snarled, knowing Joe had eyes only for his wife, but still pinched with jealousy.

When Joe only laughed again, egged on by Dex, Hart said, "So what was unexpected?"

Dex spoke before Joe could. "She's a hell of a lot more engaging than most of the women you seek out."

"Yeah." He had to agree with that. She certainly engaged him—on many levels.

"Funnier, too, with that prickly wit of hers," Joe said. "She put you in your place."

"Yeah." And Hart had to admit he liked where she put him. He glanced toward the exit.

"You could probably still catch her," Joe told him, "and apologize properly for being such a dumb ass."

"I don't know . . ." She'd made it clear how she felt about him.

"She knew I wasn't you," Dex announced. "Right off. No hesitation. Didn't you tell me that was a rarity?"

"It's unheard-of." Hart stewed for three seconds more, then bolted from the table to go after Lisa.

Joe sighed. "I guess this means I'm picking up the tab?"

Hart didn't slow down. His brother and his cousin could both afford lunch, and besides, he hadn't even eaten.

He spotted Lisa unlocking her car across the street. "Lisa!" He jogged toward her.

She looked up, shielded her eyes with a hand, and waited.

Hart had to smile at the picture she presented. Joe had nailed it—she was a challenge, and that damn tie at her throat only made him want to untie it.

"What is it?" she asked.

"A lot of things." Not touching her was impossible, so he brushed the backs of his fingers over her cheek. "I'm sorry."

Behind her glasses, her nose scrunched. "For?"

"The crack about your clothes."

"Oh." And then, "That *was* remarkably rude."

"And for being a jealous jerk."

Her eyelashes fluttered. "What?"

Damn, he couldn't take it. He cupped both hands around her neck. "I saw you ogling Joe."

She stiffened. "I don't know what you're talking about."

"Baloney. He made you all tongue-tied, when I've never seen you get that way. You're usually the most self-confident woman I know."

"I am?"

"Hell, even from the back of the restaurant I could see you blushing."

Confusion darkened her soft brown eyes, and her tongue slipped out to dampen her bottom lip. "I was somewhat affected by him."

He locked his jaw.

"I assume that you'll probably look like him one day. That's what affected me, thinking of you a few years down the road."

"Do you? Think of me?"

Her eyes narrowed, and she refused to answer. "There are strong family resemblances between you."

Hart hid his grin. "All the Winston guys have a certain look about them, or so the women say."

"I can imagine."

Hart hoped that was jealousy stiffening her lips. To keep her from running off, he changed the subject. "Did you know that my brother, Dex, is a writer? He uses the name Baxter for his novels."

She drew back in surprise. "I've read him."

"So had Christy. She even got smashed one night and quoted one of his love scenes back to him—thinking he was me. Can you imagine how she felt when she sobered up? Dex told her he was a writer, and even showed her the book." Hart grinned. "Funny shit, huh?"

"You're warped. That poor girl had to be mortified."

Hart shrugged. "I'm sure Dex made it up to her somehow." He smoothed her cheeks with his thumbs, and badly wanted to kiss her.

"Hart?"

"Hmmm." He stared at her mouth, almost tasting her. He'd always enjoyed seeing lipstick on women, but Lisa's bare lips seemed twice as appealing.

Lisa's voice shook as she said, "I don't understand you. Why are you doing this?"

"This?"

"Coming on to me." She caught his wrists, but didn't pull his hands away. "You are, aren't you?"

"Yeah." *Most definitely.*

She made a frustrated sound. "But you had your one-night stand, and you got your fill, so—"

"I didn't."

Lisa rolled in her lips, blinked, and waited.

"Get my fill, that is." His muscles all tensed; his voice went low and deep. "Damn, woman, not by a long shot do I feel done with you."

Hesitantly, she said, "I . . . You mean . . ." But she didn't finish either sentence.

"It's making me nuts thinking about you going out with that *putz* oral surgeon dude, and what you might have done with him." His voice went deeper still, rough and raw. "What I'd rather you be doing with me."

"Nothing."

Hart couldn't blame her for denying it, but he felt the damn chemistry. Still. She wanted him, maybe not as much as he wanted her, but he could work on that.

"How can you say that?" Moving closer to her, Hart hid her from view of the street with his body. He put his palm beneath her breast in the silky blouse, right over her heart. "Your heartbeat is pounding double time."

She drew a breath, nodded, and admitted, "You always do that to me."

Hell, yes. "Well, then . . ."

She licked her lips again. "I meant that I did nothing with the oral surgeon dude—who, by the way, is not a *putz* at all."

Hart grinned at how she mimicked his words, even as he felt encouraged. "Really? Nothing happened? Not even a little something?"

Her chin lifted. "If you want the painful truth, the entire night was a bust." Her eyes narrowed in accusation. "And I had looked forward to that night for more than a week!"

"Why did nothing happen?" God, he needed to know.

Lowering her head, she mumbled, "You . . . distracted me from my original intent."

Never before had a grumbled accusation made him semihard, but that confession did. "I won't say I'm sorry, Lisa. Not when I still want you."

Heat warmed her cheeks, and her expression turned chiding. "You're too bold."

The weight of her breast rested over the back of his hand, but he didn't dare cop a feel, not here, damn near in the street, where anyone could see . . .

A thought occurred to him, and he asked her, "Are my cousin and brother watching us through the restaurant window?"

Looking beyond him, she scowled. "Yes, they are." And with that, she shoved him away.

Hart sighed. "Let me pick you up tonight. It'll give us a chance to sort this out."

"There shouldn't be a 'this' to sort out."

Maybe not, but that didn't change the facts. "Let's face it— there *is* still something between us."

She surprised him by looking resigned. "Fine."

Now it was his heart thumping. He couldn't help but press his luck. Tentatively, he broached possibilities. "Given that we're both mature, reasonable people, maybe after we leave the bar, we could pick up where we left off?"

Her chest swelled with a deep breath. "I don't know."

"Yes, you do." He leaned down to put a light kiss on her mouth. "You want me, Lisa. God knows I want you. In a couple more weeks I'm going to have to leave for a training camp, and I won't be back until after the fight."

"When is the fight?"

"Not for a few months yet, and while I stay in shape, fighting shape is something altogether different. I'll put in at least six weeks of specialized training. There won't be much time for anything else."

"Ah, and you're going to be *celibate* again?"

So much skepticism. He grinned at her. "Unless you want to travel with me." Actually, that teasing comment had merit. Could a dentist get that kind of time off? He didn't know. But he fingered that frothy bow at her neck and said, "If you find time to visit, I promise to be available."

"And other than me?"

"Celibacy it is." Without Lisa, the thought of doing without wasn't all that repugnant. "You might not believe it, but the only woman I want right now is you."

"Right now," she acknowledged.

Her gaze holding his, she reached behind herself, shifted, and opened the car door. She slipped away from him and got behind the wheel. For several seconds she just sat there, appearing to be in deep thought.

Finally she closed the door, rolled down the window, and said, "All right."

Heat washed over him, tightening the coil of tension and lust. "Yeah?"

She nodded. "As you said, we're both adults. And truthfully, I haven't gotten my fill either."

Damn, the things she did to him should be illegal. He nodded with ripening anticipation. "Sounds great."

"But one thing, Hart."

Caution edged in. "What is it?"

"This time the lights stay on."

Hart moved uneasily in his seat, his gaze glued to Lisa at the bar. He'd been watching her for hours now. She spoke with everyone, flirted, and damn, she looked great. He almost regretted bringing her here. When she'd answered her door, the thought of taking her straight to bed, and to hell with their plan, had almost sidetracked him.

In fact, if it hadn't been for Lisa and her no-nonsense manner of business first, pleasure later, that was exactly what he would have done.

He hated seeing other guys come on to her. He especially hated seeing her encourage them.

Joe's elbow gouged his ribs. "Stop staring at her, will you? She's going to catch fire, you look so hot under the collar."

Dex, in typical brotherly fashion, said, "But she does look sexy as hell, Joe. How can he resist? Especially with every other guy in the bar ogling her."

Hart rubbed his chin. "She's a damned chameleon, always changing on me, one day looking like a librarian, and the next like . . . I don't know. A complete hottie."

"We wanted her to attract male attention, doofus." Joe sipped at his drink. "Although, I gotta tell you, with that fitted dress and exposed cleavage, the glasses are overkill."

"Yeah," Dex said. "She does wear glasses with a certain panache."

"It's called elegance," Hart mumbled.

Joe agreed with a nod. "She was attractive and appealing enough in the shapeless suit with matronly shoes at the bottom of those extra-long legs." He took a sip of his drink. "Like this . . . well, it makes me wonder why you're dragging your feet."

Hart's jaw worked as he gnashed his teeth together. Joe was right; no matter what, Lisa turned him on.

Tonight, she looked downright incredible. The trim but classy cream-colored dress ended just above her knees. Pearl buttons marched from the hem to the heart-shaped neckline, where she showed off the upper swells of her breasts. Her high heels made her legs look longer than ever.

"She does have great legs," Dex agreed. "Looks like most of the guys here have noticed too."

Hart scowled at them both. "I'm glad you two can have your jollies at my expense."

Joe chuckled. "Why don't you just give it up and admit you're sunk?"

"Sunk?" Yeah, he was, but he didn't need to admit shit to his cousin or his brother. "I don't know what you're talking about."

"Flattened," Dex clarified. "Head over heels. Boggled and blinded. All that good stuff."

"Don't worry," Joe told him. "It only hurts until you stop denying it, and then it's not so bad."

"Oh, shit." Hart forgot his objections to Joe's claim when Lisa slipped off the barstool. She gave him a quick, sultry glance before strolling toward a table where two men sat.

"She hasn't approached anyone else," Dex pointed out, all teasing gone. "You think those are the guys?"

Joe said nothing. He was too busy sizing up the dudes at the table. He had that certain look about him that spelled trouble.

For the other guy.

When one of the men touched her arm, Hart wasn't able to stand it. Knowing how unscrupulous and dangerous the two men could be, he didn't want Lisa anywhere near the bastards. He started to rise.

He got yanked back to his seat by Joe. "She's fine, Hart. Nothing will happen in here. Let her do her thing."

Lisa had moved out of reach with a laugh, so Hart sank back into the chair. "If they touch her again, I'm breaking their arms."

"You'll get your chance." Shrugging, Joe stayed alert, but didn't stare. "But for now, you're too obvious. I've got them in my sights, so why don't you chat with your brother or something?"

"Yeah," Dex said, taking the hint. "Tell me how you talked Lisa into coming to the bar with you. Last time I saw her, she looked ready to skin you alive."

"I reasoned with her." Hart didn't want to make small talk, but he didn't want Lisa's efforts to be wasted either.

"There," Joe said. "She's on the move again. No, Hart, you stay put. I'll trail her out and see what's what. I'll call you when I know it's clear and no one is watching us."

Dex took pity on him. "You trust Joe. You know he won't let anything happen to her."

Hart watched as Joe, staying several yards behind, followed Lisa out of the main bar area, without looking like he was following her. When they were both out of sight, it was all he could do to contain himself. He should be the man looking after her, not his cousin.

Dex tried to engage him in conversation, but Hart couldn't seem to center his thoughts on anything or anyone other than Lisa.

In a dozen different ways, he wanted her—to talk with her, protect her, laugh with her, and tease her. He enjoyed matching wits, arguing with her, and God knew he loved making love to her.

Tonight he'd have her again, and he planned to make it so memorable, she'd stop trying to push him away.

Suddenly a busty, perfumed woman stood in front of their table. She wore a short, fitted black dress that hugged every inch of her lush body, and extremely high-heeled strappy sandals. Pale blond hair and bright red lips gave her a Marilyn Monroe look.

She glanced back and forth between Dex and Hart.

Dex grinned, knowing her predicament. "Can I help you?"

She licked plump, painted lips. "You're Hart Winston, the fighter?"

Dex grinned. "No, ma'am. I'm his twin and a lowly writer. That's Hart, looking very distracted—probably about his upcoming fight."

"Oh." She turned toward Hart and smiled with giddy delight. "I didn't know you were a twin."

Hart tamped down his irritation. If this was the woman sent by the goons, then he couldn't dismiss her as he wanted to. He had to play along.

Summoning up some masculine charm, he rose from the table and held out a hand. "I'm the evil twin," he told her with a smile. "And you are?"

"Caroline Welsh." She went all giggly on him. "I'm a *huge* fan."

Hart held his smile with effort. "Thank you. I appreciate that."

"You look so impressive, I just know you're going to win your fight."

"Damn straight." It was all he could do not to glance at the goons. "Will you be attending the fight, or watching on TV?"

"I'll be there! I follow the fights all over the country. I love the excitement of a live event." She licked her lips. "And I just love hanging out with the fighters."

Great. Hart strained his good manners. "Well, maybe I'll see you there."

Turning coy, she fluttered thick black lashes and put a hand on his forearm. "Please don't tell me I have to wait months before we get better acquainted."

Hart started to answer, and his cell phone rang. He held up a finger. "Excuse me just a second, will you, honey?"

She pouted, but glanced at Dex.

Dex whistled and turned away.

"Yeah," Hart said into the phone, already knowing from the caller ID that it was Joe.

"We weren't followed, and she's in your car, waiting for you. I'll keep an eye on her until you get out here, but you should have a babe coming up to you before long."

"Exactly," Hart said. "Already done."

"Ah, she moved fast. Lisa overheard them finalizing the plan, which is why she approached to get a better look at them. Anyway, those are your boys, the ones who want to mangle your limbs. Make note of their mugs so you can identify them later, and then make a date with the chick for sometime soon, but not for tonight."

"Definitely not." He had Lisa waiting, and no other woman could compare to her.

"Lisa got their names, too, so that'll help. But we'll catch them in the act, just to make sure we have all the proof we need."

"Got it," Hart said, anxious to be done so he could join Lisa. "I'll get there as soon as I can."

After he hung up, he turned to Caroline again. "Sorry, but that was business. Now where were we?"

"You," she said teasingly, stroking his chest, "were about to invite me to join you."

"Damn, I wish I could. Unfortunately, I have to cut the night short." When her eyes narrowed, Hart said, "How about tomorrow night? Say eight o'clock?"

"Oh, that'd be perfect!" She brightened again—and stupidly glanced back at the men. "You could pick me up when I get off work."

"All right."

Withdrawing a pen and paper from her purse, she wrote down an address. "Are you familiar with the western area? I work there at a small drugstore. I could meet you in the back lot."

It was a crime-ridden area—perfect for violence—but Hart just shrugged. "No problem."

Before he knew her intent, she went on tiptoes, grabbed his neck to hug him close, and planted one on him.

She left him cold, though he tried to hide it as he caught her waist and eased her away. His damn brother sat there grinning like an idiot, with one eyebrow raised.

Hart cleared his throat and said, "Let's save that for when we have some privacy."

Caroline took several deep breaths, then nodded. "Tomorrow," she breathed with enough drama for the stage.

As she turned to swish and sway away, Hart glanced at the two men. They quickly averted their eyes, but they'd been watching, and seething.

He looked forward to annihilating them both. "Let's go," he said to Dex, who had already stood.

"Don't look at them anymore," Dex told him. "It's too obvious."

"Yeah, I know. But it'd be easier if I just went over there right now and beat them both to a pulp."

"What *will* you do?" Dex asked, knowing Hart wouldn't instigate anything. He valued his position in the fighting organization too much. "I mean, I know the general idea, but do you have someone you can trust in the SBC to make sure they're punished beyond a few punches to the face?"

"Drew Black runs an up-front operation, and he's not going to like it if they do try to carry through with their plan." They walked past the men, far enough away that they couldn't be overheard, especially not with the drone of the crowd filling the bar.

Hart could feel their burning gazes on his back. So much hostility, he thought, all because he worked hard and succeeded. Some idiots always wanted a shortcut. "I imagine Drew will kick them out completely."

"Sounds right to me."

At the door, Dex and Hart separated, with Dex hanging back to make sure the men didn't follow. Along with the street lamps and headlights of passing cars, a full moon illuminated the area and the parking lot beyond. Humidity hung in the air, making the night dense, damp.

Sexy.

Hart shook himself. Someone wanted to put him out of commission, and all he could think about was getting Lisa alone.

Somewhere in the shadows, Joe lurked, watching over her. Hart could see the faint outline of her profile where she sat in the passenger seat of his car. Waiting for him.

He inhaled the humid night air and jogged across the street.

The second he opened the car door and slid in, Lisa looked at him—and frowned. He closed the door, putting the interior in shadow once again. Moonlight shone on her glasses, and added a soft glow to her skin.

Hart wanted to kiss her, but before doing anything else, he used his cell to call Joe, letting him know the plan he'd made with Caroline Welsh.

As Lisa listened to him talk, her frown intensified. He could feel her tension in the close confines of the front seat. Jealousy? There was no reason for it, but Hart accepted it as a good sign. Never before had he wanted to deal with a possessive or jealous woman. But this was Lisa, and he was quickly realizing that with her, everything was different.

After disconnecting the call with Joe, Hart turned to her, smiled, and leaned over to take her by surprise with a quick kiss. He kept it short and sweet; otherwise, he might have gotten carried away. He wanted to be alone with her.

He wanted a bed nearby.

And the sooner he got away, the better the odds that no one would see Lisa with him. He didn't want to take any chance on the men expanding their plot to include her. As he pulled away from the curb, he saw Joe join Dex in front of the bar. Together they headed toward Joe's truck.

After they were more than a mile from the bar, with Lisa still frowning at him, Hart tried a smile. "Joe said you got their names?"

"Yes."

He raised a brow. "Care to share with me?"

"Brad Emery and Tyler Stevens."

He mulled that over, but they didn't ring a bell. Still, he didn't know everyone by a long shot, only the guys from his camp. "Never heard of them. You're sure they're fighters?"

"Brad Emery is, or so he claimed. I'm not sure about the other one." Her eyes narrowed. "You smell like strong perfume."

"I do?" He lifted his arm and sniffed. "I don't smell anything." But he actually did. Caroline had been drowning in something sweet, and she'd done her best to cozy up to him.

No way in hell was Hart going to admit that she'd taken him by surprise with a lip-lock.

Lisa made a face. "You are such a fraud."

"What did I do now?" Hell, he only wanted to get her alone, and naked and under him. Or over him. Didn't matter to him. But most definitely, the lights would be blazing so he wouldn't miss a single thing.

Her expression droll, Lisa turned to look out the window. "Did you mean what you said, Hart? That you would never lie to me?"

"Absolutely." He reached for, and found, her hand. "I admit I have plenty of flaws, honey, but I'm not a liar."

She looked at their linked hands. "So you meant it when you said you don't want anyone else?"

This was important to her, he could tell. Maybe it was time to bite the bullet and 'fess up some. He went through a green light, turned the corner—all one-handed, because he didn't want to lose the physical link with her—and slowed on the quieter side streets leading to her apartment.

"Spilling my guts here, but I don't think I've ever wanted anyone as much as I do you."

She scoffed . . . but looked interested.

"That one night together . . ." Hart whistled. "No matter how I tried to deny it, it was special. Enough so that it's kept me thinking about you far too much. Even as distracted as I've been with the SBC and training and everything, whenever I was alone, and especially at night when I tried to sleep, I'd remember different things about you: how you felt and your scent, what we did and what I still wanted to do. You've kept me awake when I should have been too worn-out from training to think straight."

She bit her lip. "If I hadn't contacted you . . ."

"I would have eventually come calling." Now that he'd admitted it to himself, Hart didn't mind admitting it to her. "I fought it, but it was a losing battle. Hell, even when I thought you might be pregnant, I had really mixed feelings about it."

Her eyes widened. "You *wanted* a baby?"

His shrug looked more cavalier than he felt. A baby that looked like him or Lisa, a little girl with her brown eyes and soft hair, or a rambunctious boy who liked to tussle.

No, the idea didn't distress him as it should.

He fumbled for the right words. "It's not that I'd plan one for right now. I mean, I'm starting a new career, and kids would really put a kink in things. But . . . eventually, yeah, of course I do."

"Amazing."

He glanced at her, unsure of her mood or her interpretation of things. "Well, you know what they say about the timing never being perfect. But I figure that no matter when they come, babies are always a blessing." He squeezed her fingers. "What I'm trying to say is that I'm glad I still have some time, but a baby with you, at any time, would never feel like bad news."

The illumination from the dashboard lights emphasized the shadows, and lit her face in a soft glow. She straightened her glasses, then peered at him with obvious confusion. "Why me, Hart? How am I different?"

He shrugged again, knowing this was important and hoping to say it right. "How I feel with you . . . being with you . . . it's easier."

Her brows went up.

"I enjoy talking with you."

She stared. "So it's my scintillating conversation you like most?"

Hart couldn't help but grin at her look of disbelief. "When I'm around you, I always want you, Lisa. Don't misunderstand that. But with you, I don't resent the time that we're not having sex."

She bit back a smile. "I take it that you've spent a lot of time seducing?"

"Or being seduced." He grinned at her. "Usually when I dated, it was with the endgame in mind."

"Interesting." She settled back and studied him. The time ticked by.

Finally, unable to take it, Hart asked, "What are you thinking?"

"I'm thinking that I believe you, that you do feel differently about me."

Relief loosened his knotted muscles. "Good."

"So then, since we do have something different going on, could you tell me why you failed to mention that Caroline kissed you?"

"Uh . . ." How did she know that?

Lisa shook her head. "Give it up, Hart. You have lipstick all over your mouth. If it didn't mean anything, if you didn't enjoy it, why didn't you just 'fess up right away?"

Five

Hart Winston not only found her desirable, but he also enjoyed her company. Lisa couldn't help but be thrilled, seeing as how she'd been secretly enamored of him forever. But she wouldn't put too much stock in anything a man said while his hormones were in charge.

If Hart had been celibate as long as he'd claimed—which had to be a record for him—then he'd likely see things in a skewed way until he'd appeased his lust.

She was ready to help him with that. Oh, boy, was she ready.

She watched as Hart pulled into the parking lot, put the car in Park, turned on an interior light, and checked his face in the rearview mirror.

"Shit." Using a sleeve, he scrubbed his mouth. "I'm sorry, Lisa. The woman grabbed me," he explained while scrubbing, "and I wasn't sure what to do, being she's probably the one I'm supposed to meet so the idiots can carry out their plot. I mean, if I'd shoved her away, or turned my face, or maybe gagged on her, the jig would be up, right?"

"Uh-huh." Lisa opened her door and got out. Like Hart would ever *gag* on a woman. He was so ridiculous, such a hedonist, how could she ever take him seriously when he spoke about his feelings?

Hart left the car, locking it with a click of the remote, and jogged to catch up with her. "What does 'uh-huh' mean?"

"It means I don't understand why you didn't just tell me about it right off." While walking along the path beneath a security light, she dug her keys out of her purse.

"I wasn't sure you'd understand."

They entered the building and headed for her apartment door. "Of course I understand. This is a delicate situation. You have to play along to expose the men who want to harm you. I wouldn't expect you to risk that just because a woman was too forward."

"So . . . it's okay? You really don't mind?"

He looked and sounded disgruntled, as if he'd wanted her to blast him with jealousy. Lisa shook her head as she unlocked her door. "I have no claim on you, Hart."

He followed her in, closed the door, and crowded close to her. Only one small light shone in her kitchen, barely breaching the shadows. His expression looked harsh, too serious, his eyes glittering and his mouth tight.

With one hand, he smoothed her cheek. "I want you to."

His look alone left her breathless, never mind the press of his hard body or the touch of his warm breath coming too fast. "What?"

"Have a claim." He cupped the other side of her face. "On me."

Lisa looked at his mouth, ready to agree to almost anything.

Then she firmed her resolve. No, she would not commit herself. If, after they'd made love again, he still felt the same, then she'd discuss it with him. "Let's go to bed."

His eyes flared—and he moved away from her.

"Hart?"

A lamp came on, almost blinding her, and then the overhead kitchen light, and the hall light.

Was he racing to the bedroom without her? "What are you doing?"

"I'm going to make sure that lipstick is washed away." Before he went into the bathroom, he looked back over his shoulder. "I'm not kissing you with another woman's mark on me."

"Oh." *So considerate. Well . . . sort of.* "I appreciate that." Truthfully, she hadn't thought of it. But now that he'd mentioned it, yes, she did prefer that he remove all signs of that woman's pursuit.

Water ran, and she heard Hart splashing, and then gargling. She smiled, dropped her purse and keys on the entry table, and headed for her bedroom. She was so anxious to have him again that she could barely contain her excitement.

She was seated on the side of the bed, removing her shoes, when Hart stepped into the room. He paused, looked at her, and then the lighted bedside lamp, and he smiled.

Coming to stand in front of her, he carefully lifted away her eyeglasses. He set them on the nightstand, and then bore her down on the bed so that she had to give up on the shoe and concentrate on his broad shoulders instead.

"I feel like a kid on Christmas morning," he rumbled before kissing her jaw, her throat, up to her ear. Carefully, he eased his weight onto her, one hand on her cheek, the other braced over her head. "Let me unwrap my gifts myself, okay?"

Her heart raced, especially when he nibbled his way to her mouth, then treated her to a deep, damp, hot kiss. She wove her fingers into his silky hair and held on, so hungry for him that she didn't care what he did, as long as he got on with it.

When he lifted his head and moved to the side of her, his hand now on her waist, Lisa said, "You're not the only one who's been celibate, Hart. So as much as I appreciate finesse, I'd just as soon get down to business."

"You went without too?"

How could she really want any other man after having him? "I'm discriminating," she said.

He was staring at her cleavage. "I'll try to make it worth the wait."

Her toes curled.

Then his hand settled over her breast, and she sucked in a breath.

Watching his hand as he cuddled her through the material of her dress and her demi bra, he said, "I love this dress. Talk about a tease, with all the buttons right there." His dark eyes came up to clash with hers. "It was the same with that damned blouse you wore. The one with the tie at the throat."

Lisa didn't understand, but with his thumb circling her puckered nipple, she couldn't even think.

"I kept imagining pulling that tie open." He gave a low growl. "I love the idea of undressing you."

Lisa closed her eyes to gather herself. "Okay. Then how about you get on with it?"

Grinning, Hart leaned down to kiss her mouth. "Yes, ma'am."

But instead, he wedged his hand into the neckline of her dress and cupped her bare breast.

"Hart!"

"You feel so damn good." He leaned down to kiss her again, smothering her protests. She reached for him, pulling him close, already on the edge of desperate need.

His tongue did wicked things with hers, and she accepted that he was an awesome kisser, the best she'd ever known. When he kissed his way down her throat to her chest, she abruptly realized that he'd been opening buttons and she hadn't noticed.

He caught the edge of her bra cup, pulled it down, and then his hot mouth closed over her nipple.

She arched off the bed with a groan.

He pressed her back down, and spent far too long feasting on her, first on one nipple, then the other. She was frantic by the time he sat up beside her and finished unbuttoning her dress, then spread the material open.

At the sight of her thigh-high hose and small panties, his eyes narrowed.

"You are so fucking sexy . . ."

Coarse language had always been an irritant to her. Now, in that guttural, affected tone, it thrilled her.

Watching his face, Lisa reached for the front clasp of her bra and unhooked it. Her breasts felt tender, swollen, from all his attention. She needed no more encouragement.

But when she started to sit up, he flattened a hand over her belly. "Let me."

He took his time stripping off her shoes and rolling down her nylons. After slipping an arm behind her shoulders, he lifted her up only long enough to remove the dress and bra, and ease them out from under her. Left only in her panties, she waited for him.

His hand cupped over her sex. He bent to kiss her belly, her hip bones.

"Hart, that's enough." She was trembling, so hot. She needed him. Now.

"Not even close."

"Yes." Tangling her fingers in his hair, she tugged him up. "I want to see you, too, remember?"

His smile was slow and wicked. "Do you need your glasses?"

"Not if you back up a little."

Standing at the side of the bed, he took two steps back, then yanked off his shirt and tossed it aside. He removed his wallet, fished out two condoms, and put them on the bedside table. Sitting again, he bent to remove his shoes and socks.

Even with her vision a little blurry, he looked too good to resist. Lisa sat up and hugged her breasts against his gorgeous, solid back. That felt so good, she came to her knees and ran her hands over him. Hart sort of froze, going very still and quiet.

She kissed his ear, breathed in the delicious hot scent of his skin, and explored all those incredible muscles in his shoulders, his biceps, and over to his chest.

He caught her hands. "Okay, woman. I get the point. Let me lose the jeans, and we're in business."

Sitting back on the bed, Lisa laughed. It was a husky, excited laugh. She watched as Hart turned to face her, opened his jeans, and pushed them—with his boxers—down to the floor. He kicked free and stepped over to the mattress.

Doing a long, slow inhale, Lisa took in the exquisite sight of him. "A man couldn't be more beautiful."

He caught her panties and dragged them down her legs. "I don't know about beautiful, but I'm so hard, I'm about to explode."

While looking at her reclining body, he grabbed for a condom, opened the package, and rolled the condom on.

Lisa held her arms out to him. It didn't matter that she was crossways on the bed. It didn't matter that she wanted to touch him, explore him more. For now, she needed him.

He was so tall that once he stretched out over her again, his legs were hanging over the side. To accommodate the position, Hart pulled her to the edge of the mattress and pushed her knees back.

Being so exposed left Lisa both shy and turned on. Her breath caught, and then she felt him against her. His big hands held her knees, pushed them farther back, and all the while he watched as his erection slowly pressed into her. It was erotic, and exciting.

Watching his face, Lisa saw the way heat colored his high cheekbones, how his eyes darkened and his nostrils flared. Muscles flexed and clenched in his chest and shoulders—and then he closed his eyes with a groan and sank into her.

Her breath caught. It felt so right to be like this with him, so perfect.

He levered down over her, saying, "Put your legs around my waist."

And then they were moving together, both of them fevered, kissing, touching, the sensations escalating too fast.

Lisa freed her mouth to cry out. He pressed his face into her throat and strained against her. Arching up, squeezing him with her legs, she held him as tight as she could—and then the most astounding climax rolled through her.

Vaguely, she heard Hart coming, too, his groan raw and deep, his mouth opened on her neck.

Minutes passed, and she continued to regain her breath with Hart's weight comfortably over her. Finally, he struggled up to his elbows and looked down at her. "Not bad. For starters."

She giggled, and then the giggles spread and she was laughing aloud.

He cocked a brow, but when she continued, he rubbed his nose against her temple, her heated shoulder. "I want to eat you up, woman," he whispered, and her giggles died a fast death.

For the next two hours he was relentless, saving, he said, the other condom by making her come twice again before joining with her.

Lisa had never known so much sexual indulgence, but she'd have no qualms in quickly getting familiar. With Hart.

And only with Hart.

It was after two in the morning when he pulled her around in the bed so that her head rested on a pillow. Like a true gentleman, he tucked her in, and even pressed a kiss to her forehead.

When he started to move away, she said, "No, you don't, Skippy. No sneaking away this time."

He leaned over her, touching her hair, kissing the bridge of her nose. "Actually, I was hoping you wouldn't kick me out. Can I assume you want me to stay?"

She was so exhausted, she said only, "Please."

"Be right back." After another quick kiss, he turned out the lights in the apartment, and then slid under the covers with her.

Lisa turned to curl into his side, and it was, by far, the most comfortable position she'd ever found herself in.

She could surely get used to this.

Could he?

When Lisa finally stirred awake, Hart sat up, ready to tackle the awkwardness of what the day would bring.

Lying on her stomach, her face smooshed into her pillow, she opened her eyes and looked at him. For several seconds she tried to focus, and then, with a jolt, she sat up and reached over him for her glasses.

Enjoying that, Hart kept her close and settled her into his side. "Good morning, sweetheart."

Chin tucked in, she mumbled, "Morning."

Yep, Hart thought. Awkward. "So," he said, trying to sound cavalier, "how late do you work today?"

"I have late appointments today, so I won't get back here until around seven."

"Damn. And I have to meet Caroline at eight." He felt her

stiffen, but didn't let her withdraw. "I know it'll be damned inconvenient, but can I see you afterward?"

She straight-armed him so suddenly that Hart lost his hold on her.

Tangled brown hair spilled over her shoulders. She had a crease on her cheek from the pillowcase. And her sleepy eyes looked extra soft behind the lenses of her glasses.

Damn, but he loved her. Every frigging thing about her, even her glasses.

"Only you, Hart Winston, would ask to come to one woman after being with another." She started to scramble off the bed, intent on taking the sheet with her, but he toppled her face-first into the mattress before she got far.

She wrestled with him, but she didn't have a chance. Laughing, Hart pinned her arms above her head and looked down at her straining shoulders, her slender back.

"I could take you like this," he whispered, pressing himself against her plump bottom. "We'd both love it."

"Hart . . ." she warned.

"I'm not going to *be* with Caroline. I'm going to meet her at that shabby parking lot, let the goons attack, and then hopefully see her arrested with her two friends."

Lisa said, "Get off of me."

Instead, he kissed a delicate trail from her nape to her shoulder—and felt her shudder. "Tell me you trust me." He nuzzled her ear. "Tell me you know I don't want any other woman, not when I can have you."

He lifted up and turned her under him. She didn't fight him, but she did have to straighten her glasses. And then her expression was so serious, so intent, he grinned.

"Tell me that you know we have something very special going on."

She chewed her bottom lip. "Define 'special.' "

One thing about Lisa—she'd never make it easy on him. "Special, as in I want to see more of you. A lot more. Tonight, and tomorrow night, and the night after that."

She said, "And the night after that?"

Damn, what did she want from him, a marriage proposal? Surprisingly, that thought didn't entirely throw him. But for now, he settled on a more diplomatic reply, saying, "For as long as we're both enjoying ourselves."

She touched her fingertips to his chest hair, as if in deep thought. "So . . . in that time, you won't be with anyone else?"

"Other than Caroline tonight." He stroked a hand down her side to her hip. "Hell, Lisa, like I told you, I don't want anyone else."

Pulling him down for a kiss, she said, "Okay."

Hart reared back. "Okay? What does that mean?"

She pushed her way out from under him, and left the bed. The sheet stayed behind. "It means that I have to go get ready for the office, but there's a spare key in a basket on top of the refrigerator. Feel free to grab it."

Now that sounded promising. He gazed at her body, cleared his throat, and asked, "How much time do you have before you need to leave?"

"Forget it, Skippy. I'm already running late, and besides, you're out of condoms."

As she sashayed off for the bathroom, Hart let out a low whistle. Tonight he'd buy an entire box of condoms. And now that she'd promised him a key, he felt like he'd made great headway.

Toward what, exactly, he couldn't say. It was incredible that his career was at risk because a woman wanted to set him up so that men could maim him.

Yet all he really cared about was understanding Lisa. He imagined his brother and Joe would get a real kick out of that.

Six

Thick humidity hung in the air, laying an eerie mist over everything. Fat clouds obscured the sliver of moon, and a steady drizzle fell from the night sky, raising noxious steam from summer-scorched blacktop. In this area of town, debris littered the sidewalks and stuffed every brick-and-mortar corner.

Hart looked at the ramshackle drugstore where Caroline said she worked. The place looked like it had been out of business for a decade, with tape on the windows, peeling paint on the clapboard siding, and shingles missing from the roof.

Despite the signs of neglect, a light shone inside. The parking lot behind the building butted up to the concrete-block side of a drive-through pony keg. Broken beer bottles were hazardous to car tires.

Lack of security lights made it hazardous to him.

But Hart wasn't worried. The only thing he felt was an impatience to get this over with, so he could return to Lisa.

Somewhere nearby, Joe had secured himself, unseen but available. He had Dex with him, and Drew Black, having been informed of the plan, awaited an update. Drew had promised that if Brad was stupid enough to use underhanded tactics to win, he'd be booted from the organization.

Hart believed him.

As he pulled around to the back of the building, avoiding the broken glass as best he could, he wondered . . . what Lisa was doing right then. Was she worrying about him? Jealous that he'd be meeting Caroline, even if only to use her to get to the men? Or had she put him from her mind?

Seeing no one in the dark, treacherous lot, he parked his car and turned off the ignition. The plan was for him to linger there until the men launched their surprise attack.

Since Hart knew about it, it wouldn't be much of a surprise, though, which changed the odds in his favor.

The sooner he got through with this, the sooner he could sort through his relationship with Lisa, so he turned up the collar of his Windbreaker and got out of the car. The slamming of the door echoed through the hushed lot.

Hart waited, his senses heightened, but nothing happened. No one approached. He heard nothing but the drip of water from the drugstore's gutter and the song of crickets enjoying the weather.

After pocketing his keys, he walked toward the back of the drugstore.

The door opened before he reached it, and Caroline stepped out under a rusty overhang. "You made it," she called out, opening a big umbrella.

Hart plastered on his most charming smile. "Am I early?"

"Nope. Just on time." Caroline strode out to him, but she looked nervous, her gaze darting this way and that.

She wore snug-fitting jeans, wedge sandals, and a frilly blouse.

If he wasn't so strung out on Lisa, he might have appreciated the picture she made, with her hair loose and curling, her lips all shiny.

Hart took her arm and turned her toward his car. As he did so, he scanned the area, but saw no one. Damn it, he wanted this over and done with. Tonight.

"So where are we going?" he asked, trying to sound natural.

She gave him a coy look. "Your place would be fine."

If she wanted to play it that way, he could go along with her. "Right to it, huh? You don't need to be wined and dined first?"

"With you, no." She sounded wistful, as if she actually wished they could get together.

Not in this lifetime. Hart opened the passenger door and waited. She turned, stared at him for a moment, then leaned up and kissed him silly.

Her lips were soft and warm, her tongue bold. With one hand she held her umbrella, and with the other she stroked his chest. She let out a small sound of yearning . . . but she left Hart utterly unaffected.

All he could think about was how Lisa would feel if she knew he was kissing someone else.

She wouldn't like it; that was for sure. But damn it, he had a role to play, so while keeping his eyes barely open, he listened hard for sounds of attack—and let her have her way with him.

Finally, without his participation to spur her on, she released him and sighed. "You really are so damn gorgeous."

Hart almost laughed—but then, for only a flash of a second, Caroline looked beyond him, and Hart knew. He spun around in time to find a masked man skulking from the drugstore—and damned if he didn't carry a ball bat!

With Hart looking right at him, the guy froze for a second, as if stunned to be caught. Then he gave a battle yell and ran toward Hart with the bat in the air.

Hart stepped away from his car and waited. He didn't run toward the guy, didn't make a sound. He just prepared.

The dude's momentum threw him off balance with the first swing of the bat, making it easy for Hart to dodge the blow and deliver a gut-squelching punch to his unprepared midsection.

Wind left his assailant in a *whoosh*, and he bent double.

Hart didn't need much more time than that. He brought his elbow down hard on the man's back, then his knee up into his face, and the idiot collapsed, his bat clattering on the blacktop. His groans were faint and filled with pain.

"Oh, no, you don't."

Hart heard Joe's voice and looked around in time to see his cousin snatch a tire iron out of another man's hand. Before the guy could recover, Joe pulled off his ski mask, and revealed Brad Emery, the fighter. The jerk on the ground had to be his cohort.

Once Brad was relieved of the weapon, Joe gave him a shove toward Hart and said, "Now see how you fare."

Hart grinned. It figured that Joe would enjoy this.

Gesturing for the man to attack, Hart waited. This guy was a little smarter, taking his time, circling Hart.

Tiring of that game real fast, Hart said, "Chicken shit, are you going to do this, or what?"

"You're a fucking punk, Winston, you know that?"

"I know I'll kick your ass. I know *you know* I'll kick your ass, and that's why you're trying this cowardly bullshit. You're afraid to meet me on the mat, man to man. You know I'd annihilate you—with ease."

That did it. Lacking a fighter's finesse, Brad launched himself at Hart, and they both went down onto the wet pavement.

Shit. Fighting on a padded mat was much easier than on the broken blacktop. But Hart, with a background of wrestling skills, and despite having smacked his head hard, twisted until he had the mount, then pounded Brad in the jaw.

His head snapped back, but Brad didn't stop fighting. He cursed and wrestled until Hart slugged him again, breaking his nose, then again, stunning him with a shot to the jaw.

Joe pulled Hart away. "Ease up, Skippy. The cops are on the way."

Hart shot a look at Joe. Catching his breath, he said, "I hope that damned name isn't catching on."

Trying to protect his head, Brad groaned and turtled up.

"I think Skippy sort of suits you." Grinning, Joe hauled Hart upright.

"How so?"

"Skipping out on women? I think that's where Lisa got it."

Well, hell. Hart scowled, but suddenly the first man started to scramble. Joe said, "Let me. Please."

Joe snagged the fellow from the back, saying, "Uh-uh, bud. Not so fast." A brief struggle ensued, but Joe had no problem subduing him. When he was held in a headlock, Joe removed his mask, revealing Tyler Stevens, the same man they'd seen in the bar.

Adrenaline still rushed through Hart. He swiped a forearm over his face, realized his Windbreaker was ripped, and took it off to toss it toward his car. Caroline still sat there, wide-eyed and distressed, watching him.

He could almost feel sorry for her, except that she'd helped to set this up.

Dex walked up with a video camera. "Good job, Hart," he said without faltering in his recording. "I got it all."

Caroline started to wail.

"What do we do with her?" Hart asked.

Lisa stepped out from behind Dex. She wore a trench coat tied at the waist and with the collar up, and held a matching umbrella over her head.

"You definitely don't let her go, or show her any sympathy, Hart Winston. Not if you know what's good for you."

Rain dripped down Hart's back and off the end of his nose, and all he could do was stare. "Lisa?"

Dex shrugged. "She insisted on coming along. Even crouched in the mud with me without complaining."

Hart looked at her feet and saw mud staining her boots and the bottom of her jeans, almost to her knees. She twirled the umbrella as if the wet conditions didn't bother her at all. Her gaze took in everything with fascination.

"I didn't expect you to be here." In fact, Hart could barely believe it. Why wasn't she at her apartment, warm and dry?

"I didn't want to miss anything." After scowling at Caroline, she smiled at Hart. "You looked incredible."

Pride swelled inside him. He always enjoyed the applause of the crowd, but praise from Lisa meant so much more.

"You're okay?" She looked him over, saw he was soaked, and shook her head. "You hit the ground really hard."

"I'm fine." Hell, he was better than fine. Lisa had come to him out of concern. That had to mean something, right? Then it occurred to him . . . had she seen Caroline kissing him again?

A police car screeched onto the scene. Dragging Tyler along, Joe greeted the officers, and to Hart it appeared he knew the men, or at least had already introduced himself.

Dex showed them some footage, and the cops wasted no time putting the men—and Caroline—in handcuffs.

Knowing his window of opportunity was limited, Hart moved closer to Lisa. "How long have you been here?"

With one disgusted look at Caroline, she said, "Long enough to know that you have deplorable taste in women."

"Not true." Looping his hands around her neck, he kissed her nose and hoped some blunt honesty would win her over. "I fell for you, didn't I?"

She froze for a heartbeat. Through the rain-sprinkled lenses of her glasses, her eyes widened. "You did?"

He couldn't blame her for being surprised. Until tonight, when he'd spent more time thinking of her than of the task at hand, he hadn't fully understood either.

Joe and Dex had known, though, the buttheads. "Oh, yeah, I did. Big time."

"Oh." She smiled and, without reciprocating, collected herself. "I suppose now the police are here, you'll have to answer questions and all that?"

Had he spooked her with that declaration? Damn it, didn't she feel the same? Floundering, Hart frowned at her. She'd once accused him of being insecure. Well, screw that. Tonight, when he had her alone, he'd find out exactly how she felt.

"The cops will want to talk to me, yeah. And I need to call Drew."

Holding the umbrella over his head, she touched his chest. "When I saw it was raining, I grabbed you a dry shirt. It's in Dex's car."

So thoughtful. "Thanks."

She bit her lip. "Do you think they'll mind if I come along?"

Tugging her closer, Hart borrowed her warmth, inhaled her scent. "It might take a while. Wouldn't you rather go home and get comfortable?"

She shook her head as she reached for his mouth, using her thumb to swipe over his bottom lip. When Hart realized she was wiping away Caroline's lipstick—again—he groaned. Until Lisa said, "I'd rather be with you, Hart." Her gaze met his. "Always."

As far as declarations went, that one nearly took him to his knees.

It was damn near midnight before they returned to Lisa's apartment. Hart should have been exhausted, but instead . . . he was anxious.

He wanted things cemented between them. And he wanted to make love to her, right now. All night.

She dropped her purse, stripped off her raincoat, and hung it on a coat tree, then set aside her dirty boots. Rolling her neck, stretching her arms, she said, "God, I'm beat. And I have to be at the office early tomorrow."

Hart crossed his arms and faced off with her. She'd said she wanted to be with him, so she could damn well start right now. "I hope you're not hinting that I should head back to my place, because I'm not budging."

Expression enigmatic, she moved to him and started working on his shirt. "Actually, after knowing how close you came to be being hurt—"

"It was never close, damn it." And that wasn't bragging, just plain truth.

"I mean, if you hadn't known about the attack." She peeled his shirt away, and her hands dropped to his waistband.

Hart liked to think he would have fared just fine regardless, but part of that was the invincible attitude he'd always had, an attitude that made him a daring athlete—and a good fighter.

Without looking at him, she said, "I'd like you to stay with me."

Hart smoothed back her damp hair. "Tonight?"

She nodded.

"And tomorrow night? And the night after?"

She raised a brow. "You're rushing things."

"I'll be going out of town soon, remember? Training, and then fighting." But Brad Emery would no longer be part of the competition. He not only faced criminal charges that would keep him busy in court, but he'd also worn out his welcome with the SBC. Brad's fighting days, at least in the best organizations, were over.

Rather than discuss his trip, she said, "We need a shower."

Well . . . yeah. That'd work. But damn it, he had important things to discuss with her. Before she could leave him, Hart caught her hand and swung her around. "I won't let you distract me with sex."

"Oh, really?"

Hart looked at her big dark eyes, at the challenge there, and gave up. "You aren't going to make this easy on me, are you?"

"Tell you what, Skippy." She smiled and draped her arms around his neck. "Define *fallen* for me, and maybe it'll get easier."

He had no idea what she was talking about.

Rolling her eyes, Lisa explained, "You said you'd fallen for me."

"Big-time," he confirmed.

"So explain *fallen*."

She wanted the words? Words he'd given only to family, words never spoken in the romantic sense?

Hart found that it wasn't nearly as difficult as he'd always suspected. "I love you."

She was so startled, her glasses slipped down her nose. "You do?"

Grinning, feeling like a million bucks, he picked her up and swung her around. "Yeah, I love you." And he stressed again, "*Big-time*."

Her bottom lip quivered. "Oh Hart, I . . ."

Tears? He winced, waiting.

"I've loved you for so long."

His tension lifted. "No shit?"

Nodding, she said, "No shit."

Her easy admission thrilled him. "That's great. So . . . we can move in together?"

"Yes." She threw herself against him. "And I want to be there when you fight. Is that okay?"

"On one condition." Hart headed for the shower. He kissed her, and then kissed her again.

Lisa pushed him back. "What's the condition?"

"Stop calling me Skippy."

Apologetic, she asked, "It really does offend you?"

Hell, yes, it did. "Joe told me why you say it, but it no longer fits." He stood her in the bathroom, wrapped her in his arms, and smiled down at her. "Because from now on, Lisa, I promise I'm staying put."

Breaking the Ice

Deirdre Martin

One

Lennie Buckley had been in Manhattan for more than an hour, and already she was excited.

She'd moved to the Big Apple to attend the Fashion Institute of Technology and get her BFA in fashion design. She'd always loved clothing, the funkier and more unusual, the better. A native of Saranac Lake, a small town in the Adirondacks in New York's north country, she'd done her best to stand out in what she thought was a straitjacketed, uniform world. She was the girl in high school who didn't worry about convention. The girl who sewed her own cool clothes. The girl people thought might go places.

At eighteen, she didn't think college was for her. With the money she'd saved from her part-time job working in a donut shop, she'd gone to Europe, where she bummed around, making enough memories to last a lifetime, but not enough money to stay. She came home dead broke and took a job with the local tailor in Saranac Lake. One year turned to two turned to three turned to four.

She'd fallen into a comfortable slacker life, surrounded by people and places she knew well. When one of her best friends died in a car accident on an icy road, it was a wake-up call: she realized life wasn't a dress rehearsal. Now twenty-seven, it was time for her to get her act together and really make her mark on the world. She applied to FIT, was accepted, and hopped a bus downstate, ready to strut her stuff in the most exciting city in the world.

She'd taken out student loans, but to save even more money, she was staying with her widowed aunt Mary in a part of New York called Hell's Kitchen. She loved the name; it sounded so gritty. Aunt Mary had always doted on Lennie, maybe because Lennie was the only member of the family who didn't think she was completely nuts. She was obsessed with her pet parrot, Rudy II. Her first parrot, the original Rudy, had died unexpectedly after close to twenty years of companionship, leaving her aunt distraught. On her most recent visit, Lennie had seen pictures of Rudy all over the apartment, and found that her aunt had even made a recording of Rudy talking that she still occasionally played. Birds had always scared Lennie a little (those shiny, beady eyes and sharp claws), but at least Rudy II didn't screech and squawk obscenities he'd picked up from Aunt Mary's late husband the way the original Rudy had. When Lennie saw that Aunt Mary still had the old Singer sewing machine she had loved playing with when she was a little girl, she decided she could put up with Rudy II.

Arriving in New York after a grueling seven-hour bus ride, all Lennie wanted to do was collapse. But Aunt Mary had other plans: after giving Lennie a quick tour of the small apartment, even though nothing had changed since Lennie's visit six months before, they were off to her aunt's watering hole, an Irish pub called the Wild Hart that was right around the corner. Aunt Mary wasn't a heavy drinker, but she *was* lonely, and the affection and enthusiasm with which she talked about her friends down at the pub revived Lennie. She dutifully walked with her aunt to the pub. They were no sooner through the door than Aunt Mary took her by the arm and started tugging her toward the bar.

She halted beside a somewhat stout, sad-looking man hunched over a battered paperback. The man looked up.

"Joey, this is my niece, Lennie," Aunt Mary said proudly. "She's going to be living with me while she goes to college."

"Lovely to meet you," said Joey, flashing a charming smile. "It's not often I make the acquaintance of charming young women like yourself, women who—"

"Can it, Mouth," a small woman behind the bar cracked affectionately. She, too, smiled at Lennie as she extended a friendly hand. "Hi. I'm Christie Gibson."

Lennie could see Christie was sizing her up. Perhaps it was what she was wearing: black Doc Marten boots, a short red tartan kilt, black tights, and a faded Patti Smith T-shirt older than she was. Lennie had also lined her eyes thickly with kohl.

"Mrs. C. has been raving about you coming for days," Christie continued. "Psyched about living in the city?"

"Absolutely."

"I just work here a few nights a week to earn some extra money. I'm a firefighter."

Lennie was impressed. "Wow."

"Where's Rudy II, Mrs. C.?" Christie asked.

"Resting at home." Aunt Mary looked at Lennie. "Usually my boy comes with me. Everyone here loves him."

"Speak for yourself," grumbled a strapping, white-haired old man behind the bar. He wiped his hands on his apron before he, too, extended a friendly hand to Lennie. "Jimmy O'Brien. My brother, Charlie, and his wife, Kathleen, own the Hart. I'm helpin' out till my nephew, Liam, gets back from Ireland."

Lennie liked his Irish accent; it made him sound soft and gentle, not the voice she expected to hear coming out of such a bear of a man.

"Let me go get them so you can meet them," said Jimmy, hastily slipping out from behind the bar.

"No, really, there's no—"

Too late. Jimmy was on his way toward the back of the restaurant. Lennie turned to her aunt. "They all seem friendly," she murmured, pleasantly surprised.

Aunt Mary frowned. "Not everyone is so friendly." She discreetly tipped her head toward a somber-looking older gentleman sitting alone at the far end of the bar. "That's the Major. Irish. Barely says a word." She plucked at Lennie's arm again, this time pulling her to the left, toward a thin, tall, scruffy man nursing a beer.

"PJ, this is my niece, Lennie."

The man smiled, revealing a row of slightly crooked, slightly yellowed teeth. *Definitely a smoker*, Lennie thought. *Maybe a coffee drinker too*. He looked a bit like a professor down on his luck, with his threadbare tweed jacket. Even so, there was an aura of charm about him.

"PJ Leary. Pleased to make your acquaintance. I must say, we all feel as if we know you; your aunt here has been talking about you for weeks."

Much to her surprise, Lennie found herself blushing.

"PJ is our resident novelist," Aunt Mary informed Lennie. "Famous."

"Well, I wouldn't say that," said PJ modestly. His brow furrowed with concern. "No Rudy?" he asked Aunt Mary.

"He's not feeling very social today," Aunt Mary replied with a sigh. "In one of his reflective moods."

PJ nodded sympathetically, amazing Lennie. Her aunt had told her how everyone down at the Hart loved her parrot, but she'd taken it with a grain of salt, putting it down to her aunt's somewhat overactive imagination. But it seemed Aunt Mary wasn't exaggerating.

Aunt Mary pointed toward a table in the dining room, where a group of four men sat laughing. "See the handsome one with the salt-and-pepper hair?" Lennie nodded. "That's Quinn O'Brien. He's a well-known newspaper reporter. His parents own this place. I won't drag you over there; he and his newspaper cronies look like they're trying to relax. But I'm sure you'll meet him eventually. He's taken, by the way. Married to a French woman."

"I'm not interested in a relationship," Lennie replied, almost meaning it. *Never say never.*

"Good," her aunt said emphatically. "You keep your head down and study."

A loud laugh went up from another table of men sitting directly across from Quinn O'Brien and his friends, drawing Lennie's attention. There were seven of them, all well built.

"Who are they?" Lennie asked.

Her aunt's eyes cut to the table suspiciously. "Hockey players. Their usual bar closed down, and they've taken to spending time here. Charlie and Kathleen say they're nice, but they look like a pack of brutes to me."

Lennie ignored her aunt's melodramatic statement. They didn't look like a pack of brutes to her; they just looked like hockey players. She enjoyed hockey, and had met lots of players over the years, since Saranac Lake was close to Lake Placid, whose Olympic Center hosted various tournaments year-round. None of the players had ever struck her as brutish.

"Ah, here come Charlie and Kathleen," said Aunt Mary with seeming relief.

Lennie decided that this time, she would be the first to proffer a hand. "Hello," she said, taking Kathleen O'Brien's hand. "I'm Lennie Buckley, Mary's niece."

Mrs. O'Brien looked momentarily disapproving of Lennie's outfit (a fleeting reaction Lennie had grown expert at perceiving), and then collected herself. "It's so lovely to meet you. We've heard so much about you."

Lennie did her best to hide her discomfort as she moved to shake Mr. O'Brien's hand. What on earth could her aunt be telling people?

"Lovely to meet you," said Mr. O'Brien, echoing his wife. "Your aunt says you're here to get a degree in fashion?"

"Yes."

"Our daughter, Sinead, dresses very fashionably," said Mrs. O'Brien. "We'll have to introduce you to her. She's a lawyer," she finished proudly.

"I'd love to meet her," said Lennie. God, all these people were *so nice.* This wasn't how she expected New Yorkers to act.

Mrs. O'Brien laid a warm hand on Lennie's shoulder. "Are you hungry? I've just made a new batch of stew."

"Oh, I'm fine, thanks."

"You're sure, now?"

"Yes."

"All right, then." She turned her attention to Lennie's aunt. "We'll walk over to bingo together Thursday night, yes?"

"Of course."

"Nice to meet you, love," Mr. O'Brien said again. He turned to his wife, gallantly offering her his arm. "Back to the kitchen for us, eh, *macushla*?"

"All work and no play, we are." Mrs. O'Brien chuckled.

Lennie turned to her aunt. "Would you mind if I went back to the apartment? I feel really zonked all of a sudden."

"Go ahead, honey. I'm just going to stay about an hour or so to catch up, then I'll be home."

Lennie kissed her aunt's cheek. "Thanks."

Her aunt smoothed her hair. "I'm so glad you're here. Though I do wish you dressed a bit more—"

"Normal? Don't worry; I do sometimes."

"That's a relief."

She and Aunt Mary started back toward the bar. Lennie could have sworn a few of the hockey players checked her out as she walked by, but she couldn't be sure.

"*To* Ivan the Terrible!"

Laughing, Sebastian Ivanov tossed a shot of whiskey down his throat as his new teammates toasted him. He'd just played his first game as a second-line winger for the New York Blades, scoring a goal in the last two minutes of the third period that propelled the team to victory over New Jersey. Assistant coach Michael Dante had commended him heartily, and head coach Ty Gallagher, a renowned hard-ass, had offered a curt "Good job." That was enough for Sebastian; after twelve years of playing in Russian and European hockey leagues, the NHL had finally come knocking— every player's dream. Acknowledgment from Gallagher was a sure sign he was getting off on the right foot. He fully intended to play his guts out to make sure he proved he could play the North American–style game.

"So, Russky," said defenseman Ulf Torkelson, slapping him on the back, "what do you think of the Big Apple so far?"

"So far, so good." In all honesty, he hadn't really had a chance to explore his new town, what with moving, training camp, pre-season, and now the actual start of the season. Even so, what he had experienced so far delighted him. The people of New York were more outgoing than he'd expected. He loved the city's unique vibrancy, so different from the mood he often encountered at home. Best of all, there was a sizable Russian population out in Brighton

Beach; in fact, his father's only brother, Yuri, lived there. Sebastian hadn't seen his uncle in years, and was looking forward to making the trip out to Brooklyn the first chance he got, not only to see his relative but also to eat some Russian food.

"You sign the lease on that apartment you checked out the other day?" asked Eric Mitchell. Sebastian had liked Eric from the minute he met him. The guy didn't take himself too seriously, except on the ice.

"Yes, of course."

He'd found a small apartment on the Upper West Side, in what the Realtor told him was "a nice, quiet neighborhood." This suited Sebastian just fine; despite being single, he was not big into the bar scene. To play well, he needed peace, quiet, rest. He was by no means a stick-in-the-mud, just disciplined.

Sebastian glanced around the Wild Hart. "I like this place," he said to his teammates. "I'm sorry I didn't get a chance to spend time in the team's original hangout."

Jason Mitchell, Eric's twin brother, grinned proudly. "Great, isn't it? Eric and me, that's one of our hobbies: finding new bars to hang out in."

Ulf snorted. "Oh, you mean like that shithole with the tiki torches a few blocks from Met Gar?"

"That place was great," Eric shot back.

"Yeah, if you're over seventy and have cirrhosis of the liver."

Another teammate, Thad Meyers, looked around. "I think this place is the perfect replacement for the Chapter House. Low key, good food . . ." He raised his beer glass to the Mitchell brothers. "Good job, Mitchy and Mitcho."

"Thank you," Eric replied smugly.

Ulf tapped Sebastian on the shoulder, pointing at the small woman behind the bar serving a gaggle of firefighters who had just come in. "What do you think of her, huh? Pretty cute."

Sebastian studied her. It was true she was cute, but she didn't stir anything in him. "Not my type."

"Not my type," Ulf repeated, mimicking Sebastian's voice. "I love the way you talk, man. You sound like The Terminator."

"No, he doesn't," scoffed the Blades' goalie, David Hewson. "Schwarzenegger is Austrian, not Russian."

"So?" Ulf shot back defensively.

"How would you like it if someone said you sounded Norwegian?" Eric Mitchell chimed in.

"I'm Swedish!"

"Exactly my point, you dick."

Ulf turned to Sebastian. "Sorry if I offended you, dude."

"No problem. You didn't offend me."

"I'll let you in on a little secret," Ulf continued, draping his arm collegially over Sebastian's shoulder, and exaggerating his fading Swedish accent. "The chicks dig the foreign accent. They think it's sexy."

Sebastian nodded thoughtfully. Over the years, he'd heard that from other Russian players who had retired from the NHL and had come home to coach or to play again for the Kontinental League. He was glad being foreign might add to his exoticism, but the players had also told him that Americans knew very little about life in Russia, asking silly questions. It mystified him, since the opposite was true with Russians: they knew a lot about the States.

"You got a girlfriend?" Thad Meyers asked.

Sebastian shook his head. He'd been engaged about three years back to a legal secretary, but in the end it didn't work out. Since then, he'd dated intermittently, concentrating instead on his career.

"We gotta get you a woman, then," Thad continued.

"I don't need one," said Sebastian with a chuckle. "At least not a girlfriend."

Ulf looked confused. "What do you mean?"

"I wouldn't mind"—Sebastian chose his words carefully—"a

female friend. Platonic, just to do things with since I'm new to New York, you know?"

"Platonic?" Ulf thrust his head forward in disbelief. "What are you, one of those celibate weirdos or something?"

"What are you, a dick?" Jason shot back at him.

"In my opinion—" Eric started.

"Which no one gives a damn about, but go ahead anyway," Jason interrupted.

"It's impossible for a heterosexual man and woman to have a platonic friendship. It just is," Eric insisted.

"You're wrong," countered Sebastian. "I have a friend back in Russia named Valerie. We're very good friends. We've never been in the least bit attracted to one another." Which was true. Of course, they'd known each other since they were five, but Sebastian saw no reason to mention that.

"Is she a dog?" Ulf asked.

Eric rolled his eyes. "How 'bout we make a deal? I'll cover your tab if you don't say another word for the rest of the night."

"Jerk," Ulf muttered.

Sebastian hesitated a moment, then decided to ask his friends' advice. "How should I try to find a girl *friend*? Someone who might be willing to explore the sights with me?"

David Hewson drained his beer. "Post a personal ad on Craigslist. You'll probably get a gazillion responses."

"Yeah, from women who say they just want to be friends, but are really hoping it will turn into a romance," said Thad.

"You ever been on Craigslist?" Jason asked him.

Thad twisted uncomfortably in his seat. "No, but I've heard that's not uncommon."

"Yeah, and I've heard if you click your heels three times, you'll be back in Kansas," said Eric sarcastically. He regarded Sebastian. "Try Craigslist. What have you got to lose?"

Two

Lennie's excitement over being in New York had transformed itself into love in just seven short days. Classes were slated to begin two weeks after her arrival, giving her time to get her bearings. Subway map in hand, she'd already figured out how to get from her aunt's place to FIT. She'd visited the Empire State Building, and roamed around Greenwich Village, losing herself in its wonderfully narrow, twisting streets. She'd also been accompanying her aunt to the Hart, and already felt part of their "family." She felt especially tight with Christie, probably because they were close in age. It was nice to have already made a friend.

Lennie was at the Hart solo tonight—Aunt Mary was home sick with a cold. She sat at the bar for a while, chatting with Christie and listening to PJ Leary prattle on about the novel he was trying to sell (something about leprechauns and magic, talking salmon). Lennie was fascinated at first, but after ten minutes, her eyes started glazing over. Eventually, she removed herself to a small table for two across from the bar so she could go through all the text messages from friends up in Saranac Lake. She was engrossed in a message from her sister, Lauren, when the door of the Wild Hart opened, causing a small breeze to sweep into the room. Lennie glanced up. Standing there was an incredibly good-looking man, his dark brown eyes intently scouring the pub. When his eyes lit on Lennie, he cocked his head questioningly, a small smile of uncertainty playing across his lips. Lennie smiled back. He looked familiar. It took her a minute to place him, but then she remembered: he was one of the hockey players who'd been at the Hart last week.

He obviously took her smile as some sort of sign because he approached her table, extending his hand. "Hello, I'm Sebastian. Are you new to New York?"

"Yes, I am."

He looked relieved. "I thought you might be."

Lennie was taken aback. How did he know that?

"I'm Lennie Buckley."

"Nice to meet you, Lennie. May I buy you a drink?"

"Sure." He was forward, but Lennie liked it. She was glad Aunt Mary wasn't here; if she were, she'd probably throw a fit at the sight of Lennie sitting alone with one of the "brutish" hockey players.

"What would you like?" Sebastian asked politely.

"A beer would be fine. Sam Adams?"

"Good choice. I'll be right back."

Lennie nodded, watching him as he crossed to the bar and placed his order with Jimmy. Perhaps he was one of the hockey players whose eyes she had felt on her when she walked past their table last week. Maybe he knew she was new to the city because he'd seen Aunt Mary walking her around and introducing her to everyone. That had to be it.

She was struck again by how handsome he was. Lovely, thick,

dirty blond hair, and those eyes—intense, yet slightly guarded at the same time. His Russian accent made him even more attractive. She'd met a couple of Russian guys when she was in Europe; they were all very polite and well dressed, priding themselves on their appearance. A little bit cocky too. She caught Christie looking at her, her right eyebrow raised inquisitively. Lennie shrugged and turned up her palms as if to say, "You got me." "Later," Christie mouthed.

Sebastian returned to the table with two bottles of Samuel Adams. He looked almost shy as he touched his bottle to hers. "*Za vashe zdorov'ye*. It means 'To your health.'"

Lennie smiled, charmed. "To your health too."

Sebastian took a sip of his beer, then looked embarrassed. "Please forgive me—I forgot to ask if you wanted anything to eat."

Lennie loved his politeness. "I'm fine. But if you want something, go ahead."

"No, I'm fine as well." He ran a hand through his hair, relaxing. "I'm glad you're here."

Lennie smiled again, intrigued. She wasn't quite sure what to say, so she let him continue talking.

"I thought you might change your mind. After all, it can be awkward meeting strangers, especially since we haven't even talked on the phone, only e-mailed." He took another sip of beer. "I was a little uneasy about going on Craigslist to find a woman who was new to the city like I was, and just wanted to be friends. But when I saw you called yourself 'New to New York' and read your e-mail, so friendly and simple, I thought, 'Ah, now here's someone I could see spending time with.' And here you are."

"Yup, here I am." *He thinks I'm someone else.* Lennie knew she should tell him that he'd made a mistake, but she didn't want to. She was intrigued that he was new to the city, just like her, and wanted to explore it with someone who was also new in town. And he was hot.

Of course, if the person who'd agreed to meet him showed up, she was screwed, but she would cross that bridge when she came to it. For now, it was kind of fun playing with him.

"I like your accent," Lennie told him.

"What accent?"

They both laughed. Lennie had to be careful what she asked him about. She had no idea what he'd revealed to the real "New to New York," or what the woman had revealed to him.

Sebastian rolled his beer bottle between his hands. "So, tell me about yourself."

"What would you like to know that I didn't already tell you?" Lennie replied carefully.

"How long you've been here, what brought you here . . ." There was that look in his eyes again: friendly but intense. Probing. Lennie felt herself responding to it as a mild current of heat made the circuit of her body. She was definitely attracted to him.

Lennie filled him in on the basic details of why she was in New York, figuring that too much info might tip him off to her being an impostor. Every time the pub door opened and a woman walked through it, she held her breath. So far, so good.

He was easy to talk to. She was nervous at first that he might think she was some kind of a flake, but no: he seemed really intrigued by the time she'd spent in Europe, and impressed that she was going to FIT. He was thrilled she liked hockey, as well as skiing and skating. With his chin resting comfortably in his palm, he never once looked bored. She was in no way bored, either, when he told her about himself.

"I was raised in western Siberia, in a very mountainous region. That's where I learned to ski."

"And hockey?" Lennie asked.

Sebastian looked sentimental. "I started playing when I was

four. My father was my coach for many years." Sentimental-
ity turned to pride. "I started playing in the Kontinental Hockey
League when I was sixteen. Have you ever heard of it?"

"No, but I take it it's a big deal."

"A very big deal. It's Russia's version of the NHL."

"When did you come here? To the States?"

"I just got here. I'm playing for the Blades. One of the best
teams in the league, you know."

"I do know." She found herself fighting disappointment as she
reminded herself that he'd placed the ad on Craigslist specifically
looking for friendship, and nothing more.

The evening flew, and much to Lennie's relief, no one had
turned up claiming to be "New to New York."

"So." For the first time all night, Sebastian looked a little shy.
"Would you like to do something next Sunday? Maybe take a
sightseeing tour on one of those buses? Unless you think that's too
corny."

"No, I would love it." She loved doing touristy stuff. In London
she'd taken a tour of the Tower. In Paris she'd gone on one of those
boat rides on the Seine.

Sebastian looked pleased. "I'll find out where the tour starts
and meet you there, yes?"

Lennie nodded as they exchanged cell numbers. "What do I
owe you for the beer?"

Sebastian looked mystified. "Nothing. On me."

"That's not right. I mean, we're friends. It's only right I should
contribute."

"Next time, maybe," he said. He came round the table and
pulled out her chair for her like a true gentleman. "It was very nice
to meet you," he said. "Shall I see you home? It's very late."

Lennie was charmed. "No, I can manage. I live right around
the corner."

He struck his forehead lightly. "That's right. With your aunt. Please excuse my forgetting."

"I forgive you," she teased. "Good luck with your games this week. I'm sure you'll do well."

Sebastian laughed lightly. "I hope so."

For a split second, Lennie thought he was going to kiss her cheek, but instead he took her hand and squeezed it warmly, causing her heart to sink with disappointment just the tiniest bit. "I'll see you Sunday. I think it will be fun."

"Me too."

"Good night, now."

"Good night."

Lennie watched him go, the handsome, intriguing, polite, athletic, charming man with whom she was now "friends." You just never knew, she marveled. She'd come in here to pass time, and the evening had ended with a social outing next weekend. Amazing.

Here one week and you're already picking up guys, huh?"

Lennie chuckled at Christie's remark. The minute Sebastian left, Christie wasted no time in frantically waving Lennie over to the bar, greeting her with a single command: "Spill."

"Nothing to spill about. And PS, I don't pick up guys."

Christie was alone behind the bar, cleaning up. Jimmy O'Brien was "dead on his feet," which was totally understandable, given his age. Still, Christie confided in Lennie that she wondered if Jimmy was just "sticking it to her." Jimmy was a retired cop. According to Christie, there had always been antagonism between the FDNY and the NYPD. The cops thought the firefighters had it too easy, sitting around "on their asses at the firehouse until called out to a fire," while they, the cops, were always out on the street, facing down danger. Jealous, Christie told her. She and Jimmy frequently traded snarky remarks. The regulars loved it.

The regulars . . . *Hell's bells*, thought Lennie. She'd already figured out the Hart was such a hive of gossip that PJ and The Mouth would tell her aunt she'd spent the night chatting away with one of the hockey players.

"What's the deal with you and the hottie?" Christie asked.

"God, isn't he?" Lennie agreed. "He's new to New York. I'm new to New York. We're just going to hang out together. That's it."

Christie snorted. "Yeah, right."

"Why is that so hard to believe?"

"Because I was watching you two. You seemed so, I don't know, connected."

"Really?" Lennie was pleased.

"Yeah, really. So, what did you find out about him, apart from the fact he's a hot hockey player for the Blades?"

Lennie told Christie all about Sebastian, trying not to sound like a breathless teenybopper.

"Sounds like a really interesting guy."

"I know."

"I bet he's good in bed."

Lennie laughed.

"Maybe you'll get to find out."

"Doubt it. He just wants to be friends."

"We'll see how long that lasts."

"Did you see his shirt? Fit him really well. Beautifully cut. I'll bet my bones it's a Perry Ellis."

"I have no idea who you're talking about, but I'll take your word for it." Christie began mopping the bar. "So—what? He just picked you at random to sit with?"

Lennie told Christie about the Craigslist screw-up. Christie looked shocked.

"You have balls, Lennie. Seriously. What if the real 'New to New York' had turned up?"

"Then I would have been in heaps of trouble. But she didn't show. Thank God." She watched Christie stack glasses. "What's your romantic status?"

"Just broke up with a fellow firefighter. Guy in my house. Talk about stupid. I'll never do that again."

"We gotta get you a man."

"No, thank you. I need time to heal. The bastard ripped my heart out of my chest and threw it to the dogs."

Lennie winced. "Gotcha."

"So your aunt—bit of a whack, no?"

"Total whack. But I love her. And she has a sewing machine."

"You really think you'll last, living with her?"

"I have to; I can't really afford to pay rent."

"How do you deal with that bird?"

"He's okay." Lennie was slowly getting used to Rudy II's squawking, more out of necessity than anything else, since Aunt Mary walked around with him perched on her shoulder most of the time. It was hard to avoid him.

"Eclectic group here," Christie mused. "But I love it. PJ plucks on my last nerve sometimes, but then I think, 'Ah, he's just lonely, poor bastard,' so I try to make an extra effort to be nice."

"Mr. and Mrs. O'Brien seem nice," Lennie observed.

"They're really nice." Christie glanced up at the clock. "God-damn Jimmy! I could have been out of here twenty minutes ago if he wasn't so 'tired.'" She stifled a yawn. "What are you and Sebastian doing together, by the way?"

"Going on one of those Big Apple tour buses. Totally lame, I know, but I think it will be fun."

"Not lame at all. I've wanted to do that since I was a little kid. You'll have to tell me all about it."

"I will."

Christie took off her apron, tilting her head in the direction of the kitchen. "Gotta go tell the O'Briens I'm done and ready to lock up. Maybe you and I could go out one night? Hang out?"

"That'd be great. I'll wait. We can walk out together."

Find a lady friend on Craigslist?"

Sebastian looked up from the locker room bench, where he sat lacing up his skates, to see Eric Mitchell regarding him with interest. Sebastian noticed that both the Mitchell brothers wore tiny gold crucifixes around their necks before every game; it was interesting to see what other players' pregame rituals were. The goalie back in Moscow wouldn't go out on the ice unless he'd listened to Queen's "We Are the Champions" at least twice. Sebastian's ritual was always to do everything from left to right. He put his left leg into his shorts first. He tied his left pads first, laced his left skate first, put on his left glove first. He'd been doing this since he was four.

"Yes," said Sebastian. "I met her at the Wild Hart last night, and on Sunday, we're going to take one of those bus tours around New York."

"No shit." Ulf Torkelson came closer as he pulled his jersey over his head. "She hot?"

Sebastian scowled. "She's attractive." *Very attractive*, he thought. "But I don't see what that has to do with anything. We're just friends."

"What's her name?"

"Lennie."

"What the hell kind of a name is that?" Ulf asked.

"It's a nickname. Her real name is Leonora."

"In that case, I'd call myself Lennie too," said Eric.

"What does she look like?" Ulf prodded.

Sebastian heaved a heavy sigh. Clearly his teammate wasn't going to let the subject drop. "She's small with short brown hair. Brown eyes."

Warm, brown eyes that often looked mischievous. A wonderful sense of humor. An interesting life story. Sebastian couldn't believe how pumped up he'd felt leaving the Wild Hart the other night, knowing he was going to see Lennie the following Sunday. When he realized he'd been playing their conversation in his head all the way back to his apartment, he started to worry: that didn't seem like something a man who only wanted to be friends would do.

"Small," Ulf mused. "She a midget or something?"

"Oh, my God," said Eric Mitchell, giving the cross around his neck a quick kiss. "You are such an idiot, Ulf." He turned to Sebastian. "You mean petite, right?"

"Yes. Petite." Delicate.

"I knew that," Ulf muttered defensively. "I was just fuckin' with him."

"How many responses did you get?" asked Thad Meyers.

"Too many to count," said Sebastian. "It was overwhelming. I couldn't read them all."

"What made you pick this chick?" Ulf asked.

"Her e-mail was very simple. A lot of the others went into very long, confusing stories I didn't have time for."

"Any good ones?" Ulf asked wolfishly.

Sebastian stared at him. "You need to get a life. You know this?"

Ulf ignored the insult. "She okay with you being a Commie?"

"Of course," Sebastian mocked. "I pulled out my wallet, showed her my picture of Karl Marx, and sang 'The Internationale' on the top of my lungs. She was quite impressed."

"Torkelson usually pulls a picture of ABBA out of his wallet when he meets women, don't you, Ulfie?" asked Eric.

Everyone laughed.

"Bite me," said Ulf, storming off with a glare.

"He can dish it out but he can't take it, eh?" Sebastian said to goalie David Hewson, who had joined them after completing his pregame ritual of throwing up.

"Yep. He's a total pantywaist off the ice," said Eric. He punched Sebastian's shoulder playfully. "You ready to rock tonight, Ivan?"

Sebastian grinned. He liked his nickname; it was so stupid it was funny, plus it made him sound formidable. He felt sorry for the Mitchell brothers; their nicknames were Mitchy and Mitcho, respectively.

"Keep playing this well, and Coach Gallagher might actually give you a real compliment," said Thad. "He give you the famous 'You have to live, eat, breathe hockey' speech yet?" The other players groaned.

"At training camp," said Sebastian. He completely understood where his coach was coming from. But at the same time, Sebastian felt he had the right to enjoy himself in his free time, especially since he was living in one of the most exciting cities in the world.

Assistant Coach Dante popped his head in the locker room door. "All right, you *gavones*. Let's get out there and play Blades hockey."

Pumped with adrenaline, Sebastian walked out of the locker room with his teammates. It was the same feeling he'd had the other night after talking to Lennie. He pushed the thought from his mind, and headed out to the ice.

Three

Lennie arrived at the CitySightsNY bus departure spot on Broadway to find Sebastian already there. She'd been looking forward to this all week. She hadn't had much time to do anything fun, since she'd been running around getting ready to start school, trying to clear up a few snafus that had cropped up.

She'd worried that it might be awkward when they spoke on the phone in the middle of the week to confirm their plans, but if anything, it was the opposite: they talked for close to half an hour. Lennie liked this guy. She really liked this guy. And maybe, if they spent enough "friend" time together, he would start to like her too.

As she knew would be the case, PJ and The Mouth had ratted her out to her aunt, telling her about the night she'd spent chatting with Sebastian. Aunt Mary had overreacted, going off on some rant about athletes, libidos, and jockstraps. When Lennie challenged her, asking if she'd ever met an athlete, all Aunt Mary could come up with was a guy her late husband used to bowl with. "Bowlers aren't athletes," Lennie countered, fleeing the apartment to the sounds of Rudy II imitating her aunt's warning of "You'll regret it!"

It was a chilly morning, but since she was dying to sit on the open, top deck of the double-decker, she'd dressed warmly but stylishly: jeans, Uggs, and a gray Aran Isle sweater.

As for Sebastian, Lennie thought he looked pretty damn cool and relaxed: black wraparound sunglasses, a weathered brown leather bomber jacket, and jeans. *He just wants to be friends,* she reminded herself. *Then change his mind, girl,* said the little devil sitting on her left shoulder.

"Hello," he said with a big smile. "You are right on time."

"I pride myself on being punctual."

He pulled out two tickets for the tour. "The bus should be here in a few minutes." He glanced around at the small crowd they were part of. "I don't think it will be too crowded."

"No," Lennie agreed. "If you don't mind, I'd like to sit upstairs in the open air."

"So would I. Are you sure you won't be cold?"

"I'll be fine. I'm from the north country, remember? Breezy is nothing."

Sebastian laughed. "Same for me. If you come from Siberia and can't handle breezy, you are in serious trouble, my friend."

Lennie gestured at the tickets in his hand. "What do I owe you?"

"Nothing."

"Sebastian, that's not right. It makes me very uncomfortable."

He looked frustrated. "How do I say this? I'm very—traditional. Where I come from, men pay, whether the woman is a lover or a friend. It's just the way it's done."

"But that's not how it's done here," Lennie pointed out softly.

"Listen to me. I'm a professional hockey player. Not to boast, but I make a lot of money. You said you are a student, yes? So let me take care of this."

Lennie agreed, but she still didn't feel right about it, even though deep down she was charmed by his old-fashioned attitude; it felt rather chivalrous. "You can take care of it this time. But next time—"

Sebastian smiled. "We'll see."

The tour lasted two and a half hours, covering a lot of territory: Met Gar, Macy's, the Empire State Building, SoHo, Chinatown, Little Italy, Wall Street, the Lower East Side, South Street Seaport, Rockefeller Center, Central Park, and more. Lennie was exhilarated, but at times she had a hard time paying attention to what the tour guide was saying, since she and Sebastian were squished close together on a bus seat for two. He was a big man; there was no avoiding their touching unless he somehow leaned away from her, which would have been extremely uncomfortable. If he was aware of how aware she was of their being in contact, he certainly didn't show it.

"This is great," Lennie enthused during one of the breaks when the tour guide wasn't talking. "I mean, all those places we've seen so far? I want to check out all of them, except the Empire State Building. I've already been there."

"There isn't much to Met Gar. I can attest to that."

"Maybe I can come see you play sometime."

Sebastian nodded slowly. Lennie wondered if she was coming on too strong; it was tough to get a read on him with his eyes obscured by his sunglasses.

She touched the arm of his leather jacket. "This is really nice. Do you know who the designer is?"

"No idea."

"Mind if I check the label?"

"Uh, no, go ahead."

She turned around on the bus seat and knelt, pulling the collar of his jacket slightly away from the nape of his neck. She caught a scent of cologne; it made her want to lean closer to his skin and inhale deeply, but she didn't dare. She focused on the label.

"Giorgio Armani. Nice."

Sebastian held out one of his arms, looking at the sleeve. "I like nice clothing."

"All the Russian guys I've ever met do."

He lowered his sunglasses, peering at her over the rim playfully. "Oh, so you know all about Russian men, eh?"

"A little," said Lennie, suddenly feeling a bit shy. "I mean, I met a few Russian guys when I was traveling in Europe. They were all really nice, but they were also into dressing well." She gave a small wince. "Am I stereotyping?"

"I don't think so," Sebastian said thoughtfully. "Dressing well? It probably comes from having so little choice available to us when the Communists were in power. Everything was so drab! I think once things opened up, everyone who could afford to, started to dress well."

"I see. Well, I'm glad I wasn't stereotyping."

"Don't fret so, *padroogah*. That's 'friend' in Russian."

"I figured. *Padroogah*," Lennie repeated slowly, trying to mimic his accent.

Sebastian laughed delightedly. "Very good! You are a natural! Maybe there's some Russian blood in you somewhere!"

"My last name's Buckley, and my mother's maiden name was Pearse. There's no Russian in the genes, believe me."

"Don't be so sure."

Lennie took a deep breath. "Can I ask you a question?"

"Of course."

"Why were you looking for a woman to hang around with?"

Sebastian laughed. "Because I play on a sports team! I have more than enough male friends! It's a nice change to spend time with a woman."

"I get that." Lennie paused. "Can I ask a favor of you?"

"Questions, favors—you're very demanding," Sebastian teased.

"You sure you don't mean pushy?"

"Maybe pushy. But that's all right. I like women—I mean women friends—who aren't shy. So what is the favor?"

"Can you take your sunglasses off? I hate not seeing your eyes."

Sebastian seemed surprised. "Oh. All right." He pushed the glasses back so they were atop his head. "Better?"

Lennie gave a controlled smile. "Much." Control was important right now. She didn't want to reveal how attracted she was to him.

The tour ended, and they disembarked with the rest of the passengers.

"I had fun today," Lennie said happily.

"Me too."

She became aware they were standing in the middle of the sidewalk, forcing exasperated New Yorkers to go around them. "We should move." They moved off to the side, standing in front of the CitySights office. "Want to get together again sometime? Maybe next week?"

"Yes, of course."

"Great." Lennie's heart was beating a gleeful tattoo. "How about I pick what we do? I already have something in mind."

"What's that?"

"A surprise."

"You're a woman of mystery, too, eh?"

"I can be." *We're flirting. He can deny it all he wants, but we're flirting.*

"I am on the road the beginning of the week. Why don't I call you when I get back?"

"Sounds good."

Sebastian nodded, squeezing her shoulder affectionately. "Good luck with school this week."

"Thank you. Good luck on the road."

He put his sunglasses back over his eyes. "See you."

"Yup."

They started off in opposite directions. Lennie had taken only a few steps when she impulsively called his name and ran back to him. She hesitated a moment, then gave him a quick kiss on the mouth before turning around and melting back into the crowd. She could feel him watching her as she made her way up the street. It had been a bold thing to do, but she had no doubt that if it was the wrong thing to do, he'd let her know next week. In the meantime, she'd never in her life been so glad she'd told a lie.

Four

"Yo, Vladimir Putin, good game tonight."

Sebastian nodded appreciatively at Eric Mitchell's compliment. The Blades had just won at home against Washington, 3–2. Sebastian was "in the zone," as his American teammates called it, the whole night.

The players were sitting at their usual table at the Hart, and Sebastian found his gaze drawn to the table where he and Lennie had first spoken. Another couple was sitting there now, clearly in love, holding hands. Sebastian felt a small, unwanted pang of envy. Ever since Lennie had kissed him, he'd been confused.

It had stunned him when she'd softly pressed her lips to his. That was no platonic kiss, and he was glad. He'd known from the night they met that he was attracted to her, and the bus trip confirmed it. Her intelligence, her sense of humor, her boldness—these were all things he liked in women. But did he really want to go down this road? Sebastian threw a shot of whiskey down his throat. He couldn't believe how much time he'd spent thinking about Lennie during his downtime while on the Blades' recent road trip. Her soft brown hair, her dancing brown eyes, her body. She was petite, but not bone thin. She had a nice-sized bust and curvy hips. He liked his women with a little meat on their bones. *His women.* This was not the way he should be thinking.

His teammates had, of course, asked him about his "date" with Lennie. He'd made a point of correcting them, saying it was an "outing" with his new friend. He'd wanted to punch Ulf when the Swedish bastard had sniggered. When they asked if he was going to see her again, he was vague. If he told them she said she was going to surprise him, sexual innuendos would fly fast and furious.

Talk settled into shop. Sebastian and his teammates were in the middle of discussing Lou Capesi, the head of Blades' PR, who was trying to convince them to do a stud muffin Blades calendar, when one of the men from the table next to theirs came over.

"Hey, guys."

"Hey, Quinn," said Eric.

"Just wanted to tell you guys you played great tonight." He looked at Sebastian. "You especially."

"Thank you."

Quinn gestured at the table where his friends sat. "If you guys ever want to hang with us, just pull up some chairs. The more, the merrier. And I promise, it'll all be off the record."

"Cool," said Eric.

Quinn nodded, and sauntered back to his table.

"Who's that?" Sebastian asked.

"Quinn O'Brien," said David. "His parents own this place, and he's a hotshot reporter at one of the local papers. The other guys work at local newspapers too."

"You ever see his sisters?" said Ulf. "Hotties."

"Yeah, especially that redhead who's married to the Irish guy," said David. "The thin, well-dressed one is some high-powered lawyer. I think she's divorced, but I doubt any woman with a brain would want to date a pig like you."

Everyone laughed while Ulf scowled. "You know, I'm gettin' a little tired of you assholes ragging on me all the time—especially you," he said, pointing to Eric. "Once upon a time you were Leader of the Pussy Patrol."

"The key word is 'was,'" Eric said smugly. "Some of us grow up eventually."

"You'll die of old age before you grow up, dickface," Ulf answered, eliciting laughs from everyone at the table, including Eric.

They made an early night of it since they had practice the next day. Sebastian was on his way out the door when a crazy lady with a parrot on her shoulder pointed at him.

"You," she barked. "I want to talk to you."

Confused, Sebastian looked to his teammates for help, but as soon as they realized they weren't the ones singled out, they hightailed it out the door. Not knowing whether he should be more afraid of the woman or the parrot, Sebastian steeled himself and walked over to the bar. "Can I help you?"

"You're damn right you can," she said, draining her cocktail glass and putting it down on the bar with a resounding slam.

"Damn! Damn! Damn!" the parrot screeched. No one seemed the least bit bothered.

"Shut up for a moment, Rudy," the woman commanded. She looked Sebastian up and down, her lips pressed together in disapproval. "Keep away from my niece. She's got enough on her plate without finding herself tangled up with some Russky heartbreaker. I know your Commie ways."

Sebastian was completely baffled. "Excuse me, but I don't know what you are talking about, ma'am."

"Lennie is my niece."

"Ah." Lennie had made no mention that the parrot woman in the bar was the aunt she was living with. Now he knew why: the woman was *shapinaya sobaka*—crazy.

"I know all about you chatting and charming her, and your bus ride around the city on Sunday. I'm warning you right here and now: you try anything funny, and you'll have to answer to me—and Rudy."

"Lennie and I are just friends."

The aunt snorted. "Till you get her drunk on Stoli and have your way with her."

Sebastian was getting angry. "Excuse me, Missus—"

"Colgan. Mary Colgan."

"Mrs. Colgan, as I said, Lennie and I are just friends. And even if we weren't, this really is nothing of your business," Sebastian said politely. "Good night."

He could hear Lennie's aunt spluttering behind him as he walked out the door. His teammates were huddled together outside the pub, eagerly waiting to know what that was all about. Sebastian told them the crazy harpy was Lennie's aunt and that she had something against Russians. They all burst out laughing so hard they couldn't even make jokes. Sebastian knew he'd never live this down. But that wasn't even the worst part. The worst part was realizing he might have just made things difficult for Lennie.

"*Please* tell me you're joking. Please."

Lennie was sitting on Christie's couch, queasiness creeping up her throat as Christie told her about her aunt calling Sebastian over to the bar and threatening him. Of course, her aunt had been on her butt about Sebastian from the moment she got home on Sunday after the bus tour. Lennie shut her down by telling her that if she didn't drop it, she was going to move out. She knew it was a harsh thing to say; but if the past two weeks were a preview of what living with Aunt Mary was going to look like, there was no way she'd be able to endure it. Since then, her aunt had been watchful but silent on the subject of Sebastian.

"Not joking," Christie said grimly. "Your boyfriend concluded by telling her that even if you were going out, it was"—Christie broke into a bad Russian accent— " 'nothing of her business.' "

Lennie groaned and put her face in her hands.

"I notice you didn't jump right in to say, 'He's not my boyfriend,' " Christie observed dryly.

Lennie lifted her head. "He's not. Yet. But I want him to be." She told Christie about kissing him; how she knew it was bold, but it felt like the right thing to do.

Christie looked uneasy. "But what are you going to do if he really, truly, just wants to be friends?"

"Die of a broken heart." Lennie twirled a strand of hair around her finger nervously. "Seriously, don't you think if he really just wanted to be friends, he would have set me straight right there and then when I kissed him?"

"It doesn't sound like you gave him a chance to!"

Lennie's shoulders sank. "True. Okay, but don't you think that if it bothered him, he would have called me during the week to tell me?"

"I don't know. Who the hell knows how guys' minds work?"

"I guess I'll find out Saturday—if he still wants to see me."

"What are you guys doing?"

Lennie perked up a bit. "I'm surprising him. There's supposed to be this really great weekend flea market on the corner of West Twenty-fifth and Sixth Avenue. I thought it would be fun; we could just walk around, talk, and look at stuff. Plus, I'm sure I could probably pick up some cool threads I can wear, or tear apart and make into something new."

"Maybe . . . if you have time . . . you could make something for me sometime?" Christie asked shyly.

"I would love to!" Lennie said excitedly. "You do dress kinda drab."

Christie's face fell. "Thanks a lot."

"I can fix that," Lennie said confidently. "Don't worry."

"Are you going to talk to your aunt about what she said to Sebastian?"

"I think I'll let it go for now. If he brings it up, then I guess we'll deal with it. I *am* going to lie though my teeth to my aunt about seeing him again, though. I'll tell her I'm studying up at the library at FIT."

Christie checked her watch. "Shoot, I'm gonna be late for my shift. I expect a full report, obviously."

"Obviously." Lennie smiled bashfully. "I hope this doesn't sound dumb, but it's nice to have a girlfriend to talk to."

"Me too. I spend most of my days with a pack of immature assholes. But at least some of them can cook." She stood up. "Catch you at the Hart, maybe Monday night?"

"Maybe even Sunday. Ciao."

This can't be the place, Sebastian thought as he stood at the corner of West Twenty-fifth Street and Sixth Avenue, waiting for Lennie. Since they'd agreed to meet at noon, he thought perhaps her "surprise" might be a well-known diner of some sort she'd heard about, and they were meeting for lunch. But no: it was a huge, open-air market.

She was two minutes late. Not a crime. He stood and watched

the dense, eclectic crowd move from booth to booth filled with junk. He didn't understand it. Why would anyone want to buy someone else's castoffs? He glanced at some of the items in the nearest stall. An ashtray in the shape of South America. An old picture of a man in what he thought might be a World War II uniform. A hideously lifelike stuffed monkey. Completely mystified, he quickly ducked across the street to a small deli to grab a cup of coffee. Deli coffee was the best, he'd discovered. Going to Starbucks seemed crazy to him. What kind of a fool paid three dollars for a plain cup of coffee, even if they could afford it?

He was walking back across the street when Lennie caught him by surprise, tapping him on the shoulder. He turned. Another surprise.

She was clad in black from head to toe. Black shoes, black jeans, black turtleneck, black leather jacket, black beret. She reminded him of a ninja, or a cat burglar—a very attractive cat burglar. Her lipstick was deep berry red. She looked so different from last Sunday, when she'd looked different from the first time they met. He assumed what she was wearing was fashionable. "Funky," she called it. But he wasn't sure he liked it. Still, the lipstick . . . it made her lips look full, delectable.

"Hey." She was cheery as they continued across the street. "Oh, wow, is that coffee? Can I have a sip?"

"Of course."

He handed his coffee to her. She took a sip.

"I hope you haven't been waiting long."

"Only a few minutes."

They made it to the corner, and stopped. Lennie gestured behind her at the flea market, a big grin on her face. "Surprise."

"Yes, surprise," Sebastian murmured, trying not to sound as unenthusiastic as he was feeling.

"I heard this place was great. I'm hoping I can find some good stuff. Maybe you can too."

Good stuff? He doubted it.

Lennie grabbed his hand, pulling him toward the first row of vendors. She liked being the aggressor, he realized. He wasn't used to it at all. Wasn't it the job of the man to pursue? And yet, there was something about her audacity that turned him on just a little.

Lennie headed straight for a stall selling secondhand clothing. "Shall we look?" she asked Sebastian.

"You look." He glanced at his watch. "There's something I need to do. I'll meet you back here in thirty minutes?"

Lennie looked disappointed. "Oh. Okay."

"I don't want you to feel rushed with me standing here," Sebastian explained. A white lie.

Lennie shrugged. "Okay." She shyly kissed his cheek. Sebastian chuckled, pulling his sunglasses down so she could see the wink he gave her. Lennie turned happily to the nearest rack of clothing as he made his escape.

He took a walk, reveling in the city's sights, sounds, and smells. Bought a hot pretzel for himself, which he enjoyed immensely. When he got back, Lennie was waiting for him, holding two big shopping bags.

"You will not believe the great stuff I got!" she said breathlessly. "Wanna see?"

"Of course."

Each item she pulled from the bags was worse than the previous one. A faux leopard coat with a long tear in the right sleeve. A sleeveless top covered in yellow sequins, half of which were missing. Stretched out, faded T-shirts. A handbag that looked like something his grandmother used to carry when she did her daily shopping. He couldn't hold his tongue.

"I don't understand."

"Understand what?" Lennie asked, folding items and carefully putting them back in the bags.

"Why would you spend good money on someone else's old clothing? If you don't have money to buy clothes, I will gladly lend you some, no problem. But this trash . . ."

"Excuse me?"

Sebastian rubbed his hands over his face in frustration. "How can I explain? You never lived under Communism, where no one had anything, and what we did have, we had to fix and recycle and repair. Nothing new. It was terrible.

"And then things changed, and finally people could buy things. New things, new clothing, not clothing that was old and out of fashion. What a luxury!" He gestured at her bags. "That is why this perplexes me. Why are you shopping for clothing as if you were poor? Why are you buying garbage? That coat is ripped. Who wants someone else's ripped coat when you can buy a new coat? Do you see?"

Lennie took his hand. "Just because something is old or used doesn't mean it's trash, Sebastian. I like old clothes. They inspire me. They're fun to mix and match. Ever hear the saying 'One man's trash is another man's treasure'? This might seem like junk to you because of where you come from, but to me, it's kind of fuel for the creative fire. Plus, to be blunt, I don't want to look exactly like everyone else."

"Believe me, you don't."

Lennie's face fell, and Sebastian immediately felt awful. "No, no, don't look sad. I meant it as a compliment," he assured her, brushing her cheek with the back of his hand. "You are a unique-looking woman, Lennie. And not because you insist on wearing these—things." Without realizing it, he had moved so close to her that her face was almost blurred. He took a step back in an effort to ward off the rush of romantic feelings engulfing him. "I'm sorry if I insulted you."

"It's okay. It was kind of interesting hearing your opinion, actually. Cultural differences, I guess."

"Would you like to continue looking around?" Sebastian offered.

Lennie laughed. "You'd hate that! No, it's okay."

"You are sure?"

"Yes, I swear."

He didn't want their outing to end so fast. He supposed they could figure out another tourist attraction they could explore together, but what he really wanted was to just sit and talk with her—privately, quietly.

"Would you like to go back to my apartment for coffee?"

Lennie looked pleased. "Yeah, I would really love that."

"Good."

"You live on the Upper West Side, right?" Sebastian nodded. "What's the address?"

Perplexed, Sebastian told her, watching as she pulled out a subway map from her rather sizable shoulder bag.

"What are you doing? We'll take a cab."

"But I can't aff—"

"I can." He took her hand. "No worries. C'mon."

Five

"I'm sorry. I don't have much furniture yet."

Lennie couldn't believe macho, opinionated Sebastian sounded sheepish as he ushered her into his apartment. Always the gentleman, he was carrying her bags from the flea market. She couldn't help but wonder what was going through his mind. He was probably grumbling inwardly about toting trash around.

"Let me take your coat."

Lennie shucked her black leather jacket and handed it to him, giving her a chance to take in his place as he hung their coats in the closet. He wasn't kidding about the sparsity: the only furniture in the room was a large, white sectional couch, a brass and glass coffee table, and the biggest high-def TV she'd ever seen. Such a guy space.

"Sit, sit," Sebastian urged. "I'll go make us coffee."

"It won't be much fun for me sitting here alone! I'll come with you; we can talk while you're making it."

"Sounds good."

She followed Sebastian into the kitchen. There was a small table there, atop which some Russian-language newspapers were scattered. An image flashed in her mind of him lingering over the paper at breakfast.

Coffee at her aunt's house was strictly a drip affair: boil water in a teakettle on the stove, pour it into a filter filled with grounds, watch it drip into a glass carafe. But sitting on Sebastian's marble counter was a sleek, modern coffee machine. Sebastian caught her looking at it and patted the top of it proudly.

"Krups. One of the best brands. It's programmable; it makes both coffee and espresso."

"Wow."

"Which would you like?"

"Plain coffee is fine, thanks."

Sebastian nodded, and set about making their coffee. Lennie was struck by how proud he was of this simple (or not so simple) kitchen appliance. To him it symbolized success. Choice.

"Your apartment is really nice."

"Thank you," Sebastian said, looking pleased. "I especially like it because the street is quiet."

"I wish where I lived was quiet," Lennie replied enviously. "My aunt's apartment is on the second floor right in the front of the building. I hear every car alarm, backfiring truck, and loud drunk who passes by."

Sebastian looked uncomfortable. "Your aunt . . ."

"I know what happened. And I'm so sorry."

"It's not a big deal. I was more worried it would make trouble for you." He tapped the side of his head. "She's touched, yes?"

Lennie laughed loudly. "I guess you could say that. She's got a good heart, though, you know?"

"That bird . . ." Sebastian shook his head. "He's crazy too."

"Well, he mimics her." Lennie swallowed. "I'll make sure my aunt doesn't bother you again, I promise."

"Don't fret. I can handle your aunt."

"I'm glad one of us can." Lennie gestured at the papers. "You must miss home."

"Yes and no. I miss my family, and some of my friends. But I don't miss"—he seemed to be searching for the right word—"how behind the times it still is in some places. Except in Moscow. You can get almost anything you want there now—designer clothes, expensive jewelry, Mercedes—it's amazing." He shrugged. "Anyway, I like to keep up with what's going on."

"Do you like it here in the States?"

Sebastian looked shocked by the question. "Yes, of course. Who wouldn't? It's an amazing place."

Lennie just nodded, recalling how when she was younger and traveling around Europe, she thought Europe was so superior to America. But hearing someone talk about the States who hadn't grown up here made her realize how much she took it for granted.

The coffee finished brewing, and they went back into the living room to sit on the couch—very close together, Lennie noticed. The sexual tension was thick, and was rapidly becoming unendurable as want of him began singing through her body. Never shy, she decided to take the bull by the horns: she put her coffee down and wrapped her arms around him. She looked into his eyes, then fused her mouth to his. She could tell he was shocked—but not too shocked to return her ardor and pull her tighter to him, kissing her senseless.

Sebastian held his breath for a moment. Then, ever so gently, he took her by the shoulders to look in her eyes.

"You're very forward, you know that?"

Lennie dipped her head to kiss the top of his hand, her gaze still seductive. "Do you dislike it?"

"No. But it makes me a little uncomfortable. I need to get used to it."

Lennie felt humiliation twist through her. "You think I'm a slut."

Sebastian's eyes popped. "Are you crazy? I think you're wonderful and beautiful." He cupped her face in his hands and kissed her softly on the mouth. "But I want to—what is the word?—savor."

Savor. That meant he still wanted to see her. Lennie was relieved, but she still wanted him to verbalize some kind of commitment. "So we're going out, then?"

Sebastian chuckled. "It would seem that way."

"Not exactly what you were looking for when you posted on Craigslist," Lennie noted sardonically.

"I didn't know 'New to New York' would be so beautiful and interesting, did I?"

Lennie coughed uncomfortably. "Yeah, about that." Time to come clean. "I'm not really 'New to New York.' I mean, I'm new to the city, like you, but I'm not the woman who responded to your ad."

Sebastian looked highly amused. "So you just pretended to be her and sat and talked to me?"

"Yes."

"What would you have done if she'd shown up?"

"Been mortified, I guess."

"Well, obviously things worked out the way they were supposed to, yes?"

"I felt a connection to you right away. Does that sound nuts?"

"Yes."

She playfully smacked his arm. "Thanks a lot!"

"I'm just teasing." Sebastian put his forehead against hers, sighing. "Are you going to hide this from your aunt?"

"No. She's just going to have to deal with it. I'm allowed to have a life."

"Maybe you should have me over sometime, so she can see I'm not a vodka-swilling Communist."

"Let's wait on that a bit."

"All right."

"So . . . can we at least make out a bit?" Lennie asked shyly.

Sebastian cocked his head. "Make out?"

"You know, kiss passionately for a while."

Sebastian grinned. "That sounds good." He wrapped his arms around her. "*Ti takaya krasivaya*. You are so beautiful."

Lennie instantly choked up. "No one has ever said that to me before."

"Then you've dated fools."

"Pretty much." She brushed the back of her hand against his cheek. "Again, I'm sorry for coming on so strong. I just—you're so sexy—"

"I know I am. You don't need to explain."

"Jerk!" Lennie said affectionately.

"That's no way to talk to your boyfriend." Sebastian nipped her neck. "Please burn those rags you bought."

"Nope."

"Then don't wear them around me."

"Deal. Now shut up and kiss me."

Do you don't think it was a whore-y thing to do?"

Lennie was sitting at the bar at the Hart, telling Christie about her day with Sebastian. Her aunt wouldn't be showing up for another forty minutes or so, so she didn't have to worry about any of her buddies/spies reporting back to her.

"What, suggesting you guys hook up?"

Jimmy O'Brien looked up quizzically from the other end of the bar.

"Could you lower your voice, please?" Lennie quietly implored her friend.

"Sorry." Christie leaned over the bar. "I don't think it was whore-y. Why should guys be the ones to make all the moves? And he made out with you, didn't he? Said you guys are going out now?"

"Yup. He said he wanted to 'savor' it."

Christie looked envious. "That's really romantic."

"I never thought this would happen—you know, come to New York and bam! Find a great guy, and a really hot one at that."

"Torture me even more, why don't you?"

"Sorry."

"When are you seeing him again?"

"Well, he wanted to get together tomorrow night, but I told him no way, unless he wants to come over and watch *Project Runway* with me and Aunt Mary."

"Yeah, I'm sure he'd love that."

Lennie's eyes cut to Jimmy O'Brien, who quickly looked away. Clearly the old man had bat hearing. Then again, it was kind of quiet right now. "Eavesdropping is impolite, you know."

Jimmy looked offended as he moved closer. "Now why would you ever think I'd care about what you two are yammering about?"

"Because you're one of the biggest gossips in here," said Christie. "All cops are—especially male cops."

"How's it goin' at the firehouse?" Jimmy shot back. "The lot of you still sitting on your arses most of the day eating donuts?"

He cast a final glare at Christie and went to tend to two new customers who'd parked themselves at the other end of the bar.

Lennie glanced toward the dining room. Sitting at a small table for two across from Mrs. O'Brien was a striking young woman, her long, dark brown hair pulled back in a sleek ponytail, her face impeccably made up. Lennie's eyes were drawn immediately to the vanilla/navy single-breasted, two-button jacket the woman was wearing. It was gorgeous. "Who's that with Mrs. O'Brien?" she asked Christie, tipping her head discreetly in the direction of the table.

"Sinead O'Brien, one of the O'Briens' daughters. She's an attorney. Kind of a workaholic, from what I hear. Going through a horrible, painful divorce. She's been coming in here a lot lately. It probably makes things a lot less painful to spend time with her family, you know? She and Quinn talk a lot."

"Is she nice?"

"I don't really know her, but the few times I've talked to her, she seemed nice. Kinda quiet and intense."

"God, look at that gorgeous jacket she's wearing."

"Is it gorgeous?"

Lennie turned back to her. "You don't think it's gorgeous?"

"Lennie, it just looks like a jacket to me."

"You have no fashion sense. I'm going to take you shopping soon, okay?"

"Be my guest."

Lennie slid off her stool. "I've got to go talk to Sinead."

"Wait! You didn't tell me when you're seeing your Russian lover boy again!"

"Don't know. But I'll keep you posted."

Lennie walked over to the table where Mrs. O'Brien and Sinead sat. Mrs. O'Brien's face lit up when she saw her.

"Lennie! How are you?"

"I'm doing really well, Mrs. O'Brien." She smiled at Sinead, extending a hand. "I'm Lennie Buckley. Mary Colgan's niece?"

Sinead looked to her mother for clarification.

"The one with the parrot," Mrs. O'Brien said.

"Your bingo friend," said Sinead.

"Yes, that's right."

Sinead smiled at Lennie. "I'm Sinead O'Brien. Nice to meet you."

Lennie fought the impulse to reach out and feel the fabric of Sinead's jacket without asking. "I'm a fashion design student at FIT. I couldn't help but notice how gorgeous your jacket is."

"Oh." Sinead seemed momentarily surprised, then smiled. "Thank you."

"You wouldn't happen to know who designed it, would you?"

"It's a Stella McCartney."

Lennie worshipped Stella McCartney—not that any of her clothing was available in Saranac Lake, and not that Lennie could ever afford a single article of Stella-designed clothing. But her designs were beautiful; unique, very feminine, with careful attention paid to small details.

"I know this is going to sound weird," said Lennie, "but would you mind if I just rubbed one of the lapels between my fingers to feel the fabric?"

"No, go ahead."

Mrs. O'Brien rose. "You girls talk clothing. I should be getting back to the kitchen." She kissed Sinead's cheek. "Don't stay up to all hours of the night working, please."

Sinead rolled her eyes. "I won't."

Lennie reached out, tentatively feeling the fabric. Cotton silk. "It's really beautiful."

"Thank you."

Maybe it was forward, but Lennie asked, "Do you wear a lot of designer clothing?"

"I do," said Sinead, not looking the least bit offended. "I'm an attorney, so I'm dressed up all the time."

"Who do you like?"

"I wear a lot of Ann Taylor. Boring, I know. That's why I bought the jacket: it's professional-looking, but just a little offbeat. I'm trying to liven things up a bit."

Lennie bit her lip. "Would you ever—I mean—if I designed something that I thought might look good on you, would you be willing to take a look? No pressure, I mean—"

"I would love to," Sinead said warmly.

Lennie almost shot to the ceiling with excitement. "Really?"

"Yes, really."

"Oh, thank you so much." Lennie had to rein herself in lest she throw her arms around Sinead's neck and give her a big kiss. Yes, she loved designing funky clothes and putting offbeat combinations of clothing together, but she also wanted to design classic clothing, stuff women could wear to work. Professional but not prissy. Professional yet feminine.

"I probably should get going," said Lennie, not wanting to make a pest of herself. "I have a lot of studying to do. How can I reach you if I come up with something for you?"

Sinead handed her a business card. "Here you go."

"Thanks again," Lennie gushed.

"Not a problem. I can't wait to see what you come up with." Sinead opened her laptop. " 'Bye, now."

" 'Bye."

Giddy with excitement, Lennie returned to the bar, told Christie her good news, and then went home to study. Her mother always said that when you're doing what you were meant to do with your life, everything falls into place. Lennie had been skeptical, but not anymore. She was right where she was supposed to be.

"Don't think I don't know what you're up to."

Aunt Mary's ominous statement to Lennie came during a commercial break as they sat together on the couch, watching *Project Runway*. Her aunt had been giving her the hairy eyeball all night. Lennie wasn't dumb; she knew it had to do with Sebastian. She'd actually been waiting to see when her aunt would bring it up. *Why now,* Lennie thought. *She's still going to be torturing me about it when the commercials are done, dammit.*

Lennie stuffed a handful of popcorn in her mouth. "What am I up to?"

"The Russky. I know you saw him on Sunday. Jimmy O'Brien told me. And I heard you on the phone with him last night."

Lennie was indignant. "Excuse me, were you listening outside my bedroom door?"

"Just passing by on my way to the bathroom," her aunt insisted defensively.

Jimmy O'Brien. Didn't any of those people at the bar have anything better to do than gossip and tattle on others? It was amazing. The next time Lennie saw him, she was going to give him a tongue-lashing he would never forget.

Lennie decided she'd try the gentle approach. "Aunt Mary, you don't even know Sebastian. He's a great guy."

Her aunt looked her dead in the eye. "You came here to study, Leonora. Not go floozing around with some hockey player."

Leonora. God, she hated that name. Floozing around? It sounded like her aunt was trapped in a bad 1930s movie.

"I'm not floozing around. I'm just dating him."

"You just got here!"

"I know—and so did he! We're exploring things together."

"Oh, I'll bet you are."

Lennie tried to keep her anger in check. "I resent what you're insinuating."

"I was young once. I know how it goes."

Just because you had to get married doesn't mean I will, Lennie thought. Her aunt probably didn't even know she knew the story behind her wedding.

"It's not like that."

"Don't like him," her aunt insisted stubbornly.

"Don't know him," Lennie returned. She huffed in frustration. "Why don't we have him over for dinner on Friday night? That way you'll get to know him."

"You know I don't like to cook."

"Then I'll cook," Lennie offered. Why did Aunt Mary have to make everything so difficult?

"Hmm." Her aunt looked suspicious.

"Look, I'm sure Sebastian would like to get to know you better too."

"And Rudy?"

"Of course."

"Hmm," her aunt said again.

"Listen, if we have him over for dinner, I promise I'll make those hats for Rudy you asked me to make."

Her aunt brightened. "Really?"

"Yes."

Last week, her aunt has asked her if she might "whip up" some hats for Rudy: a sailor's cap, a baseball cap, and a Greek fisherman's cap. Lennie had put her off. Sewing doll-sized items was extremely difficult. Still, if it would make her aunt more accepting of Sebastian, then she would make hats for a parrot, in between classes. And seeing Sebastian. And trying to come up with something that might interest Sinead. She was confident she could handle it all.

"All right, he can come over," Aunt Mary capitulated. "But no funny stuff."

"No funny stuff," Lennie agreed, chuckling. God, Aunt Mary was nuts. But as she had told Sebastian, she had a good heart, and that good heart was letting her live rent-free while she went to FIT. Having Seb over would be her ticket to peace and quiet at home. She'd call him tomorrow and invite him.

Six

"I'm surprised. I thought we were going to wait a bit on this."

"I told you: this should help get her off our tails."

Sebastian's voice was low as Lennie ushered him into her aunt's apartment. He'd been shocked when she'd called and invited him to dinner, but jumped at the chance.

He'd brought two bouquets of flowers: one for Lennie and one for Lennie's aunt, who was, thankfully, still in her room "getting ready." Lennie was touched. "You're so sweet. She's going to love this."

"Good."

Sebastian wasn't at all nervous about breaking bread with Lennie and her aunt. He knew he was a nice guy; but he also felt that deep down, it really wasn't Lennie's aunt's business if they were going out. Lennie was a woman leading her own life, not some flighty teenage girl who needed to be protected. He had a feeling that her aunt's ill will toward him might have more to do with xenophobia than anything else. Hopefully, he could set that straight.

Lennie glanced behind her, then quickly planted a hard kiss on his mouth. "I missed you this week."

"Me too." It felt like an eternity since he'd seen her. He had to admit he was smitten, which was slightly worrisome. He'd never before experienced such intense feelings so quickly.

He took in what she was wearing: ripped jeans, black high-top sneakers, a red-and-black striped long-sleeved T-shirt.

"Don't say a word about the jeans," Lennie warned affectionately. "Believe it or not, they're in style."

"You look about sixteen. It's a little disconcerting."

He was about to kiss her softly when Lennie's aunt appeared in the living room, Rudy on her left shoulder.

"Hello," she said, a trace of distrust in her voice.

Sebastian smiled, holding out his hand. "Hello. Nice to see you." He held out the remaining bouquet in his hand. "For you."

"For you! For you! For you!" said Rudy.

"Rudy, shut up," Lennie moaned.

Rudy fell silent; he obviously knew, as well as understood, the command.

Aunt Mary looked pleased with the bouquet. "How nice of you."

"Wasn't it?" Lennie said brightly. "Why don't you two sit while I put these in water?"

Consign me to the flames of hell, why don't you? Sebastian thought. But it would be for only a minute or two.

"Dinner smells wonderful," said Sebastian.

"Lennie made it. Some kind of quiche and salad." She eyed Sebastian curiously. "You eat quiche in Russia?"

"Yes, of course."

"I hear you people eat a lot of cabbage. And beets."

"You're probably thinking of borscht; it's a cold beet soup."

Aunt Mary shuddered. "Cold beets. Sounds awful."

"It is!"

She seemed to like that, rewarding him with a small smile. Sebastian studied Rudy. "He's a beautiful bird."

"Isn't he? My first one, Rudy the First, died very suddenly. It almost killed me. He was like a son to me. But within a couple of months I got Rudy the Second here. I can't imagine life without an avian companion. And he's such a good boy."

"Everyone at the bar seems to enjoy him very much."

"Oh, they love him. Love him. They loved Rudy the First too. His picture is behind the bar, you know. And his ashes. All my friends were just devastated when he died."

"Yes, I can imagine."

"Flowers are in a vase, dinner in about half an hour," Lennie announced as she reappeared in the living room. She sat down beside Sebastian, putting her hand in his. Her aunt's eyes shot immediately to their entwined fingers, but her expression was impassive, which Sebastian took as a good sign.

"I hear you cooked dinner," Sebastian said to Lennie.

"Yes, I did," Lennie said proudly, "and I think you'll like it too. It's pretty simple, but it's good."

"When I was your age, I knew how to cook a roast," Aunt Mary sniffed.

"When you were my age, you were already married and a housewife. Times were different."

"You should learn to cook a roast."

"Which would you prefer: that, or that I make a hat for Rudy?"

Sebastian's gaze slid sideways to look at Lennie. A hat for a parrot?

"Thought that might put things in perspective for you," Lennie said when her aunt had no response. She turned to Sebastian, so bright-eyed and beautiful she wished he could take her in his arms right there. "Do you want any wine or beer?"

"No, no, I'm fine."

"Aunt Mary?"

"No, thank you. I'll wait until later, when I'm down at the Hart."

"Are you liking America?" Aunt Mary asked politely.

"Of course. This is the country everyone aspires to move to, you know."

Once again, Aunt Mary looked pleased.

"Rudy learns things fast, no?"

"Very fast." Aunt Mary's expression turned back to suspicion. "Why?"

"I can teach him some Russian, if you'd like."

Aunt Mary's eyes lit up. "Really?"

"Of course. Here's one: *Dasvidanya*. It means 'good-bye.' "

Aunt Mary moved Rudy from her shoulder to her arm so he could watch her lips move. She had to repeat the phrase only ten times before Rudy started squawking *Dasvidanya! Dasvidanya! Dasvidanya!*

Aunt Mary looked proud as she pulled a treat from her pocket and rewarded Rudy. "See how smart he is?"

"Very impressive."

"Tell me another one," Aunt Mary requested eagerly.

"One more, and then it's dinnertime," said Lennie.

"*Spasibo*," said Sebastian. "It means 'thank you.' "

Aunt Mary repeated the process with Rudy, who once again picked up the phrase very quickly.

"He's brilliant," Sebastian announced with perhaps a little too much enthusiasm. Lennie's aunt didn't seem to notice: she was beaming.

He caught Aunt Mary giving Lennie a curt nod of approval. Now Lennie was the one beaming; as they followed her aunt into the kitchen, she gave Sebastian a big thumbs-up. "Thank you," she murmured gratefully. "I think you've already convinced her you're not a bad guy."

"I agree," said Sebastian. "Smooth sailing on this front from now on, eh?"

Lennie grinned. "I hope so."

Lennie knew that despite her aunt's warming to Sebastian, there was no way she was going to leave them alone after dinner. Sebastian said he didn't mind, since he had practice in the morning. Lennie realized she had a lot of studying to do anyway, plus she wanted to start thinking about what she could design for Sinead. And then there were the damn parrot hats.

To snatch at least a moment of privacy, she walked Sebastian downstairs to the street.

"What do you think? A success?" he asked, wrapping his arms around her.

"Total. Especially when you taught Rudy to say, 'Give me a drink!'"

"I thought that might break down her resistance to me completely. What's this about you making hats for him?"

Lennie groaned. "Don't ask." She fiddled with the collar of his shirt. "She was very impressed with how polite you were."

"What? Did she think I was going to come into the house and stage a revolution?" Sebastian joked.

"I don't know. She gets these ideas in her head . . . In some ways she's really sheltered, despite living in the city for decades."

"But like you said, she has a good heart."

"And a sewing machine."

Sebastian traced her lower lip with his thumb. "I'm sorry I have to leave so early. Believe me, I wish we could go back to my apartment."

"For some 'savoring'?" Lennie murmured.

"Exactly. Although maybe we could savor just a little bit right now." He skimmed his mouth over hers gently before parting her lips and slipping his tongue between them. It was so simple, yet so erotic. Lennie pulled back, biting his lower lip. Sebastian gave a small moan, which made her want to do more, but they were on the street. She didn't want them to be one of those couples who prompted passersby to shout, "Get a room!"

As if reading her mind, Sebastian loosened his hold on her.

"I'm a little uncomfortable about 'savoring' on the street," he confessed.

Lennie blushed. "Me too."

"I'll call you tomorrow, yes? Maybe we can visit another tourist attraction next weekend? One where you can't buy rags?"

"Very funny. But yes, that would be good."

He kissed her again. "Goodnight, *mllaya moya*—'my sweet.'"

"Good night."

Floating on air, Lennie went back upstairs. She didn't care if she had to spend the whole week working late into the night designing and sewing—it was worth it to have the weekend free to see Sebastian.

"*Yoo-hoo!* Sebastian!"

"*Spasiba! Spasiba! Spasiba!*"

Sebastian suppressed a cringe as he strolled into the Wild Hart with his teammates, only to be enthusiastically greeted by Lennie's aunt Mary and her damn parrot. He knew there was no way he'd be able to enter the pub undetected, but he'd been hoping that when she saw him, she'd smile discreetly or give a small wave. But no such luck: she was motioning for him to come over. *Shit!*

"I'll catch up with you guys in a minute," he told his teammates, who were snickering. Veering away from his friends, he headed toward the bar.

"How are you, Mrs. Colgan?"

"Fine, and you?"

Sebastian nodded distractedly. "Good, good." He was desperate to get away; the longer he stood there talking to Lennie's aunt, the worse his teammates were going to torture him when he got to the table.

"Having you for dinner was delightful," Aunt Mary continued. "Perhaps you could come again soon? Teach Rudy some more Russian?"

That would be hell. "That would be wonderful."

"What are you and Lennie doing this weekend?"

"We haven't decided yet." Sebastian was slightly unnerved by how fast Lennie's aunt had gone from thinking he was a KGB agent to being interested in their social life.

Lennie's aunt nodded knowingly. "I'm not surprised. Lennie's been concentrating on her designs this week, up to all hours sewing. She's almost done with Rudy's sailor cap!"

"That's wonderful," Sebastian repeated, trying to picture the colorful bird with a hat on. It was too bizarre to contemplate. He glanced quickly toward the dining room, where his teammates were now seated. "I should get going," he said congenially, patting Aunt Mary's shoulder.

"*Dasvidanya!*" Rudy squawked.

"Yes, good-bye to you, too, Rudy," Sebastian replied with a chuckle.

His friends watched him as he approached, looking as if they were about to explode from holding in their laughter. The moment he sat down, they were on him like a pack of hyenas.

"Dude, I never knew Russians were into old ladies," said Ulf with an ear-to-ear grin.

"They're not," spurted Eric. "They're into parrots."

Sebastian sighed as the table rocked with laughter. "I told you: she is Lennie's aunt. I had dinner at their apartment on Sunday, because the aunt was very displeased about her niece dating a Russian hockey player. We thought it a good idea she get to meet me so she'd see I wasn't in the country to steal state secrets."

"Whoa, whoa, back up, bucko," said Eric Mitchell. "You're dating her?"

"Yes."

Ulf sniggered. "What happened to 'I just want a lady friend'?"

Sebastian shrugged diffidently. "There was an attraction. What can I say?"

Eric thumped the table triumphantly. "Did I call it or what? Straight men and women cannot be platonic friends."

"You don't have any friends, so how would you know?" quipped David Hewson.

"She a hot little vixen in bed?" Ulf continued with a dirty laugh.

Sebastian shut him down with a cold stare. He was no prude: he'd had his share of one-night stands and boasting about conquests when he was younger. But Lennie was not a conquest, and he didn't like the way Ulf always talked about women, especially his woman, as if they were pieces of meat.

"Well, sor-ry," Ulf muttered.

"Apology accepted."

They placed their orders, Sebastian discreetly keeping his eye on Lennie's aunt. It seemed unlikely she would come over to the table, but you never knew.

"So when are we going to meet Lennie?" Jason Mitchell asked.

Sebastian shifted uncomfortably. "I don't know."

"Invite her to a game," Thad suggested.

"Let me think about it," Sebastian murmured. It might be nice for his teammates to meet her, and he liked the thought of her being able to put faces to names when he talked about them. Plus, she enjoyed hockey. He just worried about what she would wear. What if she showed up in one of her odd outfits? He would be mortified, but it wasn't like he could tell her what to wear. She would be hurt and insulted, and rightfully so.

The issue was taken out of his hands when, much to his surprise, Lennie entered the pub. Reflexively, he zeroed in on her outfit: black jeans and a red turtleneck. No trash clothing.

He watched as she approached her aunt, who pointed in his direction. Lennie's eyes scoured the dining room uncertainly. When they met his, she broke into that wide, confident grin of hers. Sebastian grinned back, motioning her over. She deposited what looked like a portfolio with her aunt, said something to the woman behind the bar, and then started toward the table.

"Check it out," Ulf murmured, his eyes glued to Lennie. "Puck bunny at ten o'clock."

"Actually, that's Lennie," Sebastian said tersely.

Ulf slumped down in his seat. "Uh . . . sorry."

"She's really pretty, bro," said Thad.

Sebastian rose, kissing Lennie as she came to his side. "Everyone, I want you to meet my girlfriend, Lennie."

His friends all introduced themselves, their smiles and greetings gracious. Sebastian couldn't believe it, but Lennie actually seemed shy, a side of her he hadn't seen before. It was adorable, but he suspected that if he told her so, she might not be pleased.

Sebastian pulled over a chair from another table. "Come on, *milaya moya*, sit down with us. Have a drink."

She looked up at him apologetically. "I just stopped in to show Christie some of the designs I've been working on. Then I really need to get back and do some homework."

"Lennie goes to FIT," Sebastian explained.

His friends stared at him blankly.

"Fashion Institute of Technology?" Sebastian tried. He was mystified. They'd all been living in the city for years; how could they not know this? Then again, the school did have to do with fashion and design, so why would they?

"Cool," said Eric, jerking a thumb in Jason's direction. "Maybe you could design my brother here some decent clothes."

Lennie smiled. "He seems pretty well dressed to me." Her shyness started to fade as she began talking to them about hockey, explaining to them about coming from "the frozen North," and how she'd actually played pick-up games at the Olympic rink at Lake Placid. "Well, you gotta come see your boyfriend play," said Thad. "He's been on fire."

Lennie looked up at him proudly. "Just tell me when, and I'll be there."

"Deal," said Sebastian.

Lennie looked mildly despondent as she tilted her head in the direction of the bar. "I really should go," she said to Sebastian quietly, squeezing his arm. She turned back to his teammates. "It was great meeting you guys."

"You too," they all chimed.

He accompanied her back to the bar.

"Ah, the lovebirds," said Lennie's aunt.

"Please don't," said Lennie. She took both Sebastian's hands in hers. "Sorry I've been MIA."

"What is—"

"Missing in action. I've been busting my ass working on some designs for the O'Briens' daughter Sinead that I wanted to run by

Christie. If Sinead likes them, I might actually get to measure her and make them for her. My first paying customer!"

"That's great."

"Your teammates seem like good guys."

Sebastian glanced back at the table. "They are."

"Can I come to one of your games?" she asked shyly.

"I'm surprised you even ask. Of course."

"I had an idea for something we could do Sunday, if you're free."

"I have practice in the morning, but after that, nothing." *Because I'm keeping the weekend open for you.*

"We could walk across the Brooklyn Bridge. There are supposed to be beautiful views, especially if you go at sunset, and then turn around and walk back to Manhattan at night."

"I would like that very much." He pictured them slowly walking hand in hand, talking and laughing. How could something so simple produce such happiness in him? Either he was a simpleton, or he was falling hard and fast.

Lennie's face lit up. "Good."

"Call me with the time you think we should go, and I will come by your apartment to pick you up."

"Can't wait!" She rose on her tiptoes and bit the tip of his nose. "Go back to your buds."

"Go show your friend your designs. And then get some sleep. You look weary."

"I'll try."

He gave her a quick kiss and walked back to his teammates, smiling. Life was very, very good.

Seven

Lennie was still flying high as she unloaded piping-hot cartons of Chinese food on Sebastian's coffee table. They'd taken their time crossing the Brooklyn Bridge, strolling hand in hand, pausing now and then to take in the views. The view of lower Manhattan was breathtaking, as was the sight of the Statue of Liberty. They could even see the Empire State Building! By the time they got to the other side, night had fallen. They lingered in Brooklyn for about half an hour, then started back. Manhattan, all lit up at night, was like an urban fairyland, breathtaking and magical. Back in the city Sebastian suggested they get Chinese takeout. One of his teammates had recommended a place not far from where he lived, and he wanted to check it out. He'd had what was called "American Chinese food" in Moscow, and was eager to try the real, authentic thing.

Lennie pulled two pairs of chopsticks from the bottom of one of the bags. "Have you ever used these before?"

"No."

"Me either. Want to try?"

"No."

She laughed at his bluntness. You could never accuse Sebastian of being indecisive or indirect, that was for sure.

She'd deliberately worn the faux leopard coat she'd bought at the flea market, just so he could see how she'd tailored it into something smart and chic. He reluctantly admitted that the coat looked much different than the last time he'd seen it. Even so, he reiterated that he would never buy used clothing in a million years.

Sebastian leaned over, peering into the steaming cartons. "Fried dumplings. Egg rolls. General Tso's chicken. Moo shoo pork. Sesame chicken."

"That's a lot of food."

"Don't worry," he assured her. "You're eating with me. It will all be gone."

The food was delicious. Sebastian, especially, seemed to take great pleasure in it. "This is nothing like the Chinese food I had in Russia," he told her. "Chicken chow mein . . . awful." He shook his head in wonder. "It's amazing how many types of food you can get here. I want to try them all: Indian, French, Italian, you name it. I've already had the Irish food at the Wild Hart, and it's very, very good." He licked Sichuan sauce off his fingers. "Hey," he said suddenly. "Would you like to try some Russian food?"

"Sure."

"I'll take you to Brighton Beach. It's nicknamed Little Odessa, because there are so many Russian immigrants there. You can meet my uncle Yuri. He's lived there for twenty years. He's a very good cook."

"I would love that," Lennie said softly, moved by his invitation. He'd talked to her a lot about his uncle, the only relative he had in the States. The fact he wanted her to meet him . . . *We're not just casually dating,* she thought happily. *I mean something to him.* This was proof positive.

Despite Sebastian's boast that he'd finish all the food, there were leftovers, though not many. They packed up the food, and as he loaded it into the refrigerator, Lennie went to the sink to wash their dishes. She needed something to do, even if it was only for a few minutes. Now that dinner was over, all she could think about was the "savoring" she hoped was to come.

Sebastian came up behind her, wrapping his arms around her waist. "I have a dishwasher, you know."

"It's not a big deal, Seb. It's only two plates, the glasses, and the cutlery."

He nuzzled her hair, inhaling deeply. "You smell nice."

Lennie closed her eyes, rinsed the last plate, wiped her hands off, and turned in his arms. "Today was great," she said with a contented sigh.

"I agree."

He came a fraction of an inch closer, his gaze pinning hers. Lennie felt herself weakening. His mouth was so close . . . she wanted to grab his face and kiss him so hard he would be stunned to the point of vertigo. She could see by the way he was looking at her that desire was rapidly building within him, too, but she waited for him to make the first move, seconds stretching out like years.

Her patience was rewarded when he cupped the back of her neck and hungrily crushed his mouth to hers. There was no hesitation: she gave in to it fully, lust burning through her as the kiss kept deepening, her body completely submissive to her mind.

Sebastian gripped the counter as if needing to steady himself as Lennie twined her arms around his neck. His eyes were dark, commanding. He remained like that for a moment before grabbing her back in his arms, holding her to him so tightly she couldn't tell whose heart was pounding faster, hers or his. One of his hands grabbed her hair, fisted there, then pulled back so that her throat was revealed to him. That was when delirium came, as his teeth nipped at her soft skin.

The kitchen counter was hard against her back, but she didn't care. All that mattered was that he kept going. Lennie momentarily took command, dragging his mouth back up to hers. Sebastian groaned with pleasure. Taking her hands from his neck, she put them on his hips, pulling him closer. Heat and friction—that was all that mattered. Heat and friction and giving herself over completely to the madness of the moment. She could have him right now, if she wanted. It would be so easy.

And yet, much to her surprise, she found herself wanting to savor.

She reluctantly tore her mouth from his, looking up into those dark brown eyes that could so easily dissuade her from what she was about to do.

"This isn't the right time," she told him shakily. "I want—I want it to be—"

"More romantic?"

"Yes."

She held her breath a moment, afraid he might get angry. But he didn't. In fact, he looked amused.

"What?" she asked. "What's so funny?"

"You were the one who was aggressive just a few weeks ago. Now you're the one holding back!"

"I know. You must think I'm really messed up," she mumbled. She'd wanted to say "fucked-up," but for some reason, she was afraid he might think she was crude. He was so traditional—such a gentleman—she didn't want him thinking less of her in any way.

"No, I don't think you're 'messed up,' as you say. Confused? Now that's a different story. But not messed up."

She could feel his hardness against her slowly waning. "Are you sure you're not mad?" she asked uncertainly.

"Not mad," he insisted.

"Disappointed," she supplied.

"Of course. I mean, here you are, in my arms, so beautiful . . ." He pressed his lips to her forehead. "But I want you to be happy. I want you to feel it's the right time."

"I want to savor," Lennie whispered.

Sebastian grinned. "Our code word."

"Yes."

"It's late. I should see you home."

"Sebastian, I can get home by myself. On the subway."

Sebastian shook his head. "No. A gentleman always sees his lady home."

"I see." Lennie was charmed. "Well, then, 'Lead on, MacDuff.' It's a line from Shakespeare," she added when he looked baffled.

"Ah. You're so knowledgeable about so many things."

"No, I just paid attention in high school English class." She tugged his sleeve. "C'mon, Romeo."

"More Shakespeare! That much I know."

Lennie laughed. "Would you prefer I come up with some Chekhov next time?"

"Hmm, let me think about it. I might prefer Dostoyevsky."

"You can teach some to Rudy."

"I hear you are almost done with his sailor cap," said Sebastian, looking like he was trying not to laugh.

"God, I should get an award for that. You can't imagine how hard it is sewing things that tiny. I'm going blind."

"You're a good niece."

"I'm a pushover."

Sebastian extended a hand. "Come. Let's get you home so you can get a decent night's sleep."

Lennie's heart swelled with tenderness. *No one has ever cared about me this way. No man has ever stolen into my heart so quickly and so fully. And I wasn't even looking for it.* It amazed her.

She took the hand of the man she intended to savor, and followed him out into the night.

Lennie tried not to fidget as she sat in the massive, quiet, climate-controlled reception area of one of New York's top law firms, Callahan, Epps, and Kaplan, where Sinead O'Brien was a junior partner. In a fit of inspiration over the past week and a half, she had sketched three different designs she thought Sinead might like. Her first instinct had been to try to catch Sinead at the Wild Hart, but then she decided that since Sinead had given her her business card, it would look much more professional for her to call. She was thrilled when Sinead told her to come in early Thursday morning to show her the designs.

Lennie smiled politely when Sinead's sharply dressed, whip-thin assistant, Simone, appeared and asked her if she wanted any coffee or tea while she waited. Lennie declined; she was wired enough as it was. Caffeine would have her bouncing off the ceiling and talking a mile a minute, which was the last thing she wanted. It was one thing to be creative, but she didn't want to come across as crazy as well.

A few minutes later, Sinead appeared in a gorgeous, navy blue business suit, looking pleased.

"I'm so glad you could come," she said, extending a perfectly manicured hand to Lennie. Everything about her was flawless and professional: her clothing, her hair, her makeup, her demeanor. Lennie supposed it had to be. "I'm really excited about seeing what you've come up with. That was fast!"

"I was inspired," said Lenny, hoping she didn't sound like an idiot.

"C'mon, I'll take you down to my office."

Lennie dutifully followed Sinead down the quiet, carpeted hallway. Lennie liked quiet; she loved sketching in silence, the only sound that of her pencil scratching against her drawing paper.

To say Sinead's office was impressive was an understatement. There was a huge teak desk in the center of the room, behind which was a floor-to-ceiling bookshelf the length of the wall, filled with lawbooks. Two other walls were of floor-to-ceiling glass, allowing amazing views of New York. There was also a gorgeous burgundy velvet couch, flanked by end tables atop which sat pictures of Sinead's family. Lennie liked the office's cozy feel. She felt like she was in a private library at an English manor house.

"Sit, sit," said Sinead, motioning toward the couch. Lennie sat, unable to resist running a hand back and forth over one of the velvet cushions. She loved velvet, but it was damn hard to work with. She'd once tried to make a velvet blazer for herself in high school, and it had come out looking like a luxury straitjacket.

"So, what have you got for me?" Sinead asked enthusiastically.

Heart pounding wildly in her chest, Lennie pulled the three sketches out of her portfolio and handed them to Sinead, who scrutinized them intently. One was a black draped cardigan made of cashmere; one was a 1940s-type pencil skirt with a back slit; the final design was a short snap jacket that would be made of rustic silk linen. Lennie tried to look interested in glancing around the office, but it was hard. Now and again, she slid Sinead a surreptitious, sideways glance, one time noticing there was an unmistakable indentation on the ring finger of her left hand, most likely from where she once wore a wedding ring.

The silence was killing Lennie. Finally, after what felt like forever, Sinead looked up. "I want all of them."

Lennie couldn't hide her shock. "Are you serious?"

"These designs are gorgeous, Lennie, and are just what I was looking for: items that are unique yet professional. You're going to have an amazing career."

Overwhelmed, Lennie didn't know what to say.

"Lennie?"

"Oh, God, sorry. I just—I'm amazed."

"Don't be. What happens next?"

Lennie fought to keep her voice steady. "Well, I'll take your measurements, and then I'll make the clothes for you."

Sinead pointed to Lennie's satchel. "I bet you have a tape measure in there."

Lennie blushed. "Of course."

Sinead stood. "Measure away."

Lennie was surprised by how talkative Sinead was as she measured her, gabbing about her family and her job, asking Lennie all about school and even about Aunt Mary. Sinead revealed that while she loved being an attorney, the job was so stressful that sometimes she wished she could just run away. Lennie wondered if Sinead's commitment to work played any role in her split from her husband.

"Done," Lennie said finally.

"Great." Sinead went behind her desk, opened a drawer, and pulled out a checkbook. Lennie gasped when Sinead handed her a check and she saw the amount.

"This is way too much money for the materials I'm going to need."

"We'll figure all that out later. In the meantime, I want you to know there's no rush on this. School should come first."

"Of course." Lennie knew she was right, but it was hard to even think about school right now when she'd just sold three designs. She couldn't wait to tell Sebastian and Christie. She wasn't so sure about telling her aunt just yet; she'd wait until she was done working on the parrot hats.

Lennie packed up her designs. "I can't thank you enough—"

"Don't be silly. I love that I'm going to be the first person to wear an original Lennie Buckley! My friends are going to be so jealous! Who knows? It could result in your selling more designs."

Lennie nodded dumbly. Already selling her designs while still in school. It was amazing.

"I'm sure I'll see you at the Hart sometime," Sinead continued cordially, showing Lennie to the door.

"I really like it there."

Sinead smiled proudly. "My folks have worked really hard to create a friendly atmosphere."

"Well, they've succeeded."

Sinead pressed her shoulder warmly. "Have a good day, Lennie. Simone will show you out."

Lennie nodded. She was still pinching herself as Sinead quietly closed her office door behind her. Things were happening so quickly, her head was beginning to spin. But they were all good things. She had no complaints.

Eight

Lennie had no idea what to expect when she and Sebastian got off the subway in Coney Island, the last subway stop in Brooklyn. All she knew was what Sebastian had told her: that Brighton Beach was called Little Odessa because of the high concentration of Russian immigrants. Coney Island blended into Brighton Beach, and as they walked toward Brighton Beach Avenue, the area's main thoroughfare, the first thing that struck Lennie was the lack of cars and tall buildings. Much as she loved living in the megalopolis that was Manhattan, being able to see the horizon was a nice change, especially since she could also smell the ocean on the breeze.

All the Russian butcher shops, delis, cafés, bookstores, and grocery stores amazed her. Even the storefront sign outside the Duane Reade drugstore had Cyrillic lettering. Clearly this was an area that didn't feel compelled to cater to tourists.

Strolling along, Sebastian said "hello" in Russian to a woman selling what looked to Lennie like small pastries. She greeted him back cheerily, asking him a question, to which he replied in the guttural language being spoken everywhere.

"What did she ask you?" Lennie asked.

"How I was, and how my uncle was. She's lived here forty years."

"What was she selling?"

"Piroshki, small pastries filled with potatoes, meat, cheese, or cabbage."

"Let's get one."

"I'm sure my uncle made some." Sebastian looked a little melancholy. "What do you think so far?"

"I feel like I've entered a completely different world."

"You have."

"You homesick?"

"A little bit. But it will pass."

At the end of the street, they made a right turn and walked the two blocks to the beach. Lennie felt content as they ambled along the pristine boardwalk. It was off-season, so it wasn't crowded. The day was chilly, yet bench after bench was occupied by old men engrossed in chess games. Groups of older women bundled up in fur coats strolled by, gabbing away in Russian. They didn't seem to mind the brisk wind coming off the ocean.

Sebastian glanced behind him at the closest group of women walking by. "That group that just passed us? They're complaining about their children."

"Isn't that what all parents do?"

"I suppose."

She'd been careful with what she'd worn, knowing that if she put together one of her more eclectic combos, it might lead Sebastian's uncle not to like her. She kept her outfit simple: jeans, a simple white button-down blouse, and a pair of clogs. She was wearing makeup, but not much. She could tell by the relief on Sebastian's face when he came to get her at her aunt's that he'd been worried she might be dressed quirkily.

"You look nice," she told him, when what she was really thinking was *God, you're sexy*. His faded jeans were tight, and he looked as though he might bust out of the black T-shirt he was wearing beneath his open leather jacket. His mirrored aviator sunglasses were the icing on the cake. He looked like a *GQ* model.

Sebastian squeezed her hand. "You, too. I think my uncle Yuri will like you very much."

"You really haven't told me much about him, apart from the facts that he hasn't really Americanized very well, he's your dad's brother, and he works as a translator."

"Well, what do you want to know?"

"How long has he been here?"

"Twenty years, I think," he said vaguely.

"Did he come here for a job?"

There was a long, uncomfortable pause. "He came because his father, my grandfather, was Jewish, so he had no future. Russia is more tolerant now, but twenty years ago, glasnost—the new openness in Russia—had barely started. He taught physics at the Moscow Institute of Physics and Technology. The discrimination became too much, so he left."

Lennie was horrified. "That's terrible."

"Yes, it is," Sebastian agreed.

"How come your father—"

"Because he was an esteemed hockey coach. People were willing to ignore the fact that his father was Jewish. No doubt if he was just a professor, the same thing would have happened to him."

"Has your uncle ever gone back?"

"No. But my father visits him here every year."

"That's good." Lennie knew it was an inadequate response, but she didn't know what else to say. All she knew was that once again, the differences between the countries she and Sebastian had been raised in were painfully clear.

Eventually, they arrived at a small, eight-story, sand-colored apartment house, and took the elevator to the sixth floor. When the elevator doors slid back, Lennie found herself enveloped in a mélange of mouthwatering smells. She tilted her head back, inhaling deeply.

"I don't know what's cooking, but it smells heavenly."

"Ah, just wait and see," said Sebastian with a wink.

Lennie realized that when she'd been outside, taking in all the new sights and sounds, she'd been able to keep her nervousness at bay. Now that they were standing in front of Uncle Yuri's door, she was hit with a bad case of the butterflies. She tightened her grip around Sebastian's hand.

"Don't worry, *milaya moya*," he reassured her. "It will be fine."

Lennie swallowed as Sebastian rang the doorbell. There was the sound of three locks clicking back; then the door swung open to reveal a well-built, silver-haired man, dressed in rumpled black pants, a turtleneck, and a lint-covered gray cardigan that had seen better days. His face lit up as he reached out to warmly take Lennie's hands between his.

"Welcome, welcome. I'm Yuri."

"Lennie."

"Yes, yes, I know. My nephew has told me about you. Come in, come in."

Lennie followed Uncle Yuri into the apartment. "See?" Sebastian whispered as he closed the apartment door behind them. "It will be fine."

Sebastian hugged his uncle, who immediately began talking to him a mile a minute in Russian.

"English," Sebastian said to him softly but firmly. "You have to talk English."

"Yes, of course." He looked at Lennie apologetically. "I'm sorry. I didn't mean to be rude."

"It's okay, I understand."

The apartment was tiny, every nook and cranny piled high with books and papers, some of them yellowing with age. Sebastian and Lennie sat down on the faded floral couch while Yuri settled into a battered leather armchair opposite them.

"When are you going to clear this junk out?" Sebastian asked him. "It's a fire hazard. I told you: I'll help you."

"And I told you to mind your business," Uncle Yuri chided affectionately. He turned his attention to Lennie. "My nephew tells me you design clothing."

"Yes. I'm going to school for it, but I just sold three of my designs this week."

Uncle Yuri nodded approvingly. "You're hardworking. That's good."

"Why don't you let her design something for you, so you don't roam around all the time looking like an old man?" Sebastian asked.

Uncle Yuri said something to him in Russian again, but this time Sebastian laughed.

"He's telling me again to mind my business, but in a more colorful way," Sebastian explained.

"Something not fit for a beautiful lady's ears," Uncle Yuri added.

Lennie nodded and smiled. The heat in the apartment was stifling. Any minute now, she was going to start sweating, not something you wanted to do the first time you met your boyfriend's only relative in the country.

"Would you like some good, strong black tea?" Yuri asked.

Oh, hell. If she drank something hot, she'd find herself sitting in a puddle of her own sweat. Yet she didn't want to be impolite.

"That would be lovely," she fibbed.

"My uncle makes good tea," said Sebastian.

Yuri rose, disappearing into the kitchen.

"You've got to open a window," Lennie quietly begged Sebastian. "It's like a sauna in here."

"I know. I can't stand it. I think he keeps it so high because for so many years, the heat in his apartment in Moscow barely worked. Now he's obsessed with it."

Sebastian crept over to the thermostat and turned it down. "That should make it better."

When Yuri reappeared, he was carrying a tray with three glasses, not cups, of tea, each glass in a holder of delicate silver filigree.

"Here," said Yuri, handing Lennie a glass. "This is the traditional way we drink it. None of those cups and mugs for us!" He held his tea glass high. "*Za fstryechoo!* To our meeting!"

The three of them clinked glasses, then settled down to talk. Having no children of his own, Yuri seemed to revel in telling Lennie stories about Sebastian as a little boy, which embarrassed Sebastian, if his eye rolling and heavy sighing were any indication. He didn't seem to mind, though, when his uncle sang his praises as a hockey player. Somehow, Lennie wasn't surprised.

"*What* was that one dish called again?" Lennie asked Sebastian as they entered his apartment. "The dumplings with the meatballs inside that your uncle made me drown in butter and sour cream?"

"*Pelmeni*—and it's supposed to be drowned in butter and sour cream! It's traditional."

"I bet I gained five pounds."

"I'm glad you didn't pick at your food like a little bird," said

Sebastian, hanging up her coat. "I hate when women do that. My uncle was very happy you seemed to be enjoying yourself so much."

"How could I not?"

The food had been amazing. Caviar served on dark, fresh, crusty bread. *Pelmeni.* Piroshki. Beef kebabs. And for dessert, blinis filled with strawberry jam.

"Do you really think he liked me?" Lennie asked Sebastian as they settled down on the couch.

"I think that's the tenth time you've asked me that." He playfully tugged a strand of her hair. "Yes. Believe me, if he didn't, you would have known it. He would have been very gruff and spoken much less English."

"It's too bad he never got married," Lennie said, sighing sadly. "Maybe we can set him up with my aunt."

Sebastian laughed loudly. "I hope you're joking!"

"Of course I am. Though it does amuse me to imagine it."

They sat together on the couch, Sebastian's arm around her, pulling her close.

Lennie rested her head on his shoulder. "I'm glad I lied to you and told you I was 'New to New York,'" she murmured contentedly.

"Me too." He turned his body toward her, his knuckles tenderly brushing her cheek, eyes full of naked emotion. *"Lyubov maya, pridi ka mne,"* he whispered.

Lennie's heart began to race. "What does that mean?"

"'Come to me, my love,'" he replied, pressing his lips softly against hers.

"What about savoring?" she asked in amusement.

"I had enough savoring at dinner," Sebastian growled. "Now I want you."

Lennie laughed, then felt herself go into free fall as Sebastian roughly pulled her to him, his mouth devouring hers. Their kiss was hard and desperate, almost feral. Emboldened, Lennie snaked her burning hands beneath his T-shirt, pressing them against his chest. So virile. So perfect. She couldn't keep her hands still. She began stroking the hard flesh, scraping her nails against the skin, circling his nipples with her index fingers. She loved it when Sebastian groaned in response. It made her feel powerful.

Wanting to tantalize him, she abruptly withdrew her hands. Then, with her eyes fixed on his, she began unbuttoning her blouse at a slow, torturous pace before tossing it wantonly to the floor. Desire surged through her as she watched his gaze travel appreciatively up and down her torso, finally coming to rest on her chest. They looked at each other a moment, and then Lennie cocked an eyebrow as if to say, *Well?* Sebastian narrowed his eyes, and then in one swift motion he leaned forward, pushed her bra up, and began to devour her breasts hungrily.

Lennie gasped as her mind quickly clouded, all reason seeping away. She wanted him to take her right here on the couch. Wanted it rough, mindless, relentless with passion. Desperate, she reached forward, yanking his T-shirt off above his head, this time letting her hands roam the terrain of his broad, hard shoulders. Sebastian groaned, lifted his mouth from her breasts. Lennie held her breath, shivering as he unhooked her bra and tossed it away.

"So amazingly beautiful," he murmured.

Lennie tried to telegraph her desperation, grabbing his face and bringing it down to hers so she could nip enticingly at his lower lip. An animal growl came from the back of Sebastian's throat as he thrust his tongue into her mouth, demanding, taking. Lennie got what she wanted: Sebastian gruffly pulled his mouth from hers, and in one fell swoop, picked her up. "In bed," he said hoarsely. "I want you in my bed."

Lennie wrapped her arms around his neck and let her teeth

graze his jawline as he carried her into his room. He was already breathing hard, his gaze dark with an intensity no man had ever looked at her with before. Heat coiled low in her belly. *Soon*, she thought. Soon the greed overtaking her would be sated.

They stripped quickly, tumbling onto his bed. He looked surprised, yet pleased, when Lennie pushed him onto his back, straddling him. All she wanted was him. All she needed was him. Greedily she attacked his lips and throat, hoping to drag him under the way she was going under, drowning in a sea of unbearable need.

Sebastian responded with fierceness, rearing up and grabbing her hair. Again their eyes met, locked, challenged. Lennie's heart thundered as she saw her own ferocity reflected his gaze. There was a pause before he pulled her head back with a hard yank, and began feasting on her throat. The move was primitive, thrilling. Lennie was glad there were no soft, tender Russian phrases falling from his lips right then. She wanted him macho and dominating, wanted the roiling desire in her blood satisfied.

There was no doubt of who was in control as he pushed her back on the bed, exciting her. They were both breathing hard. Lennie's heart was pounding as she watched him reach into the night table for protection, quickly sheathing himself. *Hurry*, she thought, need shuddering through her. But Sebastian was in no hurry; he teased and tortured at the same time, nipping her breasts before slowly slithering down her body to pleasure her with his fingers and mouth. Lennie couldn't hold back, tumbling over the edge into pleasure. Sebastian laughed darkly as he lifted his head to look up the length of her body at her.

"More?"

"God, yes, please." It was so hard to form words when all she wanted was sensation. Sebastian crawled back up her body so they were face-to-face, his large, strong hands pinning her wrists in a show of dominance. Unbearably aroused, Lennie began rubbing herself against him, a woman once again on the verge of explosion.

Sebastian kissed her roughly, then plunged into her, the slam of his body against hers rendering her momentarily senseless. Lennie felt her mind reel, blind desire unspooling within her as she bucked against him wildly, meeting him thrust for thrust. Flesh pounded flesh as the sheer animal urge to mate roared through her and she came again, the punch of her own climax a delicious blow. Sebastian looked down at her, his mouth widening into a satisfied grin, which Lennie returned. Then his mouth closed over hers and he continued moving inside her, sending Lennie spinning back into velvet darkness. She urged him on, breaking free of his grip on her wrists to embrace him, dragging her nails up and down against the smooth, muscled terrain of his back. Finally, in one lightning burst of speed, he emptied himself into her, Lennie savoring the delicious feeling of complete union with him, her *milaya moya*, her sweet.

Nine

Lennie awoke the next morning to the shrill beeping of Sebastian's alarm. She knew she shouldn't have spent the night, but Sebastian was very persuasive, and the allure of "savoring" all night was simply too much to resist. So here she was, snuggled deep and cozy under the covers, her limbs entwined with Sebastian's, the most natural feeling in the world.

Groaning, Sebastian snaked an arm out from beneath the covers to silence the alarm. The room fell back into blissful silence for a few seconds before he yawned deeply, then rolled to face Lennie, a sleepy smile on his face.

"Hello," he murmured.

"Hello." Lennie brushed the hair out of his eyes, keeping her right leg hooked over his hip. "Sleep well?"

"Mmm, very well. But now it's time to get up."

Lennie snuggled closer to him. "Do we have to?"

"Unfortunately, yes," said Sebastian, gently disentangling himself from her. "I cannot be late to practice."

Lennie rolled onto her back and sighed. "I hate being a grown-up." She lifted her head from the pillow to glance at the clock. Seven thirty.

"Oh, shit!"

Sebastian looked alarmed. "What's the matter?"

Lennie leaped out of bed, scrambling for her clothing. "I totally forgot I have an appointment with one of my professors at nine to talk about getting credit for the clothes I'm designing for Sinead O'Brien."

Sebastian was unruffled. "So take a quick shower and go. You'll make it."

"I don't have my portfolio with me," she lamented. "And I don't have her number on my cell. Shit."

"Relax. You can call the car service I sometimes use to take you home. The driver will wait downstairs while you wash up and grab your portfolio, and then take it to see your professor."

"I can't afford that. It will cost a fortune."

"I'll pay for it. I have plenty of money, and it would please me to do this for you. Please?"

"Okay."

"Good, the number is on my fridge. Go ahead and call them while I jump in the shower."

Lennie hustled out to the kitchen to call for a car. Panic quelled, she returned to the bedroom. Sebastian was already in the shower. Lennie went into the bathroom, peeking around the shower curtain at her gorgeous, naked boyfriend.

"All better now?" he asked, his eyes closed as he turned his face into the spray of water.

"We'll see." Lennie crinkled her nose. "Why are you showering when you're going to practice? Aren't you going to get there and work out and sweat?"

Sebastian looked at her and chuckled. "I can't show up smelling like sex, can I?"

"I suppose not."

He held out a hand to her. "Come on. Join me."

Lennie hesitated as she weighed his offer. *Don't do it,* the adult voice in her head said. *You have to rush back to the apartment, change, pick up your portfolio. You'll be late for your meeting.*

"You know I can't," she said, unable to hide her disappointment. "If I get in there with you, I won't be able to keep my hands to myself."

Sebastian smiled seductively. "That was the idea."

"Don't torture me, you Russian devil."

"I admire your discipline." He leaned over, giving her a shower-wet kiss. "We'll talk later, yes? I'll call you after my game?"

Lennie nodded. His games ended late, but she knew she'd still be up. She was determined to finish the clothing Sinead had commissioned as soon as she could.

"One more thing," he said, "then I'll let you scurry off."

"Yes?"

His expression was tender. "Last night was so *chudesnaya*—wonderful. I felt very close to you. I'm very—fond of you, Lennie."

"Me too," said Lennie. Too early to say the "l" word, if it ever got to that, which she hoped it did. "Talk to you later."

"Yes. Have a good day, sweet one."

"You too. Good luck tonight."

So much for Lennie's good luck wishes having any bearing on the Blades' game against Ottawa. The team was routed 5–1. Sebastian played poorly, seeming out of sync with his teammates. A step slow all night, he was penalized twice for holding. Ottawa scored on both power plays.

"I fucked up tonight," Sebastian said to no one in particular, but loud enough for everyone in the locker room to hear. He threw his helmet against a wall and slumped angrily in front of his locker.

"Forget it, Ivan. Everyone's allowed a bad night now and then," Eric Mitchell sympathized, picking up Sebastian's helmet and tossing it back to him.

"Know what I think your problem might have been tonight?" said Ulf, breaking into a big grin as he sauntered over to Sebastian, naked, with a towel slung over his shoulder.

"What?" Sebastian knew there was no point in saying "No," since Ulf would just ignore him and tell him anyway.

"You've got pussy on the brain, Ivan, not pucks." There were laughs all around the locker room.

Sebastian knew Ulf was just trying to bring him out of his funk. The teasing was just a way for his teammates to reassure him that they had his back.

As the conversations in the locker room shifted to talk of where to have dinner and what was on television, Jason Mitchell called Sebastian over to have a private word. "Just out of curiosity, does Lennie know you've only got a one-year deal?" he asked cautiously.

"No."

"You don't seem like a 'love 'em and leave 'em' kind of guy, Sebastian," Jason observed, "so I get the feeling you really like this girl."

"I do."

"Well, I don't mean to interfere, but you might want to say something sooner rather than later, so the two of you both know what you're getting into. If you really care about her, you don't want her freaking out if you end up somewhere else next season."

"Thank you for the advice," Sebastian said quietly, as he picked up his toiletry kit and walked away. Hopping into the shower, he soaped himself and thought about his future as the hot water beat down on him. He'd like to stay with the Blades, but there was no guarantee. If he didn't play well, they might not make him an offer, and he could end up somewhere else next season—maybe even back in Russia. And if he did play well, he might get a better offer from another team. With his extended family back in Russia relying on him, he wasn't in any position to turn down money for sentimental reasons.

His thoughts turned to Lennie. Not telling her about the contract wasn't lying; it was simply a small sin of omission. Still, didn't he owe her the truth? He chuckled over the irony of telling the truth to the woman who'd deceived him about being "New to New York." Right now he considered their relationship casual, but what if it continued to grow and blossom? What then?

He stepped out of the shower, toweling himself off vigorously. He had a decision to make. And soon.

Ten

Two Weeks Later

"Are you okay?"

Lennie snuggled comfortably in the crook of Sebastian's arm, her feet sprawled in front of her on the coffee table as they sat on his couch. She'd watched him play tonight, even though she knew she should probably have been home studying, or finishing up the final garment Sinead had commissioned. But that was what coffee and Red Bull were for; she'd go home and get her work done after they'd "savored."

"I'm fine," Sebastian said distractedly.

"You don't seem fine," Lennie said with concern. "You seem pensive."

"'Pensive' is—?"

"Preoccupied. Lost in thought." She stroked the side of his face. "Everything okay at home? With your uncle?"

Sebastian nodded vaguely.

"Are you mad at me or something?" Lennie ventured meekly.

Sebastian looked shocked. "Why would I be mad at you?"

Lennie shrugged. "I don't know . . . because I wore pink Doc Martens to your game?"

"Don't be ridiculous, *milaya moya*. I'm used to your 'funky' way of dressing by now, and my teammates don't pay attention to a woman's clothes," he said, forcing a smile to go along with his forced joke.

Lennie didn't bite, and instead searched his face, trying to keep her mounting anxiety at bay. "So, what is it, then?"

Sebastian gave up. "There's something I should have told you when we first got to know each other," he said quietly.

"Shit, I knew it: you're married," Lennie blurted. "You've got a wife back home in Russia. I knew it was too good to be true for you not to be taken!"

Sebastian stared at her like she'd lost her mind. "How can you say this to me?" he asked heatedly. "What kind of a man do you think I am?"

"A man who looks guilty!" Sebastian looked insulted. "Okay, I'm sorry I said that. I know you'd never keep something like that from me."

Sebastian sighed heavily. "No, I'm the sorry one." He took her hand. "Lennie, I might be gone after the season ends."

Lennie was confused. "What?"

"I have a one-year contract with the Blades. If they don't re-sign me, I'm gone."

"What does 'gone' mean?"

"You know what it means," Sebastian said softly.

"I want to hear you say it," Lennie demanded. She knew she sounded irrational, but she didn't care.

Sebastian looked pained. "I could wind up playing for another team in the NHL, or going back to Russia, or playing for a team somewhere else in Europe."

"Why didn't you tell me this when we first started going out?"

"Because I didn't want to think about it."

"Liar! You didn't tell me because you knew I wouldn't get involved with you if you did," Lennie countered angrily.

"Really? You wouldn't have gotten involved? Even though we were so attracted to one another?"

"Of course I wouldn't have!" Lennie snapped, even though she wasn't sure that was the case. She stared at him, shaking her head with incredulity. "I can't believe you deceived me."

"Look who is speaking about deception!" Sebastian retorted. "You pretended to be someone you weren't!"

"As if you minded!"

They sat glaring at each other for a moment. Sebastian wearily ran a hand over his face. "We have to make a decision."

Lennie scrambled to her feet. "We? We?"

"Okay. You," he corrected. "Now that you know, do you want to continue our relationship or—"

"Oh, it's over," Lennie fumed, slipping her boots on. She shook her head again as she laced them up. "I can't believe you lied to me!" she repeated under her breath.

"I didn't lie to you!"

Lennie jerked her head up. "You want to get technical? Fine. 'Withheld vital information.' Is that better? You withheld vital information."

"I was falling in love with you," Sebastian said quietly.

Lennie's mouth fell open. "Now?" she yelled. "You pick now to tell me you're in love with me?"

"Please stop bellowing like a madwoman," Sebastian implored calmly.

"I *am* a madwoman! A *very* mad woman!"

Sebastian cradled his head in hands, looking miserable. "This is not going well."

"How did you think it would go?" Lennie snapped. Her hands were shaking as she continued lacing up her boots. She contemplated yanking one off and throwing it at him.

"I thought maybe we could stay together, even if I left. And even if we did part, I never wanted us to part angrily."

"Ask me if I give a damn what you want, Sebastian." Lennie's jaw clenched as she tried holding back tears. "I really wish you had told me. I've been running myself ragged trying to juggle school with making sure I had enough time for you. And for what? To find out the man who claims to be in love with me couldn't even do me the courtesy of being honest with me from the beginning!"

Sebastian looked ashamed. "You are right. You deserve better than this."

"You're damn right I do." Lennie gathered up her coat and flung her bag over her shoulder. "Don't even try to talk to me at the Hart if we're both there at the same time. Got it?"

Sebastian nodded, looking pained.

"And for the record, I hope you wind up back in Siberia!"

Lennie stormed past him, slamming the door on her way out. She didn't want to think about what had just happened. All she wanted to do was get home as fast as she could, and cry.

Eleven

After storming out of Sebastian's apartment, Lennie rode the subway home, trying to sort out her feelings. She couldn't believe he hadn't let her know right from the beginning that his being in New York might be temporary. But the more she thought about it, the more she started to second-guess herself. Would she really have resisted her attraction to him if he'd told her the deal straight off the bat? She'd always considered herself a risk taker. Maybe he would have told her and she would have been okay with it, taking it day by day. Maybe.

The next morning, she decided to go down to the Wild Hart and run her conversation with Seb by Christie. Hitting the pub would kill two birds with one stone: she could spill to her friend, and she could stick around to meet with Sinead, who was stopping by to pick up the clothing Lennie had designed. "So, what do you think?" she asked Christie, who was alone behind the bar before the lunchtime mob arrived. Jimmy O'Brien's back was causing him a "world of trouble" again. Christie was pissed, but at least Mr. O'Brien was available to help out if she needed it.

"About what? Sebastian not telling you he might be gone, or your reaction to it?"

"Both."

Christie crinkled her nose, thinking hard. "I kinda think he should have told you. And I kinda think you overreacted."

"Could you be a little more definitive than 'kinda'?" Lennie pushed.

"I think you have a right to be annoyed," Christie replied carefully. "But rather than storming out, you should have stayed and talked things through with him. Breaking up with him—is that really what you want?"

"Yes. No. I don't know," Lennie whined. She wiggled around on her barstool in frustration, trying to put her thoughts into some kind of coherent order. "On the one hand, it might be good we— I—ended things. I mean, I did come to New York to study, and trying to juggle school, a relationship, and doing my own designs has been kind of crazy."

"I hear a 'but' coming."

"But what if I made a mistake?"

"Well, there's only one way you're gonna find out: go and talk to him. See if he wants to give things another try. I bet he does."

"But I told him I hoped he wound up back in Siberia," she said with a cringe.

Christie laughed. "Good one."

"Well, what if he does?"

"Lennie, which is it?" Christie huffed in exasperation. "Either you want to be with this guy or you don't. End of story."

"I need more time to think about it," Lennie muttered miserably.

"Then take time to think about it, and talk to him."

"But if I go back to him and tell him I want to get back together, he might think I'm pathetic or something. Unstable."

Christie threw down the bar towel in her hand. "Earth to Lennie, you *are* pathetic! At least right now!"

"Ouch."

"You also look dead on your feet."

"So you think I shouldn't get back with him. It'll be too much on my plate."

"You're being paranoid! And maddening!" Christie yelled.

"Sorry," said Lennie, shrinking back.

"Get some sleep tonight. Do some thinking. Then talk to him."

Lennie had been growing increasingly nervous as the time neared for her meeting with Sinead. But when Sinead walked into the pub and greeted her with a big, excited smile, all feelings of unease melted away. She knew things were going to be okay.

Garment bag slung over her shoulder, Lennie followed Sinead into the dining room. "I hope you don't mind my wanting to meet here," said Sinead, sliding into the booth.

"No problem at all. When I'm done, I can just go home and do some studying."

"And I can see my folks." Sinead rubbed her hands together eagerly. "Let's see what you've got."

Lennie's nerves crept back as she unzipped the garment bag and took out the three items she'd sewn for Sinead's inspection.

"Oh, Lennie." Sinead looked bowled over as she examined each garment. "These are perfect. Beautiful."

Lennie ducked her head shyly. "Thank you."

"How much do I owe you?"

Lennie hesitated.

"Lennie," Sinead chided, "figure out how many hours of labor went into these and how much you'd be selling these for in stores, and tell me. You're never going to be a success if you don't insist on getting paid what you deserve for work you've done."

Lennie had already figured out what she was owed. She wrote the number on a napkin, pushing it across the table to Sinead.

Sinead looked dubious. "Are you sure you're not undercutting yourself?"

Lennie put her hand over her heart. "Swear to God."

"All right, then." Sinead pulled a checkbook out of her purse and wrote Lennie's check. Lennie held it in her trembling hands, staring down at it in awe. "These are the first designs I've ever sold," she told Sinead, trying not to get teary.

"The first of many, I'm sure." Sinead gazed admiringly at the clothing one more time before zipping up the garment bag. "You know what I love about them? They're classy enough to wear to the office, yet casual enough to wear on a date."

"You're dating again?" Lennie immediately regretted saying it. Sinead hadn't said anything to her about her divorce; she knew about it only through the grapevine. But Sinead looked amused.

"Don't look so mortified. I know how fast word travels around here, believe me. I'm used to it." She checked her cell. "To answer your question, I'm not ready to start dating again. You have a boyfriend, though, right? That Russian hockey player?"

God, everyone really does know everyone's business, Lennie thought. "We broke up last night."

"Oh, I'm sorry," Sinead said sympathetically.

Lennie put on a brave face. "No, it's okay, it's for the best."

"Well, take a piece of advice from me," said Sinead, sounding more sad than cynical. "If you ever find yourself in a serious relationship, make sure each of you knows where the other stands when it comes to the big things: where you want to live, whether you want to have kids. Otherwise, you could find yourself in a major mess down the line."

"I'll try to keep that in mind."

Sinead slid out of the booth. "I'm going to want you to design some more clothing for me, so don't get too famous too soon."

"I'll try to avoid it." Lennie had already started wondering what she would do when the school year ended. The idea of going home to Saranac Lake for the summer held no appeal; she wanted to remain in the city and earn some money, even if it meant working two or three crummy part-time jobs. However, if Sinead really meant what she said, then Lennie might be able to get by with having to work only one job.

Sinead disappeared into the kitchen with the garment bag. Lennie pulled the check out of her shoulder bag, staring at it again. It was too bad she needed the money; otherwise, she would have framed it.

"*You* were great out there tonight."

Sebastian turned to Jason Mitchell, who was sitting next to him on the plane. They were on their way back from a game in Miami, where they'd played well. Sebastian had scored the game winner in a shoot-out.

"Thank you."

"So why do you look like you're on your way to your best friend's funeral?"

"I finally told Lennie about my contract," Sebastian revealed forlornly. "She did not take it well."

Jason patted his shoulder. "Sorry, dude."

"Maybe it's for the better. I don't know."

Jason nodded and opened the *New York Post,* perhaps sensing that Sebastian didn't want to go into detail about what had transpired. Sebastian kept running the scene in his head, contrasting how he had thought their conversation might go with what had actually happened.

He'd imagined Lennie being upset at first, but had assumed they would talk it through, deciding at the very least that they could still be friends if she chose not to continue a romantic relationship with him. Actually, what he'd really been hoping was for her to say, "I don't care if your contract is only for a year; you're the only one I want to be with. I love you, and whatever happens, happens. There's no reason we can't have a long-distance relationship if you have to move away."

The vehemence of her reaction had shocked him, as had her reaction to his telling her he loved her. He could see now how badly he'd miscalculated, how stupid he'd been in his assumptions. He'd been right about one thing: she did deserve better. He tried to focus on the only two positives that had come from what had transpired: one, she could now concentrate on her schoolwork; and two, he could dedicate himself fully to his game, ensuring that whatever happened next year, he'd be richer—if not emotionally, then at least financially.

Twelve

"How long are you going to avoid him?"

Lennie knew Christie had been itching to ask her for hours. She was hanging out at Christie's apartment, giving her advice on what to wear on her first date with a hottie she'd met at the bar. Three months had passed, and ever since she'd split from Sebastian, she'd been careful to stop by the Wild Hart only during the day, when she knew he and his teammates wouldn't be there. Of course, that didn't mean she didn't know what was going on with him: she read the sports pages religiously. In fact, whenever she came into the pub, Christie made a point of handing her a paper already open to the day's story on the Blades.

Not only that, but Aunt Mary always told her when the Blades were at the pub, adding, with a significant wiggle of the eyebrows, that Sebastian asked after her. The irony wasn't lost on Lennie; wasn't this the same Aunt Mary who had told her she should focus on school her very first day in the city and who had called Sebastian a "Commie"?

The truth was, she missed Sebastian. Badly. Not just their "savoring," but talking to him, laughing with him, experiencing the city together. She often sat daydreaming about him while at the sewing machine, picturing them doing this and that. Then some other thought would come darting into view and she'd snap out of it, overcome with an emptiness for which she herself was to blame. Lennie knew that if she asked him to, he would meet and talk with her, but she was held back by a huge fear of rejection. Maybe he'd decided he didn't love her after all. What if his excelling on the ice these past few weeks had to do with her not distracting him in some way?

She looked at the various articles of clothing laid out on Christie's bed. "Hmm." She pointed to a pair of jeans made by People's Liberation. Lennie liked their stuff; it was expensive, but sexy. "Those are good."

"You didn't respond to what I said. Admit it: you've been avoiding him."

"Obviously."

"He asks about you. I've told you that tons of times. He misses you."

Lennie felt a lump form in her throat. "I miss him too. But it's better this way."

Christie rolled her eyes. "Martyrdom doesn't suit you. Seriously. Talk to him."

"And say what?"

"That you miss him. That maybe you two could—"

"He might be gone in May."

"And you might get hit by a dump truck tomorrow," Christie shot back sharply. "At the very least, don't you miss his friendship?"

Lennie hesitated. "Yes. But I don't think I could be around him and just be friends."

"Because—?" Christie pushed.

"You know," Lennie mumbled.

"God, you're pitiful."

"Because I love him, okay?" Lennie burst out, her eyes filling with tears.

"Then do something about it. Life is risky, okay? Maybe tomorrow I'll get called out to a fire and lose my life. But I'm willing to take that risk, because it's worth it to me. You have to live in the here and now, Lennie. If you want him back, tell him."

"What if he doesn't want me back?"

"Then at least you'll know. Now which shirt should I wear with the jeans?"

Two nights later, Lennie screwed up her courage and walked into the Wild Hart. She'd deliberately chosen the night Aunt Mary would be at bingo with Mrs. O'Brien, knowing her aunt might make a big deal if she saw her and Sebastian together—assuming Seb would even talk to her, of course. Her gaze shot to Christie, who gave her a small smile and a discreet thumbs-up. Then, as casually as she could, she glanced toward the dining room. Sebastian was there with his teammates, his back toward her, thank God.

Lennie went to the bar. "I think I need a drink to fortify myself."

"What can I get you, girlfriend?"

"Sam Adams." The same thing she'd had the night she'd met Sebastian.

Mr. O'Brien was working behind the bar with Christie. Obviously his brother, Jimmy, had back problems again.

"Lennie," said Mr. O'Brien warmly, "we haven't seen you here in a while."

"I've been really busy with school."

"That clothing you made for my daughter Sinead? Very impressive."

Lennie was slightly taken aback. "She showed them to you?"

"Yes, the very day she got them. Lovely, just lovely. Tried them on for her mother and me. They suit her right down to the ground."

"Thank you."

"Perhaps I'll have you make a suit for me. My missus is always complaining because I've been wearing the same one since 1979."

Lennie laughed. "I would love to."

"Let's talk about it come summer, then."

"Deal." The thought of again being commissioned to design clothing and get paid for it? Heaven.

Christie handed her a Sam Adams. "Here you go."

"Thanks."

Lennie took a sip of beer, again glancing discreetly at the Blades' table.

"Get your butt over there," Christie commanded.

"In a minute." Lennie took a deep breath as nerves played up and down her spine. *Here and now*, she told herself. *That's all that matters.* She took another sip of beer, and began walking toward the Blades' table. She watched as one of Sebastian's teammates lightly elbowed him and Jason Mitchell leaned over to say something in his ear. Sebastian turned in his seat, watching her approach, his expression guarded. She wasn't surprised.

"Hey." Despite having sipped at her beer, her throat felt dry and clogged.

"Hey," Sebastian returned, standing up. "Sam Adams," he noted, picking his own bottle off the table.

"Great minds think alike," said Lennie. God, that was lame.

"Yes."

Lennie stuck her free hand into the back pocket of her jeans. "Um . . . I was wondering if we could talk?"

"Sure." Sebastian looked around the crowded dining room. "We could talk in the bar."

"All right."

Always the gentleman, he gestured for her to go ahead of him. She could feel his eyes on her back. Now it wasn't nerves that were playing up and down her spine; it was the beginning of desire.

The only table available was the one they'd sat at the night they'd met. "You know what? I don't think this is a good place to sit and talk."

Lennie's heart sank a little.

"Too noisy. Not private enough."

Relief swept through her.

"If you are comfortable with it, we could go talk at my apartment."

Lennie cleared her throat. "That would be fine."

Sebastian nodded. "Just let me tell my friends I am leaving. Then we can catch a cab."

"Gotcha."

Lennie's eyes shot to Christie, who lifted an eyebrow. "Well?" she mouthed.

Lennie smiled and crossed her fingers.

Thirteen

Lennie was relieved when she and Sebastian finally arrived at his apartment. They had been slightly awkward with each other during their cab ride, both striving to keep their conversation light and casual, both knowing that the talk they'd be having when they got to Sebastian's would be anything but.

"Coffee?" Sebastian offered.

"Brewed in your deluxe Krups coffeemaker?" Lennie teased.

Sebastian smiled faintly. "Yes, of course."

"Yes, please. A cup of coffee would be nice."

Lennie followed him into the kitchen. She was less interested in coffee than in having some kind of prop in her hand when she told him how she felt. The temptation to immediately spill her guts was overwhelming, but she controlled herself. She wanted to sound calm and thoughtful, not emotional and crazy.

"How's your uncle?"

"Well." Sebastian paused. "He asks about you."

Lennie sat at the small kitchen table, chin resting in her palm as she watched him. "What did you tell him?"

"That you're studying very hard in school."

"Does he know we—?"

Sebastian was all concentration as he measured out the coffee. "Yes."

What does he think? Lennie longed to ask. *Does he think you were a jerk not to tell me the truth at the beginning? Did you depict me as a lunatic when you told him about our breakup?*

"Give him my regards."

"I will."

Uneasy silence. Lennie rushed to fill the vacuum. "I've been following the Blades. You guys are doing great."

"We are," Sebastian agreed carefully as he glanced at her, "but we don't want to get too cocky. It's bad to make assumptions." There was a pregnant pause before his gaze returned to the task at hand. "That's something I've learned the hard way."

Lennie felt a surge of hope, but remained determined to not start talking until they were comfortable in the living room. "Do you mind if I go sit on the couch? I'm kind of tired."

"Of course, sit on the couch. I'll bring our coffee in a moment."

Lennie nodded, and headed to the living room. *It's bad to make assumptions. That's something I've learned the hard way.* Was he talking about hockey or her? Or both?

She glanced around the familiar room, looking to see if anything had changed since she'd last been there. Nothing had; it was still stark, the apartment of a man for whom decoration was a low priority. Or maybe a man who didn't want to assume he'd be staying beyond a year.

"Here we are." Sebastian joined her on the couch, two steaming mugs of coffee in hand, a prop for each of them.

Lennie marshaled her courage and took a huge gulp of coffee, which was a mistake; it burned her mouth and throat. She bit down on her lip to keep herself from yelping, but it was no good; Sebastian caught the split second of pain that flashed across her face.

"Are you all right?" he asked, concerned.

"I gulped down a little too much coffee, is all."

"There's no need to be nervous. It's just me."

"That's why I'm nervous!"

He reached out to put a reassuring hand on her knee. "Take your time."

Pure Sebastian: always so considerate, always so patient.

Lennie wrapped her hands tightly around her coffee mug. "I've been thinking a lot about how I acted the day we broke up."

"Yes?"

Lennie blushed. "I'm pretty sure I acted like a melodramatic jackass."

"Like a crazy woman."

"Okay, you don't have to rub it in." She cocked her head and closed her eyes, rubbing her forehead. "I wasn't really thinking. Just—reacting."

"I think maybe you had a right to react, though perhaps not quite so vehemently."

There was amusement in his voice, which she found encouraging. She opened her eyes. "I regret the way we parted." *Wimp.*

"So do I."

Lennie stared down into her mug. "I regret breaking up with you," she said sheepishly.

"That made me sad too."

Lennie's head shot up. "Really?"

Sebastian laughed. "Why would I say it if it wasn't true?"

Lennie put her cup down on the table, and reached out to take

Sebastian's hands in hers. "Can we give it another try? I know you might be leaving at the end of the season," she said breathlessly before he could interrupt. "But I don't care. When you love someone, you don't let it slip from your fingers. You take it day by day. Maybe our time together is limited, but I'll take it, because a finite amount of time with you is better than no time at all."

"I agree, *milaya moya*," Sebastian said softly.

"Oh, God." Lennie put her hand on her chest and breathed a sigh of relief. "I was so afraid you'd tell me that you'd changed your mind."

"You think I am someone who can fall out of love so easily?"

Lennie felt happy tears prick at the corners of eyes. "So you really—?"

"Yes. Yes. *Ya tebya lyublyu*—I love you."

"I love you too," said Lennie.

He rose, extending a hand to her, and together they went into his bedroom. She ached for him, but didn't want to rush. Taking their time, drinking each other in, they undressed each other, making love with their eyes before their bodies came together to caress and explore. There was no need for words as their mouths fused and fingers glided over naked flesh. Secrets and whispers. Sighing and longing as desire slowly built, a flicker at first that turned to a flame burning higher and higher.

By the time they lay down on the bed, Lennie's need had taken over. *Feel how much I want you*, she thought. She took his face in her hands, kissing him with an undeniable passion that could only inflame. Sebastian groaned into her mouth as he gently pushed her onto her back and climbed atop her. They locked hands, falling into each other's gazes. He slipped inside her. *This is the world I want to live in, one where there is Sebastian and only Sebastian.*

His loving gaze brought her to the edge of joyous tears as he slowly began to move inside her, Lennie savoring the feel of him against her, their bodies completely united. No thoughts of the past, no fears about the future. Just the two of them, together, now. Lennie felt as though she could touch the sky from his bed as the heat within her built. Finally it happened: the devastating, headlong rush into ultimate pleasure that she never wanted to end. But end it did, and she watched lovingly as he followed her into oblivion. When they both returned to their senses, he held her tight and secure in his arms.

Home, she thought. *Home.*

Fourteen

"To Ivan the Terrible!"

Sebastian laughed heartily as his teammates hoisted their glasses in his honor at their usual table at the Wild Hart. Though they'd been knocked out of the second round of the play-offs two weeks earlier, they still had reason to celebrate: Sebastian had been offered a contract, and he had signed a three-year deal with the Blades.

"Glad to have you on board, you Commie bastard," said Ulf.

"Glad to be on board," said Sebastian, touching his whiskey glass to Ulf's. He hadn't yet told Lennie. She was on her way down to the pub, thinking she was just going to hang out with him and his friends the way she often did. He couldn't wait to see her face when he gave her the news.

From the time they'd reunited, they'd both made an effort to ensure she didn't get behind in her schoolwork. Her academic year was now over, as was his season. They'd have the whole summer to spend together, though Lennie would be working: Jimmy O'Brien couldn't work behind the bar anymore, and she was replacing him, at least until school resumed in September. During the day she'd be designing and making clothing. Sinead had spread the word among some of her friends and colleagues about Lennie's talents as a designer. She now had enough commissions to start saving money so she could look for her own place soon.

"Where's the little woman?" asked Thad, already on his second whiskey.

"She'll be here soon," Sebastian said confidently. His eyes flew to the front door of the pub every time it opened. He couldn't help it. He was jumping out of his skin with excitement.

Uncle Yuri had wept when Sebastian told him he'd be in New York three more years. Sebastian was trying to figure out a way to help out his uncle financially without insulting him. He knew he'd never leave Brighton Beach, but if Yuri was willing, Sebastian wanted to buy him an apartment outright. Why should his beloved relative pay rent when he didn't have to? Sebastian was also intent on persuading his uncle to take a trip back to Russia with him this summer. Easier said than done; even though his uncle knew things had changed back home, he'd been deeply scarred by the prejudice he'd had to endure for years.

Jason Mitchell nudged Sebastian in the ribs. "Here's your gal." Sebastian's heart gave a thud as his eyes turned to Lennie, who had walked over to the bar to say a quick hello to Christie, her aunt Mary, and Rudy II, who was wearing the Greek fisherman's cap Lennie had made for him. Sebastian quelled his impatience, knowing he couldn't expect her to just breeze past those close to her without saying hello.

She looked beautiful. She always looked beautiful. Her long hair was loosely pinned up, gentle tendrils falling around her face. Tight faded jeans and a tight long-sleeved purple T-shirt hugged her firm, curvy body. She'd wrapped a gold scarf around her neck. He liked that she took care with her appearance— just one of the many ways they were alike.

Thank you for lying, he thought. *Thank you for pretending to be "New To New York."*

When she finally came toward him, it was with a smile that lit up the room. Gratitude again swelled in his heart. He couldn't believe that she'd chosen him, she who was so beautiful and talented she could have any man she wanted.

"Hey, you," she said, kissing him.

"Hey, you," he returned with a big hug.

"Hey, guys." Sebastian's teammates greeted her, and he could see the undeniable glint of anticipation in their eyes, which was not lost on Lennie.

"What's up?"

Sebastian broke into a slow grin. "Guess."

"Oh, God." Lennie's hands flew to cover her mouth for a moment. "You're staying, aren't you?"

"Yes!" He picked her up and twirled her around. "Three years!"

Lennie let out a whoop so loud other diners turned to look at her.

"Sorry," she apologized to the dining room, cringing a little but still exuberant. "I just found out my boyfriend is going to be in town for three more years!" She turned to Sebastian, touching him all over, as if she couldn't quite believe he was flesh and blood. "I've been praying every night, I swear to God. I even had my aunt and Mrs. O'Brien light candles at church."

"Well, it looks like it worked."

Sebastian pulled up an empty chair from the table across from them. "Come, sit down," he said to Lennie.

"Not yet," she said, taking his hand. "We've got to tell Christie and Aunt Mary the good news." Lennie was certain she was smiling like an idiot as she and Sebastian headed to the bar, but she didn't care. She was euphoric. Even though she'd been trying to take each day as it came since she and Sebastian had reunited, there had always been the nagging fear in the back of her mind that when the hockey season ended, he'd be leaving New York— and her.

She excitedly pulled Sebastian to the lip of the bar, the two of them squeezing in between The Mouth and PJ Leary, who claimed he'd found a publisher for his Celtic magnum opus.

"Hey, everyone, listen up."

The regulars quieted.

"An announcement from our comely young maiden here," said The Mouth delightedly. "It's not often—"

"Close your gob and let her talk, eh?" Mr. O'Brien's voice was chiding but affectionate. He smiled at Lennie. "Go on, love."

"Sebastian has been signed to the Blades for three more years!"

A cheer went up. "Fantastic!" said Mr. O'Brien. "Here, come round the bar, let me give you a hug."

Lennie scooted behind the bar, giddy as the old Irishman folded her in a soft embrace. "I hope this doesn't mean you're going to put off making that jacket for me, now," he teased, wagging a finger at her.

"Of course not. I'll have it to you at the end of the summer, as promised."

Mr. O'Brien leaned over the bar to shake Sebastian's hand. "Congrats. Drinks for you and your teammates are on the house tonight."

"Thank you," said Sebastian. "That's very kind of you."

"I told you he'd be here longer than a year," Christie whispered smugly in Lennie's ear.

"You did not!"

Christie chuckled. "Okay, I didn't, but aren't you glad you decided to chance it with him?"

"Yes—and I suppose in a way I do owe it all to you," Lennie admitted thoughtfully.

"You do. Which means you owe me. Which means I decide how you repay me."

"I'll make you any item of clothing you want."

Christie snorted. "Screw that! I want your boyfriend to introduce me to one of his teammates."

"Well, we'll see what we can do."

Lennie rejoined Sebastian on the other side of the bar. "Look at your aunt," he whispered, tilting his head in her direction. "She's beaming."

Lennie took Sebastian's hand and went to join her aunt, putting her arms around her neck and kissing her cheek. "I'm so happy!"

"Happy! Happy Happy!" Rudy crowed.

"How do you say 'Congratulations' in Russian?" Aunt Mary asked Sebastian.

"*Pazdravlyayoo.*"

Aunt Mary looked crestfallen. "I think that might be too much of a mouthful for Rudy to learn."

"Nonsense." Sebastian held out his arm so Rudy could perch there. Within five minutes, Rudy was squawking "*Pazdravlyayoo!*" repeatedly.

"Thanks a lot," Mr. O'Brien lamented playfully. "Now I'm gonna have to teach him some Gaelic to balance it all out. Can't have him spouting off in Russian in an Irish bar, can we?"

Sebastian returned Rudy to Aunt Mary, then took Lennie's hand, squeezing it. "Look," he said, pointing at the table where they'd had their first conversation. The couple sitting there were getting up to leave.

"Fate," Lennie declared as she quickly pulled him over to it before anyone else had a chance to nab it. She went to sit in the chair opposite Sebastian, but he was having none of it as he pulled her down onto his lap.

"So, are you new to New York?" Sebastian murmured seductively in her ear.

Lennie laughed delightedly as she twined her arms around his neck. "Why, yes, I am," she played along.

"Very nice to meet you."

"You too."

He kissed her shoulder. "Perhaps we might go out sometime."

"That would be wonderful," Lennie enthused, cupping his cheek. "Any idea on what you might like to do?"

Sebastian's eyes glinted with love. "Anything is fine as long as I get to do it with you, *milaya moya*."

Lennie wrapped her arms tighter around him.

"I couldn't have said it better myself."

Double Booked

Elizabeth Bevarly

One

Amanda Bingham climbed atop her canvas carry-on and bore down with all her weight, struggling to zip the damned thing shut before it sprang open and sent her newly purchased—and not even worn yet—vacation wardrobe flying. After four minutes, three changes of position, two puffs of chestnut curls from her eyes, and one *very* bad word, she managed—barely—to succeed. Then she carefully climbed down and held her breath, waiting to make sure it would stay that way.

She wasn't a fan of flying in the first place, and not just because her luggage was always, without fail, the last to arrive on the carousel. She'd learned a long time ago how to pack efficiently, but normally when she traveled, it was for only a few days, and she never had to take more than a garment bag. Packing for a vacation instead of business, she was discovering for the first time in her adult working life, was a whole 'nother ball game.

One week, she reminded herself. She would be gone for only a week. Some people could go away for that amount of time with a suitcase the size of an electron and do quite nicely. And it wasn't like she was going to Outer Boondoggle, where there wouldn't be any creature comforts. She'd be on Captiva Island off the Gulf coast of Florida, in a luxury condo her friends Kate and Marshall had been trying to convince her to take advantage of since they bought it five years ago.

A bikini and no worries, Kate had said. *That's all you'll need to pack*. She'd assured Amanda the condo would have everything else she'd need, right down to the sunscreen and beach towels.

Ha, Amanda thought now. Spoken like the hedonistic bon vivant Kate was. The hedonistic bon vivant with perfect skin and perfect hair and perfect everything else, who didn't need special skin and hair care products if she didn't want to break out in hives, and SPF 492 if she didn't want to spontaneously combust. Kate didn't have seasonal allergies that required antihistamines, or insomnia that necessitated sleep aids, or dry eyes that demanded artificial tears. And her vision was perfect, so she didn't have to pack things like saline solution and cleaning chemicals for her contact lenses, not to mention eyeglasses—and a spare pair, should her first pair break—or prescription sunglasses—and a spare pair, should the first pair break.

Oh, sure, Amanda probably could have bought most of those things in Florida, but who knew if the stores down there carried the same brands they did here in Indianapolis? It had taken her a long time to find products that didn't irritate her highly irritable body parts. No way was she going to risk spending the only vacation she'd probably have this decade broken out in some abominable reaction to something new. Hence the additional stuff stuffed into her bag.

Nor did Kate—or her husband, for that matter—need to stay in touch with the rest of the world when they took personal time, the way Amanda did. Kate was a painter and sculptor who did her best work in isolation, and Marshall was a tech wiz who could work from any place that had wireless access. Amanda was the assistant to the CEO of Hoberman Securities, and the only reason she was able to take this week off was because her boss was on vacation too.

As it was, she would still be on call for the next seven days, since Mr. Hoberman was never actually *on* vacation when he went on vacation. He'd expect her to call in daily with her usual reports on developments in the financial and business worlds and keep him apprised of what was going on. So she'd also had to pack her laptop and assorted other gizmos for staying in touch with the world—and Mr. Hoberman—along with any paperwork she might need to consult about projects on which her boss was currently working.

Okay, okay, so maybe her vacation wasn't going to be much of a vacation. At least she'd be at the beach. Alone. During January, a time when Indianapolis was already covered with two inches of snow and being threatened with more. With only half the work she normally had because, in addition to being Mr. Hoberman's assistant, she was also, evidently, the only person at Hoberman Securities who knew the answers to really vital questions like "Where do we keep the microwave popcorn?" and "Whose turn is it to stock up on paper clips?"

She hoped the company didn't collapse without her around to take care of such potentially catastrophic crises.

And speaking of catastrophic crises, she eyed her carry-on again, noting that the zipper was straining along its seam, and the buckles of the outer pockets looked about to blow. Always prepared, she thought. Just like the Coast Guard. Or was it the Boy Scouts? Campfire Girls? Well, anyway, Amanda Bingham wasn't the type to go off half-cocked—or with a potentially explosive suitcase. So she hefted it from the bed, carried it to the stairs leading down to the first floor of her condo, and hurled it to the bottom. It bumped and thumped to the foyer without a single stitch coming undone.

She smiled, thinking her suitcase was a lot like her. Sturdy, no-frills, under stress and pushed to the limit, but not undone. Oh, no. Amanda Bingham was *never* undone. She approached every challenge that life presented fully prepared for any mishap. And for that reason, mishaps rarely—if ever—occurred in her life.

Vacation, here I come, she thought. She closed her eyes and envisioned herself seated on the sun-drenched deck of a beachside restaurant—in the shade, of course—a pile of peel-and-eat shrimp before her bookended by a bowl of cocktail sauce and a bottle of ice-cold beer, sweaty from the heat. In the distance, the turquoise waters of the Gulf of Mexico sparkled beneath a crisp blue sky, a windsurfer clinging to a bright, rainbow-streaked sail skimming across its surface, and—

The chirping of her cell phone made the image dissolve, since she hadn't planned on including it in her fantasy. Then she realized it wasn't a part of her fantasy. Her cell phone was actually ringing. She snatched it from the nightstand, checking the number in spite of the fact that she knew perfectly well who it was. No one else ever called her.

She sighed, pushed the Answer button, and said, "Hello, Mr. Hoberman. . . . No, of course you're not bothering me. . . . No, I don't have to leave for another hour. . . . Sure, I can check on that for you and call you back tonight. Will you be at this number?"

She nodded in response to his orders, reached for the pad and pencil that were never more than an arm's length away, and bit back another sigh.

Vacation, here I come. . . . Just as soon as I finish this call . . .

It went without saying that the flight to Fort Myers was, like everything else that day, a nightmare. The call from Mr. Hoberman had led to a half dozen more, thereby using up all the extra time

Amanda had allotted herself just in case, because she always allotted extra time for herself just in case. As a result, she'd had to rush to finish dressing, rush to water her plants, rush to ensure she'd locked all the windows and doors, rush out to the cab honking its horn in her driveway, rush to the airport, rush to check in, rush to the gate, and rush to the plane.

Not that she was unaccustomed to rushing—being an assistant to a powerful CEO often required it—but once she was in rush mode, it was always difficult to slow down again. And being strapped into a tiny seat between a woman for whom it became immediately obvious that personal hygiene was an afterthought and a man who had brought aboard a meal that included what was clearly an animal long dead and never actually cooked was *not* conducive to the deep-breathing exercises she normally used to calm herself. Add to it the small child seated behind her who alternated between kicking her seat and screaming at the top of his lungs, and, well . . .

Suffice it to say that after all that, Amanda *really* needed a vacation.

She also really needed to remove her contacts because her eyes had become so irritated by the, ah, dry air—yeah, that was it; couldn't have been her seatmates—which she did once the plane was safely at its gate. She also took a few minutes to change from the tweed trousers, cream shirt, and boots the Indy weather had necessitated and into a short denim skirt, red tank top, and flat sandals she'd tucked into her carry-on to allow her adjustment to the balmy Florida weather.

As she waited for her luggage to appear on the carousel, Amanda did her best to envision the white beaches and tranquil blue water of Captiva again. And she promised herself she would take herself out to dinner that very night for an ice-cold beer and peel-and-eat shrimp. But that vision evaporated when she saw her suitcase *finally* arrive on the carousel . . . spilling half its contents. This despite the fact that someone had tried—kind of—to put it all back together again. With duct tape. That hadn't worked.

So much for the cult of the duct tape. Obviously there were some things even it couldn't fix. She sighed inwardly and hoped nothing was missing. Especially her underwear and Benadryl.

The cab ride to the condo was only marginally less stressful, and cost nearly as much as it would have cost Amanda to rent a car for the week. But she had been determined to make this a vacation in every sense of the word, and do *nothing* except sit on the beach and watch the ocean, and visit only places within walking distance, and read all four of the books she'd brought along. Provided, of course, those books weren't still circling the baggage area of some airport terminal along with her underwear and Benadryl. Oh, and of course she would also take any and all calls from Mr. Hoberman, which, she supposed, would necessitate that she work, something that rather countered the whole vacation-in-every-sense-of-the-word-thing. But you couldn't have everything, could you?

But other than the calls-from-Mr.-Hoberman part, it truly was going to be a vacation in every sense of the word. It *was*. Really. She meant it. She *did*.

Her disjointed thoughts scattered, however, when the cabbie came to a stop just below a row of gorgeous connected town houses, each painted a shade of barely-there color ranging from pearl pink to sky blue. They were perched on stilts over a row of connected parking spaces overwhelmingly populated by overpriced vehicles of some kind. Obviously, Kate hadn't been kidding about the "luxury" aspect of her condo. Her temporary neighbors clearly had money to burn.

Amanda took in the rest of her surroundings as she climbed out of the cab, noting similar complexes scattered sparsely up and down the beach as far as she could see, as well as the complete absence of any of the tacky tourist traps one usually saw woven in between such structures. The sun was dipping low over the ocean by now, staining the sky with smudges of color as soft as those of the houses in front of it, spreading fingers of gold and copper and orange across the softly rippling water. The breeze kicked up, freeing a few errant curls from what had been a tightly contained braid until the fiasco of her trip, but somehow, suddenly, Amanda didn't mind her state of disarray so much.

She closed her eyes and breathed deeply, dispelling all memory of stinky seatmates and expensive cab rides and employer's phone calls, instead inhaling the sharp, savory scent of the sea. The wind whiffled through the palms arcing over the complex, making their broad fronds whisper something soft and senseless, something that soothed her frazzled nerves.

Oh, yes, she thought as she opened her eyes. She definitely needed this. She'd been running at full tilt for too long, and it was way past time for her to take a few days for herself. No one could do their job well if they didn't take time to recharge. And what was the point of anything if one didn't do her job well?

She paid the cabbie after deftly computing fifteen percent for a tip—not that he deserved it, since he'd tossed her taped suitcase onto the ground at her feet as if it had leprosy—then collected her bag and headed for the pale yellow condo at the very end of the row, which Kate had identified as hers. At the foot of the stairs, Amanda shifted the suitcase to her other hand so she could search in her purse for the key, and in doing so, lost her grip on the bag. That inevitably freed the tape on one side and made it spill its contents *again*. On the upside, she immediately saw her Benadryl and at least one pair of underwear. On the downside—

Well, she'd just chalk up the entire day—save the gorgeous view and lovely breeze—on the downside column.

Biting back a disgruntled sound, Amanda scooped up her belongings and stuffed everything back into the bag, wrapping one arm around the bundle as best she could. Then she made her way up the steps, battled the key into the uncooperative lock, shoved at the sticky front door in a few futile efforts to open it—okay, maybe the place wasn't quite as luxurious, or at least as accommodating, as Kate had promised—until she finally managed to hurl herself against it with enough force to open it . . . and send both her suitcase *and* herself hurtling to the floor.

Okay, that was *it*, she decided as she gazed at the ceiling and did her best to ignore the pain in her shoulder that had taken the brunt of her fall. This was absolutely the last thing that would go wrong on her vacation. From here on out, she vowed, *nothing* was going to happen that would do *anything* to disrupt her R&R for the rest of the week. Nothing. Nada. Nil.

Zip. Zero. Zilch.

From here on out, *everything* was going to go according to plan. She would have nothing but peace and quiet and enjoy herself immensely and return to Indianapolis and her job fully refreshed and raring to go. The rest of the week was going to be *perfect*.

As if cued by the thought, a muffled *bump* sounded from the other side of the room, and Amanda's stomach clenched tight. Before she had a chance to process what might have caused it, a second sound followed, this one the sound of a man's voice. A man's voice singing. Singing "At the Copa . . . Copa-cabaaa-naaa." Badly.

She had managed to scramble onto her hands and knees by the time a door on the other side of the living room opened and the source of the man's voice appeared. It was coming from a man. Imagine that. A man who was cloaked by little more than a puff of quickly dissolving steam and a damp, dangerously dipping bath towel.

But it wasn't the fact that there was a half-naked man in the otherwise-deserted condo that stunned, confused, and horrified Amanda. It was the fact that she knew him. Too well.

Max Callahan, the sorriest excuse for a human being ever to come down the pike, so full of himself and his certainty that he was God's gift to women that there wasn't room in him for anything else. Anything like, oh, intelligence. Gentleness. Consideration for his fellow man. A work ethic. Stuff like that.

Or decency, either, as evidenced by the way he just stood there in the towel, his dark, wet hair falling arrogantly over his forehead, his blue eyes glittering with mischief, his broad shoulders spanning the doorway, his muscles bunching and flexing when he braced his arms against the jamb, his long, lean, torso dripping wet, sheening the taut bumps and valleys of his rock-hard abs and that mouthwateringly tantalizing curve of flesh just above his—

Uh . . . She meant . . . That is . . . um . . . ah . . .

She meant the way he stood there half naked, completely unconcerned about the fact that he was standing there half naked. Yeah, that was it.

Max Callahan, who had been a thorn in Amanda's side since high school and who always made her feel like the girl at the dance who had to stand behind the punch bowl and pretend being on the refreshment committee made her way too busy for frivolous things like dancing. Not that anyone had ever asked Amanda to dance in the first place, so it was just as well she *had* been on the refreshment committee. For every single dance.

The man who still occasionally showed up at the same social functions Amanda did and who, to this day, still made her feel like that awkward teenager who could never say, do, or wear the right thing. The man who always made a thinly veiled mockery of her dedication to her job and her desire to do the right thing. The man who never took her seriously and drove her absolutely nuts.

The man her friend Kate had been telling Amanda for years was absolutely perfect for her.

Two

It didn't surprise Max Callahan to find a woman in the condo his friends Marshall and Kate had loaned him for the week. In fact, he'd been planning on having a number of them in the condo this week. And by having them, he meant, you know, *having* them. But he hadn't anticipated one being delivered right to his doorstep the very night he arrived. At least not this early in the evening.

Then again, she wasn't exactly the sort of woman he normally ordered when he called Hottie Hut. Even through a thick veil of steam, he could tell she totally, uh . . . was not his type. There. That was a lot better than saying she was unattractive, right? Saying she wasn't his type was even better than saying she had a great personality. Who said Max Callahan didn't have a tactful bone in his body? Besides every woman he knew?

As the steam gradually began to clear, he could tell even better that she was pretty damned . . . loaded with good personality. Her hair was sticking straight up in places, her glasses were slightly askew, she was sprawled gracelessly on the floor on all fours—not that her position wouldn't afford some measure of interest from him in different circumstances—and she . . .

Wait a minute, he thought when the steam cleared the rest of the way. She wasn't just loaded with good personality; she was familiar. Too familiar. He knew her. And not in the biblical sense, which would have made this a lot less annoying.

"Amanda?" he said, not quite able to keep the disbelief—or distaste—out of his tone. But even without her answering, he already knew it was her scrambling up from the floor.

Ah, crap. So much for a vacation. Five minutes in a room with Amanda Bingham made a man want to spontaneously combust. It wasn't just that she was loaded with good personality. It was that she had absolutely no personality. None. She was a corporate drone, plain and simple, a woman who lived to work and had no interests outside doing her job well. And it wasn't like she had a job that benefited mankind or made the world a better place, like medical research or tech support or R&D for a major brewery or anything. Hell, she didn't even dance in a strip club. She was the lackey for some corporate big shot whose business consisted of making rich, powerful people richer and more powerful, and paid his own employees bubkes.

Not that Max cared or anything. Kate just liked to bitch about it on Amanda's behalf, since Amanda never bitched about it herself, being the corporate drone she was. And speaking of her job, what was she doing *here*? She never took time off from work. Not that Max cared about that, either, but it was something else Kate bitched about a lot. That and how Amanda never dated because her boss kept her hopping, and how all Amanda needed was some hot, fun guy to show her how much more life had to offer besides work. And hey, Max, why don't you ask Amanda out sometime, since a guy like you is exactly the kind of guy Amanda needs, because you could make her laugh and show her a good time and take her mind off her work for a while and . . .

And that was when Max had always had to turn to Marshall and say, "Hey, how about them Colts?" Because there was no way in hell he was going to ask Amanda Bingham to do anything. Except keep her distance. The last thing he wanted was to be infected by her workaholic, no-fun, no-personality tendencies. Max embraced the opposite philosophy: work to live. He did only the minimal amount to get by, and working as a freelance whatever-he-felt-like-being-on-any-given-week, be it carpenter or painter or mason or pool cleaner, afforded him exactly that. His needs in life were few. A soft bed, a warm woman, and the occasional beer. Or was that a warm bed, a soft woman, and a frequent beer? Depended on the day, he guessed. And today . . .

He looked at Amanda again. Today was looking to be one that required way more than bed, woman, or beer. Thank God he'd had the foresight to pack that bottle of tequila.

"What the hell are you doing here?"

Strangely, it wasn't Max who asked the question, but Amanda. Funny, but he didn't think he'd ever heard her swear before.

"What am *I* doing here?" he countered. "What the hell are *you* doing here?"

She straightened to her full height—which couldn't have been more than five-four in the scrawny flats she was wearing. He wasn't used to her being so short. Usually, she wore those power heels women wore to compensate in the workplace, but right now, she wouldn't even come up to his chin. For the first time since realizing who she was, Max took in the complete package. The reason he hadn't recognized her right off was because she was wearing glasses that made her eyes—clear green eyes he'd always thought were way too beautiful for a tightass like her—look even bigger than before. But instead of detracting from her looks, they somehow made her kind of appealing. In a sexy librarian porno kind of way. That was probably because she was also wearing a short denim skirt and skintight tank top, which was another departure from her usual corporate-drone attire. Usually, when he ran into her somewhere, she was wearing baggy, man-style trousers and baggy, man-style shirts, and her hair was always pulled back without a single strand out of place. And although it was pulled back now, too, there were plenty of strands out of place, curling riotously and making the sexy librarian look recently tumbled.

He'd never realized Amanda Bingham had such curly hair. Even in high school, she'd never worn it loose. So many mornings, he'd come to his locker, a half dozen or so down from hers, had seen that long braid hanging to the middle of her back, and had wondered what it would be like, just once, to free the band that held the woven strands together and loose the thick mass of strawberry blond.

Her hair was darker now. A rich, dark chestnut with threads of amber and ginger knit through it. It was shorter than it had been fifteen years ago, but still plaited the same way, and still long enough for her braid to have fallen forward over one shoulder. And damned if Max didn't find himself wondering, even now, what it would be like to free her hair from the scrap of red wrapped around its end.

Not that he cared or anything. He'd just heard Kate go on and on about what great hair Amanda had and how she should wear it loose sometimes. Max had really never paid much attention.

"I'm here on vacation," she told him.

He started to shake his head the minute she voiced the word *vacation*. But he echoed her sentiment nonetheless when he said, "That's impossible. *I'm* here on vacation."

She narrowed her eyes at him suspiciously. "I'm here at Kate and Marshall's invitation," she said indignantly.

"You can't be," he countered. "*I'm* here at Marshall and Kate's invitation."

"They said I'd have the place to myself."

"They said *I'd* have the place to myself."

"They told me this was the only week it was available."

"They told *me* this was the only week it was available."

He started to say more, but then it hit him. Hit him like a good, solid blow to the back of the head.

"Ah, crap," he said, speaking his earlier thought aloud. Why hadn't he listened to those alarm bells that had started ringing the minute Marshall had offered him a free week at the beach? How many times had Max asked for exactly that, only to have his friends reply that A, the condo was booked for every week Max could make it; B, it was hurricane season; or C, the place was being (choose one) painted, cleaned, fumigated, roofed, or whatever other damned thing took their fancy to keep him from enjoying the place because they didn't trust him not to trash it.

And, okay, maybe Max had a reputation for trashing places. It wasn't like he didn't clean up before he left. Or, you know, leave a check to cover the cost of replacing whatever he'd broken. But Marshall and Kate had always been adamant. Until now. Until they'd suddenly decided Max could use a week at the shore. And it was a week when they'd evidently offered their condo to Amanda too.

Funny, but he could usually smell a setup a mile away, giving him ample time to run screaming in the opposite direction. He'd just been too taken in by the prospect of a week at the beach in the dead of winter to let himself think too hard about what might be behind it.

He dropped his hands to his hips, remembered he was standing there in nothing but a towel, and realized he didn't care. Hell, it wasn't like he had anything to fear from Amanda. She hated his guts. "Did Kate tell you not to bother packing anything but your swimsuit since the condo would have everything you'd need?" he asked.

Amanda nodded.

"Yeah, Marshall told me that too."

Amanda said nothing for a moment, obviously weighing the information carefully. Then, when she must have come to the same conclusion Max had, her eyes went wide. "Are you telling me Kate and Marshall set us up?"

This time Max was the one to nod. "In more ways than one."

"Oh, no," she said adamantly, shaking her head. "No, no, no, no, no. Kate knows how I feel about you. She knows I can't st—" She halted abruptly, her eyes going even wider, two bright spots of color blooming on her cheeks.

Max smiled. He knew exactly what she was going to say. That she couldn't stand him. Which was fine with him, because he couldn't stand Amanda either. He'd never been able to understand why Kate kept harping on him to ask her out. Obviously, she must have talked to Amanda about the same thing at some point; otherwise, she wouldn't have known how Amanda felt about him. So if he didn't want to have anything to do with Amanda, and Amanda didn't want to have anything to do with him, then why had Marshall and Kate arranged this week for them to be stuck here together?

Because it was a safe bet they *were* stuck here together. Not only could neither of them have budgeted for a hotel, but there probably wasn't a hotel room to be had on the coast at this time of year anyway.

As if she'd read his thoughts, Amanda said, "They expect us to share this place for a week? Are they out of their minds?"

He started to say "Obviously," but checked himself. It was a rhetorical question, after all. So instead he said, "Look, I know you're no happier about this than I am, but there's no reason why we can't make it work. We'll just divide the condo between us. I'll stay out of your way if you'll stay out of mine."

"One problem," she said.

"What's that?"

"One," she repeated. "That's the problem."

"What are you talking about?"

"There's only one of everything," she pointed out. "One kitchen, one living room, one balcony, one bathroom, one . . ."

She halted, but he already saw where this was heading. "One bedroom," he finished for her.

She nodded. "Which means one . . ."

Again, she wasn't quite able to finish. So Max finished for her. "One bed."

She nodded again. "So who gets that?"

He smiled. "I'll wrestle you for it, Amanda. Best two out of three falls."

Three

Amanda felt the blood drain from her face. Wrestle Max? He was crazier than Kate if he thought she would go for that. Immediately, however, she realized he was only kidding. Because he started laughing irrepressibly enough to make the towel dip even lower on his hips. Just before it would have gone tumbling to the floor, he caught it, tucking it carelessly around his waist again. Though none too snugly, since it fell right back to the precarious position it had been in before, perfectly cradling that erotic curve of muscle between his navel and his—

"Hah! Gotcha," he said when he could stop laughing long enough to catch his breath.

Thankfully, that jerked Amanda's attention back to the matter at hand. Although maybe *hand* wasn't the best word to use under the circumstances. Or *jerk*, for that matter. Not considering where her gaze had fallen and how much she had been admiring the way his towel so beautifully framed his . . . ah . . .

Where was she?

Oh, yeah. Max had been laughing at her. Not that that was anything new.

"Oh, man, if you could see the look on your face," he added, punctuating the statement with a smug grin. "Relax, Amanda. I'm no more interested in wrestling *or* sharing the bed—or the bedroom, for that matter—with you than you are."

Somehow, his reassurance did little to reassure her. Maybe because, suddenly, the thought of sharing the bedroom—or the bed, for that matter—or even wrestling with him didn't bother her quite as much as it would have a few weeks ago. Or a few minutes ago. Or even a few seconds ago. Funny how a precariously placed towel could completely change the tone of a conversation.

Um, where was she?

Oh, yeah. Not getting along with Max. Not that that was anything new.

"How about we draw straws for it?" he asked. "The couch out here unfolds into a bed, and whoever draws the short straw takes the living room. How about that? That's fair, right?"

She wanted to say something about how a gentleman would automatically offer to take the sofa and let the lady take the bedroom, but she knew it would be pointless. For one thing, it wasn't unusual for her and Max to argue about women's rights on those occasions when they were forced to talk to each other, and about how he had no respect for women *or* their rights and how everything between men and women should be equal. So it would look pretty lame if Amanda talked the talk but couldn't walk the walk. For another thing, Max was no gentleman. So she only nodded her agreement. It did seem like the best way to resolve the problem.

He started to head for the kitchen to look for a couple of straws, but Amanda stopped him with a carefully worded "Don't you want to, um . . . I mean, ah . . . Before we do that, wouldn't you rather . . ."

Okay, so maybe it wasn't carefully worded. Max didn't seem to think so, either, because when he turned around to look at her, his expression was puzzled. Instead of finishing what she had been trying to say—since that would be even more difficult to do looking at his front side than it had been looking at his backside—she just turned her gaze away and waved a hand airily at the towel wrapped around his hips.

"Oh, that," he said without concern.

Oh, that, she repeated to herself. With lots of concern. Then again, he *would* be unconcerned about it. He saw himself half naked and dripping wet and rippling with muscle and mouthwatering . . . ah . . . She meant he saw himself like this all the time. For Amanda, however, this was a first. Not her first half-naked man, of course. Or even dripping-wet man. Well, not quite the first, anyway. She had, after all, you know . . . Lots of times, in fact. Well, okay, not lots. But there had been more than one guy in her life. And one of them had even showered at her place. The rippling muscle, though, was definitely a first, since the guys she dated were more fluff than buff. More rut than cut. More dip than rip.

But they all had *great* personalities. And that was what was most important.

"Seriously, wouldn't you be more comfortable if you were dressed?" she asked. Though, truth be told, it wasn't Max's comfort she was thinking about just then.

Really funny how the placement of a towel could change the tone of . . . oh, everything.

"This'll just take a second," he said with even less concern than before, continuing on his way.

She watched as he ducked behind the breakfast bar and started opening cabinets . . . then made herself look away again because she just couldn't tear her gaze from the way the muscles in his bare back bunched and relaxed and bunched again with every move he made. She didn't know why she was surprised that Max looked this good under his clothes. Of course a man as shallow and self-absorbed as he was would spend time at the gym. All he cared about was the physical. With himself and the women he dated.

Amanda pushed the thought away and took in the rest of her surroundings. Kate and Marshall had furnished the condo beautifully. Between the kitchen and the bathroom was a set of French doors that led out to a small balcony, and beyond that, nothing but sparkling white beach, glittering blue ocean, and luminous pink sunset. It was the perfect complement to the Caribbean theme of the decor. The walls were painted a brighter yellow than the exterior, and the furniture was whitewashed rattan. The accent pieces were plentiful, all splashes of dazzling color, from the charmingly primitive paintings of island houses and marketplaces to the irregularly shaped throw pillows to the thickly woven carpets scattered about the tile floor. Directly opposite the kitchen was a door that led to what must be the bedroom, and . . .

And, oh, who cares how Kate and Marshall furnished the place? Amanda thought as she turned to look at Max's back . . . ah, she meant at Max, of course . . . again. By now he was facing her, doing something on the kitchen counter that didn't seem to involve straws at all, but did rely heavily on a bottle of tequila.

"I couldn't find any straws," he said when he glanced up to find her looking at him. "So we'll have to go with swizzle sticks. And it goes without saying that there's no point in breaking out the swizzle sticks if you don't have something to swizzle them with."

"Is that a fact?" she asked dryly.

"Of course it's a fact," he assured her, continuing his task without looking up at her. "A fact you would have realized by now if you ever did anything besides work work work."

She gaped at that. "I do more than work work work," she denied hotly. "A lot more."

"Oh?" he asked dubiously. This time he did look up, but it was only to toss a lime into the air with one hand and catch it deftly with the other. "Like what?"

She started to enumerate the many and myriad activities of her daily life, but all she could come up with at the moment were things that involved Mr. Hoberman. Things like picking up his half-caf skinny latte, light on the cinnamon, on her way to work, and spending her lunch hour picking out a gift for his wife's birthday/son's wedding/daughter's promotion/mistress's college graduation/whatever, and stopping on her way home to meet for drinks with a client he wasn't able to meet himself because he had to meet with a more important client, which actually meant he was meeting his mistress. Or maybe his wife. Though Amanda doubted it.

But Max was standing there waiting for an answer, so she fudged. "I go out for coffee. And I go shopping. And I go for drinks with . . . people." She couldn't really say *friends*, because that would venture beyond the realm of fudging and into lying, since she never liked any of the clients Mr. Hoberman had her meet, and she always told the truth. Always. Except for when she fudged a little.

Max started putting things into a blender and grinned that smug grin again. "And what makes me think that all this coffee, shopping, and drinking relates directly to your job?"

She started to reply with something flip and cavalier—and hopefully honest—but he spared her having to do so by punching a button on the blender and creating a cacophony of crushing ice, lime, and tequila, thereby drowning out whatever she might say. So Amanda only mouthed a vehement, if silent, denial—It wasn't lying if you didn't say it out loud, right?—stopping the moment she saw his finger lifting from the blender button.

"So there," she concluded haughtily. Let him make what he would of that.

What he made, it quickly became clear, was margaritas. Because after filling two glasses with his creation, he came out from behind the kitchen counter with two servings of something frosty and cold, each sporting a plastic swizzle stick that ended in the shape of a cactus. But he had arranged the sticks in such a way that both were protruding from the glasses at equal angles and equal lengths.

"Being a gentleman," he said, "I'll let you pick first. Short swizzle stick gets the couch."

Amanda eyed each of the drinks carefully, but the concoction was too opaque for her to tell which glass might hold the shorter stick. She started to reach slowly for one glass, thinking maybe Max would offer some subtle body language as to whether that one held the shorter stick. But he only stood there unflinching—in his towel, damn him—holding the two drinks equidistant between himself and Amanda.

Without giving it too much thought, she reached for the glass she hadn't initially aimed for and immediately pulled the cactus out. It was full length, as evidenced by the fact that it ended in the shape of a little plastic pot and hadn't been broken at all.

"Hah," she said, holding it up triumphantly. "I get the bedroom."

Max shrugged. "Ah, well. At least I get a margarita out of it." He held his glass up. "Cheers, Amanda."

Wow. He was being a good sport. That seemed so unlike him. She touched the lip of her glass to his. "Back atcha."

He hesitated just a fraction of a second before adding, "To a relaxing week at the beach."

She hesitated, too, a bit longer than he had. "And just how are we supposed to manage that? Two people who do not get along—"

"To put it mildly."

She ignored the interjection. It wasn't like she disagreed with it. "—sharing such a tiny condo?" she finished.

He shrugged again. "We'll figure it out. Who spends any time inside when they're on vacation, anyway? I figure we'll both be out on the beach most of the time. You head south, I'll head north, and we'll probably hardly ever see each other."

Sounded like a reasonable enough plan to her. Still . . .

"Plus," he added, "I bet you're an early-to-bed-early-to-rise type, aren't you?"

"Of course," she replied automatically.

He grinned that smug grin again and repeated, "Of course." Somehow, though, when he said it, it didn't make her sound like the responsible, conscientious person it had when she said it. "I'm rarely up before noon myself," he told her. "And never in bed before midnight. So we'll probably hardly ever see each other here in the condo either."

That, too, sounded reasonable, Amanda thought. So why did she suddenly feel kind of . . . disappointed? Oh, surely not. No way would she be disappointed to avoid Max Callahan. It just went to show what a rotten day she was having.

So, "To a relaxing week at the beach," she echoed, clinking her glass softly against his.

And she ignored the little wiggle of apprehension that went up her spine as she completed the action.

It was only later, after she and Max had spent the rest of the evening avoiding each other and settling in, that Amanda saw he had, of course, left the dirty margarita glasses sitting in the sink. And when she went to rinse them out, she realized he hadn't shortened the swizzle stick in either of them. Both plastic cacti ended in a little plastic pot. No matter which one she had chosen, she would have won the bedroom.

Max had been a gentleman, after all.

Four

The second day of Max's vacation dawned with infinitely more promise than the first, and not just because he didn't have to get up in what might as well have been the middle of the night so he could make the fourteen-hour—at least the way *he* drove—trip from Indianapolis to Captiva. No, it was because he awoke to the aroma of freshly brewed coffee instead of the reek of the Dumpster below his bedroom window, to the warmth of a slant of sunlight on his bare back instead of winter's chill unabated by his busted radiator, and to the sound of the ocean beyond the window instead of his upstairs neighbors arguing about whatever was their conflict du jour.

And when he opened his eyes, he discovered yet another way this morning was different from any other in recent memory. Because what to his wondering eyes should appear but the sight of a gorgeous redhead in a satin kimono instead of some unremembered woman he'd picked up the night before and he hoped would be gone by now.

Not quite able to believe his good fortune, he closed his eyes tight, then opened them again. Hold the phone. That was no gorgeous redhead. That was Amanda Bingham. So much for good fortune.

It all came rushing back to him then. The way Marshall and Kate had set the two of them up for the week by deliberately double booking them in an island condo at the height of the tourist season. The way Amanda had come tumbling so unexpectedly through the door just as he was coming out of the shower. The way she'd been looking at him in a way she'd never looked at him before, as if she weren't A, repulsed by him; B, annoyed at him; C, disgusted with him; or D, all of the above.

Well, the joke was on Marshall and Kate. No way would Max and Amanda ever hook up. Not figuratively. Not literally. Not in any -ly way at all.

Then she turned, and he caught her in profile. She was talking to someone on the phone, and although her face was a study in contrition, the rest of her was flat-out . . . Well, he hesitated to use the word *gorgeous* again, now that he knew it was Amanda. But the morning sunlight spilled over her body in a way that was almost sacred, lighting tiny fires in the russet curls she'd piled loosely atop her head, infusing her ivory skin with an amber glow, turning her filmy robe almost translucent. And although he could tell by the silhouette beneath the fabric that she wasn't naked beneath the garment, she might as well have been, because Max was just that good when it came to mentally undressing women.

Other women, he immediately reminded himself, squeezing his eyes shut tight again to eliminate the vision that was Amanda in the morning. But when he opened them again, she was still there, still looking . . . Okay, okay. Gorgeous. Damn. She had turned back around, but the breeze was whipping up the hem of her robe enough that he caught the merest glimpse of shorts beneath. The kind of shorts women slept in, not went to the beach in. The kind made of wispy, flowery fabric and trimmed in lace. The kind that were so wispy, in fact, that the breeze could whip them up a little, too, enough that a man who had voyeuristic tendencies—And come on, what man didn't?—could also catch a glimpse of that *very* nice, *very* soft, *very* erotic lower curve of the wearer's ass.

Max squeezed his eyes shut *again*. He wasn't accustomed to thinking of Amanda Bingham's ass as erotic. He wasn't accustomed to thinking of her ass at all. Or any of her other body parts. The only time he thought about Amanda was during those unfortunate times they turned up at the same parties. And on those occasions, the only thought he gave to Amanda was to wonder what the hell she was thinking, dressing the way she did and acting the way she did and being the way she was, when any other woman who had her, ah, assets—Okay, okay, maybe he'd checked out her ass a time or two, so sue him—could be making a fortune appearing monthly in the center of a magazine with strategically placed staples. And then appearing indefinitely inside the lockers of auto mechanics, steelworkers, and frat boys all across America.

Was this a great country or what?

What it was, Max decided as he rolled onto his back and stared at the ceiling, was a weird country, where two people who had been having a perfectly good adversarial relationship as recently as a couple of weeks ago were suddenly sneaking peeks at parts of each other they'd never cared about seeing before. Or maybe it was just him being weird. Vacations had a way of making people do and feel things they wouldn't in the normal world.

He heard the soft slide of the French door accompanied by Amanda's voice, and rolled over to look at her again. She was still on the phone, looking even more apologetic than she had before. Worse, she was groveling to whoever was on the other end of the line, in a voice he'd never heard from her before. Whenever he talked to Amanda, she was assertive to the point of belligerence, antagonistic to the point of militancy. Truth be told, he'd always kind of liked that about her. That she was so passionate about her beliefs—however misguided they were—and that she challenged him in a way no one else ever bothered with. Max realized that most people considered him to be . . . well, not the sharpest knife in the drawer, if you knew what he meant. And he supposed he hadn't exactly ever tried to dissuade anyone of the idea. Life was simpler when everyone had low expectations of you. Made it easier to avoid responsibility if you could plead stupid to whatever crisis arose. And it was easier to be an observer of life instead of a participant, which Max liked a lot. Oh, he participated in the things he enjoyed—sipping a cold beer on a hot afternoon, carving a sinuous design out of a satiny block of mahogany, slow-dancing with a warm woman to the music of Keb' Mo'—but he liked to watch how life played out for other people too. He liked watching the people even more.

Which brought him back to Amanda. Who was still talking apologetically on the phone. Who had barely noticed him as she'd walked to the breakfast bar to open her laptop. Who cradled the phone between her ear and shoulder as she began to type, something that caused her robe to fall open enough to reveal a wispy, flowered top that matched the wispy, flowered shorts. A top that was so wispy, in fact, that it was drooping nearly as much as the robe, offering Max an equally erotic hint of the dusky valley between her breasts.

And waking up a certain, very masculine, part of him in a big, big way.

Great. An early-morning boner. He hadn't been thinking about how frequently he woke up in that condition when he gave Amanda the bedroom and took the sofa for himself. With her being an early riser and all—not that she was the only one, mind you . . . ahem—

he was going to have no privacy. He should have acted like the jerk she thought he was and claimed the bedroom as his right for being the first person to arrive. Who knew how long it was going to take for his, ah, condition to, ah, diminish—not that it would diminish very much, by God—especially with her running around all wispy and lacy and flowery and sexy.

No, not sexy! he immediately corrected himself. This was Amanda, after all. That realization alone should have, ah, diminished him on the spot. Instead, when he looked at her again and saw her leaning over the laptop enough to allow him an even better view of her luscious—*no, not luscious!*—curves, he did just the opposite of diminish. Very much too.

Dammit!

"Certainly, Mr. Hoberman," he heard her say ruefully. "No, I'm sorry I misunderstood the first time. Of course I should have realized you meant just the opposite of what you were saying. . . . What . . . ? No, sir, I didn't mean to imply that you didn't know what you were . . . No, sir . . . I understand, sir. . . . Yes, sir . . . I'll get right on it and be in touch later this morning. Will that be all right, sir?"

Max shook his head in disgust. Man, it must suck to be a lackey.

"Hey, Amanda!" he called out as loudly as he could, hoping her boss on the other end of the line would hear him and take the hint. "Come on back to bed, sweetheart! You shouldn't be working! You're on vacation!"

Her head had snapped up the moment she heard his voice, and now she glared at him, her eyes wide behind her glasses, her teeth gritted.

"Here, babe! Have another bloody Mary!" he shouted even louder. "You earned it after all that exertion last night!"

Her cheeks went pink with irritation, but instead of yelling back at him to shut his trap, she muttered, "No, Mr. Hoberman, that's the television. One of those awful daytime talk shows . . . What . . . ? No, I don't know how it got turned on. I never watch those. I must have bumped the television when I went past. . . ."

Then she did some more groveling, and Max shook his head again. After witnessing a few more minutes of her toadying, by the time Amanda finally hung up the phone, Max's condition had indeed diminished—though not very much, by God. Because this was the Amanda Bingham he knew—the corporate kiss-ass. It didn't matter how hot she looked in sexy sleepwear. She wasn't his type. At all.

As if wanting to drive that fact home, after hanging up the phone, she clutched the neckline of her robe and pulled it closed to her neck, then grabbed the hem and tugged it down as far as she could. She straightened her glasses and tucked her hair primly behind her ears, then stammered, "I . . . I thought you were asleep."

He pushed himself up on his elbows, mindless of the sheet that fell to his waist. Hell, it wasn't like he was naked. In light of Amanda's presence in the house, he had pulled on a pair of boxers before going to bed last night. Not that she cared. Not that he cared that she didn't care. Because he didn't. Care. At all. About Amanda. Or her opinion.

"Yeah, well, who can sleep with all that slurping going on?"

Her irritation turned to confusion. "Slurping? I wasn't slurping. I haven't even eaten breakfast yet."

"Maybe not. But you're the loudest suck-up I've ever heard."

Now her irritation returned. "I wasn't sucking up. I was doing my job."

"News flash, Amanda. You're on vacation. You're supposed to be taking a break from sucking up."

"I wasn't sucking up," she repeated more adamantly. "Mr.

Hoberman is a very powerful man. You have to talk to him a certain way, otherwise he thinks . . ."

But Max had stopped listening. He lifted one hand and levered his thumb and fingers in the internationally recognized sign language for "blah blah blah," and used the other to whip back the sheet. That, if nothing else, finally made Amanda shut up. Probably because his boxer shorts were spattered with dozens of garish colors, images of slot machines mingling with the word JACK-POT! in big red letters.

Well, he never said his underwear was tasteful. Besides, it had been a gift from a showgirl to commemorate an especially memorable night. Too bad he could barely remember it. Still, he did like the boxers.

He was about to make some flip comment—along the lines of *You should* be *so lucky*—but there was something in her face that stopped him. Amanda Bingham was—

"Holy crap, you're blushing," he said before he could stop himself.

That, of course, only made her blush even more. But she said nothing, only widened her eyes in panic and glanced away.

"You're not going to tell me you've never seen a man in his underwear before."

"Of course I've seen a man in his underwear," she said, the words coming out hushed and patchy. "I've seen *lots* of men in their underwear."

But she still wasn't looking at him. Meaning the vast majority of the men she'd seen in their skivvies had probably been in the long johns section of the L.L.Bean catalog.

Then again, this was Amanda, he reminded himself. Again. Why did he have to keep doing that? Why did he keep forgetting who—and what—she was? She probably turned out the lights when she had sex. If she even *had* sex.

Which, if she didn't, he thought, would explain *a lot*.

Biting back a frustrated sound, he reached for the khaki shorts he'd tossed on a nearby chair the night before and, with Amanda still gazing at the other side of the room—and still blushing furiously—he put them on, deliberately pulling up the zipper slowly to see if the soft, raspy sound would make her blush harder still.

Yep. It did.

Unbelievable. There was still a woman in the world who could be shy about something like a guy in his underwear. Amanda Bingham was an even bigger prude than he'd thought. And that was saying something.

So why did a warm, gooey ripple shudder through his stomach at the realization? Why did he find it kind of . . . erotic . . . that she was so unworldly?

Man, he really did need a vacation if he was reacting this way to Amanda Bingham.

"You can turn around now," he said as he finished buttoning his fly. "I'm decent."

She turned around, but she still didn't look at him. "Hah," she muttered. "That's not a word I think anyone would use to describe you."

He grinned at that. "Ah, come on, Amanda. Lighten up. You're on vacation." Before he realized what he was doing, he added, "Let me take you to breakfast. I saw a place up the road when I was driving in. Right on the beach. Bloody Marys on me."

Her irritation disappeared at that, to be replaced by . . . something. Something Max was hard-pressed to identify. Mostly because her gaze ricocheted from his and zinged to every other object in the room. "I, uh . . . Thanks, but, um . . . I can't."

He was amazed at the depth of his disappointment. What was up with that? "Why not?"

"I, ah . . ." She looked at him again, only to have her gaze once again go flying off in another direction. Very softly, so softly he almost didn't hear her, she said, "I have to work."

"*Work?*" he echoed incredulously. "But you're on vacation."

"I know, but Mr. Hoberman—"

"You're on vacation," he repeated. "You can't work when you're on vacation. That violates the most basic law of nature. If you work while you're on vacation, you throw the entire universe out of whack and we all get sucked into a black hole."

"I really don't think that's going to hap—"

"C'mon," he cajoled. "You have to eat. Breakfast is the most important meal of the day, ya know." Then he tossed her a crumb he knew she wouldn't be able to resist. Unfortunately. "You won't be able to do your job effectively if you don't eat breakfast."

And why was he so adamant that she eat breakfast? With him, no less? What did he care if Amanda wanted to spend her vacation working? Hell, it would keep her out of his hair, something that would allow *him to* enjoy *his* vacation. Hey, just last night he'd told her how easy it would be for the two of them to avoid each other, hadn't he? So why was he actively not just crossing their paths, but twining them together?

Before he could answer any of those questions—not that he had a clue how to answer them—she sighed heavily, took off her glasses to rub her eyes, and tossed them onto the countertop. Her glasses, not her eyes. That would have been really gross.

"I suppose you're right," she said wearily, sounding like someone who really needed a vacation. "But you don't have to treat. I'll pay my share."

He started to tell her to forget it, that he'd been the one to invite her out, so he was going to treat, then stopped himself. Not just because Amanda seemed to think it was important to pay her own way, but because if he—or she, for that matter—paid for both of them, then the excursion would feel more like . . . you know . . .

a . . . a *date* than breakfast—which it absolutely wouldn't be, in any way, shape, or form. And that was all it was. Breakfast. People had to eat, for God's sake.

Amanda hesitated—probably because she was trying to come up with an excuse to say no that didn't involve work, Max thought—then, with clear reluctance, nodded. "Just let me get dressed."

He started to tell her not to bother, that he'd never seen her looking better than she did wearing what she had on at the moment, but he managed—just in time—to keep his jaw clamped shut. First off, saying something like that would be sure to send this new side of Amanda back into her shell. Not that he cared, of course. And second, flirting with Amanda Bingham would be like flirting with Dwight Schrute.

So how come Max wasn't gagging the way he would be if Dwight Schrute were in the room wearing wispy, flowery PJs? And then washing his eyes out with soap and water to remove what an image like that would involve?

He pushed all those thoughts away and said, halfheartedly, "Yeah, and I'll throw on a shirt."

But it wasn't halfhearted because he regretted ever asking Amanda to join him for breakfast, which should have been the case. Instead, it was halfhearted because he didn't want to throw on a shirt. On the contrary, he suddenly wanted to shed what clothes he had on and go back to bed. Only he didn't want to go back to bed alone. He wanted to take Amanda with him. And he wanted to shed what clothes she had on too.

He told himself it was only because of his early-morning boner, that any woman would look good to a man who woke up aroused. Yeah, that must be it. No other explanation made sense. Especially the one that was suddenly trying to worm its way into his brain.

That maybe, just maybe, Kate had been right about him and Amanda.

Five

Why had he invited her to breakfast? Amanda wondered as she watched Max drag the last bite of his bacon through a puddle of leftover pancake syrup and tuck it into his mouth. And why had she accepted in the first place, when she *should* be scarfing down a muffin while huddled over her laptop keyboard, doing the work she promised Mr. Hoberman she'd have finished by this afternoon? Why was Max being nice to her? Why was she being nice to him? They'd actually managed to share an entire meal together without him calling her a corporate collective peon or her calling him a flag-waving jingoist from Macholand. And why had she put on a pale yellow sundress and taken care to brush and rebraid her hair just to go to breakfast, when she could have just thrown on a pair of shorts and a T-shirt and left her hair sleep-scattered?

But more important than any of those things, why couldn't she take her eyes off the tiny smudge of syrup at the corner of his mouth that he seemed to be completely unaware of? Why did she want so badly to reach across the table and wipe it away with her thumb or, even worse, some other body part—and maybe one of his body parts too? Maybe even *more* than one of his body parts. Maybe *lots* of his body parts. And lots of her body parts. All mingling together. In a tangle of hot, passionate . . . earthy, erotic . . . steamy, sweaty . . .

Uh . . . She meant . . . um . . .

Suddenly feeling the need to do something with her hands—something that didn't involve *any* of Max's body parts—she glanced surreptitiously at her watch. And she was surprised to realize it was the first time she'd even wondered about the time since the two of them left the condo. She was even more surprised to realize they'd been gone for more than two hours.

"Dammit," she hissed when she saw the time.

"What?"

"I need to get back to—" She halted herself before finishing with the word *work*, and quickly amended, "—the condo."

"Why?" he asked, grinning in a way that made a glint of sunlight wink off the speck of syrup. Thankfully, just as Amanda was about to lose her battle to reach across the table, he turned his head toward the ocean so that the syrup was out of sight. "I mean, look at this day. It's gorgeous. Not a cloud in the sky."

He turned to look at her again, his smile still sweet with syrup, and she made herself shove her hands under her thighs. But the victory was short-lived, because the breeze kicked up, blowing open the placket of his gaudy red Hawaiian shirt to reveal a tanned, luscious-looking collarbone beneath, and nudging a thick strand of mahogany hair over his forehead. The backdrop of cobalt ocean and sapphire sky made his blue eyes even more startling than before: clearer, deeper, more expressive. And when he grinned, it was one of those crooked, spontaneous grins Amanda had always reluctantly found charming, the ones that surfaced roguish dimples on each cheek . . .

Well. Suffice it to say her hands really wanted to be somewhere other than under her butt. Like maybe under his—

"Why don't we take a walk on the beach?" he asked suddenly.

She wouldn't have been more surprised if he'd suggested they build an atomic bomb. Walk along the beach? With Max? A man who, until forced into contact yesterday, had done his best to avoid her and whom she'd done her best to avoid? A man with whom she shared nothing in common save a double-booked condo for the week? A man who hadn't had anything to say to her from the day she met him in freshman English except to tease her relentlessly because of her good grades, her conscientious work ethic, and her desire to get into an Ivy League college?

He wanted to walk along the beach with *her*? Just how much vodka did this place pour into their bloody Marys?

"Uh . . ." she began, stretching the word over several time zones in an effort to stall while she formed an answer. Not that she had an answer for a question like that at the moment. "I can't," she finally said.

She told herself she only imagined that he looked disappointed by her answer. "Why not?"

She sighed her surrender. There was no way around it. If she said it fast, maybe it wouldn't sound like she needed to work. "There are some things I have to do for Mr. Hoberman by the end of the workday."

Now Max was the one to sigh. Only his sounded more like exasperation than surrender. "Oh, come on, Amanda. At least take a morning for yourself. Haven't you been having a nice time up 'til now? I know I have. We should take advantage of an armistice like this while we can. It doesn't happen often."

He sounded as surprised by their sudden camaraderie as she

felt, but it was true. Although she never in a million years would have guessed that she and Max Callahan could get along for two minutes, let alone two hours, they had indeed been having a nice time. Oh, sure, there had been a couple of lively exchanges during breakfast, along with the occasional raised voice when they'd disagreed on some topic. But unlike those times when they disagreed at home, their words had been civil and thoughtful, and the voices hadn't been shrill or exasperated. And they'd actually taken turns listening—*listening!*—to each other before offering a counterpoint to what was said.

"You can't work like this all week," he added. "You're on vacation."

"Why do you keep reminding me of that?" she demanded hotly.

"Because you keep forgetting," he fired back.

"Yeah, well, like you always say, Max, I'm nothing but a corporate drone. I have no life because I'm so focused on my work. And I'm the loudest suck-up you've ever heard," she concluded with more emphasis than was really necessary, since he'd been saying that just a couple of hours ago.

To hammer that point home, she lifted her bloody Mary—sans vodka, naturally, since she had to work—and slurped what little was left with as much gusto and noise as she could.

Instead of responding, Max only gazed at her in sullen silence. But then, what could he say? She'd only repeated, pretty much verbatim, what he'd always said to her before. So she stood, rifled through her purse for a handful of bills, and tossed them onto the table without even bothering to count them out.

"That's to cover my share of breakfast," she muttered. "I'll take a cab back. You can take a walk. I'm sure you'll find *some*one to keep you company." *Someone,* she added to herself, *who has about as much work ethic as you. Someone whose job doesn't depend on being available to their boss 24/7.*

As if cued by the thought, a curvy, bronzed blonde who was squeezed, just barely, into a teeny bikini and not-so-long sarong sauntered by their table, deliberately—Amanda was certain it was deliberate—brushing Max's shoulder with her hip.

"Oh, excuse me," she giggled. Truly. She giggled the words, something Amanda thought happened only in badly written novels.

"No problem," Max said automatically. But he was looking at Amanda when he spoke, something that made her wonder if he was talking to the blonde or to her.

The blonde didn't seem to realize, either, because she glanced back at Amanda, apparently expecting to see a worthy adversary with whom she would have to fight for Max's attention. One look at Amanda's face, however, and the blonde smiled a smug, victorious smile. Obviously, she didn't think Amanda would be any competition at all.

But Amanda wasn't competition, was she? Not only was she nowhere near as beautiful as the other woman, nor as curvy, and not only did she not have the know-how to deal with men that the blonde clearly had in abundance, Amanda wasn't the sort of woman Max liked anyway. Which was good, because Max wasn't her type either. It didn't matter how well they'd gotten along over breakfast. It didn't matter how much she still wanted to swipe away that syrup in an earthy, erotic . . . hot, sweaty—

The blonde made a soft *tsk*ing sound and bent over Max. Waaaaaay over, enough that her teeny bikini top became a gravitational necessity if she didn't want to be arrested by the decency police. "You have a little smidgey of syrup on your mouth," she said, giggling the words again. And then, as Amanda watched helplessly, she lifted a perfectly manicured hand to trace her thumb softly over the corner of Max's mouth, making the swiping of syrup look like something from a pornographic movie.

Unbelievable, Amanda thought. If she'd tried to do that when she wanted to, she probably would have inadvertently poked Max in the eye.

The blonde's touch finally got his attention, which was pretty amazing, considering the fact that the gravitational pull of her bikini top hadn't. And when he moved his gaze from Amanda's face to hers— her face, not the two things most men would have looked at first— he smiled and said, "Thanks, sweetheart. I appreciate it." Then he looked at Amanda again—her face, too, alas, and not the two things most men would have looked at first . . . had she had two things men might want to look at. Alas. "I don't know why no one else bothered to let me know." Then he turned back to the blonde. "I hate it when people would rather let you look ridiculous than help you out."

Hoo-kay, Amanda thought. Obviously whatever small armistice the two of them had managed to negotiate this morning was off. She wasn't sure who had violated it first, but she supposed it didn't matter. She and Max had never been allies. They were like those troops during World War I who had taken off Christmas Day to play soccer, but now, with the spirit of the season over, it was back to war.

"Oh, believe me, Max," she said. "It would take more than wiping syrup off your face to keep you from looking ridiculous."

And with that she spun on her heel and made her way toward the interior of the restaurant. She'd ask the hostess to call a cab for her. As for Max . . .

Well, she wouldn't ask for anything from him. Not for the rest of the week. Not for the rest of her life. Except maybe to leave her alone. Once and for all.

Max watched Amanda until she disappeared into the restaurant's dining room, willing her to look back, just once. But she didn't. Not once.

Dammit, he thought. Things had been going so well between them all morning. They'd been able to make it through an entire meal without sniping at each other. Even better, they'd managed to actually engage in meaningful conversation. Best of all, they'd found things to laugh about. Being away from the recollections and assumptions and expectations of their everyday lives, they'd been able to . . . to . . . to *communicate*. They'd never done that before.

He wondered why not. And he wondered why he found it so important for them to do so now. For a long moment, he sat there trying to figure out just where and when and why he and Amanda had decided to dislike each other, until the sound of a clearing throat brought his attention back to the present. When he looked up, he saw a woman standing over him, looking at him expectantly, and it took him a few seconds to remember she was the one who had just wiped the syrup off his face. Why was she still here? Had he spilled something on his shirt too?

"Um, thank you?" he said, hoping that was the proper response.

Had she asked him a question that needed an answer? He honestly had no idea. He'd been so focused on watching Amanda—and the way the sunlight had filtered through her dress, leaving little to the imagination—that he hadn't been aware of anything else. Though now that he was aware of the other woman, he realized her outfit left *nothing* to the imagination. It was all right there. At eye level. And there was a lot of it. Of them. Of her.

Oh, hell.

Normally, Max would have preferred a woman who left nothing to the imagination over a woman who made him work for it. But he'd actually kind of liked imagining that part of Amanda, even if it had been for only a few seconds. Now that he was faced with the flesh-and-blood-and-more-flesh object of what would have made a righteous fantasy, he discovered he'd rather close his eyes and think about the sunlight filtering through Amanda's dress again.

The woman smiled at him in a way that he probably would have found sexy had he not just had breakfast with a woman he suddenly found, well, sexy. "I was hoping you'd invite me to breakfast," she said.

Max gazed down at the remnants of the meal he'd just consumed, thinking it should be pretty obvious to even the most casual observer that he'd already had his breakfast. "Um, thanks?" he said again. He gestured toward the empty plate. "But I've already had breakfast."

She smiled again, and he decided that her expression actually wasn't all that sexy, regardless of whom he'd just shared a meal with. In fact, it was kind of vapid. "I haven't," she said. And then, for some reason, she bumped her hip against his shoulder. Again.

Obviously, she was a woman for whom the hip-shoulder thing and the vapid-sexy smile thing usually got results.

Then again, Max was a man who, until recently, wouldn't have needed even that much to convince himself that what he needed more than anything in the world was a second breakfast. And then a day of whatever this woman was offering, followed by a night of whatever she was offering, hopefully with a friend of hers.

Then again, that sort of thing had never happened to Max. Not the friend thing. He'd had more than his fair share of meaningless couplings with women, including women he'd just met. There was no reason why he should turn this one down. Even if she wasn't offering him more than chatty conversation over a mimosa and fruit cup, it was a damned sight better than what Miss Amanda Bingham was offering him, which was nothing but a day full of antagonism and dirty looks.

So why did he want to gracefully decline Blondie's hospitality and head back to the condo for an afternoon of Amanda's hostility? Why did he want to turn his back on this woman's ample . . . ah, charms . . . in favor of Amanda's, ah . . . less ample . . . charms? Why was he even thinking Amanda had charms in the first place?

The answer to that last question, at least, came right away, though not without a little amazement. Because Amanda *did* have charms, he realized. Not only did she look surprisingly good in wispy, flowered pajamas—even wearing glasses . . . especially wearing glasses—but she'd made him think and talk and laugh— a lot—during breakfast. For the first time Max could remember, he'd actually enjoyed doing something with a woman that didn't involve sex, and he'd enjoyed doing it for a lot longer than sex lasted.

Naturally, that made him wonder if the sex with Amanda would last longer—and be better—than sex with other women. Not that she was going to let him anywhere near her after having parted the way they had. Not unless he did something really drastic. Like . . . gak . . . apologize. Or, even more radical, be nice to her. For more than just a morning.

Hmmm . . .

That throat-clearing sound muscled its way through his musing again, and he looked up to find the blonde still gazing expectantly at him. Obviously, she wasn't going to go away until he bought her breakfast. So he gestured toward the chair Amanda had just vacated, signaled for their server, and, as the waiter cleared away the remnants of Amanda's breakfast, instructed the woman to order whatever she wanted from the menu.

What she wanted turned out to be not much of a breakfast at all—a fruit cup, dry toast, and water—making Max wonder why she bothered. Another thing about Amanda: she ate like a man. Eggs, bacon, hash browns . . . the whole nine yards.

After she completed her order—such as it was—Max tossed a

handful of bills onto the table to cover three breakfasts and a hefty tip, then told the woman, "*Bon appétit*. I'm sorry I can't join you, but I have a full day ahead of me."

And with that, Max pulled an Amanda and made his way toward the interior of the restaurant, never once turning to look back.

Six

"Do you realize you've been on vacation for three days, and I have yet to see you vacate?"

Amanda started at the sound of Max's voice, her hands convulsing on the keyboard of her laptop, making her accidentally send an e-mail she hadn't finished writing—or proofing—yet. Fortunately, it was to Mr. Hoberman's secretary, Elise, not to Mr. Hoberman, so damage control shouldn't be too difficult to manage. Except that Elise was a punctuation Nazi who would send the e-mail back to Amanda with her corrections and tell her to resend once she'd made them, and she always insisted on using commas where they absolutely did not belong and omitting them from the places where they were utterly essential. So, okay, okay, maybe Elise wasn't the only punctuation Nazi working for Hoberman Securities.

"Of course," Max added, "part of that could be the fact that I haven't seen you for most of the past two days at all."

Had Amanda had her way, he wouldn't be seeing her right now

either. Not just because she was wearing her flowery vacation jam-
mies again, but because she'd gone out of her way to avoid him
since yesterday's breakfast and had made it 'til almost tonight's
bedtime. Well, her bedtime, anyway. Probably, Max stayed up past
ten. Fortunately, avoiding him hadn't been difficult, because she'd
simply holed up in the bedroom with her laptop and . . .

She bit back a sigh. And worked. Dammit. To her credit, she'd
at least rearranged the furniture so that the desk was under the
window, and she'd been able to look out at the ocean while she
was working. That had sort of been like a vacation, since at work,
all she had to look at was the enormous eighteen-month dry-erase
calendar hanging over the desk in her cubicle outside Mr. Hoberman's office.

And she'd slipped out of the bedroom a few times when she
knew Max wasn't around, after hearing the front door close and
the sound of his V-8 roaring off into the distance, or hearing the
door to the deck *whoosh* open and closed and seeing him through
the window as he sauntered down the beach. With a beach towel
tucked under his arm and his surf jams riding low on his hips
beneath acres and acres of bronzed, muscled back. She'd had to
venture out of the room if she wanted to eat, after all. Or answer
the call of nature.

There had also been a couple of times when she'd ventured out
of the room while Max was sleeping. And if she'd taken her time
creeping past the couch to watch him, it was only because she
hadn't wanted to risk waking him. It hadn't had anything to do
with marveling at the sheer poetry of his sculpted, naked torso or
having to fight the temptation to reach out and run her fingertips
over the wisps of dark hair sprinkling his broad, naked chest.

It hadn't. Really. *Really.*

Anyway, she would have thought he'd at least have the decency
to knock before bothering her, but there he stood in the doorway

in another one of his obnoxious Hawaiian shirts and his standard khaki shorts, his feet bare, his hands tucked behind his back, the very picture of innocence.

"Are you telling me you want me out of here?" she asked. "Why? Did you invite that hot little blonde from the restaurant yesterday up to see your etchings?"

He narrowed his eyes in confusion. "Why would I ask her to see my etchings? I don't have any etchings."

Amanda sighed with frustration. "It's an old-fashioned term for . . . Never mind," she immediately stopped herself. Not just because she suddenly realized Max would have no knowledge of anything that had happened more than fifteen minutes ago, but because the last thing she wanted to bring up after yesterday was a euphemism, however archaic, for sex.

He was still looking puzzled when he asked, "And why would I want you to leave?"

"You told me to vacate," she reminded him.

"No, I didn't. I said I hadn't seen you vacating on your vacation. It was just an observation."

She was about to interrupt him again and point out that vacating and vacation didn't necessarily have anything to do with each other. But before she had a chance, he pulled his hands from behind his back, and she saw that he was holding two *very* luscious-looking beverages that she was going to go out on a limb and guess contained something alcoholic.

"You need a break," he said with much conviction.

Not that she disagreed with him, but something about having Max point that out instead of realizing it herself rankled. So she lied, "I don't have that much more to do."

He took a few deliberate steps forward and set one of the frothy drinks—had he actually mixed up something that was pink?—on the desk, well within her reach. "The point is that you have *any-*

thing to do," he told her. "You're on vacation. You're supposed to be doing nothing."

"You've obviously been doing enough for both of us," she said crisply. "You made enough drinks to keep you busy for the rest of the evening."

He smiled indulgently. "I made one of them for you. And making drinks, especially those that require the use of a blender, is an activity that has the full approval of the EPA."

She arrowed her brows downward. "The Environmental Protection Agency?"

He grinned more broadly. "The Escapism Profligacy Agency."

She bit back a smile and tried to look haughty instead. "Yeah, you need more escapism and profligacy in your life."

"No, thanks," he said. "I have plenty. It's you who needs this." He dipped his head toward the drink. "I just didn't want you to have to drink alone. That's so . . . tragic."

"Mm," she said noncommittally.

He pointed to his watch. "It's always five o'clock somewhere."

She pointed at *her* watch. "It's way *past* five here."

He reached across the table, flattened his hand against the back of her laptop screen, and began to ease it down. "All the more reason. You have a lot of catching up to do. Just pretend happy hour is just beginning here."

Oh, no, she thought. No way was she going to start pretending things. That way lay madness. She curled her fingers over the top of the computer screen and pushed it back open. "First, I have to fix a mistake you made me make."

And how could something like that come out sounding almost portentous? she wondered. She just wasn't getting enough rest this week, that was all. This week when she was on vacation. When she was supposed to be getting some rest.

Pushing the thought away, she reopened the unfinished e-mail and finished—and proofread—it, apologizing to Elise for sending an incomplete one the first time and changing the subject head to include a "Read Me First" admonition. Then she jammed her finger against the Send key—telling herself it was *not* with more force than was necessary—and started to open the next e-mail in the queue.

"Oh, no, you don't," Max said, moving a lot closer than she was comfortable with having him. He started to reach for the laptop to close it again. "You're done for the day."

But she'd already opened the e-mail, one from a new hire at Hoberman Securities that was designated highest priority. Thank goodness she did, too, because it was indeed *very* important, a notice about possible SEC violations at one of their rival brokerage firms. It concluded with a link to an Associated Press story about the investigation, which Amanda naturally clicked on, even as Max told her to c'mon, take a break for God's sake, and she countered that it would take only a minute.

But they both shut up when a new screen appeared on the computer depicting not an Associated Press story, but a YouTube video of a clean-cut young man in a black outfit with overcoat dancing and singing something about how he was never gonna give her up and never gonna let her down or run around or desert her. That was when Max started laughing. Hard.

"Oh, man," he said when he found his breath. "You got Rickrolled."

Still confused, Amanda turned to look at him. "I got what-rolled?"

"Rickrolled," he repeated, still chuckling. He must have picked up on the confusion she was feeling, because he asked, "Don't you know what Rickrolling is?"

She shook her head.

He smiled again. "Why am I not surprised?"

"I don't know. Why *are* you not surprised?"

He ignored the question and instead explained. "It's an Internet phenomenon whereby a prankster tells you they're sending you to some legitimate site, then they send you to a Rick Astley video instead, thereby Rickrolling you. It's been going on for a couple years now."

He was still smiling broadly, but Amanda couldn't figure out why. "Who's Rick Astley?"

"The guy in the video. A one-hit wonder from the eighties."

She thought about that for a minute, then said, "I don't get it."

He chuckled again. "I'm not surprised."

"No, really," she insisted. "Why is it supposed to be funny?"

He shrugged. "I don't know. It just is. It's like an inside joke on the Web."

"But I barely know the guy who sent this e-mail. They just hired him. Why would he . . . What's it called again?"

"Rickrolling."

"Why would he Rickroll me?"

Max shrugged again. "If he's new, maybe he just wants to do something that will bring him into the crowd at work. The ability to make people laugh is a great icebreaker."

"It didn't make me laugh," Amanda pointed out.

"That's because you didn't get it."

"Which is exactly my point. And even after you explained it, I still don't get it."

He shook his head, but smiled again. "And I'm still not surprised."

For some reason, his comment bothered her. "Why not?"

This time he sighed. But the sound was good-natured, not exasperated, something that surprised her. Usually when Max sighed at her, it was because he was frustrated. Right now, he just seemed to be amused.

"Because, Amanda, you never do anything that would put you in a position to be Rickrolled."

To punctuate the remark, he pushed the pink drink closer to her hand, leaving a wet trail behind it. By now, moisture was beading on the sides, trickling down to the base, making it look very appealing. She had to admit that she was kind of thirsty. And she had been working all day. By now, everyone at work would be home enjoying their lives. Even Mr. Hoberman. Amanda was the only one who ever worked this late. She deserved a break for a refreshment.

As if cued by the thought, her cell phone rang, and she automatically reached for it. But Max beat her to it and, in one deft maneuver, switched it off and stuffed it into the side pocket of his shorts, immediately Velcroing it shut.

"Hey!" Amanda cried. "That could be an important call!"

He gazed at her flatly. "Do you work for a medical research team that's on the verge of finding a cure for cancer?" he asked.

"What? No. Of course not. You know I—"

"Are you the world leader of a country on the brink of thermonuclear war?"

She made a face at him. "No, Max. I—"

"That's right," he said, feigning a sudden memory. "What you do is make rich, powerful people richer and more powerful, am I right?"

"Well, there's a little more to it than—"

"Am I right?" he asked again. In the tone of voice a preschool teacher would use with a headstrong toddler.

Amanda said nothing, figuring it was a rhetorical question anyway.

"So you don't have to be on call twenty-four hours a day," Max said. "And you sure as hell don't have to be on call when you've been granted a perfectly legitimate and well-deserved vacation."

She reached toward him, needing her phone. Badly. He might as well have taken away her right arm. "But—"

He took a step in retreat. "I'm not giving the phone back to you until tomorrow," he told her. "You're off for the rest of the evening."

She took a step forward. "But, Max, you don't understand how import—"

He took another step backward. "What I understand is that you need a break. More important, you've *earned* it, Amanda."

She took another step toward him. "I know that," she said softly.

"Then why won't you take one?" Another step back.

By now, he was at the bedroom door. This time, Amanda took two steps forward, bringing herself to where her body was nearly touching his. "I need my phone, Max."

He shook his head. Then he moved the drink he still held in front of her mouth. "Try this instead. It's way better."

She took the glass from him, set it on a table by the door, and repeated, "I need my phone, Max." She held out her hand. "Give it back to me. Now."

He dipped his head very close to hers and said, very softly, "Make me."

Without even thinking about what she was doing, Amanda leaned forward and reached for the pocket into which he had pushed the purloined phone, and managed to get it un-Velcroed before he realized how fast she could move. But her move wasn't quite fast enough, because he grabbed her wrist with confident fingers and jerked it back up, pinning her hand between his chest and hers. So Amanda threaded her other arm across her midsection and tried to snag the phone with that one. But, just as before, Max capably caught it, too, and pulled it up to join the first. Amanda tried to tug both hands free, but he held them firm, his grasp too tight . . . but somehow, in some weird way, not tight enough.

Out of nowhere, heat blossomed in the pit of Amanda's stomach, seeping upward to make her heart beat faster, and downward to warm parts of her that hadn't felt warm for too long.

"Max," she said softly when she realized what was happening, "let me go."

But he seemed to be aware of the sudden change in their postures, too, because his voice was a little ragged when he replied, "Don't you want your phone?"

Amanda shook her head, suddenly not caring. All she knew was that she needed to get away from Max before she did something really stupid. "No, that's okay." She tried to pull her hands free again, but again he refused to let go. "Max . . ." she said again. But this time his name came out sounding thready and hoarse and . . . aroused.

But then he sounded kind of aroused, too, when he said, "Amanda . . ."

Before she realized what was happening, he lowered his head to hers and covered her mouth with his, brushing his lips gently over hers once, twice, three times, four, before she even realized what was happening. She started to pull away, but he followed her, dropping her hands to curl his fingers over her shoulders as he kissed her again, more deeply this time. Instinctively, she lifted her own hands to cup them around his neck, framing his jaw with one of them. His skin was warm beneath her fingertips, rough from a day's growth of beard. He smelled of sunshine and ocean and something citrusy and sweet. He tasted sweet, too, and she realized he must have sampled the concoction he'd blended before bringing the glasses into the room.

Her last coherent thought was that this was something that had probably been coming for a long time, something the two of them had been fighting for years. Pure animal magnetism. They didn't have to like each other to be turned on by each other. In many ways, a physical response to another person was even stronger and more irresistible than an emotional one. And that was all this was—all it would be. A physical response. But there was no reason why Amanda couldn't lose herself to it completely.

She was, after all, on vacation.

Soon enough, she would have to return to the real world. But not tonight. Tonight she would do as Max had instructed, and take a break. A much-deserved, well-earned break. From her job. From her life. From her reality. From herself. Tomorrow . . .

Well, she'd just do like Scarlett O'Hara and think about that tomorrow.

Her decision made, she tangled her fingers in his silky hair and kissed him back, with all the heat, hunger, and desire that had been building forever, demanding satisfaction for them all.

She pulled her mouth away from his long enough to murmur, "It's too bright in here," then reached past him to brush her hand over the switch on the wall.

Thrown into darkness, they both seemed to lose whatever hesitation might be left. Max lowered his hand to the hem of her brief pajama top and tucked his fingers beneath it, skimming them along her lower ribs, dragging both heat and shivers in their wake. Then he hooked the waistband of her shorts and pushed them down over her hips, pulled her shirt over her head, and covered her naked breasts with both hands. Amanda fumbled with the buttons of his shirt as he gently kneaded her tender flesh, her breath catching in her throat with each new touch. He released her long enough for her to shove his shirt over his shoulders and arms, then captured her again when she moved her hands to the fly of his shorts.

Without thinking about what she was doing, she dropped to her knees before him, cupping one hand over the taut, hot flesh of his buttocks, the other curling around his hard cock. She thumbed the head gently, then dragged her fingertips down his shaft, closing her entire hand around its base. Then she moved her hand back up again, and pushed it slowly downward once more. Bathed in the pale lamplight from the living room behind him, his cock was long and shadowed, and for long moments, she only stroked him, palming the full head and dampening the rest of him with its product. When he growled his satisfaction with her touches, she moved her hand to the base again, guided him to her mouth, and pulled him deep inside.

"Oh, Amanda . . ." he murmured thickly. "Oh, baby. Oh, man . . ."

He tangled his fingers in her hair as she went down on him, circling him with her tongue, sucking him with her lips, quickening her pace a little with every long pull. She could feel him watching her as she moved her head backward and forward, felt him grow even harder whenever she took his cock deeper into her mouth. When she felt him begin to tremble, she released him, but before she could push herself to standing, Max was pulling her up and wrapping her in his arms, kissing her with a hunger unlike anything she'd ever experienced before.

For a long time, he only kissed her and kissed her and kissed her. Then he took her hand in his and led her across the room to the unmade bed, sitting on its edge and pulling her into his lap astride him, her legs spread over his. This time Amanda was the one to kiss him, looping her arm around his neck and opening her mouth over his. As she did, he moved his hand to the scrap of fabric she'd tied at the end of her braid and freed it, then used both hands to free the thick mass from its confinement. For long moments, he grasped great fistfuls of it, moving it over her shoulders, atop her head, against her back. Then, still combing the fingers of one hand through it, he lowered the other hand between her legs and furrowed his fingers gently through the damp folds of flesh there, finding the soft, sensitive bud of her clitoris and thumbing it slowly.

When she murmured her satisfaction from somewhere deep inside, he moved over her again, this time dipping a finger inside her as he stroked her. She rose up on her hips when he did, but he followed her as he had before, his mouth still clinging to hers. When she lowered herself, he drove his finger in deeper, hastening his caresses until she felt ready to come apart. Just as she felt her climax beginning to coil inside her, he turned their bodies so that she was flat on her back and he was perched between her legs. Grasping a thigh in each hand, he opened her wider, then lowered his head to taste the part of her his fingers had brought to near madness.

Over and over he licked and laved her, drawing circles with the tip of his tongue on her the same way she had with him, thrusting his tongue deep inside her the way she had taken him. She clung to the pillow beneath her head and lifted her hips higher, closer to his mouth and the havoc it wreaked, crying out his name again and again and again. He must have sensed she was near her breaking point, because after tasting her deeply one final time, he turned their bodies again.

Amanda found herself with her face turned to the pillow, her shoulders on the mattress and her ass in the air. She felt his fingers splay open over her back, then one trace down the long line of her spine, pausing just below her waist. Then he moved both hands forward, capturing her breasts in each one, rubbing the pads of his thumbs over her stiff nipples, and eased himself—all of himself—into her slick canal.

He took his time to fill her, leaning his entire body over hers to whisper hot, profane promises into her ear. His words inflamed her even more, and she heard herself speaking a few explicit, steamy promises of her own. Never had she spoken to a man so frankly during sex. Never had a man spoken so erotically to her. There was such a profound lack of inhibition between them after years of staving off too many emotions to name. She could scarcely believe she was doing this with Max—*Max!* Never in her life had Amanda felt more comfortable with another human being. Nor had she ever felt so aroused.

And that arousal grew with each new movement, each new touch, each new word spoken. They opened to each other in ways they never had before. Amanda rode astride Max, lay beneath him, took him kneeling and sitting and standing. But they had collapsed back onto the bed by the time they finally surrendered to the climax they had barely been able to keep at bay. She felt the cool kiss of the sheet under her back and wrapped her legs around his waist as he pressed into her one last time. They came together, crying out as one, their bodies going rigid as they rode out the waves of their orgasms. Then they both went limp and eased back onto the mattress. All Amanda could do then was wonder what the hell had just happened.

Well, that, and what the hell was going to happen next.

Seven

What happened was that Max kissed her forehead, murmured something about how incredible she was, pulled her close, nuzzled her hair and . . .

. . . and fell asleep.

Her heart still pounding, her brain still frazzled, Amanda lay beside him, not sure whether to feel stunned, spurned, or satisfied. What she finally settled on was confused. But, strangely, her confusion wasn't about what the two of them had just done. In fact, the more she thought about that, the less surprised she was by the development. It explained a lot, actually. She and Max probably should have realized a long time ago that they weren't battling each other so much as they were battling an attraction to each other. Even though they hadn't liked each other, they'd wanted each other. But neither had been willing—or maybe not even able—to admit that. Not until they were here, a thousand miles away from home, out of their usual comfort zones with their defenses down.

You couldn't help who you were physically drawn to. That was a chemical reaction in the brain and libido that defied explanation. Sure there were biological studies about men wanting women who were fertile and women wanting men who were providers, but Amanda thought that was BS. People had evolved a lot since prehistoric times. Why should the assumption stand that they'd held on to their primitive reproductive/protector responses to the opposite sex when the protruding forehead and unibrow had disappeared?

As far as she was concerned, the world was full of all kinds of people to whom you responded—and who responded to you— differently. Some people evoked warm, fuzzy feelings inside. Some evoked instant animosity. Some evoked no feeling at all. Some took time to warm up to. Some you liked until you got to know them. With some, you were friends. With some, you were enemies. And with some, you were . . .

Well, what she and Max were. She just wished there was a convenient label to put on it. She wished even more that there was a good explanation for it.

Chemical reaction, she told herself again. Who knew why they'd gotten turned on the way they had when they had? Why did there even have to be a reason? They were on vacation. Living practically on top of each other. They'd responded to each other passionately for years—it had just been a different kind of passion. Or maybe it hadn't.

Oh, why the hell does it matter? she demanded of herself again.

Maybe, she immediately realized, it was because she was beginning to think that, on some level—for her, anyway—there was a lot more to it than chemistry. A lot more to it than physical response. A lot more to it than passion. Maybe, just maybe, she had . . . feelings . . . for Max. Maybe, just maybe, she'd had them for a long time. Maybe, just maybe, that was why he'd always made her feel so edgy and antagonistic and fierce. Because she hadn't wanted to admit she could have . . . feelings . . . for a guy who didn't feel the same way about her.

Maybe, just maybe, what had happened tonight hadn't been the result of her physical response to him, but her emotional one. How could she know, though, if for him what had happened had been nothing *but* physical?

She scooted a little away from him and turned her head to look at him. His face was only half revealed in a slant of lamplight from the other room, his dark hair tumbling over his forehead, his thick lashes lying like silk against his cheek. The hair at his temple was damp with perspiration and, unable to help herself, Amanda pushed back a handful of dark tresses so she could see him better. She held her breath to see if the motion would wake him, but he didn't budge. She smiled at that. She never would have thought she could outlast Max Callahan at the game of sex.

God, what was he going to say when he woke up and remembered what they'd done? How was he going to feel about her now? How would he treat her for the rest of the week? Or when they got back to Indianapolis? What if he didn't want to see her again? What if he stopped attending parties he knew she would be attending too? What if he told Kate and Marshall to give him a heads-up whenever she was around, so he wouldn't have to see her?

Or worse, what if he acted like nothing had happened? Like nothing had changed? There was no way she'd ever be able to treat him the same way after what had happened tonight. There was no way she would feel about him the way she had felt before. There was too much . . . Well, just too much, that was all. And it was utterly different from what she'd felt for him before.

Very, very carefully, Amanda disentangled her body from his and scooted the rest of the way across the bed. Then, very, very carefully, she got up and searched for her clothes. She found them near the doorway and tried not to think about how they'd gotten there as she shimmied back into them. But memories washed over her of how she'd dropped to her knees so shamelessly before him and so hungrily consumed him. She hadn't felt any shame in what she had done, however. She didn't feel any now. In fact, she wanted to do it again. And she wanted Max to do all the things he'd done to her again. And she wanted to do them for—

For a long time.

Don't think about it, Amanda. Just don't think about it.

For some reason, she suddenly had a craving for one of those drinks Max had whipped up earlier. So after winding her hair atop her head and cinching it with a thick band, she made her way to the kitchen. All that was left, though, was a soupy, melted mixture in the blender and a sticky mess on the counter.

She tried not to view it as a metaphor for what her life was about to become.

Instead, she went to the wine rack and pulled out a lovely pinot noir she'd brought with her and opened it, then poured herself a generous glass and, with one more glance into the bedroom to make sure Max was still sleeping, crept to the sliding doors and— *whoosh, whoosh*—stepped out onto the deck.

Nighttime at the beach, she thought, was extraordinary. Almost surreal. Sounds seemed to carry down from the stars themselves, swirling around her ears, whispering the secrets of the universe just a little too softly to be understood. The wind whipped at her pajamas and hair, tugging loose dozens of strands to make them dance about her face and shoulders. She strode to the rail and rested her arms upon it, cradling the wineglass in both hands. Then she closed her eyes and inhaled deeply, filling her lungs with the pungent ocean air. She tasted salt on the breeze, felt the soft spike of sand on her cheeks, and far, far off in the distance, heard what sounded very much like the Sirens' call.

A-man-da, they sang, *come join us. Live as we live here in the sea. Sing the Sirens' song. Dance the Sirens' dance.* And then, after a moment—and a bit more incisively—they added, *Stop being such a workaholic, you moron. Your job sucks. Your employer is a pin-head. You have no life. You didn't even know what Rickrolling was. Leave your sorry existence behind. Go out and live. Live.*

Li-i-ive.

And then, as if the point hadn't already been hammered home by the harpies . . . uh, she meant Sirens—*whoosh, whoosh*—the door opened and closed behind her.

She turned to see Max standing there, of course, his feet and chest bare, his shorts hanging low on his hips, a glass of wine poured as generously as her own in one hand. She steeled herself for what he would say, how he would act now, how he would treat her.

And then he smiled. Not the smile he'd smiled whenever she'd seen him before. That one had always been wary and tight. As if he were bracing himself to talk to her. But then, she'd always had to brace herself to talk to him, too, she recalled. Tonight, however . . .

Tonight, there was no wariness in his smile. There was no tight-ness. Tonight, Max's face was full of easiness, warmth, and affec-tion. He was smiling at her the way she wanted to smile at him. The way she did smile at him. The way she felt inside. Easy. Warm. Affectionate.

"Hey," he said softly.

"Hey," she replied, just as quietly.

He took a few steps forward, then hesitated, as if he still wasn't quite sure where he stood with her. "I woke up, and you were gone," he said. "For a minute, I was afraid—" He halted abruptly, and she feared he might not finish whatever he'd intended to say. But he finished, even more softly, "I was afraid you'd gone."

The knot that had been coiled tight in her belly since seeing him eased at his words, allowing the rest of her to relax too. "You say that as if you don't want me to leave."

"I don't," he said quickly. His dark brows arrowed downward under his windswept hair. "Are you planning to leave?"

"No." She was surprised at how quickly the word left her mouth. At how quickly the decision was made. At how right it felt to make it. "Why would I leave?" she added with a grin. "I'm on vacation."

Evidently, they were the very words he wanted to hear, because the crease in his brow disappeared, and he covered what little distance was left between them in three quick strides. Instead of pulling her into his arms and treating her to a long, languid kiss, however, he simply leaned forward and brushed his lips lightly over hers. Then he mirrored her earlier posture, leaning on the rail, fingers woven together beneath the bowl of the glass.

"I love it out here at night," he said. "There's just something about the ocean after dark, you know? Like it's . . ."

"What?"

He turned to look at her. "You'll laugh."

Her? she thought. The woman who had just heard the Sirens call her a moron? "No, I won't," she assured him.

He expelled a soft sigh and looked back toward the whispering surf. "I don't know. Like it's . . . magic or something."

When she didn't say anything in response to that, he turned to look at her again, his expression sheepish. "You think I'm nuts, don't you?"

She shook her head. "No, actually, I don't. Just before you came out here, I thought the ocean and the stars were speaking to me."

Now he grinned again. "Were they, now?"

This time she nodded. "Yup."

"And what did the ocean and stars say to you?"

Now Amanda was the one to gaze out at the sea. She shrugged and sipped her wine, mostly because she wasn't sure what to say, but also because she wanted to hold the moment suspended in time for as long as she could. Because she knew that, someday, she would look back on this moment as the one where everything changed. Where her old life alone fell away, and her new life with someone else—with Max—began.

"Mostly," she began, "they told me I work too much."

She heard Max chuckle at that. "And this is news to you? I've been telling you that for years."

"Yeah, you have."

"So now that it's a consensus, are you going to listen?"

Was that a hopeful quality she heard in his voice? she wondered. How convenient if it was. Because she was feeling kind of hopeful too.

Without even realizing she meant to say it, she heard herself ask him, "Do you want to know why I was so focused on my grades and getting into a good college when I was in high school?"

When he didn't answer right away, she turned to look at him and saw that he was looking at her now. "Why?" he asked, his voice softer than before. Though whether that was a result of the mellow evening or the mellow wine, Amanda couldn't have said. Probably the former, since they hadn't even finished their first glasses of the latter. Still, there was something in his voice that hadn't been there before.

"It was because of my father," she said simply.

"Ah," he said. "You have one of those fathers who instills a healthy work ethic from an early age."

"Had," she corrected. "My father died the summer before I started at Notre Dame."

There was a moment of hesitation on Max's part, then an even softer, "I'm sorry, Amanda. I didn't know."

"I know," she said. "Few people do. It's not something I really talk about." Then she hurried on—hurried because she knew she wouldn't be able to say it otherwise, not that she knew why she was saying it at all. "But it was just the opposite, actually. My father never worked an honest day in his life."

There was another one of those brief pauses, then Max said, "Uh . . . what?"

Amanda sighed heavily. "He was a lot like you, Max."

Max nodded, but his expression fell a little. "So that's why I never made your A-list. Because I'm like your loser dad."

She shook her head. "No, he wasn't a loser. He was a lot of fun. Happy-go-lucky. Not a care in the world. Always smiling. Always laughing. Never met a stranger." She smiled as she remembered. "He could always make me laugh. I'd come home from school feeling horrible because I got a B on a test, and he'd always say something like, 'Mandy, it's not the end of the world. There's more to life than grades.' Then he'd tell me to blow off my homework and go to a friend's house."

Max smiled too. "And would you?"

She shook her head again. "No. I didn't have any friends close enough for me to invite myself over."

Max sobered at that. For a moment. Then he smiled again. "You coulda come to my house."

Something in her stomach kindled at his words, sputtering to life at the matter-of-factness with which he'd spoken them. Instead of replying—because she knew he was only teasing—she said, "Anyway, as nice a guy as my dad was, he couldn't hold down a job. It was always a struggle for us. There were nights when my mom had to serve peanut butter sandwiches for dinner. Sometimes all I had for breakfast was a piece of dry toast."

"Amanda—"

But she held up a hand to cut him off. "I'm not telling you this because I want you to feel sorry for me. I'm telling you because I need you to know why I am the way I am. It sucked living like that as a kid. I didn't want to live that way as an adult. I wanted to be more responsible than my dad. It was more important to me to know I could take care of myself than to . . . than to . . ."

"Than to what?"

"Than to be liked by other people," she finished lamely.

He said nothing for a moment, then asked, "Why do you need me to know all that?"

Good question, she thought. She wished she had a good answer to go with. Since she didn't, she only lifted her shoulders and let them drop in another quick shrug.

"Well, if I need to know that," he said, "then there's something you need to know too."

"What?"

"That you're well liked by plenty of people," he said. He paused again, and looked as if he were weighing carefully what he wanted to say next. Then, evidently deciding, he added, "Including me."

The spark in her belly leaped higher at that, warming her heart and making her pulse beat harder.

"But I wasn't feeling sorry for you just now," he hurried on. "A lot of people live the way your family lived. We never had much when I was growing up either. But I never felt like I was missing out on anything. Happiness is a state of mind, Amanda. So is contentment. I don't require a lot when it comes to making me happy."

She thought about that for a moment. As an adult, she had achieved and earned everything she'd thought she wanted. She had a secure position at a respected company, and she owned a home she could comfortably pay off. She lived without debt and was responsible for no one but herself. But even having reached those goals, she couldn't say she was happy. Not really. She tried to remember the last time she had been happy. Truly, genuinely happy. And she realized it had been . . .

Wow. Not that long ago, actually. Mere minutes, in fact. It had been in that incandescent moment when she and Max had climaxed together, when the joy of their coupling was coursing through her, before the seeds of doubt had started creeping in. And that hadn't come about because of her job. In fact, her job had almost prevented it from happening.

"So just what do you require to make you happy?" she asked him.

He wiggled his dark brows suggestively, snaked out a hand to tangle his fingers in her pajama top, then pulled her roughly against him for a long, deep-throated kiss. "That," he said a little breathlessly when he pulled away. "A long taste of Amanda Bingham."

She smiled at that. "You don't taste so bad yourself."

He smiled back, but there was something a little uncertain about it. "Yes, but am I enough for you to live on? I'm not exactly a well-balanced meal, chock-full of vitamins and minerals and fiber."

"No, you're not," she agreed. "You're like a box of Froot Loops."

He narrowed his eyes at that.

"Sweet and colorful and fun. And yet, somehow still an excellent source of nutrition."

Now he pulled her close again. "I can live with that," he said before dropping a kiss at her temple. He nuzzled her hair, her ear, her jaw, her throat. "And I can live with this too."

Oh, so can I, Amanda thought as she nuzzled him back. *So can I.*

She wasn't sure, but as she twined her arms around him and kissed him deeply, she thought she could hear the Sirens cheering.

Epilogue

As the morning sunlight crept into the bedroom, Max lay on his side next to Amanda and watched her as she slept. He'd had no idea sex could be so good between two people. He'd had no idea he could care about one person so much. But if he had his way, he and Amanda would move in together as soon as they got back to Indianapolis. Her place, his place, a new place, he didn't care. As long as he could be with her, that was the only thing that mattered. He didn't expect her to give up her career, but he hoped she would at least pare down her hours. And demand a raise too. That jerk Hoberman didn't realize how good he had it with her. If the guy didn't start giving her some of the perks she deserved . . .

Well, maybe once Max started showing her how important she was to him, she'd realize how important she was to other people, too; that was all.

He lifted his hand to wrap an unruly curl around his finger, marveling at how silky was her hair and how soft was her skin.

He hadn't meant to disturb her sleep, but she stirred at even that small touch, smiling when she opened her eyes to find him gazing down at her.

"Good morning," she murmured, lifting her hand to cradle his jaw in her fingertips.

"It is a *very* good morning," he agreed. "Bloody Marys on the beach in thirty minutes," he told her. "Which gives us just enough time to—"

"E-mail Mr. Hoberman," she said.

His smile fell at that. She still planned to make this a working vacation? Hell, a *no*-vacation? After everything they'd discovered last night?

"Tell me you're just kidding," he said.

She shook her head. "No. I need to do it right away."

"Amanda—"

But she was already pushing herself up from the mattress and reaching for the robe tossed on a nearby chair. "It's really important, Max," she said as she belted it.

"Yeah, I'll bet," he muttered uncharitably.

She walked around the mattress and bent over him, thrusting out her lower lip in an over-exaggerated pout. "Oh, come on. It'll only take a minute," she said in a sulky Shirley Temple voice.

He rolled his eyes. He should have realized it would take more than one night of sexual gymnastics to change Amanda's workaholic ways.

He said nothing as she strode to the desk and opened her laptop, raking her thumb across the mouse pad to bring it to life. He heard her type what probably amounted to a paragraph, then she turned around in the chair to look at him.

"How do I do that Rickroll thing?" she asked offhandedly.

Max's eyebrows shot up at that. "You're going to Rickroll your boss?"

She nodded.

"Really?"

She nodded again.

Max couldn't get out of the bed fast enough. Stark naked, he strode over to stand behind her, reaching over her shoulders to copy and paste the necessary information from her coworker's e-mail and disguise it as the link to what her e-mail had identified as a potentially explosive new investment opportunity that Hoberman should immediately forward to all his colleagues.

"He won't even click on it," Amanda said. "He'll assume it's legit and forward it to all his fat-cat pals."

"So not only are you Rickrolling your boss, but he'll be Rickrolling all his friends without realizing."

"Yup," she said. "He deserves it, that pinhead," she added. "Serves him right for making me work on my vacation." Then she powered down her computer, unplugged it, wrapped the cord securely around it, and shoved it into her bag. Her cell phone, still turned off from last night, quickly followed it.

Then she stood, turned to Max, and wrapped her arms around his naked waist. "Now, then, didn't somebody promise me Bloody Marys on the beach . . . ?"

Original Zin

Christie Ridgway

One

Double Vision

John Henry Hudson tripped on his way out of the icy-cool wine-tasting room. The October Indian summer everyone in Napa was talking about felt more like "dry sauna" to him and the shock of the temperature change made his head spin. It was either that, or the goddamn pneumonia that had nearly taken him under in August was tugging on his shirttails again.

Through the heat shimmering from the asphalt parking lot, he spied the limo that he, his sister, and her friends had taken on their tasting tour. Actually, he spied two identical black limos, but he chalked up the double vision to another bout of dizziness until he remembered Ellen ordering a second limo from the car service in case some of their party wanted to skip the last three wineries on their planned circuit.

Yeah. That would be him.

Squinting against the late-afternoon light, he headed for the first stretch vehicle. His black hair felt like a sun magnet, and the chrome handle of the limo's back door burned his palm as he yanked it open. Diving into the cool interior, he breathed in the scent of leather and a faint trace of tantalizing perfume that must be left over from the eight twenty-one-year-olds who had been touring with him.

Up front, the privacy shield was half lowered, and through it he saw the driver's cap jerk into view, as if he'd been bent over. "It's me, Carl," he called out to the man who had captained the car all afternoon. "And just between us guys, let me tell you the company of half-drunk sorority girls is not all it's cracked up to be."

Before the chauffeur could respond, John Henry continued. "Yeah, I'm sure you're more of an expert on the subject than me, so let's save both of us and get out of here. Ellen and the rest of the Sigma Woo Hoos or whatever it is they call themselves can stick together for three more rounds of swish, sniff, and slurp."

Wine tasting boiled down to just that, and he was done with it. He gazed out the side window at the surrounding hills and their orderly rows of fruited vines. The view was nice. Relaxing. He was supposed to be doing that, he remembered. "Drive me around for a while, then take me back to the Valley Ridge Resort, would you?"

The darkened privacy window rose as the limo pulled away from the curb. He thought about telling Carl to leave it down, but the trill of his BlackBerry redirected his attention. Recognizing his sister's number on the screen, he grimaced, but took the call.

"Yo."

Her voice sounded a tad put out. "Yo ho ho—"

"And a bottle of merlot," he finished for her, hoping to tease her out of her mood. "Hey, I'm funny."

Her sigh wasn't a happy one. Obviously she wasn't pleased that he'd left her birthday wine-tasting tour a few stops early. "John Henry, you're never funny."

"Wait a min—"

"You're uptight, overwound, and against relaxation in any form."

"Gee, don't bother pulling your punches."

"Tell me you aren't going back to the resort to pore over papers or check for incoming faxes instead of having fun with me and my friends."

John Henry could have defended himself. He could have told her the Sigma Woo Hoos were giving him a headache. And hadn't he told Carl not to go straight back? But the truth was, he *had* been itching to look over some reports stacked on the desk in his room. "What's this? You turn twenty-one and you're suddenly a critic?"

"I'm the woman who loves you. The only woman besides Mom, I'm guessing, who puts up with you and your workaholic ways."

He winced, despite the fact that he'd heard it before. And not only from his much-younger sister and much-exasperated mother. There'd been several beautiful ladies who had thrown up their hands and then thrown in the towel when he canceled yet another date or just flat-out forgot one.

"John Henry," his sister continued. "You—"

He coughed. God forgive him, he did it on purpose. Then he did it again.

Ellen's tone instantly changed from annoyance to alarm. "You're not feeling well?"

"Um . . ."

"You're not feeling well. Why didn't you say anything?"

Pious wasn't a natural fit for him, but he tried it on anyway. "I didn't want to ruin your birthday celebration."

"John Henry," she scolded, "you're supposed to be taking care of yourself. Two weeks of vacation, you promised Mom and me. The first week of it you spent on the resort's golf course doing business from dawn to dusk."

"Yeah, but—"

"There are only seven days left. You'd better take it easy. Isn't that what Mark prescribed?"

Mark Richards, his undergrad roommate at Stanford who was now Doctor Mark Richards and the one whom John Henry had entrusted with his health care when he'd come down with the dangerous case of pneumonia. "I believe Mark actually said I should take some time off and get drunk and get laid."

Ellen huffed, "In that case, you better stay away from my friends."

"The Sigma Woo Hoos are too young for me," he assured her.

"You're too boring for them."

He frowned. Uptight. Overwound. Workaholic. Those all sounded about right and, to his mind, not really derogatory. But *boring*?

The frown was still on his face and the word was still rattling around in his head as he ended the call with Ellen. He'd always been focused. A Type-A personality, and what was wrong with that? Sure, after his father's sudden death a year and a half ago, he'd doubled down on his hours and his concentration as he stepped into his father's shoes in the family business.

But did that really mean he was dull?

Mark had suggested he get some balance in his life, or else his health was going to suffer the way it had over the summer. He'd never mentioned that John Henry was at risk of becoming boring.

Go away somewhere, Mark had said.

So John Henry had thought of Napa, where they were relocating River Pharmaceuticals. Okay, maybe it wasn't "away" from the business, but since he'd yet to find a new house, he *was* staying at a five-star resort.

John Henry, do yourself a favor. Mark's voice echoed in his head. *Go away, get drunk, and get laid.*

His best friend should also have told him he was getting boring! Since he hadn't, John Henry had wasted one week of his vacation not seriously pursuing the prescription his doctor had ordered, damn it. There were only seven nights left, and John Henry decided he better do something with them.

Boring!

And, a quiet voice reminded him, life was too damn short for boring.

The limo slowed, then stopped due to the traffic ahead. Suddenly galvanized, John Henry slid along the black leather seat toward the front of the vehicle, at the same time reaching into his pocket to withdraw some bills. His knuckles rat-a-tatted against the smoky privacy shield. As it slowly lowered, he gave the driver new orders.

"Sorry, but there's a change of plans," he said, tossing the money onto the front passenger seat. "I need you to find me a beer. Find me a beer and a willing babe."

The chauffeur's head whipped around.

John Henry found himself staring at a pair of round blue eyes under the stiff brim of the black cap. Feathery, fairy blond hair escaped its confines to frame golden brown eyebrows and almost tangle in long eyelashes. A short nose was sprinkled with seven gold freckles. Next came a soft, pink mouth.

He wasn't Carl.

Moreover, "he" was a "she."

Zin Friday glanced at the bills on the seat beside her, then back at the man who'd thrown them there. Dark-haired, dark-eyed, with an expensive haircut that said he normally spent his days at an executive's desk and a new tan that told her he'd traded the desk for a few days in the wine-country sunshine.

In an uncharacteristic flight of fancy, Zin found herself wondering what, exactly, he wanted in a "babe." Then she remembered the single qualifying adjective he'd uttered. Her gaze slid again to the bills on the leather beside her. "Uh, that's a lot of willingness you're looking for."

He groaned. "That was supposed to be a tip for taking the driver—who I thought was Carl—off plan. Please believe me when I say I wasn't paying for . . . for . . ."

"A procurement?"

He groaned again. "My sister just accused me of being boring. You probably think I'm merely a boor, huh?"

His embarrassed expression looked sincere, and Zin had to admit his wordplay tickled her a little. "Boring, boor. You're funny."

A quick smile slashed a dimple into his lean cheek. "That's what I think."

Behind them, a horn tapped, and Zin faced forward again. The traffic in front of them had cleared, so she eased her foot onto the accelerator and continued along the rural road that led to her nearby hometown of Edenville, in northern Napa County. The Valley Ridge Resort was located on its outskirts, but it would still be slow-and-go progress as visitors leaving the wineries turned onto the main, oak-shaded route.

She checked out her passenger in the rearview mirror. He was looking out a side window, which gave her a good view of his chiseled profile. Thirtyish, she'd guess, and not only was there a nice quantity of cash lying beside her, but there was money evident in the cut and quality of the lightweight sport shirt he was wearing. His hand lifted to smooth his hair, and she couldn't miss the expensive-looking gold watch wrapped around his wrist.

As if he could feel her looking at him, his head shifted and their gazes met. She jolted, uncomfortable with getting caught staring and uncomfortable with . . . with something else she couldn't put her finger on. Reaching out, she nudged up the air-conditioning and cleared her throat.

"Are you really interested in stopping for that drink?" she asked.

"As long as it isn't a grape product—or is it taboo to want any other kind of beverage around here?"

She shook her head. "You'd be surprised how many people in Napa aren't into what we're famous for. The most celebrated vintages are out of the price range of many of the 'regular' folk, and it's a poorly kept secret that the succeeding generations of the big wine-making families often prefer a yeasty lager to a robust cabernet."

The car in front of them slowed again, causing Zin to tap the brakes. She glanced in the rearview mirror. "There's a decent tavern just ahead."

John Henry hesitated.

"You're this vehicle's last customer of the day," she added, "so you can stay as long as you like. I know for a fact they've got cold brew on tap."

Why not give the little nudge? The Napa Princess Limousine Service was owned by her friend Stephania Baci, and the business could use the extra cash that a longer booking would bring in. Zin would welcome a larger paycheck, too, of course.

The man shrugged. "Okay, then."

In less than five minutes she was pulling into the parking lot of the tavern that called itself Dave's Feed Shop. It actually had been a feed shop at one time, which explained the barnlike exterior and the straw bales stacked by the entrance. To lend an even more authentic feel, Dave and his wife, Marti, kept a few chickens on the property.

The limo scattered a couple of them as Zin braked at the rear of the gravel parking area. Then she popped into the waning heat and opened the door for her passenger. Casual loafers, followed by long legs encased in expensive jeans emerged from the car. He was over six feet, towering above her five-foot-and-hardly-anything height.

She shut the door and then turned to him. "I'll be right here whenever you're ready to leave."

"You're not coming in?"

Puzzled, she shook her head.

"Have you forgotten? I asked for a beer and a willing woman."

That charming dimple of his was showing, but she was beginning to think it rendered him only deceptively harmless, so she frowned. "A willing 'babe' is what you said. Sorry, that lets me out."

His eyebrows rose as his gaze shifted from her face to slide down her figure. Besides the black chauffeur's cap, she was dressed in a white shirt covered with a short black jacket, and black pants. Only a slight film of red Napa dust covered the obsidian-colored leather of her man-styled wingtip shoes. It wasn't babe wear.

But the way her skin prickled in the wake of his roving eyes made her feel as if she were wearing strappy sandals, a mini halter dress, and shoulder-skimming chandelier earrings. Her feet backed up until her butt met the warm side of the limousine.

Her retreat seemed to amuse him, because he smiled again and took her hand. Though he held it like a lover, he shook it like a businessman. "I'm John Henry," he said. "Nice to meet you . . . ?"

"Zin. Zin Friday." She was staring at their joined hands. His thumb rested lightly on the burn scar on top, and his long, tan fingers, a little thinner than she thought they should be, tangled with hers. A skitter of goose bumps shot up her arm.

"Zin? As in zinfandel?"

She shook her head, though that wasn't any weirder, really,

than what her oddball parents had actually named her. "Zin, as in Zinnia."

"The flower?" He blinked, then laughed. "It must be a sign, Zin-as-in-Zinnia."

"What sort of sign?" They'd been holding hands for too long, so she freed herself, tucking her fingers into the pockets of her pants.

"Doctor's orders. The words might have been slightly different, but the point's the same. I'm supposed to stop and smell the flowers."

Before she could protest, he'd popped the cap from her head. The long mass of curly hair she'd stuffed beneath the crown flowed free. Reaching out, he wrapped a fist with a swath of the stuff and lifted it to his nose. "Sweet," he said, and breathed deep.

She couldn't breathe in any air at all.

"Does the rest of you smell this good?" he asked, letting her hair fall free from his hold. The soft tone of his voice beguiled her; the admiring light in his dark eyes sent another frisson—like a puff of breath over heated skin—thrilling through her. She had a red birthmark on the nape of her neck, at the very edge of her hairline. The size and the shape of a kiss, it burned like a brand now, as if real lips had touched her there.

John Henry wasn't touching her at all.

She couldn't think what to answer—she couldn't remember the question!—and from the look of that dimple now digging into his cheek again, she thought her inability to articulate amused him. But then he hung his head, shaking it a little, and she thought he might be laughing at himself.

"I've never had this happen before," he said. "Maybe there's more to this relaxation thing than I realized."

She wasn't following him again, but this time she found her voice. "More what?"

"I—" The ring of a cell phone interrupted.

They both patted their pockets, but John Henry's hand came up first. His BlackBerry screen was lit, and he cast her a swift glance, then answered the call. "I'm here."

Zin used the moment of reprieve to take in a steadying breath. Though her mind was clearing a bit, her skin still felt supersensitized, and the throbbing at the back of her neck wasn't dissipating. It was this man's fault, with his distracting dimple and his long fingers and his glossy hair.

"Yeah," she heard him say. "I'll check the numbers right away and get back to you." He returned his phone to his front pocket.

His gaze met hers, and he grimaced. "There's this report I promised someone from work I'd look over."

"Work is important." Zin took another breath and then opened the back door for him. "I understand work."

He ducked inside the limo, then caught her hand before she had a chance to shut him safely away from her. "Zin."

"Y-yes?" Why did their twined fingers fascinate her so?

"What do you say, sweet Zinnia? Let's you and me make another attempt to get acquainted. We can do something fun tomorrow."

"I can't," she said, grateful that she had an honest excuse. Though she hadn't dated in a million years, and never at the spontaneous request of a stranger, this man presented an unsettling temptation. She tugged her hand free of his. "I don't have time."

His laugh was rueful. "That used to be my line."

"I really don't have time," Zin said once more. But it unsettled her again to realize that she actually wished she did.

Two

Double Take

Zin swallowed her yawn and passed over the customer's change and a paper bag containing her cinnamon scone. "Thank you for stopping by Bradley's Bakery," she told the gray-haired woman.

As the older lady dropped coins into the tip jar, Zin tightened the bow on the butcher-style apron she wore over her jeans and long-sleeved cotton turtleneck. It was going to be another hot autumn day, which meant long hours under the icy blast of frigid air-conditioning, even during the breakfast rush.

The customer moved off, allowing the next person to step up to the counter. "Hello, Zinnia," he said. "How's the youngest Flaky Friday today?"

"Alan," she replied, her jaw instantly clenching so the name came through gritted teeth. *Flaky Friday*. It echoed in her head as a too-familiar wave of shame washed over her. It seemed like she'd spent her whole life trying to live down that elementary school nickname. She hated to be thought of that way.

How much more she hated the two words coming from this particular man. A contemporary of her older brother and a neighbor of her parents, Alan Prescott wore his auburn hair in a brush cut and his smile was, as always, more snide than friendly. Without turning her head, she called his order to the barista. "Large coffee, extra shot of espresso." Extra black, like the jerk's soul. "Is that all you want?"

"Why, Flaky Friday . . ." He was distracted by someone he knew walking up to grab a napkin.

As the two men exchanged a few words, Zin tried loosening the muscles knotted in her shoulders. It wouldn't do for Alan to detect her tension. The bully thrived on discomfort, and it was a point of pride for her that neither he nor anyone else would see how much his needling—and that nickname—bothered her.

So she hoped she looked relaxed as he turned back to the counter. "Now where were we?"

Zin pasted on a polite smile. "I asked if there was something you wanted besides your coffee."

"Yeah, there is," Alan said, leaning close, as if to seek a measure of privacy. But the volume of his voice didn't lessen. "I want the hundred bucks that Bobby and June borrowed from me last week. They said they needed groceries."

Zin stiffened, more shame pouring like a hot river down her spine. The bakery was busy this morning, and she was supremely aware of the many people who could easily overhear the conversation. "I . . . I . . ."

"If you don't have the cash, Zin, maybe you have something else to barter."

Surprised by the smarmy suggestion in his voice, she felt heat flare on her face. She should have seen it coming, she told herself. It wasn't as if today was the first time Alan had played this particular game. Her older sister, Mari, had said he'd once threatened to call the police on the code violations at their parents' property unless she let him take her to dinner and a movie. As if that was the only thing "All Hands" Alan, as he'd been known in high school, had in mind.

Mari had told him in the crudest of terms where he could stuff his threats, but Zinnia was on the job . . . and maybe not as tough as her sister. "I don't have that much cash on me right now," she told Alan, keeping her voice low and level. "I'll get you the money as soon as I can."

"But I want it now," he insisted, that ugly smile still on his face.

She narrowed her eyes at him. "Maybe I'll call Kohl to take care of it."

Something flickered in Alan's eyes, but he didn't move. "Kohl's a loose cannon, that's true, but if you run to big brother, he could end up in worse shape than me, don't you think? I hear the cops have a special set of heavy-duty handcuffs set aside for the next time he gets in a brawl."

And wouldn't Kohl locked behind bars once again serve only to remind people just how unhinged the Flaky Fridays could be? The barista slid Alan's paper cup onto the counter in front of Zin, and she shoved it in his direction, setting a plastic top beside it. "I've got this," she told him, digging in her jeans for the cash she was carrying. She put the cost of the drink in the till, then handed everything else she had over to the man. "There's twenty bucks, counting the beverage. You'll wait for the rest."

Alan pocketed the money and picked up his drink, though didn't immediately move off. "But Zin . . . baby . . ." he started, his voice cajoling. Then he jolted forward as a hand clapped him on the back, sending hot coffee sloshing over his fingers. He yelped, cursed, then reeled around to face . . .

Zin gaped. "John Henry."

"Hey, Zin," he said easily, then directed his attention to Alan.

"Sorry, man, about that boisterous greeting. I thought you were someone I liked." He handed over a napkin, then stuffed a roll of bills in the breast pocket of Alan's shirt.

The bully frowned down at his chest while wiping at the dripping coffee. "What's this?"

"The eighty dollars I owe Zin."

She protested. "You—"

"—know how I am, Zin. Get an idea in my head and can't give it up."

Zin didn't know anything about him except that he was somehow managing to draw Alan away from her. In a manner she could only describe as smoothly masterful, he had the other man ushered out the bakery door within thirty seconds, without another veiled threat or annoying suggestion.

And without a debt to hold over Zin's head any longer.

There was a short line at the counter by the time her Good Samaritan turned around. Without complaint, he took his place at the back, shuffling forward as she waited on each successive customer until once again they were face-to-face.

"Um . . . uh . . ." Her voice drifted off, and her cheeks flared again with heat as the whole unpleasant exchange with Alan replayed in her head. How much of it had this man overheard? Obviously that Alan thought she owed him money. That her brother was not a favorite of law enforcement.

That she was one of the Flaky Fridays?

"I don't know what to say," she said.

"'Good morning' will work. And you could get me a medium coffee. Decaf." He smiled. "Or better yet, you could make a mistake and give me one that's fully caffeine-loaded so that I feel virtuous, but in actuality am getting the real substance I crave."

She found herself smiling too. "Would that make me your enabler?"

"My goddess."

It was suddenly easy to laugh. "I'm a flower, remember?"

"I did." His voice lowered. "All night long."

Zin stilled, her smile sliding off her face. She'd been thinking of him, too, ever since dropping him off at the resort the night before. It was entirely unwelcome, she'd decided in the wee hours, the little fixation she had on him, and she'd been determined to dismiss it. She had items on her agenda, work to do, a reputation to live down, and that left no room for a handsome man with dark eyes who could send a sexy shiver through her with just five simple words.

I did. All night long.

She gripped the edge of the countertop instead of fisting his shirt in one hand and yanking him toward her for the kiss she'd been wondering about for approximately fourteen hours and fifteen minutes. She didn't want to be thinking about kissing some man she'd just met—it seemed an especially flaky thing to have in the forefront of one's mind. It was hard to know whether he thought it was flaky, though clearly he knew what was in her head, because his gaze was focused on her lips. They tingled.

"We don't want to do this," she murmured.

One of his dark eyebrows winged up, and that dimple showed itself again. His BlackBerry rang, and as he reached for his front pocket, he leaned close. "Sweet Zin," he whispered, "speak for yourself."

John Henry decided he wasn't surprised to find Zin Friday on the terrace at the Valley Ridge Resort, pouring wine during the complimentary nightcap tasting late that evening. After waving good-bye to his sister and her sorority friends—they were returning to San Francisco—he'd decided on a stroll around the grounds. Catching sight of Zin's distinctive fairy curls, he'd instantly changed course. Fate had been putting her in his way, and he didn't see a reason to duck the encounter.

She seemed even less surprised to be facing him again so soon. "Hello, Mr. Henry," she said.

"It's John Henry," he replied. "The whole thing's my first name."

She blinked those otherworldly baby blues of hers. "Oh."

From his back pocket, he withdrew the envelope that had been waiting for him at the front desk. It contained four twenty-dollar bills. He waggled it. "You could have asked for me instead of leaving it with the receptionist."

Her gaze skittered away to focus on the cabernet in front of her. "Had to get to work."

"I see that." He wondered how many uniforms hung in the woman's closet. Tonight it was the black pants and manly black shoes, but this time they were topped by a white blouse decorated with a chestful of ruffles. A black band held her hair away from her pretty face. "When you claimed a busy schedule, it wasn't just an excuse to let me down easy."

She glanced up, then returned to studying the label on a wine bottle as if it were a calculus textbook. "No."

It was almost an admission that she liked him, or that she at least felt a little of the same pull that he did, and he was stupidly pleased by the small concession. He ran his hand over his hair, only to discover he was still holding the envelope, and felt stupid all over again. Frowning, he shoved it back in his pocket. John Henry had never been stupid in his life. "You didn't need to return the money."

"Of course I needed to return the money." A line dug between her eyebrows. "I hope you didn't think—"

"I hope *you* didn't think I'd hold it over you like that ass in the bakery." Just the thought of the leering SOB made John Henry see red.

"You're nothing like Alan," Zin assured him.

Their eyes met, and now all he saw was blue. He fell into it, like a lead-bearing fishing line dropping into the Mediterranean . . . or maybe it was more like a sky diver leaping from a plane into a free fall. There was a moment of helpless weightlessness, seconds of stunned panic, and then he jerked down his gaze, at the last second saving himself by changing his focus to the soft surface of her lips.

Still, his blood surged toward his cock, but this was something he understood. Lust was easy to comprehend. Simple to slake. "Go out with me, Zin," he said.

She shook her head. "I don't have time."

That same story, he thought, impatient with it, though he'd delivered it himself on any number of occasions to any number of women. "Listen—" His BlackBerry's ring intruded once again.

Without thinking, he fished it out of his pocket and strode off to answer the call, for the first time noticing the scattering of tables on the terrace and the people sitting at them while enjoying wine and snacks. "What?" he barked into the phone, moving even farther away from the small crowd.

"Your so-called vacation doesn't sound as if it's relaxed you any," his best friend said. "And if I recall correctly, that's what your personal physician ordered."

"I didn't think doctors made house calls anymore," John Henry said to Mark Richards, meddling M.D.

"Dude, this is a *phone* call," Mark replied, "and if you don't know the difference, you need a vacation from your vacation."

Maybe that would be best, John Henry thought. He was getting fixated on a woman, and that couldn't be good. "Tahiti might be nice."

Mark laughed. "I'll eat my stethoscope if you can remove yourself more than a hundred miles from River Pharmaceuticals."

"I—"

"Ellen called and ratted you out. She said you couldn't keep still or even keep your hands off your BlackBerry for a mere three hours of wine tasting."

"It was three hours with the Sigma Woo Hoos! It might as well have been three years. I needed to check in with the office a couple of times just to make sure I remembered how to start a sentence with something other than 'I took a magazine quiz' or 'Can you believe he flirted with my cousin.'"

"I feel for you, John Henry, but honest to God, you need to focus your attention on something other than what's going on at the company."

He leaned on the stone balustrade surrounding the terrace and looked out over the quiet golf course. "I was on the links every day last week," he mumbled.

"Ellen told me about that too. Those foursomes were made up of your dad's old buddies, directors from the board, competitors you might want to get into bed with someday."

"Believe me, I don't want to snuggle with some old guy in plaid pants and white shoes." His gaze swung around to Zin, who was smiling prettily at just such a one as she poured straw-colored liquid into a glass. "These are all Dad's juggling balls, and I'm just trying to keep them in the air like he did."

"Which is why he died at fifty-five, John Henry. And it's why you almost bought the farm, too, in August."

He closed his eyes. He knew it had been damn close, and truth to tell, he'd scared the hell out of himself with that dance with death. But he couldn't seem to figure out how to retrain his mind. Nothing distracted him from thoughts of this project, that report, those new plans. "I'm working on it," he told Mark.

"Jesus, John Henry, that's the whole point. You're not supposed to be working. You're supposed to be—"

"Getting drunk and getting laid," he finished for his friend.

"Is that so difficult? Figure out your priorities, man!"

John Henry didn't know how to respond, so he ended the call and stood where he was, gazing on the eighteenth hole as the terrace tables emptied. When he heard the crickets chirping instead of people's conversations, he turned around.

In his line of sight, under the golden glow of a hanging light, stood Zin Friday, folding the cloth that had covered the table where she'd been pouring. The remaining glasses were being wheeled away in a cart piloted by a busboy. They were alone, John Henry realized as he walked toward her. Stilling, she looked up.

His feet halted. She'd unbuttoned that white blouse she wore to a modest, midchest level, and it was the first time he'd seen the smooth, velvety skin of her throat. It got him moving forward again, wanting to see it from closer up, and then he realized that because of his height and her smaller stature he could detect a hint of cleavage from his new perspective.

Blood surged southward again, stiffening his cock, and he didn't feel the least bit guilty for getting off on this slight glimpse of her breasts. It felt good, it felt alive, it felt pretty damn amazing that though he had no real idea if she was a slight A cup or a more flashy C, it didn't matter.

Once again, Zin was turning him on.

He saw her swallow as he came to a stop in front of her. The narrow, bare table stood between them. "I don't have any wine left to offer," she said.

"It doesn't matter."

Her hands gathered the folds of the tablecloth to her chest, as if for protection. He frowned. "Are you afraid of me, Zin?"

"No . . . Yes. No."

He tried interpreting that as the busboy returned and deftly turned the table, released the folding legs, then walked it back inside the resort. The door shut behind the young man, and the light over Zin's head winked out. The two of them were left alone on the terrace again, with only the flickering candles on the small tables alleviating the darkness.

It felt thick as syrup as he stepped through it, stepping up to Zin to slide his hand beneath her hair and around her neck. She jolted, emitting a small, surprised sound from the back of her throat. Her hold on the tablecloth didn't ease up.

He didn't ease up either. Instead he moved in, moved closer, his head bending so he could brush his mouth against her temple and breathe in the fragrant scent of her hair. *Sweet.*

The skin of her cheek was warm beneath his lips. *Soft.*

His mouth met hers, felt it open. *Hot.*

He'd meant to be gentle, to sneak up on her with a soothing touch. But this turned passionate the instant she breathed into his mouth. His tongue plunged into the wet, smooth confines of her mouth, his fingers twisted in the tendrils of her curly hair, his other palm found the small of her back and urged her body against his.

His cock went rock hard, and fire shot through his veins as her belly brushed against the throbbing weight of him. With his forearms at her hips, he lifted her to him, groaning against her mouth as she writhed against his erection. Without letting up on a succession of hot and needy kisses, his fingers loosened from her hair and he drew them along her jaw, down her throat, and then under her blouse. Another button popped as his hand found its way to her breast.

A, B, C, what the hell did the alphabet matter? All he knew was that she moaned as his palm brushed her nipple. It tightened against his caress.

He hardened more—impossibly, painfully—at the sensation. And in sweet retaliation, he tweaked the little nub between his thumb and forefinger.

Zin shuddered, then jerked back.

Breathing hard, they stared at each other. The tablecloth was tangled at their feet, her shirttail was half out of her pants, and even in the darkness he could see her mouth was swollen. Reaching out, he ran his thumb over her lower lip.

Her tongue darted out for a quick taste, and it was his turn to shudder. "Zin . . ."

She took another step back.

He let her have her small escape. It was only temporary, he told himself. There was no way this wasn't going forward. "What are you doing now? Next?"

"I . . . I have to finish cleaning up and then clock out." She pressed her palm to her forehead as if trying to think. "And then . . . I've been up since four A.M. I've got to get home and wash my uniforms and manage some sleep."

He nodded, knowing he could push, aware the Type A in him was clamoring for action, pressure, persistence. But he also knew what it was like to work too much and the consequences of running on empty. He wanted her rested.

"Zin," he said, keeping his voice soft, "come play with me tomorrow."

"I . . ." She put her hand to her forehead again. "I have work. I'm at the bakery until after lunch, then if there's a booking, I'm on tap to drive the limo all late afternoon and into the evening."

He nodded again, deciding to let that go as well. *She has work and I have mine cut out for me.* But, he thought, this was exactly the kind of labor that the doctor would approve of. His BlackBerry chose that moment to ring, but without even glancing at the number on the screen, he powered it off.

That kiss had turned the tide. John Henry Hudson had found himself a new priority.

Three
Double-Teamed

With her toe, Zin tapped the work boots sticking out from under a late-model Mercedes. "Afternoon, Gil," she said to the owner of Edenville Motor Repair.

His reply was lost in the blast of an air compressor, but she didn't hesitate as she made her way around the building to the back parking lot that was home to four shiny stretch vehicles and led to the headquarters of Napa Princess Limousine Service. Like her, Gil worked hard, and she doubted he'd let any romantic dreams get in the way of his professional life. She wasn't going to let that happen either.

She pushed the half-opened door to Stephania Baci's duplex—aka Napa Princess Limousine Service HQ—and hung her uniform on a coatrack before moving into the kitchen. There, tall, gorgeous, and golden-skinned, her boss and best friend, dressed in a pair of cutoff jeans and a T-shirt that read *Kiss Me Cuz That's My Name*, sat at the table.

Looking up from her coffee, Stevie caught the direction of Zin's gaze. "Last year's Christmas present from my little sister," she said, plucking at the pink cotton. "I've hit the bottom of the drawer, which means it's past time to do laundry."

"Baci does mean 'kiss' in Italian," Zin pointed out.

"As if I didn't know and suffer for it already," Stevie said, rolling her eyes. "But at least it's not Zinnia."

"Ouch," Zin said, pausing in the act of pouring herself a cup of coffee from the carafe. "Is that what friends are for?"

"If you dislike it so much, you should change it," Stevie suggested.

Zin shook her head. Changing her name would be trying to take the easy way out. Altering people's perceptions of her could be done only through actions. Through work, which was why she was after a good job to offset all the flaky freakiness of her parents.

"I'm serious," Stevie continued. "Your parents picked Zinnia—"

"And Friday," Zin reminded her friend. "For the day they met, since my dad's real last name, Smith, made them feel too closely aligned with the military-industrial complex."

Stevie blinked. "I don't think I've heard that bit before."

"Try to follow me, then," Zin said, pulling out a chair and sitting across the table. "Smith and Wesson makes firearms."

"Any relation—"

"None. But they said if they used Smith, they automatically thought of Wesson, which reminded them of war. Not to mention the fuzz."

Stevie nearly snorted up her coffee. Zin reached over to thump her on the back. "Are you okay?"

The other woman nodded, even as she wheezed a few more times. "The fuzz?" she finally questioned.

"You see, the fuzz—the police—use Smith and Wesson firearms."

"Do your folks really use that term?"

"Is my name Zinnia? Is my sister Marigold? Yes, Mom and Dad still refer to the police as 'the fuzz.' I think they've watched too many *Mod Squad* reruns."

"I don't think I spent enough time at your house," Stevie said, shaking her head.

Zin had never *let* Stevie spend a lot of time at her house, which was actually a rusting double-wide on a plot of mostly uncultivated land. Their childhood hangout had been the Bacis' unpretentious farmhouse on the Tanti Baci winery property. While the Bacis were a wine-making family, they weren't a wealthy one, although their standard of living had been staircases above what the Fridays managed.

But Zin didn't want to think about the past. Not her childhood as one of the Flaky Fridays and not last night either. Last night . . . She dropped her head to her hand to rub away the memory of that kiss. Trying to forget it—and trying to forget *him*—had been the occupation of yet more sleepless hours. More dreams.

"Uh-oh, one of your stress headaches?" Stevie asked. "You need to cut out a job or two."

"I hope to," Zin answered, looking up. "I've got a job interview—for a real job using my brand-new MBA—set up for the end of the week."

"Congratulations," Stevie said, presenting her curled fingers to Zin so they could exchange a triumphant fist bump.

"I don't have the position yet." But she wanted it so damn bad. It would be as good as—better than—a name change. Finally the people in her hometown would take her seriously and would see her as something other than one of those flaky, freaky Fridays. She swallowed the rest of her coffee, then slapped the tabletop. "So tell me who I'm driving around this afternoon."

"I'd rather hear about what happened last night."

John Henry's image popped immediately into Zin's head. She tried shoving it away, but it was there, replaying in high def: his mouth approaching hers, his dark eyes intent, that masculine dimple flirting with the taut skin of his cheek.

Closing her eyes, she cleared her throat. "I don't know what you mean."

"Looks like you have a headache. I could spend three weeks in Tuscany with the bags under your eyes. Something's up."

"I kissed him." The words popped out a second before her palm clamped over her mouth. "Forget I said that," came out sounding like "Vogut ee ed dat."

Hooting, Stevie peeled Zin's hand away from her face. "What's wrong with kissing someone? As long as you're not related or it's not that ugly Alan 'All Hands' Prescott."

"Ew." Zin frowned. A kiss from John Henry wasn't remotely like what she expected a kiss from nasty Alan would be. "He's disgusting."

"You're telling me," Stevie agreed. "When I was sixteen, he caught me at midnight on New Year's Eve. Do the words 'lizard tongue' call up a pleasant image for you?"

"Really ew." Zin drew back. "You never told me that."

"We all have our secrets. I know you do."

Zin squirmed on her seat. "I would tell you if I kissed Alan."

"So who *did* you kiss?"

Maybe she could banish him from her brain if she talked about him. "A gorgeous guy. He's staying at the Valley Ridge Resort and . . . I don't know. There's just something about him." What was she thinking? She couldn't explain what happened with John Henry to herself, let alone to Stevie. She didn't date men she didn't know, and she certainly didn't kiss one like *that*. Her nipple had burned at his touch, and she'd been ready to spread the tablecloth somewhere in the surrounding vineyards or even on the lucky seventh green, and go at it right there and then.

"He's a sweeper," Stevie declared.

"What?" Zin frowned. "I think he's some sort of business guy. His BlackBerry goes off all the time."

"No, remember? We used to dream about the sweepers. The ones who would sweep us off our feet."

"We were twelve. We weren't reading *Seventeen* magazine yet, so we didn't know that being swept off our feet could lead to STDs and unwanted pregnancy. Not to mention irreparable damage to our prom dresses."

Stevie was staring at her. "Has the hot weather dried the romance right out of you? Don't you remember our campouts in Alonzo and Anne's cottage?"

Zin squirmed in her chair again. Of course she remembered their campouts in the cottage. Alonzo Baci, an Italian immigrant, had built the cottage on the winery property something like a hundred years ago for the high-society bride it was said he'd stolen from his partner, Liam Bennett.

The place held a kind of cult status for lovers in the area, due to the legendary long and blissful marriage of Alonzo and Anne, two people from such different worlds. Stevie and Zin had more than once spent the night there, staying awake until dawn talking about the men they would someday meet and marry. Silly little girls, who didn't know there was so much more to life than love.

"I think you should take him by the cottage," Stevie suggested. "Remember how we were sure we'd see the ghosts of Alonzo and Anne if the man we brought there was 'The One'?"

"Who, as I recall, we thought was Joey Lawrence."

Stevie smiled. "And I'll have my prince all to myself if you've found your one and only in this guy from the limousine."

"Wait." Zin frowned. "Did I say anything about finding the guy in the limousine?"

Stevie jumped to her feet. "No, I did. And you'll be late for the booking unless we get moving. You need lipstick."

"And my uniform," Zin said, standing.

"No. He said, um, the client asked that you not be in uniform. What you have on is fine."

Zin glanced down at her faded jeans and spaghetti-strapped tank top. On her feet was her oldest pair of running shoes. "Really, Stevie, I don't think this looks professional."

The sound of footsteps came from the direction of the front door. The door she'd found half open and left that way too. And then John Henry was there, looking as good as he had last night, and the morning before and the day before that. His smile dug that dimple into his cheek, and her heart fluttered. Her heart never fluttered. She was too busy for fluttering.

"Sweet Zin," he said. "This afternoon and evening aren't about work."

John Henry might have claimed they weren't together for "work," but Stevie had guilted her into going along with him by reminding Zin she was on the Napa Princess Limousine Service clock and that she had a job to do. John Henry had booked her services for a few hours. She'd shot her friend a dark look at the s-word but Stevie had played the wide-eyed innocent.

And then whispered in her ear as she walked out the door. "It's not a 'service' if it's your own idea to take off your clothes."

As if she was going to get naked with John Henry. So not going to happen.

Except they couldn't help but get close, because John Henry

was going to be doing the driving himself . . . He'd rented a Harley motorcycle for the occasion. It was one of the standard wine-country offerings along with wine tasting and hot-air ballooning. Almost every town in Napa County had a place where a guy—or girl—could get five hundred pounds of muscled machine between their thighs.

Before climbing onto the seat behind the client, Zin turned and raised her eyebrows at her best friend. *I'm in trouble. Help!*

Shaking her head, Stevie shooed Zin on her way . . . and for the next couple of hours she was so glad she'd complied. As they rode over the rural routes of the wine country, she enjoyed the sights with the special appreciation of someone on a busman's holiday—everything familiar was new and beautiful again.

The oak-dotted hills, the rows and rows of grapes, the homes here and there peeking over a ridge or hunkered deep in a valley. The leaves on the vines were turning gold, and everything smelled toasty and warm, as only autumn could.

Or maybe that was the strong, solid form of the man she was wrapped around. When was the last time she'd embraced someone? It might have alarmed her to be so connected, except this was the best of all possible embraces. Holding on was a necessity and didn't commit her to any other kind of closeness.

Even off the motorcycle, John Henry kept her near. When they stopped at a small roadside grocery to pick up an early-evening snack of bread, cheese, wine, and beer, he sat beside her on the bench at one of the convenient picnic tables adjacent to the parking area. Though she'd borrowed a thick hoodie from Stevie, he detected her shiver as she sipped the chilled chardonnay. In an instant, he'd draped his leather jacket over her shoulders. It was butter-soft and smelled like him, which made her shiver all over again.

He glanced down at her. "Okay?"

"Sure," she said. "The sun going down takes the temperature with it . . . or maybe it's just a goose walking over my grave."

He seemed to still for a moment, and then he smiled a little and clinked his beer bottle against her plastic, stemmed glass. "A reminder to seize the day."

"And smell the flowers?" Zin's eyes widened at her own husky, flirtatious tone. Where was that coming from? And why? She glanced away, heat climbing her cheeks.

"Oh, Zinnia."

The laugh in John Henry's voice made her look at him again. "What?"

His smile widened, and he toasted her a second time. "How you make me want to pluck your petals."

Embarrassed again—oh, who was she kidding?—incredibly aroused by the sexy sound of those words, Zin dropped her gaze to their small spread of food. She toyed with a plump grape, but its lusciousness suddenly seemed too suggestive, and she dropped it in favor of a crust of crunchy bread.

John Henry picked up the abandoned morsel of fruit and popped it into his mouth. Fascinated, Zin watched him chew and swallow, then hastily redirected her attention. She ran her right forefinger over the scar on the top of her left hand. "So, um, what is it you do for a living?"

"Shuffle papers. Sit in on meetings. Return phone calls. It's a family business that I've been accused of taking too seriously."

"You can't take work too seriously!"

"I think I've made that argument myself. But my mother and sister—to name two—aren't swallowing it whole."

"You have a sister?"

"Yep. Ellen, who just turned twenty-one. It's why I was wine tasting a couple of days ago. A celebration for her birthday." He tugged her hair from beneath the collar of his coat. "You have siblings?"

The birthmark on her neck started throbbing again. "My older sister, Mari—Marigold. And then there's Kohl." She remembered he'd probably overheard All-Hands Alan talk about her big brother. "He's a great guy," she said quickly. "A tour in Afghanistan and then one in Iraq." So his war experiences had left him a bit . . . edgy. Who could blame him? "Now he works at the Tanti Baci winery—that's Stevie's family's place."

"Okay," John Henry said. "So you and your sister were named for flowers. But why did your brother get stuck with an energy source like coal?"

She grimaced. "Not coal. K-o-h-l. The fact is, the long version of his name is actually . . . brace yourself . . . Kohlrabi."

He laughed, then sobered. "Really?"

"Really."

"Poor Kohlrabi. I thought having the whole John Henry thing was cruel and unusual."

"Bet both of you had to stand tough sometimes."

"Yeah." He nodded, then skimmed a knuckle along her jawline. "I had to prove I wasn't any sissy, while your brother had to show he wasn't a . . . vegetable? Herb? What the hell *is* kohlrabi?"

"You'd have to meet my brother to find out."

John Henry traced her bottom lip with his thumb. "I'd like that, Zin. I'd like to meet your brother and your sister the marigold and the parents who saddled you three with such names in the first place. Can you make that happen?"

No! What had she been thinking? He was so easy to talk to and sitting so close that she'd been distracted enough to reveal more than she'd intended. Now he knew about Kohlrabi and Marigold. Could the whole truth about the flaky, freaky Fridays be far behind?

Then he wouldn't look at her with that warm regard in his eyes.

"We should start back," she said, gathering up the remains of their picnic. "I have the late pouring at Valley Ridge again tonight."

But as they traveled southward toward Edenville, Zin's senses suddenly went on alert, and she was forced to ask John Henry to make an unexpected detour. "There," she said, raising her voice over the thrum of the Harley and pointing toward a narrow dirt road. "I need you to turn right there."

He glanced over his shoulder at her, but did as directed, steering them along a quarter mile of powdery ruts. Zin's nose itched, but she clutched John Henry with both hands and kept her eyes on the plume of smoke that shouldn't be there.

They emerged into a clearing and her gaze took it in, relief warring with shame. It was all as it always was, intact despite the smoke she'd spied: the rusting truck, its partner in ugliness a dilapidated ride-on lawnmower, the trashy double-wide and the detritus of the Friday lifestyle that included broken appliances, stacks of warped cardboard, and a metal, barrel-shaped trash can that was being used to burn something.

Home sweet home, Zin thought, hopping off the Harley as soon as it came to a stop. She jogged over to the trash can and peered inside.

"Everything all right?" John Henry said from beside her.

All right? "As expected," she answered. "This is my parents' place, and though it's against the law to burn leaves, Dad's a self-proclaimed rebel." Nearby she found a pail full of slimy water and started lugging it toward the smoking can.

John Henry lifted it out of her arms and doused the smoldering fire. Smoke belched, and he stepped back, almost plowing over Zin. He caught her before she could stumble, and held her tight against his side. "Do you want to knock on the door and say hello?" he asked, indicating the double-wide with his free hand. "I don't mind."

I do. "There's no one home, or they would have come out when we drove up. Anyway, you'd have nothing in common." Though everyone in the world thought Zin was cut from the same cloth.

That's going to change, she told herself. *I swear that Edenville will learn to see me differently.*

"Zinnia . . ." John Henry turned, taking her face between his hands and touching his forehead to hers. "You look upset. Let me make things better."

Their lips were inches apart, and all she could think about was the passion of last night's kiss and the solid strength of his body. She'd been leaning against him all day, and it would be so lovely to keep on doing it. But you couldn't count on anyone like that, at least one of the Flaky Fridays couldn't. So she steeled her spine and stepped away from him.

"Look, what I am is the progeny of a beauty-queen-turned-reality-dropout and an on-again, off-again organic farmer," she told John Henry, and though she still had her clothes on, just the words made her feel naked. "Which means *we* have nothing in common either."

Four

Double Whammy

When it came to Zin, John Henry didn't believe virtue was its own reward—he wasn't feeling the least bit virtuous when it came to Zin—but he thought patience had its benefits. The night before, after that impromptu visit to her parents' place, he'd left her back at the office of Napa Princess Limousine Service . . . and then left her alone. He'd stayed away from the Valley Ridge Resort's late-night wine tasting.

He'd let her believe he bought into her "We have nothing in common" speech.

So tonight, he could tell his presence at a table on the terrace surprised her. And made her nervous in a way that might rock her enough to rattle her preconceived notions about him right out of her head. She'd thought he'd be put off by what he'd seen in that clearing, which pretty much said that she'd pegged him as a shallow, you-are-where-you-come-from kind of man.

John Henry was no snob.

Except he wasn't one to work so hard to get a woman either. He'd tried deciphering that on and off all day, and now he thought that maybe it was the vulnerability on her face yesterday, or perhaps it was even simpler—perhaps it was her body and the way she'd looked in those formfitting jeans and rib-hugging tank top. She had a narrow waist and rounded hips, and her breasts were just as he'd expected . . . perfect at any size. It was the combo, he decided: the face, the body, and the way the chemistry sizzled between them when they were together.

So how had she so easily turned away from it?

It had been both heaven and hell to have her plastered to his back as they rode the Harley through the countryside. A dozen times he'd considered pulling off the road to kiss her senseless . . . to kiss her until her scent surrounded him again, and he could cup her breasts in his hands and then slide one palm down her belly and beneath those tight jeans to cup her sex . . .

Closing his eyes at the torturous thought, he groaned.

"Is something wrong?"

His eyes popped open. There she was, buttoned into her uniform, reminding him he'd been preoccupied with the woman when she was wearing man's shoes and a starchy shirt. The body wasn't what had caught his attention first.

It was the hair, the scent, the big blue eyes . . . It was Zin.

"We've closed up shop, but I saved this for you." She placed a glass of red wine in front of him, a tentative smile flashing across her face. "I . . . I didn't thank you for the motorcycle ride yesterday and . . . and everything else."

He didn't grab her around the waist and drag her onto his lap, though he wanted to, because he was so surprised that she'd made the first move. Maybe Zin felt the pull between them stronger than he'd supposed.

He toyed with the stem of the glass. "What's this?"

"It's a pretty good cab. And it offers health benefits too."

"Yeah?" He glanced up at her. "Is that part of the Napa Valley propaganda?"

"No, really. It contains antioxidants."

"So what do I have against oxidants?"

She blinked, the flickering candle on his table reflected in her eyes. Her smiled flashed on and off again. "To be honest, I'm not really sure."

"Ah, well, I'm certain my doctor will be happy." He picked up the glass and tasted the wine.

She pulled out the chair beside him and sat down. The sudden move caused him to swallow wrong, which started a fit of coughing. Zin began to rise again—probably to perform the Heimlich or make a 911 call—but he managed to latch onto her wrist and control his breathing at the same time.

"Sorry . . . about . . . that," he said, then hauled in a huge breath that ended in another couple of coughs.

Two lines had formed between her eyebrows. "Are you sure you're okay?"

"Sure I'm sure." He squeezed her slender arm, and left his hand around it. "I just—"

"You've mentioned a doctor more than once." Was that worry in her voice? "Are you ill?"

"I . . ." John Henry hesitated. "It's nothing contagious, I promise."

Her free hand covered his. It was small and butterfly-light, yet he felt the touch all the way to his groin. "But you've been sick?"

Okay, it was weeks ago. And while he still had a few pounds to gain back, Mark had pronounced John Henry hale and hearty . . . though with the added advice, of course, that he had to find some balance or he was going to find himself in the hospital again. It gave him an idea . . . a sinful idea. Though if it was in the pursuit of balance—as prescribed by his M.D.!—was it really so criminal?

Remembering how it had softened Ellen when he bugged out of her wine-tasting tour, he couldn't talk himself out of the impulse. Instead, he coughed a few more times, letting the last one die out weakly. In response, Zin again squeezed his hand in sympathy, and her chair scooted closer. He might be uptight and overwound, but he sure as hell didn't feel guilty—or not much anyway.

"Tell me the truth, John Henry."

I'm not above stretching the truth if it might get you stretched out under me in my bed. "This summer I was pretty sick."

"Define 'pretty sick.'"

"Pneumonia. It was touch and go for a few days, I guess."

Zin's other hand landed on his thigh. *Hallelujah.*

"You guess? You don't remember?"

"It's foggy in my memory." Which was true, so he didn't need to feel anything but gratified as Zin shifted even closer. He turned the hand she covered so he could grasp hers in reassurance.

"So you're still under a doctor's care?"

Mark was his best friend. John Henry figured he'd be under his "care" for the rest of his life—and the man had exhorted him just two days before to get his priorities straight. Right now, strict truth wasn't at the top of John Henry's list. "Yeah."

Zin frowned. "Then you shouldn't be out here. It's getting chilly."

But it would be downright cold if he had to return to his room alone. "Why don't we go inside, then? You could join me for a nightcap at the bar."

"No." She made a face. "The last thing I need is the other staff members seeing me fraternizing with one of the guests. I don't need to add that to my rep as a Friday."

John Henry stilled as the next natural suggestion popped into his head. It couldn't be that easy. Right? He'd been willing to work *much* harder than this to get her where he wanted. He cleared his throat, then remembered to cough instead. It came out sounding pathetic, if you asked him, but Zin rubbed his thigh at the sound, distracting him for ten too-long seconds.

Follow up, man! the devil on his shoulder urged.

"So, Zin . . ." He kept his voice casual. "If you don't want to be seen in public, I have a well-stocked minibar in my room. Care to join me?"

Her head tilted to the side in consideration. He held his breath.

"I can do that," she said.

The red-caped dude with the pitchfork and horns cheered. John Henry tried to keep any whiff of the triumph out of his smile. But surely he *was* smiling, because Zin responded with her own.

"You have the most amazing dimple," she said. "Right here." A small forefinger brushed his cheek.

All the better to seduce you with. And damn, he felt like a wolf as he led her away from the terrace and toward his room. In deference to her concerns about the staff seeing them socializing, he kept his hands to himself until they reached the deserted outdoor pathway that led to his suite.

At his door, he reached for his card key with one hand and twined the fingers of his other with hers. As he glanced back to gauge her mood, her face froze him.

It was so damn arresting in the starlight—that magical hair, those delicate features, the mouth with its soft and tempting lower lip.

A beautiful package, this woman, and he'd lied to her.

"Sweet Zin," he said, as the devil on his shoulder groaned, "I wasn't altogether up-front with you."

John Henry Hudson: uptight, overwound, and such a Boy Scout.

"What do you mean?" she asked.

"I'm not really under a doctor's care anymore. I just said that in hopes of . . . well, you know."

There was a moment of silence between them. Then Zinnia Friday's tempting mouth curved. "I do know, John Henry. And I knew out on the terrace too."

Busted! Yet . . . yet she'd still followed him back to his suite! Hmmm. Didn't that imply . . . ?

He pulled her close, gratified—hell, happy as the proverbial clam—when she didn't resist. Her body molded to him, and he knew that Zinnia Friday was going to be his lover tonight. Lowering his head, he kissed her. "I'm a very, very bad man," he said against her lips.

But he was determined to make sure Zin reaped the benefits of his sin.

Zin had decided that if John Henry showed up during the wine tasting, she would take it as a sign that she should kiss him again. And more than just kiss, if the opportunity presented itself.

The bargain had seemed a sensible one following yet another sleepless night thinking about the man while also worrying over the warning Stevie had dispensed after John Henry left her at Napa Princess Limousine Service. "Your sexual parts are going to shrivel like raisins unless you do something with them!"

To be honest, Zin hadn't been certain she knew what to do with those sexual parts anymore, but that seemed a baseless concern now that she was pressed so close to John Henry's large frame. Anchoring her to him with a hand on each of her hips, he delivered a sequence of luscious, passionate kisses.

And in response she felt as swollen and juicy as autumn's unharvested fruit.

Maybe even more so, knowing he'd been willing to lie to get her in his arms again—and then couldn't go through with the fib after all. An honest man.

Tucking her closer against him, he groaned, then lifted his head. His gaze on hers, he fumbled with the door behind him, so he could pull her over the threshold. His brows came together as he drew her into the dimly lit room. "Why are you smiling like that?"

She put her fingers to her mouth, and yes, there it was. "I don't know, exactly," she answered, laughing. A giddy euphoria was bubbling through her blood, a feeling she'd never before experienced. "Maybe because this is easier than I thought."

"How so?"

"I don't do this often, and I never do it with near strangers," Zin admitted. "I usually put a lot more thinking time into a decision like this. It's kind of, well . . . freeing just to go for it."

John Henry stepped closer. "I think, Zinnia, that 'freeing' is something we're both definitely in need of. So let's say I 'free' you from this shirt you're wearing, and then those pants, and then . . ."

His nimble fingers went to work.

As each fastening loosened, Zin felt her inhibitions ease too. Sex had always made her self-conscious—*Am I making funny faces? What if he notices the freckles on my breasts?*—but with John Henry the only thing she was conscious of was the delicious sweep of his long fingers against her skin as he removed the last of her clothing.

Naked as a baby, she faced him—still fully dressed—and could only smile again at the smug expression on his face. His fingertip touched just to the right of her nipple. "The pixies sprinkled you with their dust," he said. "I'm going to taste every one of your freckles."

He managed to put his tongue to only three of them before Zin's knees gave out. Kneeling on the plush carpet, now it was her turn to free John Henry. Her heart slamming in her chest, she opened his jeans and found him with her fingers, hot and hard, and more exciting than she'd ever considered any man.

She wasn't thinking of her freckles or her face, not of anything but what he would feel like in her mouth and against her tongue. He made a tortured sound as she stroked him wetly, and the sound rippled through her, ratcheting up her arousal. When her mouth closed over him, his hand tangled in her hair and goose bumps raced from the point of contact in woozy circles across the surface of her skin. The birthmark on the back of her neck throbbed.

John Henry was talking to her in a low voice, but she ignored the whispered words to indulge her senses in her exploration. She'd never been comfortable enough with a man to play like this, and she didn't question why it was so easy with someone she'd known for such a short duration.

Instead, she turned off her usually busy thoughts and cupped him in one hand while she used the other to steady him for the suction of her mouth. His fingers tightened in her hair and she glanced up, the greedy look in his eyes sending more champagne bubbles coursing through her bloodstream.

One of his big hands stroked down her cheek, and she closed her eyes, reveling in the soft touch on her skin as her tongue circled him again and ag—

Suddenly, he had her up on her feet and she found herself on his bed. "Hey," she protested, wiggling against the sheets. "I wasn't done."

His gaze on her nakedness, he quickly shucked the rest of his clothes. "*I* was almost done." Then he knelt on the bed to prowl his way to her body.

She giggled—Zin, *giggling* during sex!—and scrambled away from him.

He caught her ankle and drew her back, her bottom gliding

against soft cotton. She laughed again, and slid her hands under her hips. "Be careful, I'll get a bed burn."

"Then I'll kiss it and make it better." He didn't smile. "Open your legs, sweet Zin."

Which meant she wouldn't, of course, until he crawled to the pillows and kissed away the last of her playful protests. His head lowered to her breast, and he took her nipple in his mouth, sucking and tonguing it until she felt his hand between her thighs and realized they'd parted in unconscious invitation.

Silly to have put up even token resistance, because the man knew what to do with his fingers. Gentle strokes drew forth a slippery wetness that he spread over all her folds. Through half-closed eyes, she watched John Henry, propped on one elbow, seemingly fascinated with the movement of his hand and the reaction of her body. He nudged her clitoris, and she drew a sharp breath, her hips jerking against the sweet pleasure of the touch.

A satisfied smile curled the corners of his mouth, and then he touched her there again, rubbing small circles that made corresponding spirals of tension tighten inside her. "John Henry," she whispered, "you're really good at this."

"We Type A's," he murmured, his dimple cutting deep, "always apply ourselves."

She gasped as one finger slid inside her. Pleasure coiled, ready to strike. "Maybe you should . . ."

His thumb played her as another finger found its way inside her. Her breath caught in her lungs; her hips chased his touch, wanting more, more, more. "John Henry" was all she managed, trying to warn him.

He bent down to take her mouth, his hand still working its magic. "Go free, Zin," he whispered.

And she did, breaking the bonds of the tightening sexual helix in wild bursts of pulsing bliss.

He didn't give her time to gather the pieces of herself. Instead, he was at her mouth, her breasts, her sex, kissing, stroking, tasting, until she threw back her head and reveled, giddy again, liberated and lustful.

He lifted the backs of her knees in his hands, and knelt between her legs to enter her, one delicious inch at a time. When she was full, full of John Henry, he rocked his body against hers, and she rose to meet each thrust. Unfettered again, reaching for her peak without awkwardness.

Their breaths sounded loud in the dim room, and she loved the passionate sound. Her thighs tightened on either side of his hips, and he thrust harder, deeper, causing her to tighten around him. Causing him to reach between them for more of those Type-A touches.

This climax rose from her toes, rolling over her body like the sun rising over the earth to heat the air and light the sky and ripen fruit.

She burst again, and the waves of sensation pushed him over. John Henry groaned, his hips jerking against the cradle of her body. Then he was still, leaving her to pulse around him in waning aftershocks.

With a softer groan, he withdrew and fell to the pillow beside hers. "You about killed me, Zin."

She laughed.

"Hey, is murder that funny?" He rolled his head to look at her.

"I've never had so much fun in bed," she confessed.

His thumb brushed the edge of her cheekbone, the gesture tender. "Then why, sweet Zin, are you crying?"

Five

Double-Edged

Zin touched her face, surprised and then embarrassed to find John Henry was right. There were tears on her cheeks. She quickly wiped them away with the edge of her hand. The room was dim, with only the light from the foyer weakly reaching them, so she went with the cover. "You are *so* wrong. I am *not* crying."

He chuckled and rolled from the bed, padding to the bathroom, where she assumed he was tending to the condom business. She'd noticed how smooth he was about that, and wasn't surprised by it. It seemed like everything John Henry did was done well and done thoroughly. She wiggled against the sheets. All hail the Type A.

He called to her from the bathroom. "It's a fact that girls cry, Zinnia. You don't have to hide it."

A laugh was in his voice now, and she appreciated him for smoothing over the moment. Really, she was flummoxed by the whole wet-cheeks thing. "No fact, John Henry, believe me."

"You're wrong." He emerged from the bathroom and, buck naked, strolled to the minibar. She watched him pour her a glass of wine and pop the top off a beer for himself. Then he turned and walked toward the bed.

She tried to keep her gaze on his face.

"I have a sister, Zin." He slid back into bed and handed her the wineglass. "I know a lot of Sigma Woo Hoos."

Frowning, she scooted up on the pillows. "The Who Woos?"

"Not Who Woos, Zin. Woo Hoos. Sorority girls, but that's neither here nor there."

He was making her smile again. Really, she should have listened sooner to Stevie about this sex thing.

"I just want you to know," he went on, "that I don't mind about the crying. It's a cute girl thing. Like . . . I don't know. Hair bands. Thong panties. Choke chains."

What could have been postcoital uneasiness was now turning into postcoital entertainment. "Chokers, John Henry. At least that's what I hope you mean. Choke chains are for dogs."

"Maybe that's what I need," he mused, leaning back against the pillows. "I'm supposed to be looking for balance, and a dog might just do the trick. You ever had one?"

"I did." She smiled, remembering McMichael, the ebony-and-ivory terrier her dad had found somewhere and brought back to the trailer. Her parents had allowed him to sleep in her bed with her, and he'd been better than any teddy bear. "He lived a long, happy life." And given her plenty of happy times, too, now that she thought about it.

"Are you crying again?"

"No!" She frowned at him. "Honest, John Henry, I am not a crier."

His beer bottle tilted, and she watched him take a healthy swallow. For some reason she didn't think he believed her, and it rankled. Maybe every woman he had bedded had cried in ecstasy afterward. It sort of soured her mood to think of them, and it made her certain she didn't want to be just another in their ranks.

"I haven't cried since second grade."

"No way," he said, putting the beer bottle on the bedside table.

"Yes." She sipped at her wine, because she was feeling a little mad and wanted it to cool her down.

"Not even when that one guy wasn't the *American Idol* winner? Because the Woo Hoos cried their little hearts out over that and then circulated a petition on the Internet."

"John Henry, you need to stop hanging around sorority girls and start getting to know some grown-up women."

His smile expanded slowly as he took her wineglass out of her hand and set it beside the beer bottle. Then he drew her close to him so that they were snuggled together. "You read my mind, Zinnia."

Without her permission, her leg crept over his thigh. Amazing how natural that felt. Also amazing how her cheek found the comfortable resting place on his chest. His heart beat beneath her ear, and his hand sifted through her hair. It was as if they'd been lovers for a long time.

"So what made you cry in second grade, sweetheart?"

Zin breathed in the scent of him; it was warm and male and edged with an expensive cologne. Delicious. Distracting. "What?"

"Second grade. Tears."

It must have been the uncommon closeness that motivated her to confess. Or perhaps it was because the story didn't seem so dreadful within the haven of his arms. "It was because of the school field trip."

His fingers continued combing through her hair. "Pumpkin patch? Petting zoo?"

"We're country kids, for all intents and purposes, here in Eden-ville, John Henry. Plenty of experience with four-legged creatures and things growing in fields. In May, the second grade gets on buses and goes to the big city. Fisherman's Wharf in San Francisco. Ghirardelli Square."

"I didn't think children cried about chocolate."

"I cried because I didn't get to go."

"Ah, sweetheart—"

"But that's not really true," Zin said, correcting herself. "I wouldn't have minded so much missing the event, if the why of it hadn't been so humiliating." Poor little Zinnia, she thought, think-ing back to the skinny-legged, fuzzy-headed girl she'd been.

"Why didn't you go, Zin?"

"I tried saying it was because I'd burned my hand. I told my friends that's why I couldn't get on the bus." She couldn't see the scar in the dark, but the memory was indelible.

"The truth was, my parents didn't sign the permission slip and pay the trip fee. I don't know if they didn't have the money or if they forgot or . . ." It had been the first of many such incidents.

John Henry stroked her bare shoulder, and she closed her eyes, relishing the tender touch. "Poor Zin."

"Poor Flaky Friday, more like. One of the parent chaperones coined the phrase as the rest of the class tromped out toward the bus. It stuck. Transferred to Mari and Kohl, too, sorry to say. We've been the Flaky Fridays going on twenty years."

And that name had been motivating her for that long too. To do better, to overcome more missed field trips and other times when her parents' oddities made everyone in town look at *her* oddly.

John Henry lifted her over his body. She looked up, their gazes meeting. "No tears now," he murmured.

He hardened against her belly, and she made a little circle with her pelvis, thoughts of the past flying away. "John Henry, *you* are nothing to cry about."

The following night the clock read eleven twenty-two when John Henry heard a knock on the door of his suite. As he strolled toward it, he called out, "Who is it?"

"Room service."

With a half frown, he turned the knob. "I didn't . . ." His voice trailed off as he took in Zinnia, swathed in a white terry spa robe and carrying a bucket of icy Mexican beers with lime wedges poking from two that were uncapped.

"Well, well, well . . ." he said. "I didn't realize the resort had a service that knew my every wish."

"Is that right?" She smiled.

It did something to him, that smile, and he rubbed at the little crimp it put in his chest. "That's right."

Zinnia strolled past him into the room and set the beer bucket on the minibar. Taking her sweet fragrance into his lungs, he shut the door and followed in her wake. What had she done to him? Since the day they'd met, he'd been sleeping more, breathing deeper, thinking of ways to please Zin instead of ways to up the bottom line of River Pharmaceuticals.

"I took a shower in the staff lounge after my shift pouring wine. And right before I had a quick conference with the bartender in the lobby."

"That's what I mean," John Henry said. "Because here I was, just wishing I had a beer and a babe."

"A beer and a *willing* babe," she amended, turning to face him. Her hands went to the belt of the robe and loosened the knot. "And, John Henry, I'm very willing." With a shrug, the terrycloth fell, leaving her bare.

And him barely breathing.

He dropped to the floor, flat on his back.

Zin gasped, rushing to his side. She fell to her knees and leaned over him. "John—"

His name choked off as he caught her tempting nipple in his mouth. Sucking on the stiffening jut of it, he ran his hand along her naked flank. She moaned, and his cock hardened in an instant rush. It went even harder when he slid his hand down her belly and curled his fingers between her thighs, discovering she was already soft and wet.

"Hot," he said against her breast. "You are so damn hot."

He needed to taste the heat. She made little squeaks of protest as he positioned her over his mouth, but he was a man driven by lust. "Zin," he said, urging her hips lower. "This is the kind of service I'm needing right now."

His tongue swiped over her, and her taste was as intoxicating as the moan she made. His hands tightened on the hot skin of her pretty rear end as he took her flavor into his mouth. She wiggled, drawing out his name in the sweetest little wail of need, and again John Henry felt that cramp in his chest. It made him want to work harder—but more subtly than in his usual manner.

He eased up, teasing her with flicks of his tongue followed by long licks that had her trembling, and then he turned his head and nipped the inside of her thigh. She jerked, bringing that little kernel at the top of her sex to just the right spot for him to gently latch on and so take her tenderly but ruthlessly into ecstasy.

When her tremors had tapered off, he pulled her to the bed, gentle gone and urgent in its place. He threw off his clothes and then climbed up her body, sliding deep inside her with one single stroke. They groaned in unison.

It wasn't long until the explosive finish.

But the aftermath was just as explosive, John Henry thought, because it was like a bombshell going off for him to realize that holding her in his arms was becoming as addictive as the sex.

He nuzzled the top of her curly blond head, gratified when she snuggled closer against him. He'd never been a hugger, but this was so satisfying that it couldn't compare to any embrace before. "Talk to me, Zin," he whispered.

"Hmm?"

"I just want to hear your voice." He couldn't figure out why, but it was the truth. "Tell me about your day. Which of your fourteen jobs didn't—thank God—wear you out?"

He felt her smile against his chest. He smiled, too, as she told him about her shift at the bakery and her two hours driving an anniversary couple around the local wineries. "I like this place," he told her. Napa Valley, and particularly Edenville, made just the right combination of small town and sophistication. You'd know your neighbors here, relax with them, whether they were the high school sweethearts who ran the local deli or the film-producer-turned–wine maker next door.

More warmth curled through him as he congratulated himself for relocating the pharmaceutical company away from the city to this semirural enclave. *The best of both worlds,* he thought again. Balance.

His mood faltered when Zin went on to tell him about the mature man who had hit on her during the nightcap wine tasting.

John Henry frowned. "You told him you were taken, I hope." The idea that it was he who was claiming rights to her didn't even make him blink.

"Of course not."

He startled to bristle at that. "Zin—"

"I told him it was against the rules to fraternize with the guests."

It made him relax again to realize that she'd broken the rules—

and he knew Zinnia was no rulebreaker—for him. The girl who was trying to live past being a "Flaky Friday" wouldn't allow herself more than a very few infractions.

She yawned, and rubbed her cheek against his heart.

"You're tired," he said.

"Mmm."

"You work too hard, Zinnia. Can you cut the job count down to thirteen?"

"I have to help out my folks when I can, and I have grad school loans to pay off," she said sleepily. "I just earned my MBA degree in June, and I'm hoping to find the perfect job soon."

Wow. He blinked, not surprised that she held an advanced degree, but taken aback to realize that he was so out of the all-about-business loop that he hadn't been wondering about her career goals or long-term plans.

"Still, Zin, you shouldn't burn yourself out in the meantime." The words sounded weird coming out of his mouth. Maybe because they were the same ones people had been saying to him for months. But he thought it was probably because he had never let himself get close enough to be concerned for someone the way he was for Zin. He'd never found the time.

Or the inclination, really.

"That perfect job might be right around the corner. There's a new company in town, and I'd sell my soul to work there," Zin said.

He barely heard her, because he was grappling with the truth that he was changed. This time—no, this *thing*—with Zin had changed him. And it felt like a permanent shake-up of his priorities.

There was another odd sensation in his chest, and he realized it came from his heart. Opening up? Closing its door to keep Zin safely inside? He couldn't say which. He knew only that he was a different—better—man.

He took a breath in preparation to tell her—Type A's didn't like wasting time—*Zin, you're the balance I've been needing all my life.*

Instead, she spoke first. "It's called River Pharmaceuticals, and I have an interview there tomorrow."

And John Henry discovered he couldn't speak at all.

Six

Double Cross

—

Zin would have danced out the front door of River Pharmaceuticals if she hadn't thought her new boss might spy her out one of the windows and rescind the offer because of her excess exhilaration. Risking this job, this perfect job for her, wasn't going to happen.

Located in a new industrial park on the outskirts of Edenville, the company's parking lot was only one quarter full. The business was relocating from its East Bay site to Napa, and the transition team had shown up only that day. Zin was going to join their ranks ASAP. She'd even told the woman in HR that she could be there for new employee orientation the very next day. Nobody would consider this Friday flaky any longer.

With effort, she restrained herself from skipping, but ducked behind a behemoth of a truck in order to beam a great giant grin at the sky. When she lowered her head and emerged from behind the extended cab, she saw John Henry climbing out of a dark sedan just a few spaces away.

Her heart jumped. He looked like Mr. Business in a suit and tie, and for a moment it was hard to reconcile him with the naked lover who could lick his lips and make her limp with desire. Last night he'd held her over him and tasted her like a treat, and she didn't think she'd recovered yet.

Her pulse was dashing about like a happy puppy, and just looking at him made her mouth dry. "John Henry," she croaked, and she rushed toward him, calling it out louder. "John Henry!"

He started, and what looked almost like guilt crossed his features. "Zin! That was a long interview. I thought you'd already be gone—"

She stopped the rest of his words with a quick but exuberant kiss, then darted a cautious look at the office building. "You're so sweet to have worried about me and come looking. It's good news! They offered me the job, and I accepted . . ."

Her words trailed off as he dragged her to his car. "Let me take you out for a celebratory drink, then," he said. "It's almost five."

"Um, okay," she answered, as he stuffed her into the passenger seat. With a little frown, she watched him run around to the other side. "Are we in a hurry?" she asked, as he slid in and started the engine.

"Yes. No." There was a knock on the driver's window, and he glanced over. Grimaced. "Too late," he muttered, and pressed the switch to lower the glass.

It was the guard from the reception area. "I saw you through the windows," the man said to John Henry. "Is anything wrong, Mr. Hudson?"

"I'll let you know later," John Henry replied, and with a salute to the man, put the car into reverse.

As the sedan pulled out of the spot, Zin noticed that it was a reserved space and marked with a discreet sign like the one that designated the place where she'd parked. But while hers had read Visitor, this one said J. H. Hudson, President.

Her breath evaporated in her lungs and she went hot, even though she could feel the cold blast from the air-conditioning against her skin. J. H. Hudson, President. Could this be true?

The man beside her had kissed her good-bye that morning as she left his suite and wished her good luck, all the time knowing that her most fervent wish was to get a position at River Pharmaceuticals. The company that called him "President."

She felt foolish. Played. Angry and confused.

Desperate to get away from him.

What should she do now?

She glanced around, realizing they were already nearing the quaint downtown area that served both locals and tourists. A block away was the bakery where she worked. Her bank was on the corner. Across the street was the highly rated restaurant where she often dropped off visitors when she drove the limousine. Her town. Her town she'd wanted to prove something to—and now her best opportunity to do that was gone.

"I want out of the car," she said.

He glanced over. "We're going for a drink."

"I don't want to drink with you, *Mr. President*."

"Zin . . ." He sighed. "We need to talk."

"I feel too stupid to talk."

"You're not stupid." With a grimace, he pulled into a tree-shaded spot in front of Edenville Hardware. When her hand went to the door handle, she heard the snap of the door locks. "And you're not going anywhere until we have a conversation."

She folded her arms over her chest and sent him a steely glare. Her skin still felt hot, and her words burned her throat. "We could have had this conversation last night. I had no idea you're the president of River Pharmaceuticals."

"I realize that." He forked his hand through his short hair. "We can blame my father for choosing to call it River instead of Hudson."

Names had been the bane of her life. She transferred her gaze out the windshield, not wanting to look at John Henry's handsome face. Focusing on the front of the hardware store, she asked the obvious: "So why didn't you tell me?"

"Because . . ." He hesitated.

"Did I—" The question stuck in her throat. "Did I get the job because I've been sleeping with you?"

"No! Damn it, Zin, that's exactly why I didn't say anything. I didn't want you to think that we . . ." His hand went through his hair again. "I wanted you to go in and have your interview without us influencing your attitude or your decision."

She didn't know whether or not to believe him. She tried to remember if the two women she'd interviewed with had looked at her with anything beyond sincere interest. "Do Marilyn and Holly know there is an 'us'?"

"No." He sighed. "The thing is, Zin, I didn't know what the hell to do when you told me about the job last night. I couldn't decide if I should put in a good word or not say anything at all."

The door to the hardware store opened, and two people emerged onto the sidewalk. Zin stiffened. There was her father, wearing his beat-up jeans, a Grateful Dead T-shirt, and a safari-style hat that appeared to have been stomped on by an elephant. Her mother was next to him, in her floating Stevie Nicks wear, her curly silver hair reaching her elbows. They'd met as teenagers at Woodstock, and it looked as if they'd never changed clothes since 1969. A pair of passing tourists did a double take, then shared a smile.

Zin could imagine what the well-dressed couple was whispering to each other: *Hippies. Weirdos. Oddballs.*

Flakes.

The Flaky Fridays.

"But now I can tell you I'm so pleased you'll be working for us," John Henry went on. "When you called it the perfect job for you, I really hoped that would be true."

She didn't respond. Her attention was focused on her parents, because another person came out of the hardware store to talk with them on the sidewalk. It was one of the elderly twins who owned the place—either Ed or Jed, in a uniform of lightweight khaki coveralls. Zin tried to read his lips, wondering what business he would have with Bobby and June Friday that caused an expression of concern on his face.

"Who's that?" John Henry asked. "Why are you staring at them?"

"My parents," she said, watching as Ed or Jed pulled out a slender roll of bills held together with a rubber band. Shame snaked down her spine as the store owner peeled a few free. The Fridays were chronically short of cash. They'd asked Alan not long ago for grocery money . . . Were they now moving on to the two old men who ran Edenville Hardware?

"Take me back to my car," she said urgently. She couldn't witness any more of this, but short of leaping from John Henry's sedan to cause a scene on the sidewalk—and wouldn't that just improve the Friday rep?—she didn't know how to put a stop to it.

"Zin . . ."

"John Henry, please."

With another sigh, he started the ignition. "Fine. But tell me you understand why I didn't say anything about owning River Pharmaceuticals. I wanted you to know you got the job fair and square."

"It doesn't matter now," she said, her tone flat. River Pharmaceuticals had looked like her way out, but she'd messed that up by messing around with John Henry. You'd think she'd remember that there was more to life than love . . . but of course she didn't love John Henry! She just loved the way he made her feel in bed.

He pulled into the company parking lot. "Follow me back to the resort, Zin. We'll have champagne and caviar at the restaurant."

"I can't be seen with a guest," she reminded him.

"C'mon. You're going to give them notice, right?"

"Can't. Still have those student loans." Without looking at him, she reached for the briefcase at her feet.

"Zin . . ." There was a warning in his voice, then a dawning knowledge. "No, Zin."

"I'm not taking the job at your company, John Henry. Shall I call HR, or is telling you good enough?"

He groaned. "Why? It's the perfect job, you said."

"I'm sleeping with the company's owner!"

"That's our business—"

"Do you think anyone will respect me once it gets out?" The town of Edenville would surely dismiss her accomplishment, and her, with *Oh, there's that Flaky Friday who's messing around with her boss.*

"Zinnia, let's think here. We can figure out a way to make you happy with this."

He sounded unhappy and impatient. She glanced over, and saw that he *looked* unhappy and impatient, as well as sexy and rumpled, with his hair sticking up everywhere. It had looked like that last night in bed, and she'd smoothed it with her palms until he'd drawn down her hands and kissed her fingers.

Her heart had turned in her chest then. It turned again now. John Henry: steady, sexy, successful. Everything she couldn't have. Somewhere in the past few days she'd not only forgotten that there were more important things in life than love; she'd forgotten other ramifications of being a Flaky Friday. She might get into John Henry Hudson's bed, but a man like him wouldn't want a woman like her in his life for long. So now she came to her senses and made a new decision.

He must have seen something of it on her face, because his eyes narrowed. "Damn it, I'm *not* letting you give up the job at River Pharmaceuticals," he said.

"Okay, I won't."

He blinked.

She didn't have to give up the job. "Because, John Henry, I'm giving up you instead."

John Henry sat behind his desk in his new office at River Pharmaceuticals and stared out the window at the distant view of rolling vineyards, replaying the stubborn expression on Zin's face and the sting of her words. *I'm giving up you.* They still hurt like hell.

In the past, John Henry could have lost himself in work. By diving into a financial report or a product analysis, he could wrap himself in enough data and numbers to nullify negative feelings or troubling events. He'd been able to do it with a vengeance after his father died.

Of course, then John Henry had almost followed his dad down that dark path by working himself into a hospital bed.

He didn't want to do that again. And anyway, it seemed impossible to put anything between himself and thoughts of Zin. *Sweet Zinnia,* he thought with a sigh. *Who knew you could be so obstinate?*

After yesterday's pronouncement—*I'm giving up you*—he'd lost his breath and nearly lost his mind trying to reason with her. Finally, frustrated and red in the face, he'd driven off.

He was still frustrated. *But what's the big deal, man?* he asked himself. Following through on Mark's prescription, he'd gotten laid. Drunk, too: drunk on the scent of Zin. On her taste . . . So he should be ready to get back to work now, and if it was female company he was missing, well, there were other women out there.

Starting with his secretary, Pamela. He looked at her as he

passed her desk. She was a lanky, lovely brunette who'd worked with him for two years and who . . . didn't do a thing for him. Which was fine, because workplace romances obviously were not in his cards.

"I'm going for a walk," he told her.

She stared at him. "What?"

"A walk."

"You never take a walk during business hours," Pamela said, looking dumbfounded.

"Yeah? Well I need to make a change. Get up from my desk once in a while to get some exercise and clear my head. I'll be back in a while."

He felt her concerned gaze on his back as he walked away, and then pushed through the front door of the building and into the warm sunshine. The sauna heat had subsided, but it was still warm enough for shirtsleeves. He'd left his jacket back in his office, and now he unbuttoned his cuffs and rolled them up.

A car pulled into the parking lot.

John Henry watched Zinnia step onto the blacktop. Dressed in a fitted blue blouse, pencil-slim black skirt, and needle-nosed black high heels, she was businesslike perfection. Just another uniform. Armor, maybe.

But underneath all that, he knew she was funny and warm and sweet.

She should be his.

He couldn't shake the certainty as he approached her. She watched him with wary eyes, holding her sleek briefcase against her chest. When he was within speaking distance, she swallowed, then said in a quiet voice, "I'm here for the new employee orientation."

"You have an appointment?"

She shook her head, her blond hair floating over her shoulders. "HR said to come in anytime today."

"So we can talk for a few minutes."

Her eyes darted toward the office building. "John Henry, please."

"Please what?"

"Please pretend you don't know me."

The words went deep, like a knife to the chest. "Jesus, Zin." It felt like those days in the hospital, when every breath hurt like hell.

"Is that what you're going to do?" he asked, his voice harsh. "Pretend you don't know me? Pretend you've never been in my bed?"

"John Henry—"

"Pretend you've never touched my heart?"

She blinked rapidly, but he told himself those couldn't be tears in her eyes. Hadn't she sworn to him that she didn't cry? "John Henry, you had to know that you and I . . . you and I were only temporary."

"Why do I have to know that?"

She gestured between them. "Because you're you, and I'm . . ."

"A Flaky Friday." He knew that childhood nickname still bothered her, but perhaps he'd underestimated how much it motivated her actions. Yesterday, when they'd seen her offbeat parents in downtown Edenville, he'd noted the hot color of her cheeks and the embarrassed aversion of her eyes.

Obviously she was ashamed of them.

But now he saw that she felt shame for herself, too, as their daughter.

Do you think anyone will respect me? she'd asked him. She'd thought people would think less of her if she worked for the company run by the man she was seeing. She'd thought that meant they wouldn't acknowledge her accomplishments or understand her value.

John Henry rubbed at his aching chest. "Zin, listen to me. Here's the thing. No one will respect you, value you, until you respect and value yourself."

She cuddled her briefcase tighter. "I don't know what you're talking about."

"I'm talking about how you see yourself, Zin. You don't want people to think of you as being like your parents. But that's got to come from you. You have to give yourself your own value, and to hell with what the rest of the world thinks. The minute you know who you are and what you want, your priorities straighten out too."

"Where is this coming from?" Pink color suffused her face. "You don't know what it's like to be me."

"I know more than you might think. You look at me and make assumptions—just like you think Edenville does because you're a Friday."

She shook her head. "I'm not like the people in town."

"Yes, yes, you are. And I'm like you, with a twist. When my father died, tragically, frighteningly young, I tried stepping into his shoes. I worked as hard to *be* him as you've worked hard not to be your mother and father. I downplayed it before, but the truth is, I almost killed myself that way, Zin."

Her eyes were glinting again. "John Henry," she whispered.

"But I'm banking on the fact that you're way smarter than me. I still didn't learn my lesson. It wasn't until I met a beautiful blonde who made me slow down and breathe in, that I realized the kind of balance I should be aiming for in my life. Finally I know exactly what I need."

She stared at him.

Brat! She wasn't going to ask the question he was fishing for. It meant John Henry was going to have to lay it out for her.

"I want to make time for someone like you in my life. For *you*, Zin."

When her gaze didn't waver, he was forced to try again. "Don't you get it? I'm in love with you."

Seconds ticked by with sickening slowness. Her arms dropped from her chest to hang at her sides, and she held her briefcase handle in a white-knuckled grip. "No."

He groaned. "Zin . . ."

"I'm sorry, John Henry, but here's what's true: I need this job more than I need love."

Seven

Double or Nothing

Zin trudged from her car to the front door of her apartment, her gaze on her feet. Her head pounded like her footsteps against the cement. Filling out four hundred and eleven forms had made her eyes cross and her stomach burn. Remembering John Henry saying *I'm in love with you* still made her want to scream.

He was in love with her for now! she'd wanted to shout back at him. For the moment! He was rich and successful, and what did she know about that? Soon he would realize she was not on his level, and their affair would be over. She would be kicked out of his playground, and it was better to walk off of it by herself now.

"All Hands" Alan, the bully of Edenville Elementary, had proven there were times when going home was the most prudent action.

"Oh, darling," a soft voice said. "Bobby, our girl doesn't look as happy as she should."

Zin's head popped up. There were her parents on her doorstep, Dad in his Lynyrd Skynyrd Lives T-shirt, Mom in a dress made out of an Indian bedspread. Her mother clasped her hands around Zin's cheeks and kissed her brow chakra, scenting the air with patchouli.

Her thoughts and that fragrance sent Zin back to the past. She remembered coming home from school, smarting from another round of teasing on the school bus. Her mother had gathered Zin onto her lap and held her, humming an old Pete Seeger song. Now, as then, she found herself wanting to sink into that accepting embrace and let everything else fade away.

She'd forgotten the comfort of those arms.

"Hi, Mom," she whispered. She tried on a smile for her father, who was looking at her with a frown in his eyes. "How's it going, Dad?"

Without saying anything, he lifted a clay pot, putting it into her line of vision. She stared at the growing flowers, her eyes stinging. "Zinnias."

"See how happy and beautiful they are," her mother said, touching a reverent fingertip to a cheery pink petal. "That's what we wanted for you. That's why we gave you that name."

Her dad urged the pot into Zin's arms, and she curled a hand around it, feeling the clay's solid warmth. "Thanks, Dad," she said, and he smiled. A man of few words and some admittedly out-of-the-mainstream tastes, in his own way he tried. "Come on in, you two."

Her tiny front room was brightened by the pot of living flowers set on the middle of the coffee table. Zinnia dropped her briefcase on the kitchen counter and kicked off her high heels with a sigh of relief. "Can I get you something?" she asked her parents.

Her mom and dad were sitting on the couch, their hands clasped. Zinnia stared at their entwined fingers, realizing that it was often like that when Bobby and June Friday were together.

They stayed close, holding hands or at least keeping near enough to touch, even when they were working together in their garden. What she'd overlooked before fascinated her now.

"Your father and I came over to talk."

Zinnia felt a little sigh go through her. "What is it, Mom? I saw you outside Edenville Hardware yesterday. I really don't think it's a good idea to borrow money from Ed and Jed."

Her dad glanced at her mother. "We didn't borrow money from them."

"I saw you—"

"Ed asked me to deliver some firewood for him today. He was paying for the job in advance."

"Oh."

"But about money . . ." her mom started.

Zinnia swallowed her second sigh. "I know we're getting close to property tax time. I'll be able to help out, I promise. Please don't get Alan Prescott involved . . ."

"Alan Prescott!" Her normally mellow father looked angry. "I'm done giving him free vegetables from the garden. I heard he was shaking you down at the bakery, even though I'd promised to pay him back by the end of the week."

"It was nothing, Dad."

"It was something. I should have realized . . ." He looked at his wife, then back at her. "We're not going to let that happen again, kiddo."

"Okay." Zin was pretty sure it *would* happen again, but humoring her folks was easier than injecting reality into their yellow submarine.

"Because we're selling those acres we don't use behind the trailer," June said.

Zinnia stared at her. "Huh?" Her parents had been holding on to those for longer than she'd been alive, with the hope of someday establishing a little village where people would live and work communally. Zinnia had always thought the idea was forty years past its prime, but her parents clung to it as tenaciously as they did to their original Dylan recordings on vinyl.

"The neighbors to the north want to build one of those toy vineyards, and they'll pay us top dollar." Her dad said "top dollar" as if it was a phrase in a foreign language.

"What . . . what about your own plans for the acreage?"

His grin was sheepish. "We're just not that driven. We've come to realize that we're perfectly happy with our garden, and anything bigger would only cause us stress."

"Can't have stress," Zin murmured.

"And the money from the sale will take your stress away. Yours and Marigold's and Kohl's. I know you worry about how we're situated. With that cash we'll be comfortable for the rest of our lives."

If what Zinnia knew about Napa farmland was right, they *would* be comfortable. Still . . . "You'll let me look at any paperwork before you finalize the deal?"

"Of course," her mom said. "You're our business girl."

"I'm good at business," Zin said.

"We know," her father answered. He gathered his wife closer to his side. "That's why we came to congratulate you on your new job. Marigold told us about it, and it sounds perfect for you."

"Yes," she agreed.

"Like the work in our garden is perfect for Dad and me." June Friday leaned up to kiss her husband on the cheek, and he looked down at her fondly, his gaze seeming to communicate that in his mind she was still the girl who'd danced half naked to Iron Butterfly's "In-A-Gadda-Da-Vita."

Bemused, Zin watched them. For forty years they'd lived and

worked together, and yet it remained undeniable: they still enjoyed each other.

Her father rose to his feet. "Well, we've got to go. Your mom wants to try out this new recipe she found for homemade incense sticks."

Her mother stood, too, and wrapped her arm around her husband's waist. "You take care of yourself, sweetie. If you tell your troubles to those zinnias, be sure to give them an extra vitamin boost afterward. Dad will call you tomorrow and see how they're doing."

Smiling despite her low mood, Zinnia followed them to the door. "Good-bye. I think you've made the right decision about the property."

Her dad nodded, and hugged her with his free arm. Her mother's arm came about Zin, too, and they stood, a little cluster of family. Flaky Fridays, but a family.

"Make sure you've made the right decision, too, Zin," her mother said with a final squeeze. "I'll light a lavender candle for you tonight."

"Be sure not to leave it unattended," Zin cautioned as they strolled down the pathway. "Not like those leaves . . ." But she let her voice fall, because she could tell they weren't listening. Instead, they'd paused at the end of her walk to give each other a sweet, soulful kiss.

It was beautiful, really.

And that was when Zin saw something new about them. Sure, they were flaky. Sure, they ran out of money from time to time. But they knew how to love. They truly knew how to love.

Which meant that until now, she hadn't learned the best lesson the Flaky Fridays had to offer.

She glanced back at the pot of flowers sitting on her coffee table. "I hope you have a couple of hours of free time," she told them. "And at least one good idea."

John Henry experienced déjà vu as he walked out the door of River Pharmaceuticals. Idling at the curb in front of the entrance were two limousines, both with the discreet Napa Princess Limousine Service logos on the right corners of the windshields.

"Double vision?" he murmured. But he knew better this time.

Which meant he had to make a choice. Surely Zin was in one of the two vehicles.

How much of a masochist did a man have to be? Soon he'd be spending his days with her just down the hall, pretending they'd never met, pretending they'd never kissed or made each other come, and he didn't feel the least bit like hashing all that out again.

He headed for the second car, determined to avoid the confrontation. He'd make his point to the other driver—who could later pass it along to Zin—while hitching a four-space ride to his Mercedes. He was ready to get away that fast.

But he must have some kind of misery wish, because he wasn't smart enough to take a breath before shutting the door behind him. When he did, it was Zin's fragrance he hauled into his lungs. It was she who was in the driver's seat—of the second limo, this time.

"I don't want to do this," he told her.

But the privacy window rose and she pulled away, the locks clicking into place as she slowly followed in the wake of the other vehicle. He pressed the intercom that communicated with the driver. "Zinnia, I have nothing more to say to you."

She ignored him.

So he fumed silently, leaning on the leather cushions with his arms folded over his chest. Then he moved, unable to sit still, and found the refrigerator. His favorite beer was chilling there.

With a dark look at the front of the limo, he popped the top, and squeezed in one of the quartered limes he'd also found. A few swallows didn't lighten his mood.

He wasn't used to being out of control. Not of his movements, not of his feelings, not of any aspect of his life. Tension tightened the muscles in his neck and he felt his gut tighten too—all familiar sensations from those months when he'd thrown himself into work after his father passed away.

He didn't like it one damn bit, and decided then and there that the love thing was effing ridiculous. He was done with it.

There was a brief pause, then the limo turned down a narrow lane and bounced gently on a rutted track. It was dark now, and the tinted windows made it darker, so John Henry didn't know much about their location except that they appeared to be surrounded by rolling hills. Then the limo came to a stop.

He tossed back the rest of the *cerveza*, expecting his door to open immediately, but it was several minutes before he heard the distinctive click. Then Zin was there, her shirt gleaming in the darkness. "If you'd follow me . . ."

Scrambling out of the car, John Henry ascertained they were in the middle of a vineyard. The other limo was circling a gravel parking lot that was adjacent to what looked like a wine cave. The headlights brushed over a sign, and he discovered they were near the Tanti Baci winery tasting room. Stevie's family's place, Zin had told him.

"Over here," Zinnia said.

He turned his head. A short distance away, under the spreading arms of an old oak tree, was a wreck of an adobe cottage. The splintered front door was propped open, and he could see flickering flames of candlelight inside.

"Wait . . . What . . ."

But Zinnia was already moving up the shallow steps and into the place. He found himself hurrying after her, all the while keeping one eye open for falling roof tiles and the other for scurrying rats. "Why can't we talk in the limo?" he complained, as he ducked to clear the low lintel.

His feet stuttered to a halt as he took in the sight inside. On an old quilt, surrounded by votive candles, sat Zinnia. Her jacket and tie were gone, and she'd unbuttoned her shirt at her throat. So there were her gleaming skin, her fairy hair, her luminous eyes. Like the first time they'd met, like every time they'd been together, he felt this inexplicable, undeniable tug. It took him toward her now.

She patted the quilt beside her. "Be with me, John Henry."

But he didn't want to be with her! Hadn't he just decided that? It was too damn painful to put his hopes, his frickin' heart, in another's hands.

And remember, she'd already refused it. "I'll stand, thanks."

The back of her hand pressed her lips. Then she nodded. "I know how to work hard, John Henry."

"We've been through this before," he said, weary. "Let's let it go, Zin."

"What do you mean?"

"I mean I'm cool with it. You win, you're right, I'm done." He hauled in a breath and cursed himself, because even in this musty old room it tasted a little bit like Zin. "I'll pretend I don't know you, and you can pretend you don't know me."

"I didn't know *myself*," Zin whispered. "I'm sorry, John Henry. I didn't know myself or what I was missing when I walked away from you."

He stilled.

"It took your father's death and your bout with pneumonia and seven days pretending to like wine for you to get your priorities straight. Surely you can forgive me for lagging a little behind on this love deal?"

No. He wasn't going to do it. He wasn't going to unroll all his feelings for her to stomp over them like a red carpet to heartache. But damn, he couldn't help clarifying. "This . . . 'love deal'?"

"I'm in love with you too."

For sure he'd misheard, so he sank to the quilt. "Say that again?"

"It's crazy and certainly not businesslike and maybe—oh, definitely—flaky, but in almost no time at all I fell in love with a man who tossed some bills at me and asked for a beer and a babe."

"A *willing* babe." His chest tightened, his pulse going wild. He took a moment to inhale a breath and blow it out, still uncertain of what he was hearing. "It does seem a bit fast."

"My father says he fell in love with my mother on a field in upstate New York while Janis Joplin sang 'A Piece of My Heart.' They've lasted forty years."

"Those hippies had all the luck," he said, keeping his tone mild. "Imagine it: Joplin, Hendrix, The Dead . . . Then there's that whole Summer of Love thing."

She scooted closer to him and put her hand on his knee. His blood rushed toward her touch, and then was waylaid by another part of his anatomy. "John Henry," she said.

"Sweet Zin," he whispered, his voice husky. His palm cupped her face; he couldn't help himself.

"Maybe we could do a 'Lifetime of Love' thing," Zinnia said.

He was out of defenses. For just that sweet offer, she was welcome to all he had. He stroked her cheek with his thumb. "Definitely we could."

Then she was in his lap, in his arms, laughing and crying and giving him the kind of Zinnia kisses that made him happy and horny . . . and all hers.

It was a long time before he could look around him and see more than her lovely, loving face. But finally, with his woman snuggled against him the way she always should be, he could ask. "What the hell are we doing here, Zin? In this old place, I mean."

"It's symbolic."

"It's a wreck."

"Take that back. I had Stevie unlock the gate for us especially. This is the original home of Alonzo and Anne Baci, who founded the Tanti Baci—which means Many Kisses, by the way—winery almost one hundred years ago. It's a very special place for lovers, since Alonzo and Anne had a legendarily long and happy marriage, even though he was a scrappy Italian immigrant and she was a San Francisco society girl. Everybody in Edenville comes here with their sweetheart at least once in their life."

John Henry stiffened in alarm. "Are you telling me . . ." He looked down at their naked, entwined bodies, barely covered by a quilt. "If this place is so popular, maybe we'd better get moving."

"Not yet. Don't be so stuffy, John Henry."

"I can't help it," he said, settling back. "It's the name. It makes me stuffy by default. So we're going to call our kids normal things like Bill and Jane, okay?"

She rolled on top of him to stare in his face. "We're going to have kids?" she asked, a little break in her voice.

God, she was beautiful. He pulled her up for a kiss. "Anything. Everything. Always."

She lifted her mouth from his, her gaze searching the room. "Do you see them?"

He pushed her hair off her face, no longer alarmed. The mayor of Edenville and the board of directors of River Pharmaceuticals